Roz Watkins is the author of the DI Meg [barcode obscures text], which is set in the Peak District where Roz [text obscured] partner and a menagerie of demanding animals.

Her first book, *The Devil's Dice*, was shortlisted for the CWA Debut Dagger Award, and has been optioned for TV.

Roz originally studied engineering and natural sciences at Cambridge University, before becoming a patent attorney. She was a partner in a firm of patent attorneys in Derby, but this has absolutely nothing to do with there being a dead one in her first novel.

In her spare time, Roz likes to walk in the Peak District, scouting out murder locations.

The Devil's Dice

Roz Watkins

ONE PLACE. MANY STORIES

HQ
An imprint of HarperCollinsPublishers Ltd.
1 London Bridge Street
London SE1 9GF

This edition 2018

1
First published in Great Britain by
HQ, an imprint of HarperCollinsPublishers Ltd. 2018

ISBN: HB: 9780008214616
TPB: 9780008214630

For my parents.

Thank you for your support, encouragement,
and advice on how to kill people

PROLOGUE

The man clambered into the cave on shaking legs, sucked in a lungful of stale air and stared wide-eyed into the blackness. When the dark mellowed, he shuffled inside and sank onto the seat that a long-dead troglodyte had hewn into the cave wall. The familiar coldness seeped through his trousers and into his flesh. The discomfort pleased him.

He fished out his torch and stood it upright, so the light beamed up and bounced onto the glistening floor. Bats hung above him, their tiny feet grasping at the rock, furry bodies tucked into cavities.

The solitude was soothing. No judgemental glances from colleagues. No clients clamouring for his attention like swarms of angry insects. No wife shooting arrows of disappointment his way.

He placed the book by his side. Eased the cake from his pocket, pulled open the crinkly plastic wrapper and took the soft weight in his hand. He hesitated; then brought it to his lips, bit firmly and chewed fast. Another two bites and it was gone.

The air went thick. His throat tightened. He leant back against the cave wall. There wasn't enough oxygen. He gasped. Clamped his eyes shut. An image of his long-dead mother slid into his head. Slumped in her wheelchair, head lolling to one side. And an earlier one – way back when his memories flitted like fish in shining water – smiling down at him and walking on her legs like a normal parent.

He rose. Stumbled to the back of the cave, grasped at the ferns on the wall, fell against them. His stomach clenched and his upper body folded forwards. He was retching, choking.

More snapshots in his head. Kate's face on their honeymoon. Beaming in the light of a foreign island, laughing and raising a glass to sun-chapped lips. He gasped. Air wouldn't come. Drowning. That time in Cornwall, still a child. Beach huts against the bright blue sky and then the waves throwing him down. Dragging him along the sea bed, his terror bitter and astonishing.

He crashed to the cave floor. An image of a childhood cat, orange-furred and ferocious, but loved so much. The cat dead on the lane. Now a girl hanging deep in the Labyrinth, the noose straight and still. Please, not his girl.

A terrible burning, like maggots burrowing into his cheeks. He clawed at his face, nails hacking into skin, gouging into eyes.

Blackness coming in from above and below. The image of his mother again, in bed, both emaciated and swollen. Suffocating. Pleading.

Chapter 1

I accelerated up the lane, tyres skidding in the mud, and prayed to the gods of murder investigations. *Please bestow upon me the competence to act like a proper detective and not screw up in my new job.*

The gods were silent, but my boss's voice boomed from the hands-free phone. 'Meg, did you get the details? Body in a cave... almond smell... philosophy book...'

I squinted at the phone, as if that would help. Richard's monologue style of conversation meant he hadn't noticed the bad signal. Had he really said 'philosophy'? Our usual deaths were chaotic and drunken, with absolutely no philosophy involved.

Another snatch of Richard's voice. 'Scratches on his face...' Then the line went dead.

I swerved to avoid a rock and dragged my attention back to the road, which climbed between fields sprinkled with disgruntled-looking sheep and edged with crumbling dry-stone walls. A mist of evidence-destroying drizzle hung in the air. As the farmland on the left merged into woods, I saw a couple of police vehicles in a bleak parking area, and the sat nav announced that I'd reached my destination.

I pulled in and took a moment to compose myself. Of course it was terrible that a man was dead, but if he'd had to die, at least he'd done it in an intriguing way, and when I happened to be nearby. I was an Inspector now. I could handle it. *Mission 'Reinvent*

Self in Derbyshire' was on track. I took a fortifying breath, climbed from the car, and set off along a corridor marked with blue and white tape.

The path sloped up towards the base of an abandoned quarry. I trudged through the fallen leaves, the mud emphasising my limp and sucking at my feet with an intensity that felt personal. I needed to rethink my fitness regime, which mainly consisted of reading articles in *New Scientist* about the benefits of exercise. It wasn't cutting it in my chubby mid-thirties.

Through the trees I saw the face of a cliff, tinted pink by the evening light. An area around its base was enclosed by ribbons of tape stretched between rocks and shade-stunted oaks, and a police tent squatted just outside. I walked over and encased my genetic matter in a protective body suit, face mask, overshoes and two pairs of gloves.

The duty sergeant was a bearded man who looked slightly too large for his uniform.

'Sergeant Pearson,' he said. 'Ben. No evidence trampled. All under control.'

I didn't know him, but I recognised the name. According to the (admittedly unreliable) Station grapevine, he was extensively tattooed. Nothing was visible but apparently his torso was completely covered and was the subject of much fascination, which just demonstrated the poor standard of gossip in the Derbyshire force.

'DI Meg Dalton,' I said, and looked around the taped area. There was no-one who was obviously dead.

Ben pointed to the cliff. 'In the cave house.'

A narrow set of steps, smooth and concave through years of use, crawled sideways up the face of the cliff. At the top, about fifteen feet up, a dark, person-sized archway led into the rock.

'There's a house up there, burrowed into the rock? With a corpse in it?'

'Yep,' Ben said.

'That's a bit creepy.'

Ben squeezed his eyebrows together in a quick frown. 'Oh. Have you heard… ?' He glanced up at the black entrance to the cave.

'Heard what?'

'Sorry. I thought you said something else. Never mind. It's not important.'

I sighed. 'Okay, so what about our iffy body?'

'Pathologist said he died within the last few hours. And SOCO have been up.' He nodded towards a white-swathed man peering at what looked like a pile of vomit at the base of the cliff.

'Who's been sick?'

'The dog. Seems to have eaten something nasty.'

'The dog?'

'That's how they found the body. Bloke lost his dog. Searched everywhere for it. Eventually heard noises up there.' Ben thumbed at the gap in the rock. 'Climbed up, saw the body, found the dog licking something.'

'I hope it wasn't tucking into the corpse?'

'It was a Labrador, so I don't suppose it would have turned it down. But I think it was the plastic wrapper from a cake or something. Looks like it might have been poisoned.'

'Is the dog okay? Where's the owner? Has someone taken a statement from him?'

'It's all here for you. They've gone to the vet, but the dog seems fine. Only ate a few crumbs, he thought.'

'Interesting location for a body,' I said. 'I've always been kind of fascinated by cave houses.'

Ben inched towards the cliff and touched the rock. 'This area's riddled with caves. Not many of them were ever lived in, of course.' He hesitated as if wondering whether to say more, given that a corpse was waiting for my attention.

'I'd better press on,' I said, although I wasn't looking forward to getting my bad foot up the stone steps. Besides, there was something unsettling about the black mouth of the cave. 'What were you going to say earlier? When I said it was creepy?'

Ben laughed, but it didn't go to his eyes. 'Oh, don't worry. I grew up round here. There was a rumour. Nothing important.'

'What rumour?'

'Just silliness. It's supposed to be haunted.'

I laughed too, just in case he thought I cared. 'Well, I don't suppose our man was killed by a ghost.' I imagined pale creatures emerging from the deep and prodding the corpse with long fingers. I forced them from my mind. 'I was told the dead man smells of almonds. Cyanide almonds?'

'Yep, slightly. You only really get the almondy smell on a corpse when you open up the stomach.' Ben's stance changed to lecture-giving – legs wide apart and chest thrust forward. I hoped he wasn't going to come over all patronising on me. I wasn't even blonde any more – I'd dyed my hair a more intelligent shade of brown, matched to my mum's for authenticity. But I was stuck with being small and having a sympathy-inducing limp.

'Yes. Thanks. I know,' I said, a little sharply. 'So, do we have a name?'

Ben glanced at his notes. 'Peter Hugo Hamilton.'

'And he was dead when he was found?'

'That's right. Although I've seen deader.'

'Can you be just a little bit dead?'

Ben folded his arms. 'If there are no maggots, you're not that dead.'

'Okay, I'll have a look.' I edged towards the steps and started to climb. A few steps up, I felt a twinge in my ankle. I paused and glanced down. Ben held his arms out awkwardly as if he wanted to lever my bottom upwards, a prospect I didn't relish. I kept going, climbing steadily until I could just peer into the cave. A faint shaft of light hit the back wall but the rest of it was in darkness. I waited for my eyes to adjust, then climbed on up and heaved myself in.

A musty smell caught in my throat. The cave was cool and silent, its roof low and claustrophobic. It was the size of a small room, although its walls blended into the darkness so there could have been tunnels leading deeper into the rock. A tiny window and the slim door cast a muted light which didn't reach its edges. I pulled out my torch and swooped it around. I had an irrational feeling that something was going to leap out of the darkness, or that the corpse was going to lunge at me. I scraped my hair from my clammy face and told myself to calm the hell down and do my job.

The dead man lay at the back of the cave, his body stretched out straight and stiff. One hand clutched his stomach and the other grasped his throat. I shone my torch at his face. Scratches ran down his cheeks and trickles of blood had seeped from them. The blood gleamed bright, cherry red in the torch light.

A trail of vomit ran from the side of the man's mouth onto the cave floor.

I crouched and looked at his fingers. They were smeared red. Poor man seemed to have scratched at his own face. Under the nails were flecks of green, as if he'd clawed his way through foliage.

Resting near one of the man's bent arms was a book – *The Discourses of Epictetus*.

A plastic wrapper lay on the stone floor. I could just read the label. *Susie's Cakes. Dark chocolate and almond.* I lowered myself onto my hands and knees and smelt the wrapper, wishing I hadn't given up Pilates. I couldn't smell anything, but I didn't know if I was one of the lucky few who could smell cyanide.

I stood again and shone my torch at the wall of the cave behind the man's body. Water seeped from a tiny crack in the cave roof, and in the places where light from the door and window hit the wall, ferns had grown. Some were crushed where it looked as if the man had fallen against them, and others had been pulled away from the cave wall.

I felt a wave of horror. This was a real person, not just a corpse in an interesting investigation. He was only about my age. I thought about his years lost, how he'd never grow old, how his loved ones would wake up tomorrow with their lives all collapsed like a sink-hole in a suburban garden.

I breathed out slowly through my mouth, like I'd been taught, then stepped closer and pointed my torch at the area where the ferns had been flattened. Was that a mark on the stone? I gently pulled at more ferns with my gloved hands, trying to reveal what was underneath. It was a carving, clearly decades old, with lichen growing over the indentations in the rock like on a Victorian gravestone. It must have been completely covered until the dying man grasped at the ferns.

Something pale popped into my peripheral vision. I spun round and saw a SOCO climbing into the cave house. His voice cut the silence. 'We found a wallet with his name and photo driving licence. And a note. Handwritten. It said, *P middle name*.' He showed me a crumpled Post-it, encased in a plastic evidence bag.

'Has the back wall been photographed, where he pulled at the ferns?'

The man nodded.

'Okay, let's see what's under there.' I pointed at the marks I'd seen in the rock.

Together we tugged at the ferns, carefully peeling them off the cave wall.

The SOCO took a step back. 'Ugh. What's that?'

We pulled away more foliage and the full carving came into view. My chest tightened and it felt hard to draw the cold cave air into my lungs. It was an image of The Grim Reaper – hooded, with a grinning skull and skeletal body, its scythe held high above its head. The image was simply drawn with just a few lines cut into the rock, but it seemed all the more sinister for that. It stood over the dead man as if it had attacked him.

'Hold on a sec,' the SOCO said. 'There's some writing under the image. Is it a date?' He gently tore away more ferns.

I crouched and directed my torch at the lettering in the rock. A prickling crept up my spine to the base of my neck. 'Not a date,' I said.

The SOCO leant closer to the rock, and then froze. 'How can

8

that be? That carving must be a good hundred years old – the writing the same – and covered up for years before we cut the foliage back.' His voice was loud in the still air, but I heard the tremor in it. 'I don't understand… The dead man's initials?'

I didn't understand either. I stepped away from the cave wall and wiped my face with my green-stained gloves.

Carved into the stone below the Grim Reaper image were the words, 'Coming for PHH'.

Chapter 2

I emerged and climbed down from the cave, backwards, trying not to slip on the worn stone. Relieved to be outside, I jumped awkwardly down the final few steps and enjoyed the smell of damp trees and the feel of solid ground and daylight.

Ben sidled up. 'What do you think?'

What did I think? I had no idea. 'The dead man's initials are cut into the cave wall,' I blurted. 'But they look like they've been there for decades.'

Ben jerked his head back and wiped his forehead. 'No. It can't be.'

I felt a shiver of unease. 'What do you mean?'

'It's...' Ben took a step sideways. 'I don't like to talk about it.'

'Well, if it might be relevant to our body, you'd better talk about it.'

'You know the Labyrinth? On the other side of the valley.'

I shook my head. 'What about it?'

Ben opened his mouth and paused. 'Okay. It's a vast cave system below the Devil's Dice, you know, the rock formation. It's not a good place. The tunnels go for miles and miles. Some of it's underwater. And there's a noose in a cavern deep inside. Teenagers go there to commit suicide.'

I felt a flush of adrenaline, hot then cold. Why was he telling me this? I didn't want to know.

Ben continued. 'The rumour is – if you can't find the noose, it's your sign you should live.'

I stared at the light filtering through the trees, feeling the familiar thickness in my throat. I couldn't let it get to me. I was over all that now. Reinvented. I firmed up my stomach. 'And the relevance of this?'

'So, the point is, if you *can* find the noose, they say you find your initials have already been cut into the cave wall behind it.'

'Cut into the wall by someone?'

'They're said to appear on their own.'

'Have you been there?'

Ben hesitated, then licked his lips and nodded. 'We tried to save a girl. We were too late. I'm a caver – I should have got to her quicker.' He looked clammy and kind of avocado coloured. He pressed his hands against his stomach. 'I could never go back there. Never.'

I tried to stop myself picturing the noose hanging still and straight, deep inside a cavern. My hands clenched into fists, nails digging into palms. 'And the initials?'

'Well, there were initials engraved into the cave wall. Lots of them. They looked old. We didn't check for our girl's.'

'So it's not a recent thing?'

'It started in the times of the witch trials, apparently. If a girl was suspected of being a witch, she'd be led into the Labyrinth. If they could find the noose, then her initials would already be on the wall behind, and she'd be forced to hang herself. If they couldn't find the noose, she was innocent, but she had to find her own way out.'

'Jesus.'

'I know. So then in Victorian times, there was a spate of girls going in to commit suicide.'

'And this one more recently?'

He shifted from one foot to the other. 'Yes. It was about ten years ago.'

I imagined the cave wall, covered with the initials of dead people.

'If people kept hanging themselves, why didn't someone get rid of the damn noose?'

'They put bars across the cave entrance after... that girl. But you can still get in from above, if you know how.'

★

Two hours later, fully prepped and preened, DCI Richard Atkins and I walked into the incident room back at the Station. The large quantity of cops crammed into a small space had given the room the fugginess of damp trainers and wet dogs, but the electricity of a suspicious death zapped around underneath.

A board at one end was covered with photographs of the dead man and his surroundings. I stepped forward to take a closer look while Richard bustled to and fro pinning names and assignments onto a grey board opposite. Low tech, but at least it wouldn't crash.

DS Craig Cooper was peering at the photos and invading my personal space. Craig had worked his way up in the traditional manner and seemed to be the worst kind of old-fashioned police bloke – casually homophobic, with a fifty-inch TV, a subscription to Sky Sports, and a plastic-headed wife. I suspected he felt entitled to the job I'd been given, and I didn't know how to handle him. I folded my arms into a defensive position.

'Okay!' Richard strode to the front of the room. He'd removed his jacket, and dark marks stained his armpits. His face glistened. I slid into what I judged was an appropriate second-in-command spot.

'We have a male in his thirties, Peter Hamilton, found today in a cave house fifteen foot up a cliff face in Eldercliffe quarry.' Richard looked at his notes. 'Time of death around the middle of the day. We're waiting on lab results and the post mortem but early suggestions are he was killed by cyanide poisoning.'

A rumble of voices filled the room. They liked the cyanide, with its hints of Agatha Christie.

'In a cave house?' DS Jai Sanghera squinted his surprise. 'Fifteen foot up a cliff face?'

Jai was a lapsed, un-turbaned and de-bearded Sikh. He'd always appeared mild-mannered, but was apparently prone to occasional explosive incidents which no one had ever witnessed but everyone seemed to know about.

'Yes, Jai,' Richard said testily. 'It's a cave, and people used to live in it. You have to climb steps to get there. We're pretty sure he went up alive.'

'Unless the murderer was the reigning Mr Universe,' Craig said.

'Yes, yes, or the victim was a zombie, climbing glassy-eyed and un-dead up to the cave house.' Richard was in a creative mood.

'Did it to himself then.' Craig's tone was scathing. He clearly had little time for the suicidal.

'We don't know. There were some odd things about it. Meg'll fill you in.'

I moved sideways into the hot spot; steeled myself. An unnerving smirk crept across Craig's fleshy face.

I told them about the probably poisoned cake, the carving on the cave wall, and the strange fact of the man's initials appearing under it.

'Was it home-made or shop-bought cake?' Jai jiggled his leg up and down as if he was keen to sprint off and get started.

'Bloody hell, Jai, have you been on the speed again?' Craig said.

'We don't know for sure.' I ignored Craig. I'd noticed that was what Richard did – his years of experience hadn't given him a more advanced strategy. 'The wrapper had a paper label stuck to it saying "Susie's Cakes" and it had a "best before" date months away.'

'Interesting,' Jai said, also ignoring Craig. 'What's the history of the cave house?'

'That bit of cliff hasn't been quarried since pre-Victorian times.

They think the cave house was created in the mid 1800s and people lived in it until about fifty years ago.'

Jai said, 'I heard it was supposed to be haunted.'

Craig snorted.

'It could be relevant,' I said. 'If it affects people's behaviour.'

'It's why no one goes in there,' Jai said. 'No kids or tramps or anything.'

Craig made ridiculous *X-Files* noises. But Jai was right about no one going in the cave house. There'd been none of the usual beer cans, fag-butts or tortured teenage poetry.

Richard elbowed me out of the way. 'Thank you, Jai, but I don't think this man was killed by a ghost. Anyway, back to the cake.' He swung his gaze around the room like Derren Brown about to reveal something astonishing. 'We've already tried to trace "Susie's Cakes" and there seems to be no such company. Unless it's incredibly obscure.'

'Won't be obscure for long if they put cyanide in their cakes,' Jai said. Gentle snickering passed through the room. Richard shot Jai a disapproving look.

'Okay.' Jai pursed his lips as if to emphasise that he was now being serious. 'So someone put cyanide in the cake and made it look like shop-bought so he'd think it was okay and eat it? So, we're talking murder, not suicide?'

'Bit hasty there, Jai.' Craig folded his chunky arms over his fledgling beer gut. 'It could be suicide but he made it look like murder so his dependants still get his life insurance.'

'If he gave a shit about his family, he wouldn't have killed himself,' Jai said. I took an audible breath before I could stop myself and Jai glanced at me, his face turning purple. I smiled weakly at him and mouthed reassurances. I didn't want people walking on eggshells around me.

'Yes,' I said, trying to take control again. 'It could be murder or suicide or deliberate contamination of cakes.'

14

'If it's not suicide, it's probably the wife.' Richard had recently been through a difficult divorce.

'Yes, I'm keeping an open mind too.' I couldn't let that go, but statistically speaking he was probably right.

'Who found him?' Jai was bouncing his leg again, probably just to annoy Craig now.

'A Labrador. It was after the cake.'

'Is it okay?'

'Didn't think your lot liked dogs,' Craig said.

I smiled at Jai. 'He's fine. We think he only ate—'

'The dog's fine, Jai.' Richard rocked on his heels. 'It's admirable that you're all so concerned about our loyal canine friends, but we do have a dead man as well as a slightly queasy dog.'

'So he died in a haunted cave,' Jai said. 'And there was a hundred-year-old carving on the cave wall that seemed to predict his death?'

I gave a slow, deliberate nod.

Jai had stopped fidgeting. 'Do we need to call an exorcist?'

★

We ended the briefing and everyone dispersed to do their stuff. I turned for another look at the photographs, and sensed Craig standing behind me, too close again.

'I hope you're up to this,' he said.

I spun round. 'Why wouldn't I be?'

He raised his eyebrows and shrugged.

I felt the blush come over me, hot and sharp like needles.

'Are you alright?' Craig said. 'You're sweating like a paedo in a Santa suit.'

'Yes, thank you, Craig, I'm perfectly fine.'

He took a step closer. His breath smelt of mint and stale garlic. 'Don't worry,' he whispered. 'I'll be keeping an eye on you.'

Chapter 3

I retreated to my work-station and sat staring at my screen. Sweat prickled my back. I'd come to Derbyshire to get away from this. To make a new start, wipe the slate clean, and various other clichés. I couldn't let an idiot like Craig get to me. I sat up straighter in my chair and forced my shoulders back. I'd just have to show them I was up to the job. I had a good brain. I was a good detective.

My little pep talk sounded unconvincing even to me – like those motivational posters you see on the walls of ailing companies, or the pseudo-profound positive quotes on your most depressed friends' Facebook pages. But I forced myself out of my chair and went to find Jai. He and I were visiting the victim's wife that evening.

'What a total arsehole Craig is,' he said. 'He'd be having a go at me if he wasn't so scared of the PC brigade.'

I felt my shoulders soften. 'Yeah, maybe.'

'And if he hadn't heard I was a psycho.'

I laughed. 'Maybe I need to get more violent.'

Jai smiled, but then his face creased into concern. 'Watch him though. He can be a nasty bastard. Just... I don't know. Be careful.'

★

By the time Jai and I left the Station, the clouds had lifted and a streaky sunset lit the sky as we drove through the rock-strewn hills towards Eldercliffe. Mum lived on its outskirts, so I knew the town a little. Its jumbled, narrow streets hunkered down in the base of the valley, as if defending themselves from the advancing quarries.

We headed away from the main town, up a lane so steep it made my ears pop. On the right was a farm and on the left was the rim of the quarry, the ground falling away behind it into nothingness. Just one house sat on the edge like an eagle's nest – a cottage made from the same stone as the quarry, as if it had grown out of the rock.

'That's his house,' Jai said. 'Crazy place.'

'Yeah, not somewhere to live if you suffer from suicidal thoughts.' I immediately wished I hadn't said that.

'Wife's a doctor,' Jai said. 'Kate Webster. Has she been told?'

I nodded. At least we didn't have to do that. I pictured Hamilton's face, lacerated by his own nails. How would you cope with knowing your husband's last minutes were spent trying to claw his skin off?

We walked up to the cottage, and the door was flung open to reveal a small woman in jogging trousers. Her body was thin but her face was puffy as if it had been lightly inflated.

I showed her my card.

'Oh, right. I'm Beth. Peter's sister.' She gestured us into a long hallway which smelt of beeswax and vanilla. The kind of place where they employed a cleaner.

'I'm so sorry,' I said.

Beth gave a quick nod. 'Kate's in the living room. Go through. I'll make some tea.'

We walked into a room dominated by a vast inglenook fireplace and a picture window overlooking the shocking drop into the quarry. The curtains were open to the darkening sky. Two squidgy sofas sat at right angles, one facing the fireplace and the other with its back to the window. There was space to walk around, unlike in my living room where you had to move around in a crab-like shuffle to avoid gouging your leg on the corner of something.

A slender woman stood by the window with her back to us.

'Dr Webster,' I said. 'I'm sorry for your loss.'

She turned and gave us a cautious look. Her eyes were red but she looked delicate and composed in her grief, like a Victorian consumptive.

'It must be a mistake.' She took a couple of steps towards us. 'Please tell me you've come because it's a mistake.'

'I'm sorry. We'll need to formally identify him, but he had his driving licence on him. And he matched your description exactly.'

A tear dripped onto her T-shirt. 'What the hell happened to him?'

'Are you able to answer a few questions?' I asked. Jai and I walked across the oak-boarded floor and sat on the sofa facing the fire. I hoped she'd follow our social cue. She didn't.

'How did he die?'

'I'm afraid we don't know yet. When did you last see him?'

She started pacing up and down by the window, shoulders hunched and arms crossed. 'I saw him this morning. He was work-ing from home which he always does on Mondays. It was all totally normal, for God's sake. They say he was found in a cave or something?'

'Yes, it's about fifteen feet up, cut into the rock.'

'What the hell was he doing in there? He's supposed to have a quick walk to clear his head, not sit around for hours in a cave.'

'We don't know. Did you know about the place?'

'I knew there was supposed to be a cave. The locals say it's haunted. They're a bit like that round here. They say our house… Oh, never mind.'

Beth returned with a tray of tea and digestive biscuits. She lowered it onto a rather splendid coffee table made from old painted floorboards, and sat down. Kate stepped across the room to sit next to her.

Jai took a mug of tea, got stuck into the biscuits, and made notes.

'What were you saying about this house?' I asked.

'Oh, just that everyone said it was bad luck,' Kate said. 'That we shouldn't come here. But we took no notice. How can a house bring bad luck? But now I'm thinking—'

'Come on, Kate.' Beth's tone was sharp. 'It's terrible about Peter, but it's not the house's fault.'

'But what about those other people? Before we moved here?' Kate turned to us. 'No one would buy the house. It had been empty for ages.'

Jai paused with his biscuit halfway to his mouth. 'What happened to the other people?'

'The man fell off the cliff outside, or threw himself off, no one knew. And then his daughter… Oh, it was horrible.'

'It's not relevant,' Beth snapped. 'We need to find who killed Peter.'

'She was only fifteen,' Kate said. 'She went off to this horrendous underground cave system on the other side of the valley and killed herself. Everyone said the house was cursed, but we thought we were so clever, we were above all that. We got it cheap.'

'I remember that,' Jai said. 'Section tried to get her out, but—'

'It's not relevant,' Beth said. 'Kate's just upset. There's nothing wrong with the house.'

I remembered Ben Pearson telling me about the girl he'd failed to rescue. 'Was she the girl who hanged herself in the Labyrinth?'

'Yes. It was awful. And the Victorian who originally built the house threw himself off the cliff.' Kate sat forward on the sofa and spoke fast. 'And other people have died here. Even Peter's grandmother said there's a curse. Something to do with witches. She said the spirits of the witches can push you off the cliff out there, so you shouldn't get too close to the edge. Not that Beth takes any notice when she's tending that horrendous rock garden.'

'It's bloody ridiculous,' Beth snapped.

Kate turned to me. 'Why do people who live here keep dying?'

Beth folded her arms. 'My grandmother's in the early stages of dementia. I can't believe we're talking about a ludicrous old wives' tale when my brother's just been killed!'

I made a note to talk to the grandmother. My ears always pricked when relatives laid into one another. They'd sometimes forget we were even there. Beth obviously hadn't forgotten us though. 'Sorry,' she said. 'This is all irrelevant. What do you need to know?'

I smiled at them both. 'Do either of you know why he'd have gone in the cave house?'

'He always liked caves,' Beth said. 'But I didn't realise—'

'Hang on.' Kate stared right into my eyes. 'Was someone else there with him? Is that why he went to the cave house?'

I shook my head. 'We don't think so.'

She looked down at her tea. 'Right.'

'We'll need to take his phone,' I said. 'And his laptop. And we'll have to get people to go through the house.'

Kate sighed. 'Yeah, do whatever.' She hesitated. 'Just so you know, there's, well, emails on his laptop from me saying I've had enough.' She shook her hair off her face. 'But it wasn't serious. Normal marital stuff, you know. He's been difficult recently. But I didn't kill him.' She gave a slightly hysterical laugh. 'If I had, I'd have deleted the emails, wouldn't I?'

I mentally noted her assumption that she could access her husband's emails. 'Where were you today?'

'What? I was at work all day. You don't seriously think I might have done it?'

'Just a formality,' I said. 'What did Peter do for a living?'

'He was a patent attorney. You know, with inventions.' She leaned forward over the coffee table, took a biscuit and looked at it with horror before dropping it back on the plate. I'd observed with the bereaved, the thin ones never ate the biscuits.

'It looks like he'd had some chocolate cake. It was in a plastic wrapper saying "Susie's Cakes" – is that something you bought?'

'No, never heard of it. But Peter loves cake. He'd never turn it down if someone offered. Was anyone else seen in the woods?'

'We're checking that.'

'I can't imagine him buying it for himself. There are no shops on the way down there.' She tapped her fingers against her knee.

There was a buzzy energy about Kate Webster. Not the usual

flatness of someone who'd lost a relative. I noticed my toes were curled in my shoes as if I was clutching the floor with them. 'You say he'd been difficult recently?'

'Oh, I don't know. Yes. I mean, he'd been grumpy with me. And drinking too much. I thought he was hiding something.' Her voice caught in her throat. 'Oh God, it's going to turn out he was having an affair, isn't it? I can't bear it.' She rose, walked again to the picture window, and stood with her back to us.

I kept my voice gentle. 'I'm sorry to ask but I don't suppose, if he *was* having an affair, you'd have any idea who it might possibly be with?'

She turned and stood silhouetted against the evening sunset, leaning against the window in a way which made me nervous. 'Christ almighty,' she said. 'Of all the questions you hope you'll never be asked. Who could your husband be having an affair with, in case they...'

'I'm sorry.'

'Look, he didn't socialise on his own outside work and they're mainly men at his office. There was a client he mentioned a couple of times, Lisa something, but he didn't even like her. No, he wasn't interested in her.' She rubbed her nose. 'Oh God, he would give that impression, wouldn't he? I can't believe this is happening. How can this be happening to me?'

Beth stood and walked to the window, gently touched Kate's arm, and led her back to the sofa. 'Peter wasn't having an affair,' she said.

I took a biscuit. It seemed to relax people when you ate their biscuits. At least that was my story. 'Can I ask,' I said, 'how was his sleeping? And eating?'

Kate crossed and uncrossed her legs. 'He was always eating. Loved his food. But actually he'd lost a bit of weight recently. And I suppose he had been a bit more tossy and turny over the last year, always dragging the duvet off me. He's had a few nightmares. I put it down to work stress.'

I turned to Beth. 'Did you notice anything?'

She shook her head. 'He seemed okay to me.'

'Was he on anti-depressants?'

'No,' Kate said. 'He hated drugs. Ironic, given his job.' A tiny smile twitched at the edges of her lips. 'He thought they were a sign of feeble-mindedness.'

'When did you get worried about his drinking?'

'I wasn't exactly worried. But, well, it started about a year ago and it's got worse recently.' Her lower lip shook. She took a deep breath and continued. 'I'd get home and he'd be in front of the TV with a beer. He'd claim he'd only had one but sometimes he'd stagger when he got up. And he was hiding the bottles. And other times he smelt like he'd been smoking. Not tobacco either.'

'Can you imagine him ever wanting to harm himself?'

'What? No, no.' She shook her head like a dog shaking off water. 'No. He wouldn't do that to me.'

Of course, relatives always said that. But some of us knew better.

I stood. Something caught my eye in the wood-burner. It was an expensive cast-iron thing with a glass front. The fire wasn't lit, but inside were several half-burnt logs and a few pieces of paper, visible through the sooty glass. They were almost completely singed black but the end of one piece of paper was still intact and had handwriting on it.

'What are those papers?' I asked.

Kate jumped up and lunged towards the fireplace. 'Oh, nothing!' She grabbed a poker and reached for the door of the wood-burner.

'Leave it!' I shouted, as if she was a dog heading for a picnic.

Beth flashed angry eyes at Kate, who froze in a poker-wielding stance. She turned her head slowly towards me, as if wondering whether I had the right to do this. Presumably, she decided I did; she put the poker down on the hearth and stepped back. 'Sorry.' She retreated to the sofa. 'It's nothing. Just some old papers I was using as scrap.'

I exchanged a look with Jai. 'Okay, I'd like our people to see them.'

I left Jai to finish the interview, and asked to see Peter Hamilton's study. According to Kate, he'd usually worked there before he went on his walk, and it certainly looked like he'd been planning to return – no suicidal tidying was in evidence. The room had a slightly musty but not unpleasant smell that reminded me of the libraries of my youth. An antique-style desk was strewn with papers covered with handwritten notes, much crossed out. The messiest page was headed 'Claims', and chemical formulae spidered their way across it.

Bookcases lined the walls, crammed with unappealing books about biochemistry and patent law, many covered with a layer of dust. But the bottom shelf caught my eye – a collection of photograph albums. I crouched and gently pulled out one of the albums. It was filled with holiday snaps. Kate Webster and Peter Hamilton, very much alive. All bright smiles, white villages and sunny skies. The other albums were similar – happy holidays, any discord well hidden. I eased out the album that looked oldest. The pages were stiff and the plastic sheets that were supposed to keep the photographs in place had yellowed and lost their stickiness. I turned the pages slowly, holding them at their edges.

The early part of the album included wedding photos – a man and a woman, presumably Hamilton's parents. A later photograph showed the same couple, with two boys and a younger girl who must have been Beth. The woman now sat flaccidly in a wheelchair. On her knee was a cat of such a vivid orange it stole the light and made everything else look grey. All three children stared adoringly at it.

I flipped through pages of later childhood photographs – scorched lawns and yellow Cornish beaches; no mother in these. Then the university years – punting on the river and lounging in Cambridge college gardens, surrounded by glistening turrets and pinnacles. Most of those photographs featured a rather beautiful girl. Her huge, dark eyes gazed out of the photographs right at me. She was the central point, like the sun to the other people's planets. She stared at the camera and Peter Hamilton stared at her. Even after I looked away, her face was in my head.

I stood and looked again at the papers on the desk. I lifted the one headed 'Claims'. Something was written on the back. I turned it gently. One word covered the paper, written maybe one hundred times, in different-sized lettering and at different angles and with different pens.

Cursed.

Chapter 4

We pulled away from Kate Webster's house. My mind was swirling with witches and curses and poison, and flashes of Peter Hamilton's blood-stained face. I glanced back towards the cottage, perched resolutely on the cliff with the quarry falling away all around it. An outside light shone on a little rock garden which sprawled over the stone to the side of the house. I pictured the drop onto the rocks far below, and wondered if the cottage would ever surrender itself to the quarry, as if on an eroding coastline.

'Did you find anything else useful?' I asked Jai.

'Not really. Apparently he goes for a walk every Monday when he works from home, but not always in the quarry. He was a greedy sod who'd take cake from anyone, but no one would have wanted to harm him.'

'Clearly.'

'All that stuff about a curse on the house was a bit weird. You wouldn't think a doctor would fall for that.'

'Or a patent attorney. It's odd though, if people who live there keep dying. Did you ask if anyone had died recently?'

'Yeah. No. Last one was that girl ten years ago.'

'Ben Pearson told me about her yesterday. The duty sergeant. That Labyrinth is supposed to have the initials of the people who died cut into the rock.'

Jai glanced at me. 'What, like in our cave?'

'Yes.' I steered the car down the steep hill towards the town centre, praying we wouldn't meet anyone coming up. 'So, it's pretty strange that the girl came from the same house, don't you think?'

'Hmm, yes. And there was something else his wife said.'

'Oh yes?'

'Okay, so when I asked if either of them knew about the carving in the cave, the wife started saying something that I didn't quite catch, and the sister shut her up. Then the wife made out she hadn't said anything. And you know how sometimes your brain pieces together later what someone said – well, I'm thinking she said something about the basement.'

★

I dropped Jai at his house in Matlock and took the A6 towards Belper. It was late and dark and the drizzle had morphed into a diffuse fog that distorted the headlights of the oncoming cars. Either my eyes were getting worse or driving at night had always been an act of faith. I squinted into the gloom and wished I was in bed.

Back home, I let myself into my tiny, rented cottage. The heating was on and the hallway felt cosy for once, the long, rust-coloured rug warming the stone-flagged floor and books sitting in chaotic piles on the shelves. A phone balancing on one of the piles flashed a tiny red light. At what point in my life had answer-phone messages transformed from exciting to depressing? I kicked off my shoes and pressed the button. Mum's voice. The usual stuff. How was I? How was work? Was I eating? (Seriously, had she not *seen* this body?) There was something about her voice – high-pitched but breathy, as if she was trying not to be overheard. She'd seemed different recently, as if she was worried about something, but I was damned if I could get her to tell me what it was. Probably just the strain of looking after Gran. A wave of guilt and helplessness washed over me. I probably wouldn't find time to visit her tomorrow. I'd be up to my neck in the investigation.

I glanced into the living room, then walked to the kitchen with the message still playing. Hamlet burst through the cat flap in a haze of black and white fur. I leaned and scooped him into my arms, somewhat against his wishes, and buried my face in his soft belly. He purred grudgingly and wriggled out of my grasp. I gave him food even though he'd have been stuffing his fat face at my indulgent neighbour's house all evening, grabbed a glass of water, and sat at the kitchen table with my laptop.

I eventually found it on a website about Derbyshire myths and legends – the story of the Labyrinth, the witches and the initials on the wall, just as Ben Pearson had said. It was classed 'not verified'. The cave house was also mentioned. It was said to be haunted by a woman as thin as a skeleton, who wailed for her lost lover. I snapped my laptop shut, and rubbed my arms to get rid of the goose pimples. I didn't believe in ghosts.

I climbed the steep stairs, Hamlet forming a trip-hazard at my ankles, and tried to resist the compulsion to check the upstairs rooms. I had to stop doing this. I closed my eyes and leant against the wall of my tiny landing. I pictured the noose deep inside the Labyrinth. Straight and empty. That other image flickered at the edge of my consciousness. A young girl hanging. I squeezed my eyes tight shut and forced my fists into my temples. She faded away.

I poked my head into the chaotic study and the overflowing spare room, glancing up at the ceilings, as always.

Chapter 5

'It'll be that one.' Jai nodded at a Georgian building which had a smug look and stood out from the shabbier buildings on the street, as if lit from below. 'You can just tell it's stuffed full of fat-cat lawyers.'

He was right. The weak morning sun shone on a brass plaque which announced, *Carstairs, Hamilton and Swift – Patent and Trade Mark Attorneys*. I shoved open the heavy door, and we walked into a surprisingly modern reception.

The receptionist sported the kind of permed hair that surely went out in the eighties, and a badge saying *Wendy*. I silently applauded Carstairs and Co for employing someone so far from the archetypal Barbie-esque legal receptionist. Her eyes widened at the sight of our ID, and she said, 'Ooh yes, you're here to interview the suspects. Let me show you to the conference room.'

She led us towards an oak panelled door on our right. As she reached for the handle, a woman burst through the front door from the road, swerved, and knocked me in the stomach with a pointed elbow. 'I need to talk to someone about the cases Peter was handling.' She had one of those sharp, rodenty faces common in the girls who'd bullied me at school.

Wendy turned to her with a tight-lipped smile and said, 'I'll be with you in a moment.'

I bashed the woman with the oak door as we entered the conference room, and added her to the list of suspects.

The room wouldn't have looked out of place in a minor stately home. Hefty books lined the walls and stern, lumpy-nosed old men gazed disapprovingly from gold-framed portraits.

'What did I tell you?' Jai settled himself on an upright chair facing a Georgian window overlooking the road outside.

'Yeah, you'd be quivering about the charges if you were a client.' I sat round the corner of the table from Jai, so we weren't lined up in battle formation, and removed my coat and my special, crazy scarf. It was far too long but my sister, Carrie, had knitted it for me, vowing to keep knitting until she could knit no more, so I wore it even though I had to coil it in a bizarre double loop to avoid it dragging on the floor.

Wendy returned with coffee and biscuits.

'Do you have a moment?' I said.

She put her tray on the table and puffed up like a courting bird. 'Yes, of course.'

'We were just wondering what Peter Hamilton was like to work with?'

'Oh, he was very nice. Such a shame. He was the nicest of the three partners. The other two can be terribly difficult. Although poor Peter had been somewhat moody recently.'

I caught Jai's eye. *You take over, and charm some dirt out of her.* He stepped in beautifully, with a sympathetic smile and an intimate tone. 'You must have to put up with a lot. So Peter Hamilton had been a bit moody?'

'Only in the last six months or so. Snapping at me about things.'

'Have you any idea why?'

'Not really. They all get very stressed. And of course the other two partners—'

'That's Felix Carstairs and Edward Swift?'

She nodded. 'Yes, they were concerned about Peter.'

'What makes you say they were concerned?' Jai was good. Wendy rested one leg and leant against the door frame as if she was chatting to a friend.

'They've been having meetings, just the two of them. Between you and me, I think they were trying to get rid of him.' She took a tiny in-breath as if realising the implications of what she'd said. 'Oh, no, not like that. I mean, trying to get him to leave the firm. I think Peter was behind with his work. Apparently Edward was snooping through his files when he was on holiday. Edward's a funny one though. A little bit on the spectrum, if you know what I mean.'

'The autistic spectrum?'

'A teensy bit.' She held fingers up to give a visual representation of *teensy,* and lowered her voice. 'And make sure you ask Felix about StairGate.'

Jai leant forward to encourage her, and spoke quietly. 'What was that?'

'Oh, it's just what we called it. Like Watergate, you know, but it all happened on the stairs out there. Felix was shouting at Peter and then it was terrible – Peter fell.' She took a step towards us and whispered. 'We think Felix must have pushed him.'

'Really?' Jai's tone was conspiratorial.

'Oh yes, Felix isn't the easiest man. He ran over a cat in the car park out the back and he didn't seem upset at all.'

'That's not good.' Jai sat back.

I put Felix to the front of my list of suspects, ahead of pointy-elbowed-woman. 'And who's that in Reception?'

Wendy looked like she'd eaten vinegar. 'The one that's having a tantrum because her patent attorney had the cheek to die on her? That's Lisa Bell. I think *she's* part of the problem. I heard one of the secretaries saying Peter had been undercharging her, and the other partners weren't happy.'

So that was the client Hamilton's wife had mentioned. Lisa something. Could he have been having an affair with her? It would take a brave man to tackle that woman.

An assertive knock rattled the door, and a man strode in like he owned the place, which he possibly did.

Wendy jumped. 'Oh, I'd best get back.'

The man held out his hand. 'Felix Carstairs.' He sat opposite Jai, round the corner of the table from me, and spread himself out, stealing space in an alpha-male kind of way. I could practically see Jai's hackles rising, but there was nothing overtly offensive about the man. He had a symmetrical face and the sleek plumpness of a well-groomed show pony.

'Terrible news about poor Peter.' He spoke with the slow diction of those brought up to think everyone listened to them. Whereas I'd learnt to spit it out quick before someone interrupted.

'Yes, terrible,' I said. 'Do you mind if we ask you a few questions about him?'

'Of course not. Happy to help.' Felix smiled, his confidence cocooning him like a magic cloak. He was the kind of person everyone had assumed I would meet at Cambridge, but in reality I'd been drawn to a group of fellow comprehensive school students, as if by an invisible magnet.

'When did you last see him?'

'Friday. Oh, and I was at work all day Monday. Wendy in reception can verify that.'

Interesting that he was getting his alibi in before I'd even asked. Jai wrote in his notebook and eyed Felix with deep suspicion.

'Okay, thanks,' I said. 'Had you noticed anything unusual about him in the last few weeks?'

'I wondered if he was a little depressed. It was suicide, I assume?'

I took a bite of a caramel chocolate digestive and settled back in my chair. 'Were you close?'

'We were up at Cambridge together. But, you know what men are like – we don't talk about anything important. I suppose I should have found out more about his life.' He sounded almost bored. 'Is there anything else? I have a pile of work to get through.'

'Peter's cases? I gather he was behind?'

'Oh, not especially. We're just all extremely busy. Taking on any extra work tends to put us under pressure.'

'So, were you worried about Peter's performance?'

He looked me in the eye. 'Not from our point of view. We were a little concerned he was feeling stressed.'

Felix could have been awarded a prize for *Most Innocent-Looking Witness Ever*. At least according to traditional thinking. No fidgeting, leg-tapping or shifty eyes. It was too good a performance.

'So, was his behaviour affecting the business?'

'Oh no. It was his welfare we were concerned about.' Felix knotted his eyebrows together. 'We didn't like to think he was struggling.'

'But we heard you argued on the stairs and Peter fell?'

Felix stiffened and lost the Mother Teresa look. 'Who told you that?' His tone was cold. 'We hadn't argued. Peter's been clumsy recently. I helped him when he fell.' He seemed to get control of himself and pointedly relaxed back into his chair, but if he was a dog, you would not approach. Jai scribbled something in his notes.

'What about his charging?' I said. 'Were you concerned about that?'

'Not really. He'd charged out fewer hours recently but it's normal to have ups and downs.' He had himself back inside the cocoon, firmly zipped up.

'So, was there anything else you noticed?'

'Not that I can think of.'

I fought a wave of annoyance. He was giving us nothing.

'Can you think of anyone who might have wanted to harm him?'

'No, of course not. But surely it was suicide?'

★

'I remembered something else,' Wendy said. We were in Reception arranging a meeting with Edward Swift, the *teensy bit autistic* other partner, who was working from home. 'It's probably not relevant, but a man came here one lunchtime last week asking for Peter. Rather an odd man.'

32

'Odd in what way?' I said.

'He was wearing a straw boater hat which was very inappropri-ate, and he had on a floppy coat like tramps wear and shoes that looked too big. He looked like a tramp in fact. And he definitely smelt like a tramp.'

'And he wasn't a client?'

She smiled. 'No. I mean we do get some clients who look like tramps, but he wasn't one of them. He said his name was Sebastian. I remembered because of *Brideshead Revisited*. I loved that on the television. Anyway, Peter came down and hurried him out. I heard him say he shouldn't have come here.'

'What did you think they were up to?'

'I really had no idea. He seemed a funny sort of person for Peter to be spending time with. And Peter was angry. He was trying to hide it but I could tell by the colour of his face.'

Chapter 6

'I bet he's a shit if you get on the wrong side of him.'

I'd been right. Jai was not a fan of Felix Carstairs. I pulled out of the car park and set off towards Edward Swift's house. He lived in a much resented new development a few miles south of Eldercliffe.

'Murderous type of shit?' I said. 'Or just your common-or-garden one?'

'Hard to tell. But if he did murder you, I reckon he'd do it neatly and competently, with no excessive emotion involved.'

'What, you mean like poisoning in a cave, for example?'

'That kind of thing. Although with colleagues like Felix Carstairs and clients like that woman in reception, maybe the poor bastard did top himself after all.'

We arrived at Edward Swift's house – a mock Georgian hunk of a building, squatting at the end of a curved driveway, in a gated complex of similar houses like something from *Desperate Housewives*.

'I'll lead on this one,' I said. 'I'm used to strange, slightly autistic types.'

Jai laughed. 'I'm glad your Oxbridge education wasn't wasted.'

We pulled up in the expansive parking area and headed for the pretentious, columned entrance. The door opened and a hefty, well-groomed woman took a step towards us. She had the look of someone scaring off raccoons. When she saw our ID, her face softened but it looked fake-soft, like quick-setting concrete.

'DI Meg Dalton and DS Jai Sanghera,' I said. 'Here to see Edward Swift.'

Her cheek twitched. 'Oh yes. He won't like being disturbed. He's doing an urgent draft.' She had an American accent with a southern twang.

'We know. Are you his wife?'

'Yes. Grace Swift.' She stood stiffly as if wondering whether to let us into the house. Then she relaxed. 'Sorry, come in, come in. So sad about Peter. What a terrible thing to happen. Edward's in his office. I'm just with the children in the living room. Actually, I know Alex would love to meet you, if you have a moment?'

'Alex?'

'Our son. We home-school him. And he's decided he wants to be a detective when he grows up.'

'Right.' Him and half the other kids in the land. 'We'll need to talk to your husband first, then if we've got time, we'll have a chat with Alex.' I could feel unenthusiastic vibes emanating from Jai, but I thought it was always best to keep wives on side – they often knew more about their husband's lives than the husbands themselves did. Besides, Jai was the kid-expert. He had two of his own.

We stepped into a hallway the approximate size of my house. A child of about ten bounced into view. He had spectacularly orange hair and the luminous skin that so often went with that look. 'Mum! I've finished my calculus. Can we do—' He stopped abruptly and stared at us as if we were biological specimens.

Jai spoke first. 'Alright, mate?'

The child gave him an uncertain look.

'Alex, these people are detectives,' Grace said. 'They've agreed to have a little chat with you if they have time, after they've spoken to Dad.'

The child had a bird-like fragility. If he had the misfortune of being good at maths as well as ginger, he'd be the main prey-animal in the playground. Maybe home-schooling made sense. 'I'm going to be on next year's *Child Genius*!' he said.

I winced as if I'd been caught out. The programme had been a guilty pleasure for me, watching with wine in hand, booing at the most horrible parents. The children were pitted against one another like fighting cocks, trying to win the title of Britain's cleverest child.

'Oh,' I said weakly. 'Make sure you find time to play outside with your friends as well.'

A flash of annoyance crossed Grace's face before it reverted to the placid mumsy look. 'This way,' she said.

We followed her into a vast kitchen complete with granite worktops, slate floor and the aroma of fresh bread. It was the kind of kitchen you see in those awful, aspirational homes magazines at the dentist, the ones designed to make you dissatisfied with your perfectly adequate house – if indeed you have an adequate house, which I didn't.

Grace installed us at the table and asked if we wanted coffee. I nodded and she popped a sparkling burgundy capsule into a sleek, black machine.

'I know they're an ecological disaster, but…' She looked round and shrugged. I shrugged back – the shrug that defined the whole of Western civilisation.

She presented us with coffee, disappeared from the room, and reappeared a few moments later. 'He's outside staring at his fish. Would you like to go out or shall I bring him in?'

Jai and I exchanged a look. 'Staring at fish?' I said. 'I thought he had urgent work to do.'

'It's based on the optimum efficiency of the human mind. He works for a set time, takes a short break, walks, works, stares at his fish. He has a timetable mapped out so he operates at peak performance. He's a wonderfully diligent and organised man.'

'Wow. Okay.'

'Here he is.'

A man stepped through an open patio door from a bright garden and approached the kitchen table, notepad and pen in hand, as if he'd come to interview us. He had a startled look, with prominent raised eyebrows above pale blue eyes, and light blond hair with just a hint of his son's ginger. 'Can we be quick?' he said. 'I have some urgent drafting to do.'

Grace slipped out of the kitchen.

'So we gather,' I said. 'And we have a possible murder to investigate. So let's press on, shall we?'

He pulled out a wooden chair and sat facing us. He steepled his fingers in a show of confidence but couldn't seem to pull it off, so resorted to picking up his pen and making as if to write notes on my performance. 'If I don't get this draft done by the end of—'

'When did you last see Peter?'

He glanced at Jai and then gave me a huffy look. 'On Friday at work.'

'And did you notice anything unusual?'

'No, but I only said hello in the corridor. He looked fine.' He tapped his pen against the table.

'Did you and Peter get along well?'

'Yes, well enough. We went into business together.'

'But that was five years ago. What about recently? I understand Peter had changed recently.'

Edward cleared his throat. 'He seemed to have become a little careless, yes.'

'And what were the implications of that?'

'It could be very serious in our profession.'

With some witnesses, you could set them going and they'd be off like the Duracell bunny, revealing every tiny detail of the victim's usually tedious and irrelevant life. The problem was shutting them up, but at least you had something to work with. This was clearly not going to be the case with Edward.

'Why is it so serious?'

'Patent work is very deadline-driven. In most branches of the law, if you miss a deadline, you can extend it, no one's harmed. But we have certain deadlines where if we miss them, that's it. An invention potentially worth millions isn't protected any more.

And if the client's disclosed the invention, you can't ever get valid protection.'

'Had Peter missed one of these deadlines?'

'Look I can't really say much. It's all confidential. I don't see what this has to do with his death.'

'Why? What do you think *is* relevant to his death?'

'I really have no idea.' He wouldn't catch my eye.

'So how do you know this isn't? And don't you care?'

Edward put his pen down and then picked it up and started the annoying tapping again. 'Yes, of course I do. I am sorry about Peter but he had been a pain in the neck recently. I'm not going to pretend otherwise.'

'So, had he missed an important deadline?'

Edward sighed. 'He may have done.'

'Where were you yesterday?'

'I was in work all day. I didn't even go out at lunchtime.'

'Why do you think Peter got careless?'

'I don't know. I wondered if he was drinking. Not in the daytime but in the evening, and then feeling under the weather in the daytime.'

'Why were you going through his files when he was on holiday?'

Edward blushed and the pen froze mid-tap. 'Oh, that.'

'Yes, that.'

'I was checking he was on top of his work. Which he wasn't. Or his partnership duties.'

'What partnership duties?'

'Look, can we continue this another day? It's bad enough having to take on half Peter's clients without losing more time.'

'Tell me what partnership duties he'd neglected.'

'He hadn't renewed our professional indemnity insurance, which was pretty serious given the state of his work. We trusted each other to do things. You have to in a small firm – you can't be checking up on each other all the time or you'd never get your work done.'

'Was that serious? Not renewing the insurance? I imagine it was.'

Edward gave a humourless laugh. 'You could say so. We're still a traditional partnership, which means we have unlimited liability. We could be personally bankrupted by one of his mistakes.'

'Was that what you and Felix Carstairs were discussing?'

'What do you mean?'

'I heard you had discussions, just the two of you.'

Edward put the damned pen down and looked straight at me, but didn't quite meet my gaze. 'We were concerned about Peter's performance, yes, and this indemnity insurance issue was very alarming.'

'Did you consider asking Peter to leave?'

'It's not that simple. We'd have had to find a lot of money.'

'Why would you have had to find a lot of money to get him to leave?' I leaned forward in my chair.

'We'd have had to buy his share of the business – worth several hundred thousand. And we'd probably have had to pay him a year's salary, too.'

'And do you have to buy his share in the business from his beneficiaries now?'

'Yes. But we have insurance to cover that. He didn't let that one lapse.'

'You've checked that already?'

'Of course.'

'So, it's actually quite convenient that he's dead?'

Edward examined his hand, the one without the pen. 'Yes, actually, it is. It's easier to pick up his clients between us than to manage his mistakes.' He wiped his large forehead. 'Look, they've probably told you I'm not good with people and I'm also not a good liar. It is convenient that he's dead but I didn't kill him.'

I sat back in my chair. 'Okay, we'll leave it at that for today. We may need to talk to you again.'

Edward grabbed his notepad and bolted from the room.

I rocked my chair recklessly onto two legs, and turned to Jai. 'I wonder how many levels of bluff a man that intelligent could handle.'

'Enough to fool your average cop,' he said.

Grace reappeared and offered us another drink, which we declined.

'Do you have time to talk to Alex today?' she said. 'It's fine if not. I know you're very busy.'

I grimaced. Did some mental calculations. 'Okay. I'll have a word with Alex while my colleague asks you a few questions.'

'Oh, thank you so much. He'll be thrilled. Do tell him if he's being too precocious. We're really trying to avoid that. It's just… he didn't get on well at school. I so want him to have a happy childhood.' She hesitated. 'And to be brought up with Jesus in his heart.' She beckoned Jai from the room and he followed her, glancing back and giving me a theatrical, *Don't-make-me-go-with-the-Nutter* look.

I ignored Jai, and sat back and closed my eyes against all the weirdness.

I heard the thud of approaching children. It sounded like at least four. I opened my eyes unwillingly.

Alex appeared in a cloud of ginger. He bounded over and sat on the chair opposite me, his elbows pushed forward onto the table. 'I'm going to be a detective when I grow up.'

A girl of about fifteen followed, clutching a mug of tea, and sat next to me, legs crossed. She looked at me and rolled her eyes. 'Lucky you, getting to talk to Alex. He'll probably ask you to do his stupid logic problem.'

'This is Rosie,' Alex said. 'She comes for extra maths because she's not that good at it.'

I gave Rosie a sympathetic look.

'It's true,' she said. 'But at least I'm not a spoilt brat.'

Alex's eyes darted back and forth between Rosie and me. 'Oh,' he said. 'I'm sorry. Mum told me I should think about other people's feelings. Sorry, Rosie, it's not your fault you're no good at maths.'

Rosie laughed. 'Thanks, Alex. I feel so much better now.' She looked at me. 'He doesn't actually mean to be rude. It's a disability.'

I smiled at Rosie and turned to Alex. 'Did you want to ask me about being a detective?' I was keen to move the conversation away from poor Rosie's ability or otherwise in maths.

'Yes,' Alex said. 'Do you use deductive logic?'

I felt a frisson of panic. I was used to questions about dead bodies and Tasers. 'Yes, I suppose so. Maybe more often inductive.' I wasn't sure I could fully remember the difference. 'Why do you want to be a detective?'

'I want to see corpses and use my intelligence to solve crimes.'

I suppressed a laugh. 'That's what we do. Plus a bit of paperwork.'

'I think I'd be very good,' Alex said. 'Rosie and I are arguing about a logic problem. Would you give us your opinion?'

'Er... I could do with getting going really.'

'Please,' Alex said. 'It won't take very long.'

I sighed. 'Okay. Two minutes.'

'Hurray!' He whipped three playing cards from his pocket and handed them to me – two kings and an ace. 'Shuffle them,' he ordered. 'Please.'

I complied and passed them back to him. He dealt the cards face down on the table, giving me one card and himself two. 'Leave your card face down,' he said, picking up his two cards.

Rosie folded her arms. 'No one cares but you, Alex.' But she stayed at the table.

Alex scrutinised his cards and laid one of them on the table, face up. A king. The other card he laid face down next to it. So, there were two cards face down – mine and his – and one card face up, which was a king. 'What's the probability of you having an ace?' he said.

'It's got to be fifty percent,' Rosie said. 'Two cards face down: one ace, one king.' She lifted her mug and took a sip.

My mind was occupied with the ridiculousness of being sucked into playing a clearly contentious card game with a suspect's child. But I still saw it immediately, with that odd brain of mine, some-times so sharp it cut itself. I glanced at Rosie. I really didn't want to make her wrong and Alex right. But I couldn't bring myself to get it wrong either, even in front of children. What did that say about me?

I sighed. 'It's one in three.'

Alex threw his arms in the air. 'Hurray! See! Detectives have good brains.'

Rosie dropped her mug. It crashed onto the floor, flinging tea across the room in an arc and sending shards of porcelain skating across the tiles. She jumped up. 'Oh God! I'm always dropping things. I hate it!'

Grace appeared in a flurry of mops and reassurances, Jai following behind, raising eyebrows at the carnage. The children slunk off. Grace cleared up the mess while Jai and I packed up our stuff.

'That didn't work out so well,' I said. 'He didn't find out much about the job.'

'Thank you for talking to him anyway.' She put the mop back in a tall cupboard and smiled at me. 'It was good of you. I know you must be terribly busy. And sorry about the tea. Rosie can be a little clumsy.'

'No problem,' I said. 'She seemed like a nice girl.'

'Yes, she is. I'm helping her with maths. It's a shame – she used to be excellent but she's struggling now. She's Felix's daughter. You know, Edward's other partner.'

I nodded. The cat-killing, stair-pushing partner who was so determined Peter had committed suicide. 'Do you teach Alex every day?'

'No, we share it between a group of parents. It means I can work too. I have a small business. Edward's happy with the arrangement provided I don't neglect the household duties.'

Jai shot me a look.

I cleared my throat. 'Oh, what do you do?'

'A small jewellers in Eldercliffe. I enjoy it and it's a little pin money for me. I'm calling in there now actually. I need to catch up on some repairs.'

I'd visited a jeweller's in Eldercliffe only last week to get a replacement for a brooch Mum had lost. Swift's Jeweller's. Of course.

'I think you're making a brooch for my mum,' I said.

Her face lit up. 'Oh, the one we've made from an insurance photo? What a small world! It's ready actually, we were going to call you.'

'Great. I'll call in for it when I'm in Eldercliffe later.' I stood and placed my mug on the gleaming countertop. 'What kind of fish are they?'

'Koi. Do you want to see them? Some of them are quite beautiful.'

I nodded, unable to resist interesting animals. Jai gave me a despairing look, but followed us through the glass doors onto a weed-free sandstone patio overlooking a raised pond about the size of Grace's kitchen. I peered into the still water. Koi flitted to and fro – mainly silver and orange but some multi-coloured, and one with what looked like an image of a spine running down its back. Their lithe bodies cruised under the surface, clearly visible between bobbing water lilies.

'They're stunning,' I said.

'Yes, some of God's most lovely creatures.'

Chapter 7

Outside, it smelt like fresh-cut grass, and the front lawns looked recently manicured, their edges trimmed and compliant. I turned the car carefully, aware that metaphorical net curtains were twitching, and we left the gated complex to set off for the Station.

'My God,' I said. 'Are the 1950s on the phone wanting their good housewife back?'

Jai snorted. 'But surely every wife asks her husband's permission before going out to work?'

'Unbelievable. I'm still in shock. Is she on Valium or something? The effort of keeping my mouth shut almost killed me.'

'He was weird too,' Jai said. 'Seemed quite chuffed Hamilton had done the decent thing and pegged it.'

'Did you find out anything more from her?'

'She confirmed he was home all evening on Sunday watching TV. And as far as she was aware, he was at work all day yesterday, but obviously she doesn't know that. And she comes from Alabama originally.'

I pulled onto a muddy lane, noticing sheets flapping in the garden of a cottage on the corner, and an old wheelbarrow in the driveway stacked with logs. It was reassuringly messy after the clinical pristineness of Edward and Grace's estate.

'Alabama? Maybe that explains the Stepford Wife thing?'

'She was definitely a bit Stepford. Do you think she could be programmed to kill?'

I laughed. 'That feature'll be in the next software update. She'd probably lie to cover for him though. All part of being a good little wifey.'

'And the comment about the child genius having Jesus in his heart.'

'I know. Sounds painful. Do you think they can sort that with an operation?' I glanced at Jai, checking if I was offending him. Not clear-cut either way.

'And you managed to upset the kid so much he chucked a mug on the floor?' he said.

'Something like that.' I pictured Alex's smug face when I'd confirmed his view of the card game, and poor Rosie's disappointment. Why couldn't I have just said I didn't know? 'Did Grace tell you anything else?'

'She met Edward when he was travelling round the US after he graduated. His car broke down when he was passing through her town, and she rescued him, and they were soul mates.'

'How romantic. Do you think Edward could have done it?'

'He's coldly logical,' Jai said. 'I could kind of imagine him disposing of the inconvenient.'

'And he'd do it intelligently, with no unnecessary blood and gore. Just like the other partner. Could they have done it together?'

In Eldercliffe, sandbags were piled high in an alleyway between cottages. I knew during stormy weather, water ran in streams down this road and sometimes into the living rooms of the houses. But I hadn't heard a storm forecast.

'Both partners have got a financial motive, if Hamilton had been screwing up at work,' Jai said. 'Sounds like something's changed in the last year with him.'

'An affair?'

'Sounds like more than an affair to me.'

'I don't know. If he was sleeping with that client who was

expressing her grief by complaining loudly about her patent cases and elbowing me in the ribs, it could be quite traumatic.'

'Love works in mysterious ways.' Jai wiped at a smear on the passenger window. 'Or maybe he finished it with her and she bumped him off.'

★

Back at the Station, I was intercepted by Fiona Redfern, the new DC – all young and keen and untarnished by cynicism. She bounced after me as I limped into my room.

'We found some drugs in his office,' she said.

I sat heavily in my chair. 'What? *Drugs* drugs?'

I waved vaguely at another chair but Fiona stayed standing. 'Medical drugs. We haven't identified them yet. Two different types – one looks like it might be an anti-depressant and we've no idea about the other one.'

'Are you sure they weren't to do with his work? He files patent applications for pharmaceuticals.'

'They were in a locked drawer with personal belongings and one of the other partners said it wouldn't be normal for him to have samples of drugs he's working on. So I don't think they're for work. I'm going to talk to his GP.'

'Okay, good. Anything else?'

'I asked my granny about that cave – you know, the rumours. I know it's not really haunted, but if people think it is…'

'It's okay. I agree. What did she say?'

'She said the ghost was a healer who lived there in Victorian times. She starved herself to death after her lover died. You can still see her in the cave when the wind gets up in the quarry…' She licked her lips. 'Sorry, I know that's silly. There was nothing recent or relevant.'

'Okay. Thanks for checking it out.'

Fiona smiled and seemed to loosen up a bit. It occurred to me that she was nervous of me. I didn't want that. I liked Fiona. I'd even discovered she and I had been on the same march in London, although we hadn't known each other then. She obviously shared my feelings about a Chinese 'festival' that involved boiling live dogs.

'Don't worry about telling me stuff that might be silly,' I said. 'I want you to say what you think. In fact, if you're not making ridiculous suggestions on a regular basis, you're probably not contributing enough.'

She gave an uneasy laugh. 'Okay. Right. Thanks. Well, we got the results on those papers from the fire in their house.'

'Oh yes?'

'The very top of one piece of paper was legible and it just had one word on it. *Tithonus*.'

'What's that?'

'An ancient Greek in a myth. He got older and older but could never die.'

★

I spent some time sticking information into the computer and browsing through what others had entered. My thoughts kept drifting to the girl in the Labyrinth. Hanging deep inside a cave where they used to take witches, the initials of dead people cut into the rock behind her. The last thing I needed in my head was an image of a girl hanging from a noose, but could it be relevant? She'd lived in the same house as our victim, and it was a strange coincidence that his initials were also cut into the cave wall behind him.

I hauled myself out of my chair and wandered off to track down Ben Pearson, the reactive sergeant from the day before. I found him at his desk, fighting with an online form. He seemed glad to be disturbed.

'Yesterday's victim lived in the same house?' He touched his beard as if it was a lucky charm. 'As the girl who committed suicide in the Labyrinth?'

'Yep. His poor wife thinks the house is cursed.'

Ben swallowed. 'I did hear a rumour. The girl's father died at the house, of course.'

'What exactly happened to the girl?'

'She went in to the Labyrinth. It...' He scraped a hand through his receding hair. 'Sorry. It took us too long to find the noose. It's way deep inside and we kept taking wrong turns, again and again. It was horrendous. Almost as if the tunnels were moving around while we were in there. But she'd found it all right.'

I tried to keep it business-like, to not picture her. But Ben wasn't helping.

'The noose is an old, old chain.' He shuddered. 'Hanging from a hook high up on the cave roof. And there's a big square rock under it, almost the height of a man. The noose hangs down above the edge of the rock. So, you can climb on the rock, reach forward, take the noose and put it round your neck. And then just step forward off the rock.'

'God. And it's been like that since they used to hang witches?'

'I think the chain's from Victorian times. They've been hanging witches in there longer than that.'

'And this girl? She'd... She'd already done it.'

Ben hesitated. He was very still. 'Yes. We were too late. Took too long finding her. She was gone.'

I was holding it together. Pretending I was okay. But I couldn't talk any more about the girl. 'And this happened after her father died?'

'Yes. He either fell or committed suicide, off the cliff at the side of that house.'

'Where there's a little rock garden?'

'Yes. He didn't leave a note, but there was something else. I'm not sure if they decided it was relevant.'

'What was it?'

'He left a sketchbook full of drawings of the Grim Reaper.'

Chapter 8

I left Ben and headed back to my desk, my mind feeling tangled and confused, as if I was staring at equations I couldn't solve. I knew a house couldn't really be cursed, but what if people believed it was? It could be like Pointing Bones or clusters of suicides or the placebo effect. Belief in the curse could make it true. I remembered reading about a man who'd been diagnosed with cancer, and obediently died, only for the post-mortem to reveal that the diagnosis had been wrong. There was no cancer, and the man was in good health, other than being dead. Your own brain could kill you.

'What were you talking to *Tat* for?'

I jumped and looked up to see Craig looming over me.

'Sorry? Who?'

'*Tat.*'

I deliberately misunderstood. I wasn't going to call the poor man *Tat,* even if his entire body was covered in them.

'Ben Pearson,' Craig explained as if to a small child.

'He was the duty sergeant.' Why was I explaining myself to Craig? I turned to my screen.

Craig laughed unpleasantly. 'Don't try to get him through any metal detectors. It's not just tattoos. There's all sorts going on in there.'

I was wondering how on earth to deal with Craig, when Jai appeared. 'I don't think Meg's as fascinated by Ben's piercings and tattoos as you clearly are, Craig,' he said. 'Have you got some kind of homoerotic fantasy going on?'

Craig swore at Jai and sloped off.

'You handle him so well,' I said.

'I've had lots of practice. He's unpleasant but he's not that bright, fortunately. Did you find anything out from Ben?'

'There's something odd going on at that house. The guy who died ten years ago left a sketchbook full of drawings of the Grim Reaper.'

'Like the carving on the wall of the cave?'

'Sounded like it.'

'And his daughter hanged herself in the Labyrinth where initials of dead people are carved into the wall.'

I nodded. 'You've got to admit, it's a bit sinister. But there'll be a rational explanation. I'm going to talk to his brother. He's a doctor. I don't suppose he'll believe in curses and witches.'

★

Mark Hamilton's farmhouse sat at the end of a short, stony drive, surrounded by barns and abandoned machinery. It was in a craggy region to the west of Eldercliffe, and the Peak District hills were visible in the distance, laced over with pale stone walls.

I parked in a gravel area and climbed out of the car, and a bunch of fluffy chickens marched over and gave me a bit of a talking to. They seemed to have something important on their minds, but they scattered when I made my way to the house.

Close up, the house was run-down but lovely, the old stonework held together with crumbly lime mortar and the windows forming odd reflections with their original warped glass. I was just beginning to feel calmed by its demeanour when a ferocious growling erupted from inside and something crashed against the glass of the door. I jumped back. Was he keeping wolves in the hallway?

The door opened a fraction and a man's face appeared through the gap. He was holding back waves of dogs like an animal-loving King Canute. Tails wagged and tongues lolled. My breathing slowed. 'Sorry,' he shouted over the frenzied barking. 'They're a bit excited. Hang on, let me get leads.' But he didn't actually move.

'I like dogs,' I yelled. 'Don't worry, assuming they're friendly.' One of my senior colleagues in Manchester had told me: 'If you admire someone's dog, you own their ass.' Setting aside the fake Americanism (watching too much *CSI*), he'd had a point.

The man let the door open. Christ, that was a lot of dogs. Barking and leaping and hurling droplets of slobber at my face. He rushed out after them, flapping his hands. 'Sorry! Get down!'

His clothes looked like they'd been recycled out of the laundry bin – a look I wasn't unfamiliar with – and he hadn't shaved that day.

'Mark Hamilton?' I said.

He gave a quick nod. I folded my arms and ignored the dogs, who quickly went from jumping to wiggling and wagging. I showed Mark my card.

He held out a hand, then pulled it back and examined it. 'No, don't shake my hand. Just been preparing dog food.'

I smiled and whipped my hand back. 'I'm sorry for your loss. Do you mind if I ask you a few questions? I know it's difficult but the sooner we can get onto this—'

'Yes, I understand. Come in. Sorry about the mess. Peter's death, it's thrown me. And sorry the place reeks of dog food. I do it in bulk – cook it, bag it up, freeze it. I have so many, it saves money, but it's a bit gross.'

'It's fine,' I said, although there was a rancid smell in the air.

'It's taking my mind off things today,' Mark said. 'They made me take the day off but I'm not sure it's good to be at home with my thoughts.'

We waded through dogs into a farmhouse kitchen. I glanced into a pantry rammed full of industrial-looking junk. There were bits of old pallets, the ends of gutters, wellies with their feet chopped off, mouse-chewed cardboard boxes.

'I can't throw anything away,' Mark said. 'I think it's almost pathological.'

In the kitchen, piles of papers and cats sat on all the surfaces and more cats covered an Aga. An elderly dog lay in the corner, draped over the side of his basket like one of Dali's soft clocks. Unwashed crockery filled the sink and a fly graveyard decorated the windowsill. This wasn't just one day's worth of mess. Gran would have said he needed a good woman. She hadn't realised you could no longer rely on women for unpaid cleaning duties.

'Sit down,' Mark said, waving his hand in the direction of a scrubbed pine table. All the chairs were covered in papers or cats, some both. Was I supposed to sit on top of them?

'Oh, you can move her.' He pointed at a grey cat. 'Oh no, not her.' I snatched my hand back. 'This one. Here.'

I plonked myself down and allowed the ejected cat to climb onto my knee.

'I'm sorry. I take on far too many animals. Especially the older ones.' Mark walked to the sink, ran water over his hands and wiped them on his trousers. He'd obviously read the research about excessive hygiene being bad for you. He collapsed onto one of the chairs, lifting and scooping a cat onto his knee in a practised motion.

The formalities out of the way, I said, 'Can you think of anyone who might have wanted to harm your brother?'

'You know, I really can't. He was so normal. Not involved with any dubious characters. Everyone liked him.'

'There's been a suggestion he might have been depressed recently? Or possibly drinking too much?'

Mark looked at the cat on his knee and stroked it gently. 'Yes, maybe he has been a little down.'

'Do you know why?'

The cat stood, arched its back, and re-settled on Mark's knee. He rubbed under its chin. 'Just pressure of work, I think.'

'And, well, could there be any possibility he was having an

affair?' I tried to say this sensitively but it was hard not to speak ill of the dead when conducting these kinds of investigations.

'Peter? I'd be really surprised. I don't know when he'd have time apart from anything else. He was terribly busy.'

'And what about the relationship with his wife, Kate? Was it good?'

'Yes, I believe so.' Mark's stroking became jerky and the cat looked up at him with an irritated expression.

'Don't you work in the same medical practice as Peter's wife?'

'Same building, different practices.'

'And do you get along?'

'We get along all right, yes.' He gave a pointed sigh. 'Look, I'm going to be totally honest here. Peter and I had an argument. I feel terrible. The last things I said to him weren't nice. But I didn't kill him.'

'What was the argument about?'

Mark looked startled as if he was surprised I'd asked this obvious question. 'Oh, as I said, he's been very moody recently. It was just about his behaviour.'

'What had he done, specifically?'

He scraped his chair away from me. 'Nothing in particular – just general irritability. Work stress mainly, but he shouldn't have taken it out on Kate or me.'

I spoke very gently. 'Is there any possibility he could have taken his own life, do you think?'

Mark's eyes widened. 'Oh no, he wouldn't do that. No, I'd feel terrible if he'd done that. After we'd argued. No, he didn't kill himself.'

There was something I liked about this man, with his chaotic kitchen and impractical quantities of animals. At that moment, I felt like blurting out my own confession. To a stranger, even though I'd told no-one, not even Mum or my oldest friend, Hannah. But of course I didn't. I kept it professional.

'What about the rest of your family?' I asked. 'Do they live close?'

'Beth lives in Ashbourne, and she visits Peter and me quite often. Dad lives near Stanton Moor, with Granny in an annexe. I'm afraid our mother died when we were children.' I remembered the woman in the wheelchair, in the old photograph in Peter Hamilton's study.

'Oh, I'm sorry.' The cat dug its claws into my knee. I tried to shift it into a better position. 'Peter's wife said something about their house. About there being some kind of…' I hesitated to show him I appreciated the odd nature of my question. 'Curse. Do you know anything about that?'

Mark froze. It was as if the air around us went colder. 'Oh, for goodness' sake.'

'I realise there isn't actually a curse,' I said. 'But sometimes there's a reason behind these rumours. And Kate said nobody had wanted to buy their house, and there have been a few deaths there.'

'It's utterly ridiculous. You know what people are like. They can't handle coincidences. You always get clusters of deaths sometimes, it's the way probability works. It's like these cancer clusters people get so hysterical about. Just the result of randomness.'

'So you've no idea what the so-called curse is about?'

'Of course not. It's nonsense.'

'And what about Peter? What did he think?'

'I'm sure he heard the silly rumours, but he was a scientist. He didn't believe in a curse any more than I do.'

★

The road swept steeply down to Eldercliffe, the jumbled roofs and spidery lanes spreading below me like a toy village. The hills rose beyond the town, and the old limestone quarries shone white, as if a monster had taken bites out of the apple-green hillside. I wound my way into the marketplace, and parked on a slope which made me nervous about my car's handbrake.

I wanted to check Mark Hamilton's and Kate Webster's movements for the day before. The surgery where they worked was on a side street which climbed from the town centre, and I struggled up between stone cottages so tiny they looked like Hobbit houses. I wondered if there was a kind of medieval witch trial system in place, because anyone capable of making it up the hill to the doctor's clearly wasn't particularly ill.

The surgery sat like an ugly boil amidst the loveliness of the other buildings – a concrete edifice overlaid with square windows like a messed up Mondrian. The early evening sun emerged briefly from behind the clouds as I arrived, sending a shaft of light onto the front of the building and further emphasising its hideousness. I tutted about planning laws, and walked through automatic doors into a spacious reception area that smelt of bleach and sickness.

Both walls were lined with patients – mainly docile-looking older people, but also a child who was removing toys from a plastic box and spreading them around the waiting room with a furious enthusiasm. His hollow-eyed mother glanced up with a dairy-cow expression before returning to her copy of *Hello* magazine.

I showed my card to a receptionist labelled *Vivian*. 'Could I have a quick word please?'

'Yes. What's it about?' The woman folded freckled arms across her stomach.

'I just need to check Kate Webster's and Mark Hamilton's movements for yesterday please.'

The woman sighed audibly. 'Oh, of course. Dr Webster's husband.' She pushed wire-framed glasses up her nose towards her eyes. 'They'd be prime suspects, I suppose?'

'What makes you say that?'

'Oh, nothing.' She lowered her voice to a whisper and glanced at the patients sitting glumly in the waiting room. 'The police always suspect the wife, don't they?'

'So, yesterday?'

'Oh, yes.' She twisted to look at a screen to her right, and tapped on a keyboard in a slow, two-fingered style. 'Well, they were both here all day from about 8am to about 5pm, according to the computer.'

'And did either of them go out at all during the day?'

'It doesn't look like it from the computer.'

'But do you remember?'

'Oh, no, I don't remember. I can't keep track of what they all do. But the computer should say if they went out. Health and Safety. Unless it's been *tampered with*, of course.'

Well, she was a loyal employee. 'Who could tamper with it?'

'Well, any of the partners, I'm sure.'

I suspected the lovely Vivian was going to be less helpful than she appeared. 'Thank you,' I said. 'One of my colleagues will come and take a statement from you.'

I retreated through the waiting room and out of the doors, tripping on a plastic lorry which the child pushed into my path. The glass doors shushed to a close behind me, and I glanced backwards. A young woman had followed me.

'Are you a detective?' the woman asked. She had long, blonde hair and a charity-shop-chic look.

I nodded.

'I heard something last week and thought I should tell you, in case it has a bearing on the investigation.'

'Okay, go ahead.'

'I've got to be quick. I should be inside.' She looked over her shoulder. 'I overheard Dr Webster, the dead man's wife, on the phone. I don't know who she was talking to, but she sounded panicky. I forgot to knock and she slammed the phone down when I went into her surgery.'

I was a big fan of people who forgot to knock. 'What did you hear?'

'I heard her say something about typhus, and then she said *we need to be careful, the police have been sniffing around*. I remembered because of her saying about the police.'

'She mentioned "typhus"?'

'That's what I heard.'

'I know times are hard in Derbyshire, but typhus? Surely not.

Wasn't it spread by lice? In medieval times and World War One trenches?'

'I don't know. I just do the filing. I'm going to uni next year though and doing law.' She gave me an appraising look. 'I might be a detective actually. I heard something else, too.' She certainly seemed well suited for a career in detection. 'Something a bit weird.'

'Weird?'

She nodded. 'I heard Vivian, you know, the receptionist, on the phone. She sounded upset. She said Dr Webster was doing *the Devil's work*.'

Chapter 9

I walked back down to the marketplace, wrapping Carrie's scarf tightly round my neck against the bitter wind. My car was still in the car park and hadn't plunged down the hill into the side of a shop, as per my imaginings. I had my hand on my key when I remembered about Mum's brooch, ready for me to pick up from Grace Swift's jewellery shop. It was just over the road, and probably due to shut as it was bang on five o'clock. I dashed over the marketplace as fast as my dodgy ankle could carry me, ran in front of a driver dopily looking for a non-existent parking spot, and burst in.

The shop was empty. I glanced back at the door and saw the sign – *Open*. Oh dear, the other side must have said *Closed*. But the door had been unlocked, and I needed Mum's brooch.

'Grace!' I called.

No answer. A distinct clunk came from the door. I jumped. It had sounded like something locking. I gave the door a shove. It didn't move. I twisted the handle and rattled the door, a feeling of unease squirming inside me. I was locked in.

'Grace?' I tried to keep my voice calm.

I could hear a ticking noise, like a loud clock. I was sure there hadn't been any ticking when I'd first walked in. It had started when the door clunked and locked. I told myself to think calmly. There had to be an innocent explanation.

I looked around the small shop. Glass cabinets were filled with standard fare – watches and so on – but one cabinet caught my eye. It seemed to glow. Inside were pendants and bracelets made from a precious stone I didn't recognise. It had a kind of magical luminance – colours swirling and mixing and seeming to change before my eyes. A top shelf contained pale, bright pieces and a lower shelf darker pieces, both beautiful.

Where was Grace? The hairs on my arms pricked and I remembered there was a murderer somewhere in this unlikely community.

I noticed a door at the back of the shop, behind the till. I walked round and pushed it. It resisted, then swung open with a creak to reveal a small workshop. I stepped in, trying to avoid knocking over any of the vats of noxious-looking chemicals. The air was thick with the smell of burning metal.

Grace was hunched over soldering equipment. She looked up and her soldering iron fell and clanged on the floor.

'The door was open,' I said. 'But then it locked me in.'

'Oh, I'm so sorry!' Grace stooped and retrieved the soldering iron. 'I set it to lock at five. My assistant must have left early.'

'Yes, there was no one around. Aren't you worried about leaving the shop unattended?'

'God wouldn't let me be burgled.'

I replayed the words in my mind, trying to work out if I'd misheard. I hadn't noticed God taking a hands-on role in crime prevention in the area.

'And the cabinets are electrified after five,' Grace said.

'Electrified?' I said weakly. Obviously God wasn't quite up to the job on his own.

'Yes. With a simple electric fence set-up.'

I remembered the clicking I'd heard in the shop. 'That sounds dangerous.'

'Oh no, it's quite safe. It's high voltage but the pulse duration is short, so the energy transmitted is low. Like a fence for horses.' She put down the soldering iron and led me back into the shop. The clicking sounded more ominous now.

'You're not going to make me stop are you?' Grace said. 'It would only affect someone who tried to steal something. It's off when the shop's open.' She reached forward and touched the edge of the cabinet containing the lovely jewellery. A spark cracked the air and she pulled her finger back sharply. 'There! I'm still alive. Try it if you like.'

'No thanks. Look, just make sure no one can wander in the way I did, and put some signs up.'

'Yes, of course. I'll switch it off and get your mum's brooch.' She tapped a code into a keypad behind the counter. The clicking noise stopped. I let out the breath I'd been holding.

Grace reached under the counter and pulled out a box, which she handed to me. I opened it up and the brooch was spot on – exactly like the original. 'It's beautiful,' I said. 'Perfect. It was her grandmother's and she was so upset to lose it. I know it's not quite the same to have a new one but I think she'll be pleased.'

Grace smiled, put the box into a plush velvet pouch, and tied it with a silver ribbon. 'Have one of these too.' She took a magazine from a pile on the cabinet of lovely things and popped it into an expensive-looking paper bag, with the brooch. 'I do hope your mother likes the brooch.'

'She will. I can't believe she was so careless, but she's been a bit forgetful recently.'

'What a shame. Do you see her often?

'Not as much as I should.'

'Oh, I was the same. I should have done so much more for my father when he was still alive.'

Her eyes glistened. I wasn't sure what to say. I gestured at the cabinet. 'Your jewellery's beautiful. Do you make that yourself?'

'Yes, it's rather special.'

I walked a step closer to the cabinet. 'It's lovely. Like nothing I've ever seen.'

'Well, it's a rather unusual type of jewellery.' She opened her mouth as if to say more, but then hesitated.

'Oh?' I leant to peer into the cabinet.

'You might have heard of it. I call it *Soul Jewellery*.'

'No, I haven't heard of it.'

'You may have heard the term *Cremation jewellery*. I know it sounds strange but people kept asking for it. I wasn't sure at first, but I like it now. It's made from loved one's ashes.'

I stepped back. Dead people's ashes. I shivered.

'Those ones aren't for sale, obviously. They're for the relatives. But do you see the different colours? That tells you so much.'

'Oh, what does it tell you?'

'You can see from the colours those who have led good lives versus those who haven't.'

'Sorry?' I glanced at her face. She had the Stepford Wife look again – eyes wide, slightly vacant expression, not a touch of irony. I swallowed. 'You mean the light ones versus the dark ones?'

'Yes.' She smiled and a little dimple appeared in each cheek. 'Well, that's how I see it anyway.'

★

As I was in Eldercliffe, I decided to drop Mum's brooch round. It would be an excuse to check she was okay and moderately assuage my ever-present gnawing sense of guilt.

I drove up the hill and navigated the lanes to the more modern side of the town. Leaving Eldercliffe was like travelling in time, as the buildings progressed from medieval through Georgian and Victorian, past 1930s semis and finally to the 'executive' new-builds which sprawled around the town's edges. Mum lived in the semi-detached zone, in a dull but reasonably affluent suburban street, where men washed cars that weren't dirty and mowed stripes in their lawns, and women did everything else.

I pulled up outside Mum's house, and was surprised to see that her car wasn't in the driveway. She must have nipped to the shops. I decided to let myself in and wait for her.

I walked through the privet-enclosed garden, turned the key and gave the front door a shove. A crash came from the direction of the kitchen. She was in after all – dropping things again. Maybe she'd left the car at the garage.

The door slammed behind me, as if a window was open somewhere in the house. That was strange, in this weather.

'Mum,' I called. 'I've got your brooch.'

No answer. That was really odd. Mum must have surely heard the door slam, and would have come into the hallway, or at least shouted a greeting. I hoped the crash hadn't been her falling. They always said the kitchen was a potential death-trap and best avoided.

I heard a soft thud, like the boiler room door closing. I figured she must be okay if she was fiddling with the heating. I headed towards the kitchen. 'Mum, are you there?'

No answer.

With a flush of adrenaline, it occurred to me that it wasn't Mum in the house.

Chapter 10

I froze and stood in the hall, ears straining. I contemplated calling for help, but it would take too long for anyone to arrive and I'd feel an idiot if it was just Mum having one of her moments.

I retraced my steps to the front door and picked up Mum's cast-iron boot jack. Gripping it in my right hand, I edged towards the stairs. I had to check Gran was okay. She was now a professional ill-person and was virtually immobile, lying helpless in bed. I crept up to her room and gently shoved the door open. She was asleep, snoring gently, and I could see no evidence of an intruder. My own breathing slowed.

I tip-toed back downstairs and paused outside the kitchen. I could hear nothing but my own heart, which was surely beating more loudly than it should have been. I inched the door open.

The room smelt of washing up liquid and vinegar, and under that a trace of burning. There was no one there.

My gaze flicked over the clear work surfaces and tiled floor. All looked normal, except that a window was wide open, leaving gingham curtains fluttering.

I stepped over to the boiler room, clutching the boot jack with rigid fingers, and pushed the door. The room was empty. I rushed to the back door and out into the garden, but could see no one, so ran round the side of the house and looked up and down the road. It was tumbleweed-level deserted.

I stood stupidly in the road, looking back and forth, feeling my breath rasping in and out. Who could have been in Mum's kitchen?

I hurried back to the house. The study was locked and the TV and DVD player were still in the living room. I checked Mum's bedroom, and it looked pristine and untouched, her jewellery still hidden in the first place a burglar would look. She kept the study locked up like a fortress but her jewellery was in her underwear drawer. There was something forlorn about her Mum-pants, folded neatly around her rings and necklaces.

I padded back downstairs, still half-expecting to see an intruder lurking in the shadows. But I'd seen enough burglaries – glasses smashed, bins upended, clothes strewn everywhere – to know this wasn't one. I must have arrived just in time.

I took out my phone to call it in. And had a moment of doubt.

I returned to the kitchen, and noticed Mum's little metal horse on the floor. It lived on the windowsill, and could have been knocked off by someone climbing through. I looked around with a forensic gaze, but could see nothing else out of place.

Something loomed at the window, visible in the corner of my eye.

I gasped and jumped back before spinning round to look. The neighbour's cat perched on the sill and stared at me with dazzling green eyes.

I let out a huge sigh. 'Alfie. Oh my God. Did you jump up onto the windowsill and knock the metal horse on the floor?'

Alfie blinked – a fluffy ball of tabby, admitting nothing.

I sank onto one of Mum's wooden chairs. It was just the bloody cat. Mum must have left the window open. She'd been absent-minded recently. I felt like a melodramatic idiot for charging around the house and garden with an offensive boot jack.

I tried to laugh at myself, wishing someone was there to share the story. *High-flying detective terrified by tabby.* Hannah would think it was hilarious. What I'd thought was the boiler room door closing must have been Alfie jumping off the windowsill back into the garden. Thank God I hadn't called it in. I could do without the *Pink Panther* cracks.

I imagined myself telling Mum, and started to rehearse a comic tale. I felt a coldness inside. No matter how light-hearted I tried to be, she wasn't going to find this funny. I pictured her face crumpling with anxiety. She'd understand it was the cat, but deep down she'd think it was something else.

I stood and paced the kitchen. I couldn't tell her. It would be cruel. She wouldn't feel safe here any more, and all because of the neighbour's cat. I'd have to keep my mouth shut and pretend it had never happened.

Like someone twisting a knife, a little part of me pointed out that I wasn't absolutely sure no one had been in the house, that I really should tell Mum and call it in – persuade them to take fingerprints, just in case. Was I being selfish by not telling her? Saving myself the trouble of coping with her if she got scared.

I felt the familiar tearing inside, my job tugging me one way, Mum and Gran the other. The job was like a new baby, demanding total commitment and unsociable hours, especially with the Hamilton case. I couldn't bear to fail. I had to prove I was good enough for the opportunity I'd been given. If Mum got more anxious, how could I find the time to be with her? And we needed my salary. Without the money I contributed, Gran couldn't have a private carer. It had been so upsetting for her when she'd had a different one each day, someone she didn't even know, doing the most intimate and unspeakable things to her.

Alfie jumped down with an un-catlike thud and disappeared into his own garden. I closed the window, found the key in the kitchen drawer and locked it.

The front door clicked. 'Meg, is that you?'

'In the kitchen,' I shouted.

She appeared and gave me a hug. She felt more solid these days – almost my size. She'd always been skinny when I was a child, seeming insignificant next to Dad's bulk.

'You left the window open, Mum. You need to stop doing that. I shut and locked it.'

'Oh, did I? I've been a bit forgetful recently.' She put her bag on the floor and leant against the kitchen counter. 'I burnt the toast and opened it. I must have forgotten to shut it. I nipped to the garage but they've got no milk.'

'Well, be careful, Mum. I worry about you. Are you alright? You don't seem yourself at the moment. Are you anxious about something?'

'Oh, I'm fine, Meg. Don't fret about me.' The skin of her face was greyer than I remembered.

Worry nagged at me. 'I can ask Tracy to do some extra hours.' I could manage. Just.

'No, no.' She turned away from me and fiddled with the kettle. 'You mustn't. I'm fine.'

I hesitated. I'd been so sure there was someone in the kitchen. Maybe it wasn't fair to keep it from her. But, no, I'd been silly. It was only the cat. 'I'll nip up and see if Gran wants a word.'

Gran had obviously just woken up. It shocked me each time I saw her now – her face creased like an old apple and her scalp shining through a fuzz of hair, almost like a baby's head. She'd been so proud of her hair, treating it to blue rinses and Silvikrin hairspray that Carrie and I had secretly mocked.

A cloying smell hung in the air, and a sick bowl nestled half under her bed. She levered herself up on the pillows and fixed me with her still-demanding eyes. 'Got yourself a new boyfriend yet, Meg?'

'Hello Gran, good to see you.' She clearly hadn't heard me charging around with the boot jack.

'Better get a move on, all the decent ones'll be gone. You'll be on to the second round – divorcees, and they're a menace with their ex-wives and spoilt brats. And if you want children…'

'Come on Gran, you know that bit of my brain's missing. I'm not bothered about having kids.'

'Ach, you're probably right. I sometimes wish I hadn't bothered

66

myself.' I loved the way Gran came out with such un-grandma-like comments. Her mind was still sharp, although the tact-and-diplomacy-lobes had shrunk.

'Yeah,' I said. 'Most people spend their lives making themselves miserable doing work they hate, to make money for the sake of their kids, and then their kids grow up and do the same thing over again for *their* kids. I don't see the point. Besides, I'm quite capable of making myself miserable all on my own, without doing it for the kids.'

'Ah, well, you modern women, you're right, you know. Who wants to depend on a man? There aren't many good ones.'

She stared into the distance. Not that there was any distance in her life any more, stuck in this room, with nothing to look at that was further away than the TV. I couldn't imagine knowing I'd never again look at the vastness of the sea or even the Peak District views I took for granted.

'Anyway, how are you feeling? You look well.' I could smell the lie as it slithered out of my mouth.

'I'm not going doolally if that's what you're wondering. But my damn stomach does hurt and I can't keep the painkillers down. If I was a dog, they'd have put me down long ago.' She closed her eyes. 'Your mum should…'

'Gran?'

She didn't reply, and sank lower into the bed. I hugged her, not too tight for fear her bones would crumble. 'I'll see you again soon, Gran.'

I crept out and padded downstairs to the kitchen.

Mum made tea and we sat together at the table. A memory from long ago popped into my head – the four of us having supper at our old house. Before Carrie got ill. I'd been a babbler. I'd ask 'Why?' until most adults were ready to bash my little blonde head against the table. Except Dad. He'd have answers for every question, and then he'd have some of his own for me. 'Why do you think the sky's blue?' 'How many stars are in the universe?' (I guessed fifty, which was a big disappointment to him.) 'How far away do you think the sun is?' 'How long do you think the light takes to get from that star to here?' Mum and Carrie would sigh, roll their eyes and serve the sprouts.

'Your dad makes the important decisions in this family,' Mum used to say. 'Like whether the universe is expanding and whether we should throw our hats in for string theory or loop quantum gravity. And I make the unimportant ones like what we have for supper.'

'Here. I've got your brooch.' I fished it out and pushed the velvet bag into her hand. 'You can forget you ever lost it.'

She opened up the little box, and the brooch sat and sparkled.

'It's lovely,' she said.

I took the box and had another look. 'Did you know they made jewellery out of dead people's ashes?'

'Oh, that's nice.'

'Really? A bit ghoulish, isn't it?'

'Don't worry, I won't suggest it for your gran.'

I smiled, wondering if Gran's ashes would come out light or dark, according to Grace Swift's insane theory. 'Mum, is she in a lot of pain? She said we'd have put her down if she was a dog.'

Mum stood and walked to the window. 'I don't think she really means that. She can be a bit incoherent.'

'She was pretty coherent about my lack of a boyfriend. But I was serious, do you need more help looking after her?'

'No.' She knew the financial situation. 'I'm okay. Tracy's great. She bathes her... and everything. But some days it's hard. Sometimes I have to force myself not to just shut the door and forget about her.' She wandered back and sat at the breakfast bar with me. 'Anyway, how are you?'

'I'm on this new case. You'll have seen it on the TV.'

'I haven't really been watching the TV. Let's talk about something other than work.'

'Haven't you been following it at all? It's the most dramatic thing to happen in Eldercliffe for about four hundred years. It's normally all sheep down mineshafts round here.'

'I know, love. I don't like bad news.'

'He was some kind of lawyer. His wife's a GP just up the road. Are you at her practice? Kate Webster?'

'No. I said let's talk about something else.'

It wasn't like her to get snappy. I sensed she was hiding something from me. I felt as if the world had lurched, like a ship. 'Are you alright? Mum?'

'I'm fine. I don't know her. I'm at the other doctors' surgery. I don't know the name.' She picked a piece of fluff off her cardigan.

'Are you sure?'

'Yes. Never heard of her. Poor woman. You're not working too hard, are you? You know what you can get like. Have you found time to see Hannah recently?'

I felt a stab of guilt. 'I'll see her at the weekend. But Mum—'

'Could you nip out and get me some milk, love?'

'Yes, I suppose so.' The shop was only five minutes' walk away, although half of this was spent plunging down a periously steep set of steps to the main road. I sensed she was trying to get rid of me, but when Mum didn't want to talk, there was little point in persisting. I grabbed one of her coats from the rack by the door, shoved a fiver in my pocket and let myself out the front.

The road was dimly lit and the houses were set back – all in their own lonely spaces, behind hedges and cherry trees, so the street-lamps cast long shadows onto their lawns. This area was a complete contrast to the tiny lanes, steps and alleyways of the old town a few minutes away. I walked in the direction of the main road, still feeling spooked by the Alfie-cat experience. I looked down at the cracked slabs of the pavement. When I was a child, someone had told me if you avoided the cracks, terrible things would never happen to you. I'd always avoided the cracks. So much for that theory.

I thought I heard the patter of footsteps behind me. I whipped my head round but there was no one there. Just the tree branches ruffling in the breeze. I pulled my coat tighter around me and increased my pace.

I reached the top of the steps which tumbled down towards the town centre. They were cut into the rocky hillside which separated the old town from the newer area where Mum lived. Their stone surfaces were worn, their edges curved and uneven. Ornate iron railings had apparently once graced both sides, but they'd been taken in the war to make something deadly, and never replaced.

I paused to curse my bad ankle before tackling the descent. A street lamp shone behind me, and my body cast a spindly, elongated shadow down the steps, my shadow-head almost touching the road far below.

My phone vibrated in my pocket. I fished it out. Kate Webster. I touched the screen. Her voice blasted out, high pitched and frantic. 'I found an email from him. Just now.'

'Slow down, Kate, it's okay. What have you found?'

'I hadn't checked my emails since before he died. Your lot have got my laptop. I just checked them on Beth's. He sent one that morning saying…' She tailed off.

I pressed the phone hard to my ear. Shadow-Meg did the same, her movements exaggerated and distorted by the shape of the steps. 'What did the email say, Kate?'

I heard the footsteps behind me again. Coming up fast.

Chapter 11

Someone was behind me. I gasped and tried to spin round, but my foot slipped over the curved edge of the top step. My legs shot out from under me and I slammed onto my hip. A flash of adrenaline exploded in my stomach.

There was a burst of frenzied barking and snarling.

I was falling. I tried to grab onto the steps, but my fingers slipped over their smooth surfaces. I crashed all the way to the bottom and bashed my head against the final step with a sickening crack.

I lay crumpled and astonished. Pain stabbed into my ankle, hip, shoulder, and skull.

Something was careering down the steps. I wanted to scream. I couldn't move. I shielded my head with my arms.

A wet tongue licked my face. I tried to lift my head but a jolt of pain shot through my neck and I sank back down. I heard panting and snuffling.

I lay on the pavement. My throat felt solid right down to my chest and a whooshing noise flooded my ears.

I groaned and levered myself into a sitting position. The world pitched. Moist breath warmed my ear. It was Mrs Smedley's German Shepherd – Freddie, the escape artist. He licked my face three times, then shot off up the steps.

I tried to piece together what had happened. Someone had run up behind me, really close, then Freddie had appeared and done his wild-wolf impression, I'd fallen down the steps, and the person had run away.

I looked around, my gaze flitting back up the steps, panic just below the surface. I couldn't see anyone. But what if they came back, now Freddie was gone? My breath came in sharp bursts.

I needed to be on my feet. I needed to be able to run. I hauled myself up and stood shakily with my legs apart trying to get my brain to work. A wave of dizziness came over me like a blanket of mist, and I sat back down on the bottom step.

'Fuck,' I said. 'Fucking hell.'

I knew I should probably call the Station, but what would I say? Someone came up behind me and I fell down the steps, like an idiot? I didn't even see their face. I'd never hear the end of it from Craig. My new name would be *Eddie the Eagle.* And besides, I needed to be sick. I had to get back to Mum's.

I took a first tentative step. Everything seemed to be in working order, albeit painful, so I carried on and started climbing back up towards Mum's house. One foot after another. My head throbbed and something wasn't right in my hip either. About ten steps up, I paused for breath and glanced back down towards the road.

I gasped and collapsed onto the step. It was the flashback again, smashing itself into my consciousness like an attack from a vicious animal. First the feet, dangling. Dangling like feet weren't supposed to dangle, level with my face. Everything wrong – the feet, the ladder, incongruous in the middle of her bedroom. My brain unable to make sense of it. Staring at the feet for an endless moment, a low cry already building in my throat, terrified to look anywhere but the feet. Then the point my gaze flipped up. Carrie's head slumped forward. The shape of her skull through wisps of hair. Me screaming, climbing the ladder, scrabbling, pulling, sobbing. Then falling. Finally, always the falling.

Chapter 12

Hannah sniffed the air. 'Ugh! Hospitals. You could have chosen somewhere more interesting for a mini-break. I spend half my life here.' She wheeled herself up to my bed.

My head was mushy. 'At least it's wheelchair-friendly. Anyway, I'm not staying. I hate hospitals.' They smelt of guilt and dejection. I forced those feelings away and attempted a smile. 'Nice of you to visit me, Hannah.'

'I was worried about you.' She frowned at me. 'I did have someone else to visit too.'

'Good to know I'm such a priority in your life. Who were you visiting?'

'It doesn't matter. When are they discharging you?'

'I don't care what they do, I'm leaving today. I've missed a day of work already. I can't believe I've been here last night and most of today. What a waste of time.'

'What the hell have you been up to anyway?' As if I'd done it deliberately.

'I fell down some steps, and bashed my head.' I swivelled to show the bump.

'Jesus. How come?'

'Someone ran up behind me.' I hadn't meant to say that.

'Oh my God. Maybe it was a rapist or something. What did he look like?'

'I didn't see. Honestly, it was most likely just some idiot in a hurry. It gave me a fright, that's all. And I fell down the steps.'

'Why didn't they help you then? If it was a normal person?'

She had a point. Something wasn't right about the whole incident. But the thought of reporting it as suspicious filled me with exhaustion. I had no information. I'd seem pathetic. The last thing I needed now, with Craig hot on my tail, was to appear vulnerable. 'I'm not saying anything to Work or to Mum about the person coming up behind me. It'll only worry them. Don't mention it, Hannah, I mean it.'

'But it's kind of scary. What if they're after you?'

'Stop it. Seriously.' I remembered the flashback. It hovered in the back of my mind like a caged animal, scratching to be let out. I couldn't let it out. I couldn't go back to how I'd been in Manchester. I was over all that. 'Anyway, who were you visiting?'

'Oh, I met someone through that group. She campaigns for stuff for disabled people. She's had pneumonia and I came to visit her. That's all.'

'Oh. You never mentioned her before.'

'Why do you always have to be so negative?'

'For Christ's sake, Hannah, I wasn't being negative.'

'Your face says it all. Besides, I know your views. What was it you said about that group? *The devout manipulating the disabled?*'

That did sound like me. I kept my voice even. 'Look, I don't want to argue. Let's not talk about it. It's not worth falling out over.'

'Okay. I know you don't like that group. But they're only trying to stand up for vulnerable people and unborn babies who have no voice.' Hannah swallowed. 'Nowadays most people would abort a baby like me with Spina Bifida.'

God, I didn't have the energy today. I shifted on my pillows. 'I'm not sure that's true, or a good way of looking at it. You're—'

'They showed us pictures of babies at the age they can still kill them.'

'They're bloody manipulating you, Hannah, can't you see it?

74

Did they show photos of babies screaming after their twentieth operation too?'

Hannah shifted her chair back an inch.

I reached for her hand. 'I'm sorry. I just wish they wouldn't show that stuff.'

'They're trying to make things better.'

I pulled my hand away. I couldn't understand why Hannah had been sucked in by them, but I didn't want to repeat the argument.

'Just forget it,' Hannah said. 'You're right. I did have lots of operations on my spine but I can't remember. My baby photos would have been more at home in *The Lancet* than in a family album.'

'Oh Hannah, I didn't mean you. Of course I don't think you should have been aborted.' I looked over at Hannah, so lovely and full of life. I'd never admitted to her that being paralysed was one of my worst fears; that it woke me sweating in the night, tangled in sheets and gasping for breath; that I probably would abort a baby like her if I ever had to make that terrible choice.

Hannah looked up and I followed her eyes. Jai, striding towards us.

His voice sounded like he was being lightly strangled. 'Meg, what happened? They say you bashed your head.'

'I'm okay. It's no big deal.'

'I was leaving anyway,' Hannah kissed me, somewhat frostily, and did a kind of wheelchair handbrake-turn before gliding away.

Jai sat on the chair by my bedside. 'Seriously, are you alright?'

'I'm fine. How's it going with the Hamilton case?'

'Oh, there's a suicide note. Richard's wrapping it up. You don't need to be involved.'

I sat up, with some difficulty. My brain chugged. I'd forgotten. Just before I fell. The call from Kate Webster. 'An email,' I said hesitantly.

'Yes, an email. All fairly clear cut.'

No, it wasn't. I was sure it wasn't clear cut. 'What did the email say?'

'It was the usual stuff. Sorry, sorry, you're better off without me and all that.'

'How do we know someone hadn't hacked his account? It just doesn't have the feel of a suicide to me.'

'He'd been behaving strangely, acting depressed, saying he was cursed. Richard's happy with suicide.'

'Come on, Jai.' I could feel my brain clarifying. 'One, have you ever tried to get cyanide? You can't pick it up from Asda. Two, cyanide's not a nice way to die—'

'I thought they put it in those pills for spies.'

'It's quick, not nice. And C—'

'You were doing one, two, three, not A, B, C.'

'Give me a break. I've had a head injury. Three, have you seen where he lives? He could have just chucked himself off that cliff any time. Why bother with cyanide-infused cake?'

'Trying to make it look unclear so it's an open verdict and the wife gets the life insurance?'

'Why the email then?'

'You make a persuasive case for a woman recently bashed on the head, but it's Richard you need to convince, not me. And he's not expecting you in till Monday.'

I sank back on my pillows. What I hadn't said to Jai was – four, Mark Hamilton is a nice man with lots of dogs and cats, and he had an argument with his brother who is now dead, and I *cannot* let him think his brother committed suicide if it's not true. No one should have to go through that.

'I'll go in tomorrow,' I said. 'And persuade Richard.'

'Be careful, alright?' He reached out and touched my arm. I instinctively pulled away and Jai withdrew his hand as if he'd touched a hot stove. I wanted to say sorry, I didn't mean to pull away, but the moment was gone.

Chapter 13

My eyes flipped open. It was brutally dark – no trace of dawn. Something was pressing on my chest. I opened my mouth to scream, and felt something soft touch my face. I smelt fishy breath. I reached and flipped on the bedside light. Hamlet. He looked into my eyes, purred and kneaded my face. I released my breath.

I'd been released late the night before into the caring arms of my Mum. The medical people had confirmed I wasn't bleeding from my brain or anywhere more vital, but had told me to come back if I experienced any of a long list of symptoms. They'd allowed me out on the basis that Mum stayed with me overnight and checked I was still breathing and at least normally coherent in the morning.

For a few minutes I lay staring at the ceiling, trying to absorb Hamlet's feline calm. What would have happened if the dog hadn't turned up at the top of those steps? Had someone been coming for me? Was it something to do with the Hamilton case?

I slid out from under the duvet and eased myself into a sitting position. I reached for the bedside table and grabbed my painkillers, feeling my brain bounce within my skull when I moved. I gulped down two of the super-strength pills the hospital had doled out.

I crept down my sloping floorboards to dig out clean clothes, feeling like I was on the high seas. The lack of right angles in my crumbling, ancient house didn't help. Bending over was the worst

– my sense of balance was gone and my brain was clearly a little too big for my skull.

Mum was asleep in the spare room, but I could do without her fretting and forcing gallons of tea down me. Besides, it was stupidly-early o'clock, so I left her to it and tottered downstairs and into the kitchen. Hamlet followed me and bumbled around while I made tea, then followed me through to the living room at the front of the house. The heating hadn't come on yet and it was bone-numblingly cold, but by the time I'd sunk onto the sofa, I was too exhausted to get up again and do anything about it. Besides, Hamlet had parked himself on me and it was a life rule of mine not to move when catted.

A lump of plaster was coming away from the wall in the damp corner. I sighed, reached for the remote and stuck the TV on with the sound down low, praying for a programme that didn't involve educationally challenged people from Essex copulating on a remote island.

I reached into my bag and fished out the magazine Grace had given me what seemed like weeks ago. Her disturbing but gorgeous jewellery would be a good distraction.

'Ugh.' I dropped the magazine. It wasn't about her jewellery – it was a religious thing, the lead article, '*How to be a Godly Business Woman*'. I kicked it aside and closed my eyes. The pavement rushed towards me. My insides felt untethered as if I was in a lift going down too fast. The memory of the flashback shimmered like a distant threat.

I forced myself to think about the Hamilton case. Pressed my fingers to my temples and started mentally sifting through the evidence. I took a deep breath and realised I was feeling better.

My gut told me it wasn't suicide. Of course I could never admit that to Richard – he'd accuse me of being illogical. I'd argue it was my subconscious pulling together all the threads and seasoning them with years of experience. I could point him to numerous articles in *New Scientist* about the supremacy of intuition when there were lots of factors to consider, but if I did, he'd throw something at me. Probably a cactus. Cacti were his thing.

I searched my memory for the word Fiona had mentioned from the paper in Kate Webster's fire. *Tithonus.* Why would Peter have scrawled that name on a piece of paper which his wife seemed so keen for me not to see? I reached for my laptop, prised open the lid, and googled it. This was what I needed – to focus on work.

I took a slug of tea and scrutinised the search results. According to the Greek myth, Tithonus was a Trojan, who was kidnapped by Eos (clearly a proto-feminist, reversing traditional gender roles) to be her lover. Eos asked the Gods to make Tithonus immortal. But she only asked for immortality and not eternal youth, so poor Tithonus got older and older but never died. I read that, *Tithonus indeed lived forever… but when loathsome old age pressed full upon him, and he could not move nor lift his limbs… she laid him in a room and put to the shining doors. There he babbles endlessly, and no more has strength at all, such as once he had in his supple limbs.* In some accounts, he eventually turned into a cicada, eternally living, but begging for death to overcome him.

I shuddered, put the laptop down and manoeuvred Hamlet onto my knee. I leant and breathed in his subtle, nutty cat smell. What a terrible story. Poor Tithonus, shut away, suffering behind closed doors so nobody had to witness his torment. It was kind of what Mum had admitted wanting to do with Gran. It sickened me, but I knew it was in me too – the desire to shut away anything too painful to confront.

Hamlet, with blatant disregard for my emotional needs, climbed off my knee and wandered through to the kitchen in the hope of a snack. I followed him through, dished out something exotic and organic for him, and made more tea for myself.

I leant against the sink and stared out into my garden. Took in the cracked patio splattered with puddles, the lawn tangled with weeds, the sprawling hedges, the wisteria that scaled the back wall of the house and leant over as if it was trying to escape into next door's better-cared-for environment. I noticed the little organised patch I'd created two weekends ago. Dug nicely and planted with three robust, un-killable shrubs. They were looking good.

The sun emerged from behind a slab of cloud, all bright and surprising, beaming through the dust and cobwebs on the kitchen windows and casting shadows on the black-and-white tiled floor.

I spun round, wincing at the pain in my head and hip. Nobody was after me. And I would *not* let the flashbacks return. I was fine. I'd carry on working and forget all this ever happened. I left Mum an appreciative note and set off for work.

★

I hobbled down the corridor and into Richard's room. My ankle had flared up in sympathy with my head, and I must have cut a pretty sad picture.

Richard was at his desk, poring over something which he hastily shoved in a drawer. He was shielded by piles of documents, all neatly stacked and aligned in rows in front of him. Each pile was topped with a tiny cactus in a pot, like a prickly paperweight. It was very strange, but we'd got used to it. He looked up at me, but his shoulders stayed low, giving him the appearance of a giant turtle. He invited me to sit opposite him in a psychologically disadvantageous lower chair.

'Yes. Meg. I wasn't expecting you in. And seeing you now, you'd better get off home.'

'I'm fine. I just want to look into the Hamilton case a bit more. Can you give me some time to—'

'I'm taking you off that one. Craig can help Jai wrap it up.'

'No, please, just give me a few days. I don't think—'

'You've had a head injury. I can't risk it.'

The chair was trying to engulf me. I hoped my predecessor wasn't in there. I clawed myself up a couple of inches. 'Why would he commit suicide in such an odd way? It makes no sense.'

'We know the man was unstable. He'd decided he was cursed,

chose to commit suicide in the haunted cave. He even wrote a note. Suicidal people do odd things.'

Did Richard's clear-up rate need enhancing or something? 'What if someone hacked into his account?'

'You've had a knock on the head.' He picked up a cactus and pointed it at me. A tiny red flower sprouted from the top. 'You're not fit to be at work.'

I straightened my back and tried to look healthy, not sure if the cactus-pointing was supposed to mean something. 'Do we know he sent the email? Anyone could have logged into his account.'

'It's not your problem. You're off the case. If there are any loose ends, Jai and Craig will follow them up.'

I noticed a framed photograph on Richard's desk. A blonde woman. Young. Hopefully his daughter, although she was more attractive than you'd expect for someone with Richard's genes. It occurred to me I knew nothing about his private life.

'No.' I made my voice forceful. Not the voice of someone who'd recently bounced down steps on her head. 'I'm really okay. Let me carry on.'

Richard coughed. 'I know you've had some personal issues in the past…' He gave me a helpless look.

I wanted to scream. I'd left the Manchester force to get away from all this.

'I'm fine,' I snapped. 'I had some time off. It happens. I'm fully recovered.'

'Well, I don't want to be responsible…'

I wondered if he'd be like this if I was a man. 'Yes, I had some personal issues. And now I'm better. It has nothing to do with anything.'

Richard glanced at the photograph of the girl. 'But if it's not suicide…'

'So, you're not totally convinced it was suicide.'

He gave me a look so full of exasperation I'd only previously seen the like pass between relatives. I sensed he was weakening.

The phone rang. Richard glanced at it and twitched. Looked at me. Looked back at the phone. 'I'd better get this.' He snatched it to his ear.

I sensed an opportunity. 'So, okay, thanks. I'll carry on with the Hamilton case then.' I jumped up as best I could and limped out of his office, leaving Richard sitting with his mouth open.

I hurried down the corridor, my brain still feeling foggy and sore. The brutal lights stabbed at my eyes and there was a shimmering in my vision, like the beginnings of a migraine.

Craig slithered out of a doorway and stood in my path. 'So, are you off home then?'

'No, Craig, I'm carrying on investigating the Hamilton case.'

'You're off that. Me and Jai are tying it up. It's suicide.'

The shimmering expanded. Craig's face was distorted like something in a hall of mirrors. 'No. Richard said I could carry on.' Well, sort of.

Craig's breathing was audible. 'No. That's wrong.' He was like a pug that thought it was a Rottweiler.

I looked into his pale eyes. 'Check with Richard if you must.'

'What did you do? Offer to shag him?'

My hands curled tight and hard. 'Oh, for Christ's sake, Craig. Leave me alone.'

'Oooh, touchy!' He took a step back. 'That's the problem with you women, isn't it? You get all upset about nothing.'

I was sick of representing the whole of womankind. Why couldn't I just cock up on my own account, like a man could? 'I'm not upset,' I said. 'You're the one with a vein throbbing in your neck.'

He shot me a look of pure venom. 'Real cops don't have time off with "stress".' He put air quotes around the word, and said it in a ridiculous, high-pitched voice.

'Get out of my way, Craig. Real cops don't act like arseholes either.' I pushed past him, shoving him harder than I'd intended against the wall.

'Just because your sister—'

82

I spun round and lunged at him. Imagined smashing my fist into his smug face. But I held back and kept my voice low. 'If you mention my sister *ever* again…'

There must have been something about the level of my anger that cut through even Craig's obliviousness. The blood drained from his face. He turned and walked quickly away.

I stormed to my office and threw myself into my chair. I was so furious I felt pins and needles in my veins, almost as if my blood was fizzing. It frightened me how much I'd wanted to punch Craig.

I rubbed my eyes and realised the migraine was disappearing, fading into a few tiny shreds of light in my peripheral vision. I shoved Craig's puggy face from my mind and focussed on my breathing for a couple of minutes, preparing myself to get back up to speed with the case.

I logged in and looked for the 'suicide note'.

Chapter 14

I stared at the screen, scrutinising every word of the email.

Dearest Kate,

It's getting worse. It's survival of the fittest and I'm not fit. I
should have shared more with you and I'm sorry. I won't destroy
your happiness and dreams. I know that I am spoiling your life.
Please say sorry to Mark too.

All my love,

Peter

I printed a copy and went to find Jai. He was perched sideways on
his chair, squinting at his computer screen.

'We're back on,' I said.

He looked up, and winced. 'You don't look so good.'

I waved his concerns away. 'I never look that great, to be honest.'

'Yeah. Not sure about that. Your face isn't normally actually
green.' He pulled up a chair beside him. 'So what do you reckon
about the suicide note?'

'I think it's dodgy.'

'Me too. And something interesting's come up.'

I shuffled closer to his overflowing desk. 'Tell all.'

'You know the task force have been searching the area around
the cave house. Well, they found something odd.' Jai tapped on

his keyboard and brought up a photograph of a fallen tree in some woods. He zoomed in. 'This tree's about fifty feet from the cave house. It looks from the footwear marks as if he stopped here.' Jai pointed at the screen.

'By an old tree?' I leant closer. 'Is it hollow?'

'Yes. Well spotted. And can you see there's a metal casket inside the hollow bit?'

'A *casket*? What are we in, *The Merchant of Venice*?'

'Don't try and impress me with your literary references. Call it a metal box if you prefer.'

'No, no, casket's good. Did anyone else go to it?'

'It looks like some medium-to-large boots, probably wellies, go near it.' Jai walked his fingers across the desk as if illustrating the path of the boots. 'Not huge, but probably men's.'

'Was there anything in this casket?' I moved closer to the screen and zoomed right in. 'Is that a combination lock?'

'Yes, it is. Word-based. They're working on it, trying to get in without smashing it if possible.'

'So he might have taken something out of the casket? Just before he went to the cave and died?'

Jai looked up from the screen and nodded.

I folded my arms. 'That's no suicide.'

★

Fiona and I drove away from the Station, following directions to Felix Carstairs' house. Richard had grudgingly agreed that the casket changed things, and I could carry on investigating, which was just as well since I already was.

'Are you feeling okay?' Fiona asked in a hushed voice. 'Did you fall right on your head?

'I'm fine, thanks, Fiona. Did you look at the notes from Felix Carstairs' and Edward Swift's interviews?'

'Yes. They were inconsistent. And Felix was rather cagey.'

'Indeed. And very keen for us to think it was suicide. Let's see if we can get any more out of the bugger today.'

I pulled left to let an insane motorcyclist shoot past me.

Fiona tutted. 'Honestly, they deserve to end up as road-kill.'

'Well, they probably will. I just hope they don't take us with them.' A whole posse was trying to pass, engines revving aggressively behind us. 'Did you find anything more about the history of the cave house? And the carving?'

'Not much,' Fiona said. 'There was a reference to a healer living there in Victorian times, who starved herself to death. I wondered if she was the ghost my granny was on about.'

'Oh yes?'

'But there was nothing about the carving at all. I can't find anyone who knew about it, or any mention in the history books.'

'But our experts are adamant it's old?'

'Yes, Victorian.'

'It's hard to believe it's not relevant in some way. And the man who chucked himself off the cliff outside their house ten years ago left a book full of sketches of the Grim Reaper.'

'I saw. It's so creepy. And the cave had the dead man's *actual* initials carved into the wall. What's the chance of two different people having the same three initials?'

'Very roughly fifteen thousand to one. I worked it out. I thought the odds would be better than that, given how few people have names beginning with "x" or "z" or whatever, but it turns out "h" isn't that common. Unless they were related, of course.'

'See. You are a geek.'

'Who said I was a geek?'

'Oh… Just Craig.'

'I don't suppose it was a compliment.'

We passed through Matlock Bath, the shimmering limestone crag of High Tor piercing the horizon on our left. I peered upwards, whilst obviously also paying attention to the road. 'That's supposed to be the last place in England where eagles nested.'

We turned off the A6 before the improbably named Whatstandwell and climbed into open countryside. After a couple of miles, we found Felix's house, approached by a long driveway edged with pristine post and rail fencing and surrounded by glistening green fields.

'Wow,' Fiona said. 'It's like the road to Chatsworth.'

We parked in a courtyard in front of a huge barn conversion. A woman emerged from a block of stables and approached us, looking like one of the *Made in Chelsea* crowd when they were in their country gear. And was there something familiar about her?

We left the car and I introduced us. 'Is Felix Carstairs in?'

Her face fell. 'Oh, about poor Peter. Of course. I'm Olivia, Felix's wife. Felix and I were so upset to hear what happened. Suicide, wasn't it? How terrible.'

'Did you know Peter Hamilton well?'

She hesitated a moment too long. 'We were all at uni together. Felix and I lost touch with him for a while but obviously since they set up the firm together, we've seen more of him.'

I walked a few steps across the courtyard to lean against a fence overlooking fields. The countryside spread away below us, woods and valleys patterned bright and dark by the shadows of the clouds drifting above. In the distance, a cloud the colour of charcoal was moving in our direction. Olivia moved over to stand next to me. I sent *Relax and Tell Us All Your Secrets* vibes to her. Fiona popped in next to us.

'Where did you go to uni?' I asked.

'Cambridge.' She said it the way I tended to. Studiously casual, with a touch of apology. I remembered why her face was familiar. She was the beautiful girl in Peter Hamilton's university photographs.

'What did you study?'

'Maths. But I didn't finish. I got pregnant with Rosie. I know, I know – how dumb is that? My periods were always light and they didn't stop, so by the time I knew, it was...' Olivia paused. 'Oh, I'm giving you far too much information, aren't I? Felix says I always talk too much.' She looked away. 'Anyway, we have Rosie so it was

87

worth it, even if I don't have a fancy career. I suppose I could get a job but it all seems a bit pointless when Felix earns what he does. And it's not so easy to get back in if you didn't even finish your degree.' She ran a delicate hand through her hair. 'Oh, sorry, I'm doing it again. You don't seem like a detective.'

'No, no, carry on.' These kinds of witnesses were great. Whole life story and we'd only just met. And that was my speciality – not seeming like a detective.

'What else do you need to know?' Olivia said.

'Do you know Edward Swift from university as well?'

'No, Felix met him when they were doing their patent exams. They bonded through the trauma of it all.'

'So, are Felix and he good friends?'

'Well, I'm not sure *good friends* is quite right. But we end up doing quite a few things together. Work things and some social stuff. You know men, they don't make friends outside work. Edward's a bit odd though. Not much fun, to be honest. His wife's the same. Apparently she was brought up by religious nuts in America, so she's not your classic party animal. Not that I am either but, you know, I can let my hair down.' She gave me a quick smile, showing neat, white teeth. 'Grace is okay though. She gives Rosie extra maths lessons.'

'Oh yes,' I said. 'I met Rosie at Edward and Grace's house.'

'Being driven mad by Alex I suppose?'

'She was, actually.' I glanced up at the sky. The black cloud was moving closer and lower. 'Why don't you help Rosie with her maths?'

'Oh, she won't take it from me. Grace is very patient and her maths is decent. She's freakishly intelligent actually, and a techno-wizard, just like Edward. She fixed our burglar alarm when it conked out and it was an utter mystery to me. She's not your average hick from some Deep South town full of fundamentalist loons.'

I laughed, reminding myself not to warm to the witnesses.

Olivia led us to the front of the house, our feet crunching on the pristine gravel. Something caught my eye in one of the first-floor windows. A girl, pressing her face to the glass, but looking up rather than down at us. She was incredibly still. My eyes kept being drawn back to her. I didn't want to stare but there was something uncanny about her pose. She still hadn't moved.

'Is that Rosie up there?' I tipped my head in the direction of the window.

Olivia looked up. 'I think that's the picture, not the girl.'

'Sorry?' I couldn't stop staring.

'Oh, Rosie drew a picture of herself looking out of the window. She leaves it in the window to creep people out.'

'That's a bit strange.' It had worked. It was creeping me out. It was a damn good picture.

'Yes, she's been a bit of a teenager recently.'

The face moved. Fiona grabbed my arm and I jumped backwards. We exchanged a quick, embarrassed look.

'So now we're all accustomed to thinking it's the picture, she must have put her face there instead.'

Olivia pushed open a heavy door and let us into a spacious hall. An oak staircase swept away from us, and Rosie appeared at the top. 'Did I freak you out?' she shouted. She looked younger than I remembered – gangly and long-limbed but small.

'Not really,' Olivia said, before whispering, 'Best to ignore it,' through the corner of her mouth.

'I drew a picture of Medusa, and then when I saw it, it made me turn to stone.' Rosie started to descend, more slowly than I'd expected.

'Well, I'd better make sure I don't look at *that* picture.' Olivia turned to me. 'Rosie's developed an interest in Greek myths, the more gruesome and sinister the better.'

'It's not my fault. We did them at school.' Rosie gave me a shy smile. 'Daddy won't want to see you.' She reached the bottom of the stairs, but lost her footing and tripped down the last step. She looked up at us. 'There's something wrong with me. But nobody knows what it is.'

'Nothing not being a teenager wouldn't cure,' Olivia said.

'I have mood swings and depressive incidents,' Rosie said. 'And I keep dropping things.'

'All right, Rosie, this isn't about you. Where's your father?'

'I wouldn't fancy disturbing him. He's in the foulest mood.'

'I'm sure the detectives are accustomed to dealing with difficult men.'

I laughed. 'Have you met our boss?'

'He threw a mug at the wall,' Rosie said.

Olivia stiffened. 'Where is he, Rosie?'

'He didn't even clear up the mess. He said this is all he needs and it would have helped if Peter hadn't been so fucking behind—'

'Okay, Rosie, that's enough.'

Rosie raised her eyebrows. 'Just repeating what he said for the detectives. He's in his office.'

Olivia gave us a nervous smile. 'I'm sorry. He'll be fine with you. Come through. He gets a little... stressed. About work. He takes it very seriously.'

She led us down the high-ceilinged hallway, tapped on a door at the end and nudged it open. 'The detectives. To talk to you about Peter. I'll bring you some coffee.'

Oak bookshelves lined the walls and an antique desk faced the door. These weren't the sort of people who'd had to buy their own furniture.

Felix sat behind the desk like a monarch on a throne.

'Take a seat.' He waved at a pair of antiquey-looking chairs angled in front of the desk.

I instinctively brushed non-existent cat hairs from my trousers before sitting down, wondering if the wicker seat was rated for my weight. Fiona sat lightly next to me.

'Okay,' I said. 'You told us the other day everything was fine with Peter. But others have said he was drinking, not performing well, that you and Edward Swift were worried about—'

'He was a bit behind but nothing we can't handle.'

'But you've just hurled a mug at the wall.'

Whoa, that changed things. The shiny, happy shell shattered and Felix projected a wave of anger so strong I braced and clutched the arm of my chair. I was definitely jumpier since my fall. More alert to the menace in things.

'I did not hurl anything at the wall.' Felix's voice filled the room. 'I dropped a cup. Rosie's being utterly ridiculous at the moment.'

'But there were problems with Peter's work, weren't there?'

'Oh, for God's sake.'

'You were concerned he'd missed a deadline.'

'I give up. So much for trying to preserve the poor man's good name.'

'Come on, you know better than that.'

'He was an alcoholic and he was having an affair with one of his clients. Happy now? Maybe they can put it in his obituary.'

'Who was he having an affair with?'

'That appalling Bell woman.'

'Lisa Bell? The one who was in your office when we met the other day? How do you know they were having an affair?'

'He was under-charging and it was obvious when you saw him with her. His wife may have found out – she went and stayed with her parents in Bakewell for a week. They were having problems. Got the impression she wanted kids and he didn't. You know. The usual tedious stuff.'

'And he was drinking too much?'

'I'd say so. Since he couldn't walk down the stairs without falling over and his secretary had to check his drafts for stupid errors.'

'Okay, thank you. That's very helpful. Can you think of anything else that might be relevant?'

'No. Can I get back to this urgent work Peter's left me?'

'What size feet do you have?'

'Why?'

I let the silence sit between us.

'Size nine,' he said at last.

'And do you possess any wellies?'

'No.'

'No wellies?' I looked out of the window at the acres of land which he clearly owned.

'Since you ask, they disappeared from our shed a couple of weeks ago.'

I raised my eyebrows. 'Just your wellies?'

'Yes, I'm sure I left them in there, but it's never locked. Anyone could have taken them.'

I sighed. 'Okay, I'll let you get on. Please do let me know if you think of anything or if the wellies turn up.'

Felix took my card and we left his office.

Olivia appeared in the hall. 'Oh, I'm sorry! I forgot the coffee.'

'Don't worry.' I noticed a Georgian bureau sitting by the door. 'You have some lovely furniture.'

'Oh, it's all from Felix's family.'

If these people were landed gentry, due to inherit millions from *Downton Abbey*-esque relatives, then a financial motive for Peter's killing seemed less likely.

'Lucky you,' I said. 'It must be nice to have well-off relatives who give you furniture.'

She grimaced. 'You haven't met his mother.'

I laughed. 'Could you show us the shed?'

We followed her out of the front door and to a wooden shed standing on its own across the courtyard. Olivia pulled open the unlocked door.

'Why do you want to see the shed?'

'Is this where the wellies went missing from?'

'Oh. Yes, that's right. And some gloves disappeared too, I think.'

Now we were away from the main house, I seized my opportunity. 'Olivia, does your husband have a bad temper?'

She was silent for a few seconds, then spoke firmly. 'Not really, no.' She touched the high collar of her blouse, then whipped her hand away. 'Nothing out of the ordinary.'

Chapter 15

We pulled onto the lane outside Felix and Olivia's house. The charcoal-coloured cloud had landed overhead and was dumping rain on us as if it was being paid by volume. The car steamed up within seconds, and the wipers were squeaking and not clearing the windscreen properly. I swore at myself for not fixing them. Why was I such a procrastinator?

I wiped a smeary visibility-hole and drove through a puddle that turned out to be a pothole, jarring all my aching bits. 'Ouch,' I said. 'Why don't they ever repair the bloody roads? I'm always driving into potholes.'

'How's your head?' Fiona asked.

I touched my bump. 'Oh my God, it's the size of an orange now.'

'Are you sure you're okay?'

I wasn't sure at all. I had a shocking headache and an underlying feeling of dread. My worries about Mum clouded my brain like fog. But it was better to keep busy. 'I'm absolutely fine, thanks.'

Water was running in streams down the lane. I kept to the centre. I knew these deluges eroded ditches in the grass verges. They filled with water and concealed themselves as puddles to trap unwary drivers. I thought of the sand bags back in Eldercliffe, and hoped they'd stuck them in front of their doors.

By the time we arrived at the Station, it was raining so hard that the trip from car to building was enough to make us look like we'd been dunked head-down in a fast-flowing river. Fiona disappeared to perform a mysterious grooming ritual which would make her look like an Olay advert again, and I headed for my office, wishing there was a bath in there.

Jai appeared in the corridor. 'God, life's tough. You dive down stone steps onto your head, and then someone chucks a bucket of water over you.'

'Thanks for the sympathy,' I said.

'You should have parked in one of the marked police vehicle spaces, like Craig does.'

I laughed. 'Do we have any towels here?'

'Towels? What do you think this is – a luxury hotel? You'll have to stuff your head under the hand-dryer in the bogs like everyone else does.'

I took his advice and went off to the toilets, muttering about the Derbyshire weather, which was even worse than sodding Manchester.

When I returned, I found Jai leaning against the edge of my desk. His inability to sit still combined with his lanky body made me imagine he slept perched on a post like a large bird, rather than in a bed like a normal person.

I grabbed my chair and wheeled it close to the radiator, so I could quietly steam.

'Looking glam,' Jai said. 'Seriously, are you okay?'

'I'm fine. Anyway, what did the post mortem say?'

Jai gave me a despairing look. 'Okay, I give up trying to ask you if you're alright. Let's talk about the corpse instead. Oh my God, is that where you hit your head?'

'No, Jai, I always had a protrusion the size of a grapefruit on the back of my skull. I was born like it. Nearly killed my poor mother.'

'Okay, okay, the post mortem confirms it was definitely cyanide poisoning. The pathologist was quite excited.'

'Potassium cyanide?'

'Yep, in the cake but not in the cannabis. Time of death between

11am and 2pm on Monday.' Jai shifted to sit on the desk, with his feet on a chair. 'And we confirmed his business didn't have professional indemnity insurance. Peter did forget to renew it. It's back in place now. And there's a life insurance policy with his two partners as beneficiaries, to the tune of half a million each.'

I whistled. 'Wow. That could come in pretty handy. Especially if he made a cock-up which left the firm exposed financially. I can't imagine Felix or Edward taking to a life of poverty.'

'So they both have a motive.'

'Unless they have huge wealth from somewhere else – which we need to check. Felix and his wife, Olivia, knew Peter at university as well. I get the feeling there's a bit more to that.'

Jai looked at me through narrowed eyes. 'Between Peter Hamilton and Felix's wife?'

'Possibly. There was something about his photographs of her. And she hesitated when I asked her if she knew him well.'

'Interesting. We checked alibis for Monday and also for Sunday night. They think that's when the casket was placed in the tree trunk.'

'Oh yes?'

'Everyone's pretty solid for Monday. Sunday evening Kate Webster was watching TV with Peter. Felix Carstairs and Edward Swift were also at home watching TV and their wives back them up.'

I sighed. 'So the alibis are rubbish.'

'Well, yes, you could say that. Wives aren't as bad as mothers, but they could be covering for their husbands. They could even be in on it.' Jai leant back and knocked over one of my stacks of paperwork.

'Bloody hell, Jai, there was a system in that.'

Jai pushed the papers back into a pile, shuffling them all together. 'Sorry, am I mixing the Jurassic with the Cretaceous period of your filing system? This one's actually bleached from the sun. You've only been here a few weeks. How did you manage that?'

'I think Richard's passed me all his crap to deal with. I assume you couldn't find Susie and her special cakes? She could have a viable niche business there, you know.'

'There definitely doesn't seem to be a "Susie's Cakes", so it looks like it was just to make the cake look shop-bought and safe to eat.'

'Right,' I said. 'No Susie. What else?'

'You smell of wet cat.'

'Thanks a lot, Jai, that's good to know.' I shifted away from him.

'It's not so bad. Better than wet dog.'

I spun my chair round to warm the other side of myself but the radiator had gone cold. 'Christ, aren't we even allowed heating now?'

'Public expenditure cuts. They'll be taking the chairs next and making us jog on the spot or dance to keep warm.'

'Don't make me imagine Craig and Richard dancing.' I rubbed my hands over my arms. 'Did the forensics around the body show anything?'

'Nope. No alien hairs or whatever. Nothing that didn't come from the victim. But there's more about the casket they found in the fallen tree.' Jai examined a note on the table. 'The combination was the word HENRY.'

'HENRY. Does that mean anything?'

'Not so far,' Jai said. 'And the plot thickens. Inside the casket was another closed box, also with a word-based lock.'

'Really?'

'Yes, really. But there seemed to be a clue in the outer casket, which possibly led to the combination for the inner box. A piece of paper with some weird riddle on it.'

'What did it say? Look, I want to go again to the quarry – approach it from the direction Peter Hamilton would have done and see where this casket was found.' I glanced out of the window. Couldn't see much but decided to adopt a positive mental attitude. 'It's stopped raining now. Do you want to come with me and you can tell me this stuff on the way?'

Jai jumped up, always happy to leave the Station.

Once in the car, I stuck the heater on full and we set off for Eldercliffe. I'd park near Hamilton's house so we could walk down the footpath into the woods.

'Wipe the windscreen for me, can you Jai?' I shoved a cloth into his hand.

'My God, what have you been doing with this?' He smeared the admittedly grubby cloth over my windscreen. 'You need to clean the glass every few years or so, you know.'

'Yeah, yeah, you can still see through it, can't you?' I peered through a small, non-misty area of the screen. 'So, there was a second, smaller box inside the casket?'

'Yes, and they found a trace of the cake in there – like a smear of chocolate that must have got onto the outside of the wrapper.'

'So, the cake could have been in the smaller box and that was inside the casket.'

'Yes, and it also backs up the cake being home-made and put into the plastic wrapper.'

'Of course Hamilton could have got the cake from somewhere else and opened the casket up with traces of cake on his fingers.'

Jai sighed. 'I know. He could. But there's no trace of cake on the outer casket. I think we should explore this. We haven't got much else.'

'I agree. But let's not get obsessed with it. Anyway, what else?'

'Well, there was a cheap compass inside the inner box, with Peter Hamilton's fingerprints on it, and a piece of paper with the date of his death and the word *Hamster22*.'

'And you said there was a piece of paper in the outer casket with some kind of riddle on it. What did it say?'

'Can't remember. It was gibberish. They've sent it off to some weirdo who doesn't wash but can solve these things. We keep him in the basement.'

I laughed, although I was frustrated Jai had forgotten the riddle, which I was itching to hear. 'Oh yeah, I think I met him nicking my milk once. So, Hamilton found the casket and he opened it, which means he knew the outer code, HENRY, and he found the piece of paper with the clue to the lock on the inner box, solved that, opened the inner box and took the poisoned cake. And possibly left the compass in it?'

'Looks like it. There are no fingerprints apart from his.'

'And he might have left the *Hamster* piece of paper in there, or it might have been in there already.'

'Yes, it had his fingerprints on, but of course he could have just looked at it.'

'So, let's suppose the killer invented "Susie's Cakes". Printed off the label and packaged up the cake to look like shop–bought. And left it in the inner box, inside the casket, for Hamilton to find and eat. But why would Hamilton even go to the casket?'

'Why do you think?'

'You're not fooling me, Jai. I do realise that's what parents say when they can't answer their kids' *why* questions.'

'Okay. Busted. Truth is I have no idea why he would have gone to the casket and taken the bloody cake.'

'Well, we know he was a greedy sod who wouldn't turn down cake, if he found the casket for some reason. Have we any way of tracing the printer the cake label came from, or the plastic wrapper?'

'They're looking into it, but it seems he used a black-and-white printer without the steganography markings. And there's not much to go on with the wrapper.'

'The murderer was clever. What about tracing the source of the cyanide?'

'They're working on it.'

I pulled up on the lane, not far from the parking spot outside Peter Hamilton and Kate Webster's house. It was still blessedly dry outside but the sky was black so we donned waterproofs and set off to find the footpath down to the quarry.

Kate Webster had said Hamilton would have cut through a tiny alleyway between two houses, to access a path which led down to the woods at the base of the quarry. This area of Eldercliffe was known for its confusing arrays of tiny stone cottages, dotted seemingly at random on the sloping hillside. The cottages, alleys and gardens were thrown together according to no obvious plan, and you could never follow the same route twice.

We took a path with a drop on the left so steep we could see down the chimneys of the houses below. I glanced over the side and remembered crashing down the steps outside Mum's house. I leant against the wall and breathed out slowly through my mouth.

'Are you okay?' Jai said. 'Is it your head?'

'It's alright.' I took a step away from the wall.

Jai squinted at me. 'Are you sure you're up to this?'

I kept my gaze fixed ahead and started walking. 'I'm fine. Come on.'

We spotted the alleyway, which was more like a tunnel, since the first floors of the two houses were joined together, forming a little bridge. Instinctively hunching over, we crept through and were surprised to find a grassy path which took us down a steep slope straight to the woods in the base of the quarry. We followed the main path, as we assumed Peter Hamilton would have done. Although it had stopped raining, water fell off the trees in fat globules, and a musty, loamy smell thickened the air.

'Were there any traces of cyanide on the swabs from Hamilton's house?' I asked.

'Not that we could find. The wife's got to be a possible though. We found evidence on his laptop that they'd recently increased his life insurance to nearly a million. He's worth a hell of a lot dead, that man. And there's evidence of arguments. In one email she says she's not sure she can take it any more.'

'And she's been pushing us towards the cursed house thing. Maybe that's to distract us.'

I skirted around a muddy patch on the track. A path to our left had been fenced off, and a sign shouted *DANGER* and featured a flailing man. I looked through the trees, and in the distance saw a lake of the most vivid turquoise, against a backdrop of sheer cliffs. I nudged Jai. 'Look at that.'

'It's the old quarry that's filled in. Idiots die swimming there every now and then. A kind of local natural selection.'

'It's so… blue,' I said. 'Even though the sky's grey. I can see why people are drawn to it.' The fencing wouldn't have stopped me in my younger years.

Jai obviously wasn't tempted. 'Chemical pollution,' he said.

'Okay, the wife. She did mention arguments, but claimed it was normal marital stuff. Of course she would say that. What about the brother, Mark? I wondered if there was something going on between him and Hamilton's wife. And there's the comment the student made at the health centre. Something about typhus and the police sniffing around. Why would Kate Webster have made that comment if she had nothing to hide? And what about the client who he was doing free work for – Lisa Bell? You talked to her, didn't you? Could she have poisoned him in a cold-blooded fit of jealousy?'

'I grilled her pretty hard about the possible affair and she was all astonished denial. She seemed more pissed off that he'd died in the middle of the patenting process than anything else. She's not a top scorer on rapport-building, that's for sure. She was alibied for Monday, but she was another solitary TV watcher on Sunday night.'

'What did she say about him reducing his charges?'

'Just that he'd been slow recently, so he'd agreed to charge out fewer hours than he put in. She did seem a bit evasive though. I definitely got a sniff of something odd going on.'

'Jesus, it's complicated.' Water was running down the back of my neck. 'Is everyone putting everything into HOLMES?' You had to admire whoever contorted the initials of our crime-busting computer system into that acronym.

'Yes, I think so.' Jai splashed through a puddle.

We were nearing the cliffs where Peter Hamilton had been found. The wind was getting up, rattling the branches above us. We approached the taped-off area, and a thick-necked uniformed officer nodded us through. 'Good to see some human life,' he said. 'There's more people on the moon than in these woods.'

We were about ten feet from the fallen tree. The hollow where the casket had been found was obvious when you were close, but you'd have had to look for it.

The uniform put his phone in his pocket. 'Found the bastard who did it yet?'

'Not yet.'

'Well, don't you worry, I've stopped the seething hordes rampaging through the crime scene.'

Jai snorted. 'Yeah, not the most exciting spot for you.'

'Christ, no. Can't even get a sodding coffee. I did fend off a couple of young idiots this morning though. Tried to get to the fallen tree, you know, where they found that box thing.'

I looked at him with more interest. 'They'd come past the outer tape?'

'Yeah. Ghouls I suppose.'

'We haven't released anything about the fallen tree,' I said. 'What made you say they were trying to get to that?'

'Seemed to be looking on their phones, like they were following something on there. I wondered if it was that stupid Pokemon thing. They didn't see me at first, and I didn't see them until one of them said something about the tree.'

'What exactly did he say?'

'Something like, "Near that fallen tree, I think". Then their heads popped up from their phones and the other one said, "Holy crap, is this where they found that body?" Then they saw me, I shouted at them to stop and they pissed off. I didn't want to leave here to chase after the little bastards.'

'That's weird,' I said. 'It doesn't sound like Pokemon. So, why would they be following directions to come here, and yet be surprised that it's where the body was found?'

The uniform shrugged and turned slightly away, as if he had something more interesting to do.

'Come on, Jai,' I said. 'You should have a look in the cave.'

I walked to the cliff where the steps led up to the cave house. 'You go first. I'm slow with my ankle.'

Jai climbed nimbly up the steps and I followed, less nimbly.

We flashed our torches around the walls and floor, and breathed the uniquely cave-scented air – a musty mix of damp and bat droppings. I directed my torch up, hoping to see bats sleeping, but there were none. Just a tiny spider, which scuttled away from the light.

Jai was more interested in the carving. 'Oh. My. God.' He stood and gazed. 'That is so damn spooky. How the hell could it predict Peter Hamilton's death?'

I walked further into the cave, feeling the temperature fall. Looking at the carving made my lungs feel tight, as if the air had gone viscous. 'It can't,' I said, then added helplessly, 'Well, I don't know. It has to be relevant in some way. If he found out about it and thought he was cursed? Or the killer found out about it and thought it was a good distraction.'

Jai swung his torch around the rest of the cave. 'I'm not sure it would be my choice of place to come and relax and read philosophy.' He stepped towards the lighter area near the entrance and switched his torch off. 'Shall we get going?' He turned towards me. 'Holy shit!' He leapt back, eyes wide.

'What the hell?' My heart banged against my ribcage. 'What is it, Jai?'

Chapter 16

'Look behind you.'

I took a step towards Jai and turned slowly. I gasped and felt my hand go to my mouth.

A skeletal woman was running from the Grim Reaper. I stared at the cave wall, blood rushing in my ears.

'It's the ghost,' Jai whispered. 'The woman who starved to death.'

Once I'd calmed down, it was clear what it was. 'It's the shadow from the tree in the window, isn't it?'

Now our torches weren't shining on the back wall of the cave, it was lit only by sunlight from the cave door and the window. Jai was blocking most of the light from the tiny doorway, and the position of the sun must have been just right to beam through the window. A tree had grown across, and it cast a spindly shadow on the cave wall, next to the carving of the Grim Reaper. The shadow looked like a stick-thin body, which moved when the tree was battered by the wind.

'Yeah,' Jai said. 'It's a shadow. But I can see why people don't come here. That's uncannily like a person. Let's get out of here.'

'Okay, okay. You go down first.'

Jai squeezed through the entrance and shuffled round to descend backwards. Just as his head was about to disappear, he froze and looked up at me. 'Oh my God. I think I know how the killer got Peter Hamilton to the casket.'

I stared at him, silhouetted in the cave entrance, and spoke softly. 'So tell me.'

'Let me get out of this hell hole first.'

'Go on then. Hurry up.'

Jai navigated the steps down from the cave house, with me following as fast as I could.

Once Jai was safely at ground level, he turned to me. 'Geocaching. Have you heard of it?'

I'd heard Hannah mention the term, but couldn't remember what it meant. Possibly I'd been drunk when she told me. 'Not exactly. Let's head back and you can tell me.'

We set off along the path, and Jai continued in a smug tone. 'Basically it's a way of getting your *World of Warcraft* types to venture out in the daylight for a change. It's like a treasure hunt. You log on to these websites and they give the GPS co-ordinates of a place where the treasure – the cache – is. Then you go out and try to find it. Or something like that.'

I paused before a particularly muddy spot. 'So that could be a way to get someone to go to a specific location in the woods?'

'Well, that's what I'm thinking.'

'And open a casket?'

'Indeed.'

★

We arrived back at the Station in the early afternoon. As we walked down the corridor towards my office, Craig popped out of a doorway and blocked our path. 'Richard won't like the idea of two detectives going off to the woods, will he now?'

It was just as well we didn't have guns because I would have taken mine out and shot him right between the eyes. Twice. I suspected it wasn't healthy to feel this way about my colleagues.

Jai took a step towards him. 'Oh give it a rest, you slimy little—'

Craig puffed up like a poisonous snake. 'Our role is *strategic*, isn't that what Richard says? We're not paid to blunder around in—'

'I'm not sure he meant *you* when he said that,' Jai said. 'We all have to play to our strengths.'

Craig looked baffled for a moment before his potato-head flushed pink.

Jai adopted the tone of someone speaking to a backward child. 'Oh, sorry, Craig, was that too subtle for you?'

Craig righted himself and turned to me. 'How are you feeling after your little accident? It's a shame your limp makes you prone to falls.'

I kept my tone even. 'Can I have a word with you, Craig? Shall we nip into my room?'

Craig lost his bravado. 'Whatever.' He followed me down the corridor.

My anger had left me and I felt very tired. 'Craig, have I done something to offend you?'

'No,' he said. 'I was concerned about your welfare. Didn't want you getting into trouble with Richard. Or over doing it. I know you can be a bit, how would you say it, fragile.'

Anger sparked inside me again. I suppressed it. Told myself to play the long game. Call his bluff.

'I'm fine. I appreciate your concern. I'd like us to get along.'

He gave me a confused look which morphed into a smirk.

I was on a tight rope. I really didn't want to fall out with him and have him hijacking me. But with men like Craig, there was almost no line between keeping them sweet and letting them think you were weak.

'Since you want to help,' I said. 'There's some number plate data that I'd like you to apply your expertise to. I'll send you an email.'

He opened his mouth as if to say something, then shut it again and left the room.

I sank onto my chair and put my head in my hands. My bump

ached and my mind churned with all the different information. I could do without belligerent colleagues to add to the mix.

I turned to my computer and stared at the information on HOLMES, trying to make sense of all the threads. Several people could have wanted Hamilton dead. But why use the casket, with or without geocaching? And I kept coming back to the carving on the cave wall. No one seemed to know anything about it but I couldn't believe the matching initials were a coincidence.

I wanted to see Peter Hamilton's father and grandmother. One of them must have known something about the carving or the curse. I grabbed my case and headed for the exit.

Fiona intercepted me on the way out. 'Guess what? Felix Carstairs' parents aren't rich any more. They were Lloyd's Names.'

'Really? So they lost their fortune in a blaze of sinking ships and asbestosis claims?'

'Something like that. He and Olivia rely on the income from his patent attorney firm just like normal people.'

'And she doesn't even work.'

'No. If the firm went under due to Peter's mistakes, they could lose everything.'

★

The sky had brightened and there was even a patch of blue up ahead. I wound the window down and inhaled the smell of fresh, rain-soaked countryside. I wished I could shift the feeling of unease that lurked at the back of my mind. I couldn't help thinking the incident on the steps had something to do with the Hamilton case, as if someone was trying to get rid of me. But no one even knew it was me pushing against a suicide verdict. It must have just been an accident. I rubbed my strained shoulder and took the road towards Bakewell.

Most of the villages in this area were picture-perfect tourist honeypots of stone cottages and tea rooms. But just a few miles away you'd come upon a remote settlement full of rusting machinery, bags of cement, feral collies, and farmers who'd stare blankly at you as if they'd never previously encountered someone from outside Derbyshire. I was confident Peter Hamilton's father would live in the first kind of village, but his house actually stood on its own, a symmetrical Georgian pile on the road between Birchover and Stanton in Peak.

I was met at the door by a nervous-looking woman in her sixties. I showed her my ID and followed her through a gloomy hallway lined with hunting prints (or possibly originals). She led me into a room which was almost completely dark. Thick curtains covered the windows and there was no artificial light. The woman proclaimed into the room. 'It's the lady detective to see you.'

I squinted into the darkness. My eyes gradually adjusted and I could make out oak panelling on the walls near me, but still no person.

'Come over and sit down, for God's sake.' The voice emanated from a far corner. 'Mrs Brown, would you make tea?'

'Can we put a light on?' I asked.

'Oh, oh, yes. He likes the dark.'

A lamp flicked on and I saw him hunched in the corner. I blinked, not sure if I was seeing him properly in the strange up-light of the lamp; not sure if I was seeing his body or if he was under a duvet or cushions.

I walked closer. There were no cushions – it was all him. Under hooded brows there was what once must have been a distinguished face. His gaze was still sharp, but his features were engulfed in fat. He wasn't just a bit overweight – this was a case of *Take the Side off the House to Get Me Out When I Die*. I tried not to stare.

I perched on a Chesterfield chair opposite him. 'Mr Hamilton?'

'Well, I'm Peter's father if that's what you mean, but we have different names.'

'Oh, okay.'

'Yes, there's no feminist like a seventies feminist, and Lily didn't want to lumber herself or the children with my name. Can't blame her really.'

A musty smell touched the back of my throat, reminding me of Gran's mouse-eaten attic in her old house. 'Right,' I said, wondering just how bad his name would be.

'It's Laurence Winterbottom. Yes, I was bullied terribly at school. Lily was right not to pass that on.'

'Right. Thank you.' He'd disconcerted me – taken me off my planned initial-words-of-sympathy route. 'I'm so sorry for your loss,' I said.

'You understand why I like the dark now you've seen the size of me?'

I panicked and attempted the non-committal head wobble they did so well in India. *Yes or No or Maybe, or whatever you want me to say.* There didn't seem to be much point in doing the usual thing with fat people and telling him he wasn't fat.

He flicked the lamp off again. I could just see his outline in the half light from the slits between the curtains. It was barely light enough to make notes, but I didn't have the heart to complain.

A deep sigh rippled through his flesh. 'Have you found who did it yet?' The voice was monotone.

'Not yet. I was wondering if I might ask you a few questions?'

A faint rustling came from behind him. What the hell was that?

'Yes, go ahead,' he said.

'Er, yes.' I was distracted by the rustling. 'When did you last see Peter?'

'He visited the Saturday before he died. With Kate. For afternoon tea.'

'And did you notice anything unusual about him?'

'No, not at all. He seemed perfectly normal. Talked about work and current affairs.'

I jumped. Now my eyes were fully dark-adapted, I could see a white rat snuggling into Laurence's neck and another one squatting on the curve of his stomach. The rustling came from an enclosure behind his chair, where several more rats pottered around on wood shavings.

'Meet Frederick.' Laurence pointed at the rat on his shoulder. 'And Fosdyke.' He gestured towards his stomach. 'They're friendly.'

Frederick glanced at me with sharp, pink eyes, then sat on his hindquarters and groomed his face, his bald tail draping over Laurence's neck.

'Oh. Er… they're sweet. Unusual pets, though?'

'One of Peter's clients gave them to him. They were redundant lab rats and he felt they deserved a break. My sons are both rather soft. But Kate wasn't keen to have them in the house and Mark has too many cats, so they came here. They make excellent pets.' He turned and made a kissing gesture to Frederick, who stopped grooming himself and nestled closer to Laurence's face, burrowing into the flesh of his neck.

Mrs Brown bustled into the room and placed a tray on a table between Laurence and me. She must have had night-vision contact lenses or something. She poured us tea and offered me a plate of flapjacks. I took one. She didn't offer the flapjacks to Laurence.

He shifted in his vast chair. 'Now, what else did you want to ask me?'

'Others have suggested Peter had been depressed recently, or anxious about work, maybe even drinking too much. Did you notice anything?'

'No, he seemed normal to me. Who do you think could have done this?'

'We're working on that. Did you know he used to visit a cave house in the woods?'

'Where he was found? No. But I'm not surprised. He was fascinated by caves as a child. He was always making up stories about odd creatures which lived in them. Preferred caves to beaches actually, especially after he nearly drowned in Cornwall.'

'Have you ever been to the cave house?'

Laurence paused a little too long. 'No. I had heard there was one in those woods but I've never been. I'm not disposed to going hiking in woods these days.' He gave the flesh of his stomach an aggressive poke, as if angry with it. 'I assume you've spoken to Felix. They've been friends since they were at Cambridge. Although they drifted apart after that terrible accident.'

'Accident?'

'Yes, in Cambridge. Did Felix not mention it? I suppose it's not relevant.'

'No, he didn't.'

'That sounds like Felix. Never liked the boy much. But, yes, one of their friends was killed. I suppose it's ancient history now.'

I looked expectantly at him. He must have known I'd want details.

He took a deep, wheezy breath. 'He was killed falling off a roof. You know boys, they can be silly. He was indulging in a spot of night climbing and he fell.'

'How horrific. Were Peter and Felix there?'

'No, he was on his own. Awful shock to them when they found out the next morning. Peter had to come home for a few days. He was most upset.'

'And he and Felix drifted apart after that?'

'Well, yes. Until years later, when they were both doing patent exams.'

'Did they fall out?'

'I don't know exactly what went on. I did sometimes think Peter was bottling something up. He wouldn't say. Maybe if his mother had still been alive...'

Frederick snuffled at Laurence's ear.

I smiled randomly into the gloom. 'I know this sounds strange, but it seems Peter may have thought he was... cursed? Do you know anything about that?'

Laurence was very still. Even the rats paused their grooming activities. 'No. Of course not. I don't know what you're talking about.'

'You've never heard talk of a curse?'

'No. I can't believe you're asking me this. Peter wasn't killed by a curse.'

'Okay. I wonder if it would be possible to have a quick word with your mother? Is she well enough?'

'She's not in, I'm afraid, and she's not very coherent these days. No, I don't think there'd be any point in speaking to her.'

'Would she know about the curse?'

'Don't believe everything my mother says. She's not really compos mentis any more.'

'Where is she?'

'She'll be on the moor. She goes up to the stone circle.'

'How do I get to the moor?'

'I really don't advise talking to her. She won't want to see you. It's a surprise she's even up. She's become largely nocturnal in recent years. She wanders around in the dead of night and only eats fish she gets free from the butcher for her non-existent cat.'

'It'll only be a quick word.'

Neither of us spoke for a moment. Fosdyke gave me a disapproving look.

'Well, if you insist,' Laurence said. 'There's a shortcut across the garden. It's over the hillock. Mrs Brown will show you. It's best not to mention my wife, Lily. Mother gets upset. She might have one of her turns.'

I thanked Laurence and found Mrs Brown, who gave me directions to the moor. Laurence seemed so keen for me not talk to his mother, it made me especially eager to see her, compos mentis or not.

Chapter 17

I pulled my coat tight around me, and followed a path over a bleak, windswept, heather-coated area which led up to the higher ground, where I knew I'd find the stone circle. No sign of blue sky here. The clouds hung low and grey, and gusts of wind whipped through the surrounding silver birches. Something darted in my peripheral vision but when I snapped my head round, there was nothing. My muscles felt taut like piano wires. The knock on the head must have done something to me – I wasn't normally jumpy like this.

I paused as the Nine Ladies stone circle came into sight. The stones dated from the Bronze Age and were reputedly created when nine women were turned to stone for dancing on the Sabbath, which seemed harsh. Their presence was greater than their size, which was less than waist height. I felt a tightening in my chest, as if I was being squeezed. The place had an eerie stillness. Even the rustling of the trees and the birdsong quietened as I approached.

A woman stood at the centre of the circle, looking up at the sky. She was straight-backed and, like the stones, she seemed to still the air around her. She turned and looked at me with a cold, bird-like stare.

Her cut-glass voice sliced the silence. 'Are you that dreadful woman from social services?'

Well, that snapped me out of my dreamy state. I walked closer. 'No, no, I'm the detective. I'm so sorry about your grandson's death.'

I held out my hand but she ignored it.

'I'm not eating those meals. My fish is perfectly good.'

I stared stupidly at my extended hand, before retracting it and stuffing it in my coat pocket. 'I'm not from social services.'

'I know why he died. Who are you again?'

'The police,' I said. 'Do you mean you know why Peter died? Should we go back to the house?'

'You can go back. I'm not. I come up to the moor to get away.'

'What are you getting away from?'

'My family.'

I jumped as a flurry of leaves spun past. Why had I thought it was a good idea to interview an insane old woman on a deserted moor?

She stabbed a long finger at my chest. 'I know I'm old and losing my mind. And I do get confused sometimes. But I remember everything from the old days.' I saw a glimpse of how she must have been in those old days, her wealth and privilege wrapped around her like a silk cloak – she the lady of the manor and my sort tending pigs or pulling swedes. She was still intimidating, even though she was tiny and frail. Not that size had anything to do with it, as the neighbour's Great Dane once told me after an encounter with Hamlet.

She strode surprisingly briskly to one of the 'ladies' and leant against it. 'It's a bad thing with Peter, but I wasn't surprised.'

I followed her over to the stone. 'Why not?'

'Because of the curse.'

The breeze touched the hairs on the back of my neck. 'The curse?'

'I told Laurence, he should never have married that Lily.'

'So what is the curse?' I couldn't believe I was taking this seriously. But something about the old woman and the stone circle on the bleak moor made a curse feel all too possible.

'They've been cursed since they accused a young woman of being a witch.' She spat the words into the breeze. 'Ridiculous, of course – there were no witches, just women who upset the wrong people, defied the church or stood up to boorish men. They took her to the Labyrinth and...' She shook her head slowly. 'Ever since then, terrible things have happened. And that house...'

I huddled deeper into Carrie's scarf. 'What terrible things have happened?'

'People die young. Like her. Died an appalling death, and Laurence never recovered. Look at him now.'

I remembered the woman in the wedding photo, flushed and happy, and later in a wheelchair. Then missing from the photos. 'What do they die of?'

'Everything.'

'What do you mean, everything?'

She ignored me. Stared out towards the lower ground to the east. The heather shone an unnatural purple in the orange evening light, standing out against the black clouds behind.

'Do you know about the carving in the cave house?' I asked. 'The Grim Reaper?'

She whipped round and blasted me with a gaze that felt like a punch. I stepped back, my foot catching in a tuft of grass, so I staggered and almost fell. She mouthed something but I couldn't hear the words. Her lips moved almost as if she was praying under her breath. Then she started coughing. Her tiny frame shook, and I felt a wave of panic.

'Cursed. Still cursed.' She whispered the words between coughs. 'And now she's pregnant. Nothing good will come of that.'

'What? Who's pregnant? Are you all right?'

'Leave me now.' She gasped and clutched the stone at her side. 'Leave me.'

I took a step away and regarded her cautiously. She stopped coughing.

I waited to check she was okay, then asked, 'Who's pregnant?'

She waved her arm in a gesture of dismissal.

I tried again. 'Was Peter affected by the curse? What happened to him?'

'I'll say no more,' she said. 'Leave me alone now.'

I did as she asked and walked away across the rough grass, breathing heavily. I glanced back as I lifted myself awkwardly over the stile to Laurence's house. She looked like a witch herself, standing by the stones. A bird had landed next to her – a crow or a raven. Goose pimples tingled on my arms.

I rapped on the kitchen door and Mrs Brown appeared. 'You look like you've seen a ghost.'

I felt like I'd seen a ghost. 'I'm fine,' I said, and told her about the coughing. She promised to check all was well, and told me to go through to Laurence.

I tapped on the door and walked into the drawing room, which seemed even darker after the brightness of the moor.

'Did you find her? Are you alright?'

'Yes. She did talk about the curse.'

'Bloody nonsense.'

'What does she mean though?'

'It's just the ramblings of an old woman. I told you – she's losing her mind. There is no curse.'

'She mentioned someone being pregnant. Do you know who that would be?'

'Oh, she blathers on sometimes. I've no idea.'

'What did your wife die of?'

He paused and sank deeper into his chair. 'A kind of motor neurone disease.'

'I'm sorry. How awful.'

'Yes.' I detected bitterness and resignation in his voice. It was strange how the dark made me more aware of the subtle inflections of tone. 'It hit the children very hard. Towards the end we couldn't do anything for her and she eventually suffocated.'

'That's why Mark can't abide suffering,' I said quietly.

'You're right. Any lame duck that wanders past, Mark'll take it in. And he won't let it suffer. It's better to be dead than suffer, he says. Having seen what Lily went through, I'm inclined to agree.'

★

Driving home, I called Jai on the hands-free. 'Could you check something out?'

'Yes, I'm fine thanks, Meg. How are you?' Jai's voice was breaking up, but the tone was still clear.

'I'll probably lose the signal at any moment so just consider the niceties done, can you? A friend of Peter's and Felix's apparently got killed in an accident in Cambridge. It could be nothing, but did anything come up in the background checks?'

'Well, we didn't find that. But Edward Swift and Felix Carstairs, the two partners – they both have criminal records.'

'Really? What on earth for?' I swerved to avoid a pheasant, his red and gold feathers reflecting my headlights as he ambled onto the road. He should have been safely tucked up in bed in a tree. He wouldn't survive for long with that attitude. Bred to be easy to shoot, the poor sod.

Jai's voice filled the car. 'Edward for rowdy behaviour outside an abortion clinic and Felix for small-scale dealing of cannabis.'

'Oh. Right. Interesting. Could you check about a student falling off a roof in Cambridge? And I still have a signal. How are you Jai? Are you having a nice day?'

'Yes, I've been consoling myself with a bit of Epictetus.'

'The stuff Hamilton was reading in the cave?'

'That's right. I'm only supposed to keep company with those who uplift me.'

'Oh, really?'

'Yeah. So I'll be off now.' The line went quiet. I cursed Jai's sense of humour. Then he was back. 'No, it's all about not getting mithered about stuff outside of your control. And living in the present like a dog.'

'Do we know if he's always been into this sort of thing? I didn't notice any other books on philosophy or personal development in their house.'

'I checked with the wife and she didn't know about it.'

'So, why's he suddenly reading Stoic philosophy? And has it got anything to do with Tithonus who can't ever die? Or with him thinking he was cursed? His grandmother thought he was cursed too.'

'He wasn't killed by a curse, though, was he? Some bugger left poisoned food in a casket in the woods and he ate it. We checked all the other foot sizes. Mark Hamilton's are huge – size twelve, Edward Swift's are size ten, Kate Webster's size five and the two other women size seven. All had wellies present and correct except Felix, which you already know about.'

'So, probably any of them could have worn our wellies except Mark Hamilton or Kate Webster.'

No answer. Damn. Lost him.

The countryside around Birchover was eerie in the evening light, random rocks jutting from the hillside like statues that just might come alive at night. I reached the strangely named Via Gellia, not a Roman road as you'd expect from the name but a winding motorcyclist's death trap which I usually enjoyed driving. The trees loomed over the road, meeting in the middle above it and forming a tunnel. The ground never dried properly, even in high summer, hence the problem with motorcyclists periodically having to be scraped off the tarmac. Tonight the road seemed forbidding and I struggled to see its shining surface. I hoped the head injury wasn't messing with my vision.

I finally arrived home, let myself in, and stretched as I hobbled along my tiny hallway. My shoulder ached where I'd wrenched it falling down the steps.

Hamlet trotted up like a little clockwork toy, his fluffy undercarriage swinging from side to side.

'Come on, let's feed you,' I said. 'And maybe even me too.'

I did my room checks, cursing myself for being so ridiculous when getting up the stairs was such an ordeal, and returned to the kitchen. The windows would never shut properly, and it was freezing. The boiler fired away ineffectually, sounding like it could take you to Mars but failing to heat the tiny house. I spooned out some *Duck with organic vegetables* for Hamlet, stuck the kettle on and leant down to rummage in the freezer. Whilst fully intending to cook something wholesome and low carb, I was drawn to pizza and chips. Oh well, it was comfort food, and surely justified in view of my injuries.

Armed with pizza, chips and large quantities of tomato ketchup (one of my five-a-day) I retreated to the slightly warmer living room with the laptop, and googled *geocaching*. Jai had been right. It was apparently a kind of treasure hunt, where participants used GPS systems to hide containers, called *caches*, which other participants then found. A typical cache was a small, waterproof container containing a logbook with a pen or pencil. The geocacher entered the date they'd found it and signed it with their code name. Sometimes the cache contained items for trading, usually cheap toys.

So, it made sense if Peter Hamilton had left the little compass in return for the cake. He may have wondered why there was no log book, but it probably wouldn't have worried him, and maybe he left the dated piece of paper instead. And the cake looked shop-bought and had a long sell-by date so, although it might be unusual to leave cake, he wouldn't have had any reason not to eat it.

My mind wandered to how I'd felt on the high footpath. I'd never been scared of heights – slightly uneasy perhaps, but not scared. That was all I needed. The flashbacks returning and now a fear of heights too. Surely if I'd been going to develop a phobia, it would have happened at the time, not twenty-five years later.

Chapter 18

I woke after a difficult night. When I peered into the bathroom mirror, I was expecting the Elephant Man to gaze back at me, but I actually looked relatively normal. I chucked down some more of my hospital pain killers, pulled on clothes, and hobbled down the steep staircase.

I made tea, sat at the table with my mug, and called Jai.

'Sorry I lost you yesterday. Is there any progress with the geo-caching thing?'

'We've got people checking the relevant websites and seeing if any of his contacts are into it. It turns out there's a thing called a mystery cache where you have to solve a puzzle, either to get the co-ordinates where the box is located or to get into the box when you get there.'

'So the answer to the puzzle could be the code to get into the casket?'

'Yep, that's what I reckon. We really need to find out if he went on any geocaching websites. The hairy geeks are looking into it.'

'You mean our esteemed Digital Media Officers?'

The weak sunshine highlighted dust motes in the air and smeary marks on the window. Once this case was over, I'd do a spot of cleaning. 'I think we should talk to his wife again,' I said. 'Would you come with me? I was going to go straight there this morning. I'll ring in to the Station.'

Jai lived in a flat on the outskirts of Matlock, surrounded by other recently separated males. He was waiting outside when I turned up.

'Alright?' I said, the normal Derbyshire greeting, which should be followed by a repetition of, 'Alright?' rather than an actual answer.

Jai shunned the greeting convention. 'No,' he said. 'Just got the post. Letter from the solicitor. How can the nice person you marry turn into an evil psycho-bitch from Hell?'

'Maybe she was always an evil psycho-bitch and you just didn't see it?'

I'd heard about Jai's ex-wife from Fiona. Apparently she judged other women according to a formula involving their husband's earnings divided by their clothes size. Jai was well out of it. If he was going to be shunned by his family for marrying a non-Sikh, he could surely have chosen someone more worthy.

Once we were in my car and on our way, Jai reached to flip on the radio. Alanis Morissette's 'Ironic' came on.

'It's not bloody ironic, is it?' Jai said. 'Rain on your wedding day.'

I laughed. 'No, Jai, it's not. It's just a tad unlucky. And a traffic jam when you're already late?'

'Par for the sodding course, I'd say.' But he'd perked up a bit.

'Isn't it ironic?' warbled Alanis.

'No, it's not!' we shouted.

Alanis faded to a conclusion. An image of Kate Webster's god-awful, cliff-hovering house slid into my mind. I realised I didn't want to be in it, hanging over the side of the quarry. I'd still go, but I felt the need to share my pain. Should I tell Jai? Would he tell Craig later so they could add this to the string of piss-taking options? I decided to risk it. 'I've been feeling a bit weird about heights,' I said. 'You know, since I dived head-first down those steps.'

'Like a vertigo thing?'

'A bit. But if you mention this to Craig, I will, in all seriousness, kill you. After disembowelling you.'

'I'd never do that.' He sounded quite hurt.

'Sorry. It's... Oh, don't worry. Anyway, I was just thinking about Kate Webster's house jutting over the edge of that sodding quarry.'

'You've got me to hold your hand.'

I looked round at Jai, and he reddened slightly.

'Yes. Thank you.'

I drove up the narrow lane out of Eldercliffe, my car engine grunting with the strain, and pulled into the parking space by Kate's house.

Kate appeared at the door with dishevelled hair, in a dressing gown. 'It's a mess in here and I'm not up, I'm afraid. Maybe you could make an appointment to come back later?' You only got that kind of comment from the middle-class suspects.

'We'd prefer to come in now, if that's all right. We don't mind about the mess.' I inched my foot inside.

'Okay, whatever.' She moved away from the door into the hallway. It had degenerated visibly since we were last there. Dust and hairs drifted in loose clusters over the floorboards like dandelion clocks and the air was sweet with the smell of decaying cut flowers.

We followed Kate into the living room. The TV blared. Kate shuffled over and switched it off.

'I was watching *Extraordinary People*.'

'Oh, I watch that,' I said.

'These two girls have only got one body between them. They seem so happy. Even have boyfriends.'

'I remember that one. Incredible.'

'Puts my problems into perspective.'

I did the same as Kate. There's nothing like two girls sharing a body or a man with ten stone testicles to make you pull yourself together when you're feeling a bit hard-done-by.

'Right,' Kate said. 'How can I help? Do you want tea?'

'Yes please, shall we go into the kitchen?' I had to get away from that picture window.

We walked through and settled ourselves around her beautiful kitchen table, which was made of a selection of different coloured, faded, aged planks. I was coveting this woman's furniture again.

I ran my hand over the waxed table-top. 'So, what did you think about the suicide email?'

'Well, at first I assumed it was from him, obviously. But the more I thought about it, the more I realised it wasn't his style. I think someone must have hacked his account.'

'Did anyone know his password?'

'Well, he wasn't that careful.'

'Do you know it?'

She pulled her dressing gown tight around herself. 'He uses a few different ones. I'd have a good chance I think, yes. You do know if I'd murdered him, I wouldn't be saying he didn't commit suicide, don't you?'

I smiled, processing all the negatives. 'Yes, we got that. Did Peter ever go geocaching?'

'Oh, that stupid thing with co-ordinates?'

'Yes, that's right.' My pulse quickened. She was going to say yes. We were onto something. Finally.

'Yes,' Kate said. 'He used to check for caches and find them on walks at the weekend, or sometimes on his lunch break on Mondays I think, if they were nearby.'

Bingo. I glanced at Jai and saw a look of triumph flit across his face. 'Right,' I said. 'Thanks. Did you ever go with him?'

'Why? Has this got something to do with his death?'

'We're looking into it.' I hoped she'd be satisfied with my complete non-explanation.

'Oh, thanks for clarifying that,' Kate said. 'That's on a par with East Midlands Trains telling you the train's delayed because it was late leaving the last station.'

I smiled. 'We can't say at the moment. Did you ever go with him?'

She rolled her eyes. 'Fair enough. Well, no, I never did. But he used to go with Felix and Edward about once a month, and one or more of their wives too, I think. Oh, and Mark sometimes used to go with them.'

'Do you happen to know which website he looked at?'

She tapped long fingers against the table. 'No, but I'm sure your people will be looking at his browsing history.'

'Did you ever go on the geocaching websites?'

'No. I left him to it. I always thought it was a bit odd.'

'Did Peter ever mention a friend called Sebastian?'

She looked up sharply. 'What, from his Cambridge days?'

'We're not sure. Who was he?'

Kate fiddled with a strand of dark hair. 'Oh, you know Peter...' She paused. 'Sorry, you didn't know Peter. Somehow he managed to befriend this homeless guy when he was in Cambridge. I don't really know how it happened but it's typical Peter. If someone talked to him, he'd be too polite to ignore them. I think Sebastian started chatting to him one day on Parker's Piece and it turned out they both came from round here. So they hung out together a bit. It was the summer of Peter's second year, after the exams.'

'And had Peter kept in touch with him?'

'No, it all fizzled out. And of course Felix hated Sebastian. Thought he had a crush on Olivia. He was insanely jealous about her.'

Kate jumped up to get us tea.

'You were saying Felix hated Sebastian,' Jai said, once Kate had sat back down.

'Yes.' She crossed her legs and adjusted her dressing gown. 'And Peter wasn't too sorry to let the friendship go, because he found Sebastian's glue-sniffing friends unnerving. Ironically, Felix didn't mind them, but then Peter said Felix always maintained a few dodgy friends so he could get hold of drugs when he wanted them.'

'Sebastian sounds an interesting character.'

'Yes, I think it was a bit of an eye-opener for Peter. Sebastian's main aim in life was to get arrested. He liked being in police custody because he got fed sausages.'

It was good to know we were doing all right by our criminal underclass.

'So, was Peter ever scared of Sebastian?'

Kate frowned. 'No. He found him a bit strange I think, but never threatening.'

'Okay, could we ask you about the recent increase in the life insurance on your husband,' I said, gently again.

Kate fiddled with her hair, combing a knot with her fingers. 'It was at his instigation,' she said. 'It was actually because we were planning to have a baby. And he'd been talking to his granny. She's always been a doom-merchant. I can see it looks suspicious, but also a bit too obvious, don't you think? If I was going to do it? I'm not stupid. And we did it on me too, not just him.'

'It's for nearly a million pounds. A lot of money, especially when you don't have kids yet. Did you have immediate plans?'

'Yes. Well, we did. Peter got cold feet about a year ago but he was coming round again. And life insurance is actually still quite cheap at our age and we thought we should sort it out now. Once the baby was on the way, we'd have other things to focus on.'

Kate stood and walked to the kitchen window, turning her back on us. 'This is actually quite hard to talk about.'

'I'm sorry,' I said. 'We have to ask these questions.'

'So,' Jai said. 'We heard you went and stayed with your parents in Bakewell for a while? Were you and Peter having problems?'

She whipped round and spoke to Jai. 'Oh, for God's sake, are you playing Bad Cop? Who said that? My parents are dead. I went to install a burglar alarm at our holiday cottage.'

Obviously Felix had got completely the wrong end of the stick, which seemed consistent with his level of interest in Peter's personal life. 'You have a holiday cottage in Bakewell?' I said.

'Yes. It's an old windmill. It was too much hassle to rent it properly so we just use it to get away, and let friends and family stay there – Peter's partners and Mark, mainly.'

'You like high places then.' I felt a little odd.

'I always used to. Although this house – well, I don't feel so good about it now. But the windmill's stunning. You can go right up to the top. There's a spectacular circular room up there with huge windows overlooking the moor.'

I tried to look enthusiastic.

'We were thinking of re-instating the milling mechanism actually,' Kate said. 'We're both interested in that sort of thing. There's still the space in the tower for it and a hole in the floor of the upper room. Anyway, that won't happen now. So, no. No serious problems with Peter. I only went for a few days.'

'Okay, that's fine.' I hesitated. 'Peter's grandmother mentioned someone being pregnant – could that be you?'

She looked confused for a moment. 'Oh, I don't think so.'

'Right. Thanks. Just one more thing. The paper we took from the fire – that you said was scrap. It had a word on it in Peter's handwriting – *Tithonus*. Does that mean anything to you?'

Kate breathed in slightly before saying, 'No. Nothing.'

'Are you sure? Why would Peter write that word?'

'I really have no idea. A crossword maybe?'

'And why had you burnt it?'

She looked away. 'No reason. We often use scrap paper to start the fire.'

I waited, but she pursed her lips and made it clear she was saying nothing more.

'Okay. Before we go, could we have a quick look in the basement?' I didn't actually know what was down there, but was now imagining an insane, wild-haired relative living in the bowels of the rock.

'Oh,' Kate said. 'Do you think it's relevant? I don't know why we didn't get rid of it. I used to think it was an interesting feature, but now…'

'Can we go down?'

Chapter 19

Kate rose stiffly and reached for a huge key hanging on the kitchen wall. 'I know this is silly because there's nothing valuable in there, but I like to keep it locked.'

She led us into the hallway and shoved the key into a heavy oak door on our left. The key clunked and she pushed the door open. It creaked like something from a horror film. Kate flipped on a light, illuminating worn stone steps plunging downwards. A moist draught touched the hairs on my arms. I shot a look at Jai, and he raised his eyebrows.

'I'll be in the kitchen,' Kate said. 'I can't look at it since… you know. It's on the back wall, straight ahead.' She shuddered and walked away.

I tried to make myself step firmly and confidently, even though I had the urge to creep. Jai followed close behind. The light bulb was near the top of the steps, and as we walked past it our bodies cast shadows which danced on the walls.

I reached the bottom and took a step into the musty room. The back wall of the basement came into view. I stumbled away from it, knocking into Jai. He grabbed onto my arm before hurriedly letting it go.

'What the hell?' Jai's voice seemed too loud in the echoey space.

'Another one,' I whispered.

It was very similar to the image in the cave house, but rather than being hewn into stone, it was painted in faded black onto the lime-washed wall. The pose was the same – axe raised high, grinning skull, skeletal body hunched forward.

'A Grim Reaper in the cave where he died,' Jai said. 'A Grim Reaper in his basement...'

I steeled myself and walked over to the image. It looked at least decades old. 'And a book full of sketches of the Grim Reaper by the other dead man who fell off the cliff outside.'

'It's actually creeping me out a bit,' Jai said. 'I'm not surprised his wife won't come down here.'

We took photographs and left. Kate was sitting at the kitchen table staring at the floor.

'Thanks.' I handed her the huge jailer's key. 'Do you know the origins of that?'

She looked up and stared through me for a moment, before taking the key. 'What? No. It's always been here. Horrible isn't it?'

'Why didn't you show us this when we were here on Monday?'

She stood and we walked into the hallway. 'Oh. I didn't see the relevance. And Beth hates people seeing it. She reckons it perpetuates this whole curse thing. She says if we... sorry, I... ever want to sell the house, people need to stop going on about it being cursed.'

'And what's your view on the curse?'

Kate hesitated. 'I thought it was rubbish, of course. But now... I'm not so sure.'

'Did you say the man who originally built the house died?'

'Yes. He was actually one of Peter's ancestors. It was built in Victorian times.' She glanced at us as if to gauge whether we were interested. I gave her an expectant look, and she carried on. 'He threw himself into the quarry. A strange little man from the bookshop in town called round when we first moved in and told us about him.'

'Does anyone know why he killed himself?'

'He was some kind of Victorian industrialist, and he'd had this house built but it wasn't so near the edge of the quarry then.

Apparently it was surrounded by beautiful rhododendron gardens. Anyway, something went wrong and he lost his money, and sold off chunks of his garden to the quarry company. They were still quarrying at this end in those days and they chipped the ground away around it, which is why the house is now perched right on the edge. His family and friends turned against him and he ended up throwing himself to his death.'

'Poor man,' I said, picturing him tumbling over and over as he dropped into the quarry.

'I know,' Kate said. 'So many people have died.'

★

We stepped out of Kate's house into the mist of grey drizzle that plagued high places in Derbyshire. Some creature was making the noise the BBC use to indicate you're in the countryside and possibly about to get murdered.

'Christ, that was sinister,' Jai said. 'I'm not surprised she's gone off the house. I wouldn't live there on my own.'

I smiled. 'Scared of ghosts?'

'Don't try and tell me you weren't freaked by it. I saw your face.'

I laughed. 'Let's walk down to the marketplace for a coffee and a think.'

Jai squinted at the sky. 'Leave the car here?'

'Yeah. We can cope with a bit of rain.' Even though I had a cluster of exciting new injuries to complement my long-term limp, and would most likely have been shot if I'd been a horse, I liked to walk. You noticed things when you walked. Besides, it was a relief to be outside and not in a grim basement surrounded by rock and ominous pictures.

We arrived at the town square – Georgian buildings crowded around a cobbled marketplace like teeth that needed braces. And a coffee shop in a nice old building that hadn't had its windows ripped out.

I pushed through the swing door and took a gorgeous breath of coffee-infused air. Chunky tables sat on wooden flooring planks, and chalkboards listed bounteous varieties of coffees and exotic paninis. A jumble of old-fashioned, carved walking sticks sat in a wicker basket by the window. At the counter, I surveyed a selection of muffins each the size of a small child's head.

'A skinny latte,' I said. 'And one of those lemon things, the ones with "heart attack" drizzled on them in yellow gunk.'

Most of the tables were occupied. Young people peered at phones and avoided conversation, and a harassed-looking woman corralled two blonde, androgynous toddlers in a corner. We sat ourselves near the window, in a flurry of damp coats and scraping chair legs.

Briefly, I luxuriated in the sheer pleasure of sitting in a coffee shop with a muffin and a latte, even a stupid skinny one. But soon, the transitory joy of the first few mouthfuls passed. My rising panic about the confusion of the case and lurking unease about Mum and the step-falling incident returned.

'I should have let Richard kick me off this damn case,' I said, rubbing the bump on my head.

'He's not as bad as you think, you know.' Jai took an enormous bite of panini. He'd chosen a caramel latte and a slab of cheesecake for afters, in the manner of skinny men.

'Sorry?'

'Richard. He's had some difficult personal stuff going on.'

'I don't think he's that bad.' I took a swig of the latte. Should have gone for full fat. I'd read the low-fat craze was making us fatter anyway.

'Did you know his daughter used to be his son?'

'No, you're kidding!'

'I shit you not. The photo on his desk – Natasha. Used to be William.'

'She's way too hot to have been a man.'

'What are you saying? Actually, William wasn't even Richard's son – he was his wife's kid, but it was Richard who was supportive of the sex–change thing. The wife couldn't handle it.'

'Jesus. How do you know all this?'

'Well, not through Richard. He keeps it very close to his chest. One of my friends knew him through a golf club. This friend told me Richard used to hang around with some people he met at church, but when it came out that William wanted to be Natasha, most of them dropped Richard and his wife like a stone. My friend was one of the few not to disown them, but then he's an atheist and doesn't give a rat's arse about the son–daughter stuff. He said it was shocking how the others behaved.'

'And Richard stood by the kid?'

'Yes, even when his wife freaked out. I think Richard had always been a casual Christian, you know, weddings and funerals and stuff, and had never really thought about it that much. Whereas his wife and her friends were on the more serious – well, bordering on loony – side.'

'Jai… Surely you were brought up religious?'

He hit me with his full-on big-brown-eyes stare. 'I was. I ditched the turban and the beard a long time ago, but sort of hung on to the religion. But then when I wanted to marry an English girl… Oh, you know, it all turned nasty with my family. And I suppose I blamed their religion for it. Anyway, it emphasises for me how decent Richard was about the Natasha thing.' He gave a hollow laugh. 'I can imagine how my parents would have reacted if one of us boys had decided we wanted to be a girl.'

One of the blonde children removed a walking stick from the wooden basket and bashed it repeatedly on the wooden floor, as if to applaud Richard's actions. His mother mouthed an apology generally at the room.

I fiddled with my unused sugar packet. 'Do you not have any belief then?'

Jai sighed. 'Not really. I kind of abandoned it all. How about you?'

'No belief. I seem to have the guilt of a Catholic though.'

Jai raised his eyebrows. 'What do you have to feel guilty about?'

I hesitated. 'Oh, Mum, mainly. She's looking after my gran, and she seems a bit weird at the moment. Anxious about something, but she won't say what. I should spend more time with her but work always takes over. And then… Oh, never mind. Family can be a bit weird.' I couldn't tell him the whole story. Not in a coffee shop in the middle of a murder investigation. 'But Richard's friends disowning him – that's bad.' I gave the mother of the stick-bashing child a reassuring smile.

'Yeah, they were pretty hardcore. I think they were members of some group, euphemistically termed Life Line or something, which is basically anti-everything they don't like the sound of. And that most definitely includes starting life as a boy and ending up as a blonde woman called Natasha.'

'Oh God, I know that group. My friend Hannah went to a few meetings. They were trying to recruit disabled people to their anti-abortion views.'

'Well, she wants to be careful. They can turn on you.'

'So, what happened between Richard and his wife?'

'They split up in the end. She stuck with her religious friends, and doesn't have anything to do with Natasha or Richard. She still lives round here though. Works at the health centre in Eldercliffe.'

'Not Vivian, the receptionist?'

'Yes, I think she is called Vivian.'

'I knew she was a nasty piece of work. We took a statement from her. She'd been dropping hints about Kate Webster being up to something but when Fiona spoke to her, she wouldn't say a damn thing. It could just be that Kate's willing to sign off abortions, and in the cold light of day Vivian realised the police didn't regard that as the Devil's work. I can't believe she disowned her own son. Daughter, I mean. Now you've made me feel sorry for Richard.'

'So you should. He's intimidated by you.'

'What?' I paused with my muffin halfway to my mouth.

'He worked his way up the ponderous route. He's not dumb but he's not sparkling either. You know he's always trying to do *The Times* crossword? He fancies himself as a bit of a Morse but he's not quite up to it.' Jai shovelled his pudding into his mouth. I envied his casual, guilt-free relationship with cheesecake.

'Is that what he's always hiding behind his piles and cactus towers?'

'Yes. He probably wouldn't want you to see. Being a known smartypants with a law A level you did in a spare five minutes, and a poncy Oxbridge University degree.'

'He does know there's no Oxbridge University, doesn't he?'

Jai laughed. 'Yes, I'm pretty sure he does.'

'Okay, okay, I'll try to be nice to him. But he does patronise me.'

'I'm sure he does, but it's clearly more complicated than him just being a sexist moron. I think he gets a bit mixed up knowing how to deal with you.'

'Yeah, I'm so tricky.' I wiped crumbs from my face. 'Anyway, could you have a chat with the man at the bookshop who Kate mentioned? You know, about the Victorian ancestor. All this talk of curses and so forth, I wonder if it might shed some light.'

Jai nodded and scraped the last few blobs of cream from his plate.

'Lick it if you want,' I said. 'I don't mind.'

'You may have licked plates in Manchester.' He was dying to lick it, I could tell.

My bag vibrated on my lap. I grabbed my phone. 'Meg Dalton.'

'It's Fiona. The farmer opposite Peter Hamilton's house saw a woman, not the wife, visiting him on his working-from-home days.'

'Who was it?'

'We're looking into that. And I've spoken to a detective in Cambridge. He handled a case where a lad fell off a roof. A friend of Felix Carstairs and Peter Hamilton.'

'Oh yes?'

'He thought Felix and Peter were lying about what happened.'

Chapter 20

It was Saturday and Richard had promised to sack me if I didn't have a rest. I decided to drive down to Cambridge to talk to the detective who'd been involved in the death of the student roof-climber. Although perhaps not technically a rest, I could take Mum with me to look at my old college and pretend it was a relaxing day out. I figured Mum would have calmed down enough about my fall that I could cope with a day of her company.

'Are you sure you're well enough to drive?' she said, before we'd even left her house. Uh oh, maybe I'd been wrong. 'Your head. I'm worried about you. And remember how you were a couple of years ago? I don't want you overdoing it.'

'I'm fine, Mum. Get in the car. Did you bring your sat nav?' Mine was playing up and I thought we might as well use the one I'd given her for Christmas. I doubted it had enjoyed many outings. I probably should have been able to find my way to the college where I studied for three years, but I was suffering from sat nav-induced learned incompetence.

Mum baulked before getting into the car. 'Have you got a big bruise?'

'Yeah, bowling ball size.' I opened the passenger door and shoved her in. 'Come on, let's forget about it and have a nice day, shall we?'

I got in the car and stabbed at the sat nav, accidentally bringing up the recent destinations. The last one was in Chester. 'What took you to Chester?' I asked while putting in the Cambridge details.

'What was that, love?'

'The last place you went with the sat nav. I didn't know you'd been to Chester.' I pulled away and headed out of Eldercliffe in the direction of the M1. I glanced at Mum and saw a flush rising up her neck and onto her face. 'Are you okay, Mum?'

'Yes, of course, Chester. Well... Oh yes, I lent it to Sheila next door when she went to see her friend.'

I could no more imagine Sheila next door using a sat nav than I could Hamlet. 'Really? Did she manage to work it okay?'

'Yes, I think so. Us older folk aren't as dim as you think.' She crossed her arms and took three audible breaths. 'Anyway, remember when we came down here after you got your offer?'

I breathed in sharply, surprised she'd mentioned this. Our trip to Cambridge had been a rare, sweet day when Mum and Dad had seemed content in each other's company. They'd spent my teenage years not so much together as trapped in different parts of the same web of grief and guilt. Eventually Mum couldn't bear it any longer and had asked him to leave, and I'd spent many years suppressing my bubbling resentment over this. But that day, they'd sat in the front of the car chatting like proper parents whilst I bit my nails in the back.

'Yes,' I said. 'It was a good day, although I was fretting I wouldn't get the grades.'

'Oh, you poor thing. You always so wanted to impress your father.'

I glanced at her. She rarely mentioned him and tended to stiffen and walk away if I did. 'I wanted to impress both of you – not just him.' I turned the wipers to intermittent. 'Well, okay, mainly him.' I stared at the rain smearing over the windscreen. 'I do miss him, you know.' My voice was quiet against the noise of traffic on the wet road.

'Yes, of course. But it was his choice to move to Scotland.' She looked straight ahead. Back to the usual.

I was too hot, and the car smelt of wet cat. How did I carry that smell around with me? Hamlet hadn't even been in this car. I turned down the blower but the windscreen immediately steamed up. I pulled over to the inside lane.

'I bet you don't miss his moods,' Mum said. 'I still catch myself stacking the dishwasher the approved way.'

I had a flash of memory – Dad on one of his dark days. All of us creeping around him as if he was an unpredictable carnivorous animal. But because it was my fault about Carrie, it must have been my fault Dad had been so miserable, and Mum so distant. I knew this wasn't really true, but it was a compelling story I told myself.

We peeled off the A14, headed into Cambridge, and found somewhere to park in a back street. We could wander around my old college before heading into town. The detective who'd been in charge of the enquiry into the student's death had agreed to meet me in The Eagle for lunch, and Mum assured me she'd be happy sampling the tea shops.

I felt guilty and unentitled walking into Newnham, and even had my ridiculous CamCard to hand to prove my authenticity if challenged. But the porter laughed and waved us in. We stepped through the door from the Porter's Lodge into the gardens – a sanctuary enclosed on three sides by delicate red buildings – and were hit with the smell of wet plants and clean air.

My mind shifted to our earlier conversation. 'Dad wasn't really that bad before he left, was he, Mum? I mean, everything was awful anyway after Carrie.'

'Well, either way, you'll probably feel a lot better if you stop fretting about his opinions. He's made it clear he's not that interested.'

I winced. That was a bit unnecessary. I blinked and looked over at the intricate college architecture. 'I'm not trying to impress Dad. I hardly even talk to him.' I could feel the shake in my voice. 'I just want to do a good job.' I glanced at my watch. I should have been heading off to meet the detective.

'And when you were here,' Mum said. 'You were always so worried you were going to fail, even though you were doing fine.'

How much time had I wasted worrying about failing? I'd never just rested in the sunshine in these stunning gardens – always in the back of my mind was the worry that I should be working, that I didn't understand my work, that I was stupid. We'd all felt stupid. At school, we'd been the brightest in the class, but then we were thrown in with hordes of seemingly far better-educated public school kids. I'd only realised later they felt stupid too, but like wild gazelle they'd learnt not to reveal any weakness for fear of being eaten alive.

I looked at Mum. 'Well, since we're having this conversation, I worry about you too. Caring for Gran's getting too much for you. I want to help more, but work's so busy.'

'I'm okay. I know you do as much as you can.'

'You've seemed a bit anxious about something recently. Is everything okay?'

Her voice was firm. 'I'm fine.'

I pictured Mum's window wide open, curtains flapping. 'Are you absolutely sure?'

'Yes, it was all getting a bit much, but I'm alright again now.'

'And did Sheila next door really go to Chester?'

She stiffened. 'Yes, of course. Don't you need to get to your meeting with the policeman?'

'Yes, I'm late. Are you walking into town with me?'

She spoke quickly and didn't look at me. 'No, I'll use the toilets here and walk down on my own. You always walk too fast for me anyway, despite your ankle. I may as well saunter, and have a walk along the Backs.'

'Are you sure you know where you're going?'

'I'm not an idiot, Meg, I can find my way.'

'Right, I'll call you when I'm done. Have you got your mobile with you?'

She gave me a stern look. 'Yes. And I've even worked out how to switch it on.'

★

I immediately identified DI Andrew Carter in The Eagle, via my unfailing police detection sense, which was sadly shared by criminals. He introduced himself as if he had the weight of the world on his shoulders, his handshake warm and dry but somewhat limp.

I bought us drinks and sandwiches, and we settled ourselves in a quiet corner.

'You want to talk about the student that fell off the roof back in '99?' He sat with his head hunched forward like a depressed bird of prey.

'Yes, we're investigating the death of one of his friends. I wondered if you thought there was any more to it than just an accident?'

I'd ended up on a wooden stool with no back. I adjusted my position and crossed my legs.

'They're all bloody idiots, of course,' Carter said. 'Supposed to be the cream of English youth.' He tutted and took a deep swig of his pint. 'If that's the case, God help the rest of them.'

'So, you get quite a few of them climbing on the roofs?'

'Oh yes, it's quite the thing. Some of the stupid sods have even written books about it. But there's two types of climber. There's the reckless idiots who go on to kill themselves in the Alps, and then there's the cretinous drunks who grow up and become stock brokers and bankers, and make millions bankrupting the rest of us.'

'Right. Which category was the boy who died in?'

'Matthews? He was in the drunken category. Actually we found drugs in his system too. And I reckon—'

'What kind of drugs?'

'Cannabis and a touch of amphetamines.' Carter sat back in his chair. 'And I reckon those other two boys were with him on that roof. But they weren't admitting anything.'

'Carstairs and Hamilton?'

'Yeah. Which one's dead?'

'Hamilton.'

'That figures.'

'Oh?'

'He was the easily led one.'

Our sandwiches arrived. Carter picked at his. 'What's wrong with a bit of ham and tomato? It's all brie on a bloody raspberry coulis these days. What the hell's this?'

'I asked for ham and tomato. So, you think they were on the roof with Matthews? Where did they say they were?'

'In bed. Not together.' Carter let out a homophobic snort. 'Alone. No one could confirm. The toff—'

'Carstairs?'

'That's the one. I reckon he bullied the other one into keeping shtum. The toff was cool as you like but the other one, he was shitting himself. We had a bit of fun with him, but couldn't get anything out of him. He was more scared of the toff than he was of us. Can't afford to really frighten the little buggers nowadays can we?' He laughed unpleasantly. 'Not when Daddy owns half of bloody Kent.'

'What made you think they were on the roof with him?'

'We found their fingerprints and scuff marks from their shoes. But they just said they'd been up there the night before and Matthews must have gone up again on his own. No bugger saw anything so we had no proof.'

'So, if they were there, do you think it was anything other than an accident?'

'Who knows? We drew a massive blank. No one knew anything.'

'Did you test Carstairs and Hamilton for drugs?'

'No, we had nothing on them. We couldn't allocate a lot of resources to it, since it looked so much like an accident. Nasty though. Iron railings. Spikes. Like something out of *The Omen*.'

I winced. 'Was there a motive to kill Matthews?'

'Nothing obvious. Reckless, young, spoilt, drunken wankers with an added dose of speed? It could have been anything – a comment about a girl, a badly timed insult. Or a pure accident and they just didn't want Mummy and Daddy to know they were stoned on a roof in the middle of the night. My gut feeling was there was a bit more to it than that, but we never found anything, so I'm not sure I can help you. I'm sorry the nicer one's dead. He seemed like a decent enough kid. For a student tosser.'

I didn't think there was anything more to be extracted from Carter, so I let him share a little more of his sunny world-view while we finished our lunch, and then made my way out.

I called Mum, more in hope than expectation, and she answered with her loud, panicky mobile-phone-voice. She was in a tea room on King's Parade, and I agreed to meet her there.

I walked between the ostentatious buildings and replayed my conversation with Carter. I tried to sift through the other information about the murder, but kept getting drawn back to my conversation with Mum. Was I still trying to impress Dad, even though I hardly ever saw him and, as Mum so tactfully pointed out, he clearly wasn't interested? And was I using murder investigations to feel better about myself?

Deep in my maudlin thoughts, I nearly walked straight past Mum's tea room. I glanced up and saw her inside the window. She looked up from her phone and caught my eye. Was she *texting?* I blinked and made my way inside.

'You were lost in thought,' she said, and raised her head to alert the waitress.

'Yeah, just solving crimes, you know.' I squeezed myself onto a chair in the small gap opposite her at the table. 'Were you texting? Have you entered the twenty-first century?'

'Ha, ha. Maybe I have.'

The café had a French, rustic look and smelt of roasting coffee. My spirits lifted, and I noticed Mum had lost the tightness around her eyes.

'Who were you texting?'

'Oh, nobody you know.'

'You haven't got a man, have you, Mum?' I had to admit, this seemed highly unlikely. Mum ignored me and tucked her phone away in her pocket.

'I've had a lovely time,' she said. 'A little walk along the Backs and then I sat in here and read my book.'

'Sounds appealing. I talked to a dour policeman about the death of a young man. Er, a latte please.' The waitress took my order and was about to leave. 'Oh, and a coffee cake. Sod it.'

'Stop worrying about your weight,' Mum said. 'When you're my age, you'll look back and realise you weren't fat. Did you get anywhere with your police stuff?'

'Not really. But that wasn't the main point. I wanted a day out with you. And I am a bit fat. I know it's stupid, and we're all being brainwashed by the media into being unhappy with our bodies so we'll buy more crap we don't need. And Hannah's told me how she feels when idiots like me who are a little bit plump moan about how much they hate their bodies. But I'd still like to shift a few pounds. Anyway, I'm glad you've had a nice time.'

She smiled. 'It's been good. When you were here, I never seemed to have time to look around.'

'Neither did I.' I realised how ridiculous that sounded, given that I'd been there in term time for three years, plus the summer I'd worked as a very bad silver-service waitress for college conferences, burning delegates with hot plates and spilling soup.

A beep in my pocket – a text from Fiona. *Woman seen by farmer, visiting Peter Hamilton's house – Olivia Carstairs.*

Chapter 21

We finally arrived back at Mum's house. I was exhausted with the effort of avoiding the speed cameras on the A14, and driving had aggravated the shoulder I'd wrenched when I'd fallen down the steps.

'Will you have a cup of tea.' Mum was the opposite of today's youth. Although this was strictly speaking a question, her inflection made it a command.

I hauled myself from the car and hobbled after Mum to the door. A buddleia sprawled over the lawn and scented the air with honey. There was a different smell layered underneath. A distant part of my brain knew it was a bad smell, but I didn't immediately identify it.

Mum pushed the door open, and we walked in.

That smell again. I froze in the hallway.

Gas.

'Mum! Get outside. You've got a gas leak.'

She turned to me, looking confused. 'Did I leave the gas on? On the hob?'

'Get outside. I'm calling for help.'

'But your gran…'

'Can't you smell it, Mum? It's really strong.' I fumbled my phone from my pocket. 'Don't switch on any lights.'

She ignored me and headed for the stairs. 'It'll kill her, Meg. She's so frail.'

My fingers were lumps of meat. I managed to dial Jai. He picked up and I shouted incoherently at the phone. He'd know what to do.

I raced after Mum into the hallway, the rotten cabbage smell thick in my throat, and followed her up the stairs and into Gran's room.

I rushed to Gran's side. She was either asleep or unconscious. We shook her and shouted but she wouldn't wake.

'She's going to die.' Tears streamed down Mum's face. 'I'm not ready. She can't die now.'

I ran and opened the window. I knew gas wasn't poisonous as such but it could kill you if it displaced too much oxygen, and Gran was so old and frail. We had to get her out.

I wedged my arm under Gran's chest and dragged her sideways towards me. How did her tiny bird bones weigh so much? My shoulder spasmed. I had no faith I wouldn't drop her. My arms were usually strong, thanks to exercises I did with Hannah, but my muscles were torn and bruised from my fall.

I glanced at Mum. She was at Gran's feet. She gasped, 'How can she be so heavy? I can't lift her.' Her arms looked hopelessly fragile, pulling feebly at Gran's ankles.

I relaxed for a moment, to regain some strength. I took a deep breath, and the gas smell made me want to gag. 'Mum, what time does your heating come on?'

She looked up and spoke slowly. 'Any time now. I set it later than usual. I knew we'd be back late.'

Could the boiler ignite the gas? I didn't know, and wasn't eager to find out.

My shoulder was sending scorching pains through my body. I didn't know how we were going to get Gran out. I felt like collapsing on the floor and crying with despair at our helplessness.

Then a tiny voice whispered that it could be okay to die like this, blown up in an explosion. It would be quick. Gran would be spared a death from cancer, and I'd be spared all my guilt and my desperation to do the right thing, even though I never seemed to know what the right thing was. Mum wouldn't have to grow old.

I was so tired. It could be a relief. It would be relaxing to be dead. Nothing more to do. Nobody to worry about. My knees felt wobbly and I had the urge to lie down.

Was this me, or the gas in my brain? I felt befuddled. Mum took a step away and sat on the chair.

We had to get out.

'Come on, Mum. We can do this.'

I pulled Mum from the chair and put her hands on Gran's feet. I dragged Gran off the bed, feeling the agony of her weight wrenching my injured shoulder. I wanted to scream. Mum supported her legs as much as she could, and we didn't drop her, although her middle sank towards the floor.

Mum's breath was rasping like sandpaper and her face was crimson. 'I can't… The stairs.'

'Put her down a minute.'

We laid her as gently as we could on the floor, with more of a thud than I'd hoped for. She muttered something.

'Gran,' I shouted. 'Are you awake? You need to wake up.' I wanted to slap her, shake her, force her into life.

Her blue lips moved and her eyes flipped open.

'Grab one side each,' I said. 'Maybe she can help us.'

We each took one frail arm and heaved her up on to her feet. She managed to take some of her weight herself, and we shuffled her towards the stairs.

Like a strange and ungainly beast, we lumped down, stair by stair, panting and grunting and swearing.

We reached the bottom of the stairs and dragged ourselves along the hallway to the front door.

I tripped on the step and fell, pulling Mum and Gran down on top of me. I realised I was crying. 'Get up,' I mumbled. 'Get out.'

But we were all tangled together, a mess of limbs. I pictured the boiler preparing to fire up.

I was seized with anger that this was happening. On top of everything else we had to cope with. It gave me a burst of strength and I hauled myself to my feet, dragging the others with me. The three of us hobbled onto the lawn.

'Come on.' My breathing was so fast I could hardly speak. 'Get away from the house.'

I filled my lungs with the buddleia-scented air, and collapsed onto the cold grass.

Chapter 22

I dreamed I was dragging myself away from an unknown terror, pulling something heavy and unspecified behind me, my limbs like lead and my heart hammering. I woke early, my brain full of disbelief about the day before.

I reached for the phone and called Mum from my bed. 'Are you okay?'

'I'm fine,' she said. 'I called the hospital and your Gran's going to be alright. They're just keeping her in for a day or two, to be on the safe side. What about you?'

'Don't you have a headache? I feel like someone's taken my brain out, diced it like steak, and put it back with all the bits in the wrong places and the knife still in there with it.'

She hesitated. 'Oh no, love, I feel okay.'

'Are they sure the house is safe? Why don't you come here?'

'It's fine. They fixed it all last night. They're adamant it's safe now. Some connector thingy on the boiler had come loose.'

'Hadn't you serviced it, Mum?'

'Well, I did. A while ago.'

'Jesus, Mum, you've got to look after yourself better. I can't be worrying about you all the time. It's driving me nuts.'

'I know. I know. It's just hard work with your gran. And your father used to sort out boilers and those sorts of manly things…'

'This sexism could kill you, Mum.'

I couldn't think clearly with this knife in my brain. Couldn't work out whether to raise my worry level about Mum from Standard to Red Alert. If there had been an intruder in her house the other day, they could have tampered with the boiler. But the boiler man had just blamed a loose connection. I realised I was being ridiculous. Gas leaks happened, especially if you expected your ex-husband to sort out boiler servicing despite him living in Scotland and you never seeing him or so much as mentioning his name. I vowed to keep a closer eye on matters relating to household safety.

I heaved myself out of bed and climbed down the perilous staircase in my nightshirt to make tea. It was freezing, and the kitchen windows rattled in the breeze. The cat flap clattered and Hamlet shot through with a mouse, but I was so tired I couldn't even be bothered to argue with him about it. I'd see a small pile of glistening giblets later, with any luck before I trod in it.

The milk was on the turn but I stuck it in my tea anyway, grabbed my laptop and carefully climbed the stairs to go back to bed.

At about half past ten, a knock on the front door snapped me out of my thoughts. Shit. I wasn't dressed. But Hamlet's food came by mail order and I was nearly out of it. I pulled on jeans, stuck a fleece over my nightshirt and almost fell down the stairs.

I flung open the door and my heart sank. I was seriously not in the mood for this. Two young women with the round, self-satisfied faces of the born again, one clutching a pile of magazines adorned with rainbows and happy people. I registered the magazines as familiar but couldn't immediately think why.

'You're wasting your time here,' I said. 'I'm irredeemably atheist. Going to burn in hell for sure.'

I knew that wouldn't cut much ice. I'd once worked with a Jehovah's Witness and she'd confessed they got credit for the amount of time they spent trying to convert people, regardless of the hopelessness of the venture. She'd tried to open my eyes to the light of Jesus every morning for five years.

I started to ease the door shut.

'Wait!' The older one of the two took a step towards the closing door. 'You're the detective investigating the death of Peter Hamilton, aren't you?'

I opened the door again.

'We have some information you should know.'

Holy crap, was I going to have to invite them into my house? I battled a wave of exhaustion and stepped back. 'You'd better come in.'

It wasn't proper procedure, of course. I wasn't prepared. I didn't even have a bra on. I should have told them to make an appointment at the Police Station. But they looked potentially flighty, so I led them into the damp living room and sat them down. I hoped this wasn't a ploy to try to convert me after all. I sat on the chair nearest the draughty window and listened to Hamlet charging around upstairs. That poor mouse.

'How can I help?' I said.

'We have information about Dr Webster – the dead man's wife.' The slightly older one sat forward on the edge of my sagging sofa. She had dark hair that looked like she cut it herself, and a wide-eyed gaze, as if she'd recently been hypnotised or smacked on the head.

I grabbed a notepad from my Stationery-Fetishist's stash in the desk by the window, and took a few details from them, to cover myself just a little bit. The older one was called Dawn and the younger one Charmaine.

'She's killing her patients,' Dawn said. 'Going against God's will and taking lives.'

'Life is a sacred gift from our Creator,' Charmaine said. 'For the terminally ill, there is God's marvellous promise of a resurrection to a paradise of health and life under God's Kingdom.'

'Okay, okay,' I said. 'Forget the Bible study. What have you seen her do? With your own eyes?'

Charmaine sat back and let Dawn take over.

'She killed my neighbour's mother.' She sat up straighter in the chair. 'Dr Webster gave her more morphine than she needed, and the woman died. I overheard my neighbour talking to her friend in the garden.'

I sighed. 'Was the woman dying anyway?'

'No one can tell. We don't know when God will choose to take us.'

There was a scuffling in the corridor, and a mouse ran into the middle of the room, hotly pursued by Hamlet. He cornered it by my foot and I managed to scoop it up and dash from the room and through the kitchen to the back door, cradling its shaking body with both hands. 'Can one of you come and open the door?' I shouted.

Charmaine appeared, looking shocked.

'Turn the key clockwise and open the door,' I said.

She did this and I hurled the mouse towards the end of the garden and shut the door and the cat flap before Hamlet had a chance to follow.

'Just saving the life of one of God's precious creatures.' I rinsed my hands. 'Of course if they're badly injured I bash them with the frying pan of death to put them out of their misery.'

Charmaine's jaw was slack. 'You hit them with a frying pan?'

'Yes, there's a Le Creuset that's perfect for the job. Nice and heavy. Only if they're paralysed or something. It's the kindest thing, don't you think?'

I wasn't sure why I felt compelled to torment her, but it had been a tough week. She edged away from me and made her way back to the living room.

I followed. Hamlet came along too and loudly sniffed the spot where the mouse had left the floor, glancing up at me with a resentful expression.

'What was wrong with the woman Dr Webster gave the morphine to?' I asked.

The two women looked at each other. 'We think it was cancer,' Dawn finally admitted.

'Was your neighbour angry with Dr Webster?'

'I don't know. But this isn't the only case. Everyone in Eldercliffe knows she'll do it, and that she killed her husband too.'

'What makes you say she killed her husband?'

'A woman like that. Playing God.'

This wasn't getting me anywhere. 'Have you any other reason to believe she killed her husband?'

Both women looked at me with distant expressions as if searching their memory banks for Bible quotes.

'Thank you,' I said. 'I've got your statement. We'll take your comments into account.'

I stood, but they didn't.

'Aren't you going to prosecute her? What she's doing isn't legal you know.' Charmaine actually settled deeper into my chair. Was I going to have to forcibly remove them? Wield the frying pan?

'We'll look into it. Thank you. I need to get on now.'

I walked towards the door. They both rose and followed me from the room.

They baulked a little in the hallway.

'Here, I'll take a copy of your magazine on your way out.' This sentence didn't really make sense, but I hoped the mix of bribery and suggestion would do the trick.

It did. There were extra *Get-on-the-Bus-to-Heaven* points for giving out magazines.

I took a deep breath and closed the door behind them. And locked it for good measure.

So, that must be what Vivian at the health centre had meant by *the Devil's work*. Kate was prepared to help patients die. But was it relevant to our enquiry? Okay, it wasn't legal but was it really so bad to help some poor bugger who was dying of cancer check out a bit early? I suspected the majority of doctors would do the same.

I wandered into the kitchen again, wishing I had milk that wasn't off. Maybe I'd combine a milk mission with a visit to Hannah. Take my mind off gas leaks and dead people.

The phone rang. Mum. I stuck the magazine on the kitchen table and picked up.

'Just to let you know, they've decided to discharge your gran today.'

'Wow, that was quick.' I sat down, realising why the magazine was familiar. It was the same one Grace had given me in her jewellery shop. Having no desire to be a godly business woman, I chucked it in the direction of the recycling bin.

'Bed shortage, probably,' Mum said. 'But she's fine.'

After chatting some more about Gran, I decided to ask her again about Dr Webster. I was sure she'd recognised her name. Maybe she'd heard some gossip.

'On a different subject, Mum, you know Dr Webster? The wife of the dead man?'

'Look I have to go. I...' She trailed off. We both knew she didn't have any pressing engagements.

'Mum, it's kind of important. Had you heard her name before I mentioned it the other day? It might be relevant to this murder investigation.'

'Sorry, Meg, I don't know anything about her. Speak soon.' And she hung up on me.

★

A text established Hannah was in, and had cake. I grabbed my coat and mobile, and set off up the cobbled street towards the hill that led to her housing estate. It was drizzling but I left my hood down and went hatless so I'd hear if anyone crept up behind me.

The road climbed steeply between terraced stone cottages. I wished I'd taken the car. My ankle ached and my head throbbed, and I'd never previously noticed all the alleyways and dark corners on this route.

I wrapped my coat tightly around me and quickened my pace, knowing I'd panic if I ran. I tried to distract myself by rating the cottages for original features like lime mortar and sash windows, with extra points for old glass, but I was too jittery to commit to the game.

Finally, the houses turned from old to new and I took a left into Hannah's cul-de-sac, glancing behind me even though I felt melodramatic doing so.

Hannah's house had never looked more welcoming. I felt a pang of envy for her double glazing, cavity wall insulation and damp proofing. This was ridiculous of course. Hannah only lived in this bungalow because of the easy access and low maintenance. I could hardly envy her reasons for that.

She buzzed me in and I walked through to the kitchen, where she sat in her wheelchair, wearing a vest top and the self-righteous look of the recently exercised.

I checked the feel of the air, and it was clear our almost-argument in the hospital was forgotten. The slight tension in my stomach disappeared.

'You look smug,' I said. 'Have you been doing pull-ups?'

'Yeah, do you want to do some with me?'

I blasted her with my best astonished look. 'I know I've been sharing your quest for amazing upper body strength and a sylph-like figure, but not today.'

'Okay, okay. You're convalescing.'

The kitchen was all clear counter-tops and built-in appliances, with sparkly-clean windows overlooking her tiny lawned garden. I looked out and saw the neighbour's cat squatting in Hannah's flower bed again. It had been an ongoing bone of contention that the cat ignored its own sprawling, chaotic garden and chose Hannah's pristine one as its toilet.

'Mum reckons in the future we'll look back and realise we weren't fat after all,' I said, easing myself onto one of her leather-backed chairs.

'You might. When I looked at my BMI on the chart, there was a skull and crossbones next to it.'

'Yeah, you're not supposed to use your height when you're in your wheelchair. Does that mean you're not going to offer me cake?'

'Oh, sod it, I did do some exercises.' Hannah rooted in a low cupboard and emerged with an enormous carrot cake which she slapped onto the table. 'Cut us some of that. It's practically a vegetable. Anyway, how are you? Did you work out any more about what happened? With the nutter running up behind you?'

I shook my head. Carefully. 'No. But it's made me ridiculously jumpy. It's pitiful. And then Mum had a gas leak yesterday and we had to drag Gran out of the house.'

'Bloody hell, Meg. It hasn't been your week. Are your mum and your gran okay?'

'Yeah, they seem fine. But if there'd been a spark, it could have been the end of all three of us. And the house.'

'Jesus.'

'Mum's apparently not been getting the boiler serviced.'

'Oops.'

'So, that's another thing for me to worry about.'

'Well, you are an expert.'

'With boilers?'

'With worrying.'

Hannah seemed to have forgotten the drinks, so after cutting us each a slab of cake, I tried to work out how to use her espresso machine. I had an inability to work the most basic household gadgets that was shared with most Cambridge science graduates.

'Put the little capsule in the top and press the button, Meg. It's not rocket science.'

'All right. You're supposed to be doing this. You're the host.' I got it sussed though, and produced two espressos.

'Let's have a look at your dating site,' Hannah said with an enthusiasm I didn't share.

One of my Manchester friends had signed me up with the site and in a ridiculous demonstration of people-pleasing, I'd gone along with it. I'd so far avoided actually going on any dates, but Hannah had taken it on as a personal mission to get me out there risking my life meeting potential psychopaths in Derby bars. She reappeared with the laptop, logged into the site and started browsing through profiles.

I took a sip of coffee. 'Okay, let's see what hotties the computer's selected for me this time.'

Clutching my cup, I wandered round to stand behind Hannah and peered at the laptop. 'What about that one?' I pointed semi-randomly at a man whose picture was blurry enough to leave room for hope.

'No way. Look at the age thingy. He's forty-two and he's looking for a woman twenty-five to thirty-eight. Tosser.'

I put down my espresso, and leant in towards the laptop screen. 'These guys all look the same, Hannah. Slightly balding blokes who like going to the pub and watching TV. Seriously? And how can I tell if they're psychopathic control freaks?'

'Is that what you're after?'

'Well, in a break from the norm, I thought I'd avoid them this time around.'

'Hmm… Maybe we need to refine your search.'

'Anyway, why do I even need a man? This bicycle doesn't need a fish.'

'I think it's the other way round, Meg. You're the fish.'

I walked back to the other side of the table and sat down. An image popped into my head – the earnest faces of my morning visitors. 'Hannah,' I said. 'Do you think doctors should be able to… help patients die, you know, if they're suffering really badly?'

'Wow. That was a change of tack.'

'Anything to avoid discussing my love life.'

Hannah put down her coffee cup and folded her arms. 'Well then, no. Actually, I don't.'

'Vets do it all the time. We wouldn't let an animal suffer, if it was dying anyway.'

'Why do you ask?'

'We've had reports of a doctor doing it. I know I'll have to log it and everything, but I've been mulling it over. Is it actually wrong?'

'You can't just let them get away with it. They might be like Harold Shipman.'

'I don't think it's anything like that. More like people who are dying of cancer anyway. Just hurrying it up to avoid them suffering too much.'

Hannah's tone was sharp. 'Well, you'll clearly think what you want, but I think it sends the wrong message to disabled people.'

I looked up, remembering that Hannah had been to the Life Line group, and that my morning visitors had given me a Life Line magazine. She was the wrong person to talk to, but it was too late to take it back now. 'I don't want to fall out over this,' I said. 'What message does it send to disabled people?'

Hannah's shoulders dropped, and she picked at her cake. 'Sorry. I didn't mean to be funny with you. It's just… Oh don't worry, I don't want to get all heavy on you. You don't need it right now.'

'It's okay, Hannah, what are you saying?'

'Well, a lot of people think if you're in a wheelchair, you'd be better off dead.' Her mouth twisted. 'Especially nowadays. If you're a burden—'

'No one could think you were better off dead. Or a burden. What do you mean?'

'That if euthanasia's legal, disabled people might feel obliged to end it, you know, to take the pressure off relatives and the NHS.'

'I thought that bill they tried to get through was only for terminally ill people?'

'Who can say if you're terminally ill? The next step'll be people deciding our lives aren't worth living. Or, more to the point, aren't worth all the medical costs.'

I bit the inside of my lip. 'I hadn't thought about it like that.'

'Yes, well, you'd be surprised the things people say. I hear them sometimes, when they assume I'm deaf and stupid as well as in a wheelchair. *You'd just top yourself, wouldn't you?* Those sorts of comments.'

'People say that to you?'

'About me, not to me. And my friend who's almost completely paralysed – even the doctors say it. It's no wonder she's worried about what would happen if we had assisted dying.'

'Jesus, Hannah.'

'I'm sure there's two sides to it anyway.'

I tried to keep my tone balanced and curious. 'Your friend – is she the one you visited at the hospital? The one you met through that group you go to?'

'Yes. She can hardly move now, but she says her life's still worth living.'

'What condition does she have?'

'It's a genetic thing with a weird name. You won't have heard of it.'

'I think the people who told me about this doctor might go to the same group. They looked like the Amish – would you know them?'

'There's a few look like that. I don't know everyone – I've not been that many times. And anyway, you'll be pleased to hear I've decided to stop going.'

'Oh.' I wasn't sure what to say.

'They're not loonies, Meg. There's a receptionist from the health centre and people who run their own businesses and all sorts. But it turned out it's more of a religious group than a disability support group. And I'm not really religious, and then it all got a bit angry at the meeting on Tuesday. I didn't like the feel of it. But I'll keep in touch with my friend.'

'You're well out of it,' I said. 'I heard they turned against my boss because his daughter's transgender.'

'Yeah, that does sound possible, to be fair. That's the kind of thing I didn't like. And they were demonstrating outside abortion clinics. I don't agree with that.'

'Oh, Jesus, don't get me started.' I crunched so hard on my lip it bled. The last thing Hannah needed was a huge rant from me. But honestly, these people drove me mad. So rabidly against abortion that they'd make women risk their lives carrying dying babies to term, but fine about lab experiments on primates, and guns for everyone, and *the death penalty,* for God's sake.

'Calm down, Meg, I've left the group, okay?' Was she reading my mind?

My phone rang. Work. I picked up.

'Meg! There's been another death.'

Chapter 23

The base of the cliff was in deep shade. I trudged along a damp footpath from the parking area, my mind torturing itself with its own special toxic blend of guilt and panic. A second death was bad. Really bad. Second deaths set the internet buzzing with hysterical tweets about incompetent police and serial killers, and Oh My God, are *children* even safe any more in this town. A second death meant I hadn't done my job.

A flash of *déjà vu* hit me when I saw the tape fluttering in front of the vertical slab of rock. I half expected to see the cave, and Peter Hamilton lying dead, his hand clutching his throat, cherry-red blood seeping down his cheeks. But we were in a different part of the quarry, in a place I'd imagined but not seen – a hidden place, away from the footpaths, surrounded by trees whose branches tapped in the wind like anxious fingers. We were directly below his house. I glanced up and saw it far above, silhouetted against the evening sky.

The scene was secured, and uniformed officers and SOCOs buzzed to and fro. I donned a scene suit and stepped through the tape, a hollow opening up inside me at the sight of the body. This shouldn't have happened on my watch.

She was about ten feet from the cliff edge, on her front, with one arm reaching out to the side and the other tucked under her. She looked tiny and forlorn, like a baby bird fallen from its nest.

The pathologist crouched over her, and looked up as I approached. I'd met her over a previous corpse – she was called Mary something. 'Well, this is a strange one,' she said, with an inappropriate amount of enthusiasm. 'On the face of it, it looks like an accident or suicide. No injuries other than those caused by the fall.'

An accident or suicide. The guilt-monkey in my head wasn't having that. And anyway, I sensed a *but*. 'How long's she been dead?'

'Not long.'

I leant to look at the dead woman's face. Her cheek was scuffed but otherwise she looked unharmed. Apart from being dead, of course.

'It's definitely Beth Hamilton,' I said. 'The sister of the man who died last week in the cave house. How awful. Two people in one family.'

'Looks like some of the rocks have come off the cliff.' Mary wasn't about to get distracted with sympathy. 'It could have crumbled under her.'

'She liked to tend the garden on the edge,' I said. Beth's thin fingers were curled into loose fists, her nails caked with mud. 'Her sister-in-law told her it was dangerous.'

Could it really have been an accident? I peered up at the little rock garden, but the light shone in my eyes and nothing was clear.

I walked carefully around the body. 'Is that something in the dirt?'

Mary unfolded herself into a standing position. 'Yes, that's what I was going to say. It's quite intriguing. She must have been alive for a few moments after she hit the ground.'

'Is that even possible?'

'Yes, the impact doesn't always kill them immediately. It's dependent on the height of the fall and the consistency of the landing. Fascinating subject.'

I looked at Mary's bright face. She was treating this like a cross-word puzzle, rather than a person's life. I sometimes wished I could do that. 'Poor woman,' I said. 'Her last few minutes must have been terrible.'

'You see what she's drawn?' Mary pointed a booted toe, as if I wasn't already looking at what was drawn in the dirt.

I stepped closer, careful not to tread on anything important. The letters were large and loopy, almost child-like, some parts pressed deeper than others. I imagined poor Beth, gasping her final breaths through battered ribs, determined to tell us something.

'I think she used that.' Mary pointed at an egg-sized stone near Beth's extended hand. 'There's mud on it and it has a sharp edge.'

I stared at the roughly drawn letters. The breeze tickled the back of my neck, and I shivered and pulled up the collar of my coat. '*GR*,' I said. 'She wrote *GR*.'

'Do you know what it means?' Mary said. 'Do you know a *GR*?'

I pictured the carving in the cave. Thought of the man who'd died here ten years ago, leaving behind his sinister sketchbook. Remembered our trip into the basement of the house that now loomed above me, squatting on the cliff-edge, almost like a living thing.

I said nothing.

★

Jai met me by the cordoned area outside the house. 'Oh, it's *Death-Wish Woman*,' he said. 'What's it to be today? We've had falls and gassing with the threat of explosion. There's still plenty more ways to injure yourself.'

'Why are you so God-damned perky? Beth Hamilton's dead. Besides, you took your time getting any help to us. What did you expect me to do? Leave Gran in there to die?'

I walked towards the flapping blue-and-white tape and nodded at a uniformed officer. SOCO were scratching around like hungry hens, in the area of the rock garden.

Jai followed me over. 'I'm just kidding. You did well to get your gran out.'

'Yeah. And my shoulder won't let me forget it. So, what the hell's gone on? Another death at this house?'

'Kate's in a bit of a state,' he said. 'Fiona's with her. And Mark Hamilton. Do you want to see the rock garden?'

'Have you been down to the bottom?' I gestured in the general direction of *Off-the-cliff*. Someone was chain-sawing trees in the woods far below.

Jai shook his head. 'Is your mum alright? And your gran?'

I nodded. 'Yeah. A bit shocked.'

'They can't tell for sure if anyone else was here,' Jai said. 'No marks, but obviously they can't get much off rock anyway and Kate and Mark rushed around destroying evidence before they realised what had happened. It looks like the edge is crumbly. So she may have just fallen. It's pretty windy to be hovering around the edge of a cliff.'

'You've not seen the letters she scratched down there?'

'I haven't been down, Meg. What letters?'

I hesitated and glanced towards the nothingness beyond the cliff edge. The sky was a palette of greys, the nearer clouds racing in front of distant ones. I felt a moment of dizziness and took a step back. '*GR*. In the mud next to her.'

'What? As in Grim Reaper?'

I shrugged. 'I suppose it could mean any number of things.'

'Christ almighty.' Jai leant forward towards the cliff as if he could peer over and see the body. He clearly couldn't.

I grabbed his arm. 'Get back, Jai. We could do without losing you as well.'

He shook me off, then gave me a quick, apologetic smile. 'Same as the guy ten years ago?'

'Well, he drew sketches.'

'Why would she do it? Is it something to do with the curse?'

'What curse though?' I felt panic rising up in me. How could we find a killer if a curse was to blame? How many more people would die? 'I mean, seriously Jai? What is the bloody curse?'

★

'I told you! It's this house!' Kate shook Mark's hand from her arm. She was sitting on the sofa but her legs were solid as if she was about to leap up.

I sat on the other sofa. I'd left Jai outside, poking around the rock garden.

'I'm so sorry.'

Mark tilted his chin upwards in a brief nod. 'Thanks.'

'Are you okay to tell me a bit about what happened?'

'Oh, God.' Kate sank back in the sofa and folded her arms across her stomach. 'I know a house can't be cursed, but why do people keep dying?'

Mark turned to Kate. 'Just tell her what happened.'

'I was at work. We do some Sunday surgeries now. Beth wanted to come and mess around with that horrendous rock garden. So, I said come over and I'd see her when I got in.'

'She had a key to the house?'

Kate nodded. 'And then, when I got back about four, there was no sign of her. And I just knew she'd fallen off that cliff. It can crumble away underneath you. I kept telling her. I put a fence up years ago, but that went over. Anyway, I went out and tried to look down, but I couldn't see anything.'

I nodded sympathetic encouragement.

'So,' Kate said. 'I phoned Mark and he came round and we looked at the rock garden again and it was obvious she'd been weeding right near the edge. Her little fork was there. And then we drove to the bottom car park, because it's actually quite far to walk down from here. And we went along the path…'

Mark wiped his cheek. 'We tried to resuscitate her. But it was too late.'

'And we called an ambulance,' Kate said. 'But we knew. We're doctors. We knew.'

'I think she probably did just fall,' Mark said. 'She was always reckless on that cliff.'

'Had she said anything to you about Peter's death?' I asked.

'What do you mean?'

'Look, I'm not saying it wasn't an accident. We've no reason to believe it wasn't, but—'

'You think whoever killed Peter could have killed her too?'

'I'm not saying that.'

Mark sighed. 'Well there was something, I suppose. I don't know if it has any relevance.'

'What?' You need to tell me, even if you think it's not relevant.'

'Well, okay. She suspected Felix.'

My pulse quickened. 'What? Why didn't she talk to us?'

'I got the impression she wanted to talk to him first. She didn't want to go around making accusations.'

'When did she tell you this?'

'Thursday, I think it was. She didn't seem very sure. It was more of a passing comment. You don't think he…'

Kate had been very quiet through this. But I glanced round and noticed her face was white. 'Felix can be nasty,' she said. 'Peter told me.'

'What do you mean?'

'He just isn't a very nice person. I'm not saying he's a murderer.'

'But?'

'Well, I don't know if any of this stuff relates to people too, but you hear it, don't you, about serial killers?'

'What have you heard, Kate?'

'Well, there was that cat he ran over. Peter loved cats and he couldn't believe how callous Felix was. And then…'

'Was there something else?'

'Well, again, it may not be relevant but it shows you what kind of person he is. Anyway, years ago, they had problems with mice in their student house. And Peter didn't want to kill them. So he got some humane traps and tried to catch the mice, but the mice seemed to work out how to get the cheese and get out again.'

'They're not as dumb as people think.'

'No. Anyway, in the end he bought this fancy, big trap that was supposed to catch several mice at a time. And it did.'

'And?'

'He got home and found Felix had taken five mice out of the humane trap and dumped them in a bucket of water to drown. Peter was horrified, but Felix thought it was funny.' She paused. 'Stuff like that. Not exactly evidence of psychopathic tendencies – just, well, not quite normal.'

Chapter 24

'Beth Hamilton.' Richard stood in front of a board of photographs, shoulders back, chest thrust forward. 'The sister of Peter Hamilton. Worked as a solicitor in Nottingham.'

I'd slept in and missed breakfast, and I felt grotty even for a Monday morning. My head throbbed with a dull urgency.

'Found at the bottom of the cliff outside her brother's house,' Richard continued. 'So far, we have no reason to believe this is anything other than a tragic accident.'

I opened my mouth, then shut it again. I'd get my chance to speak.

'What is it with that house?' Fiona said.

'You'd better ask your granny.' Craig's voice oozed unpleasantness. I couldn't work out if it was reassuring or depressing that he acted like an arse around Fiona too.

'We've kicked off house-to-house,' I said. 'And we're checking what CCTV we have, and looking at motives. So far, we've found no evidence that anyone else was on the cliff with her, but of course we found no forensic evidence around the cave where her brother was found. If it's the same person, they're careful. And the rock doesn't show up prints or footwear marks. Plus, her brother and sister-in-law trampled all over the area anyway.'

'What about the Grim Reaper thing?' Jai said.

'Seriously?' Craig's forehead creased above his monobrow.

I ignored Craig. 'The victim appears to have scratched some letters in the mud with a stone before she died. The letters *GR*.'

Fiona gazed at me with her wide, guileless eyes. 'Was it definitely her who scratched them?'

'Yes,' I said. 'Almost certainly.'

'Didn't that man ten years ago leave sketches of the Grim Reaper?' she said. 'And isn't there a picture of it in the basement of the house?'

'Yes, and of course on the wall of the cave where Peter was found.'

'Come on guys.' Richard folded his arms. 'These people weren't killed by a curse.'

'No,' I said. 'I suspect the curse is a distraction.'

'This Grim Reaper thing has to be about something,' Jai said. 'It's too much of a coincidence.'

'I agree,' Fiona said.

Craig narrowed his eyes. 'Oh, well, that clinches it. If you've decided—'

'Drop it, Craig,' I snapped.

Jai turned to Craig. 'Did you not get your shag this month?'

They were spiralling out of control. 'Right,' I said in my most assertive voice, which was probably not very assertive at all. 'We also know the victim mentioned Felix Carstairs. She had some suspicions about him in relation to Peter's death. In her wisdom, she decided to talk to him first instead of coming to us. Fiona, could you find out if she did talk to him, and check his alibi again? And Craig, you can look into all the *rational* reasons several people might have died in and around this house, possibly people from the same family. And work out why Beth Hamilton might have scraped *GR* in the mud.'

★

Jai was at his desk on a chair, which was unusual. Two steaming mugs of coffee sat in front of him.

I reached for one of the coffees. 'Is this for me?'

'No, I've taken to making two. Since we're only allowed breaks "at the exigencies of duty" whatever the hell that means. Need to get my caffeine in.'

It was cause for much griping that we had no formal breaks and no canteen, and weren't even allowed a radio due to some bizarre copyright issue.

'Oh, for God's sake. Give me one of them.' I dragged a chair across our new eco-carpet, and sat next to him. 'You said you'd got something new on Peter Hamilton? If someone did kill Beth, it's most likely the same person who killed Peter.'

'Yes.' Jai passed me a mug. 'Do you want to hear the clue that was in the casket.'

I felt my headache fading. 'Of course I do.'

Jai shuffled forward, put his mug on a stained coaster, and peered at a ragged piece of paper held down by a grey stapler. 'It's word-based again. Here goes. *My first constant is an old friend who gives us circles, you'll find; my second is a constant which brings oil to mind; my last two abbreviate the scale when tectonic plates aren't aligned.*'

I squinted at him. '*Oil*, as in, what you put in your car?'

'What, you mean you actually put oil in that rust-bucket?'

'No, I get my sergeants to do it when they get on my nerves.'

I leant over Jai's desk and peered at his notes.

'Don't worry about me. I wasn't looking anyway.' He shifted backwards in his wheeled chair. 'We've had some other stuff back from the computer geeks. Peter Hamilton logged onto the website PeakDistrict-Geocache.co.uk, at 12.30pm. Just before he went on his walk. And guess what his username was.'

I felt a flush of excitement. We were right about the geocaching. '*Hamster22*? He left a note of his name and the time because there wasn't a notebook in the casket?'

'Nobody likes a smart-arse.' Jai rocked back in his chair.

I took a slurp of my coffee. 'I've seen those chair-legs snap, you know. Just don't knock my mug when you go down.'

Jai pivoted back further. 'They only snap when Craig's in the chair.'

I glanced over at Craig's desk. No sign of him.

Jai's chair teetered, and panic flitted across his face before he allowed himself to crash back down, causing papers to flutter on his desk. 'Anyway, we contacted the owner of the geocaching site and asked him if he could check the history. See if there was ever a cache located in the old quarry. And he found one. A mystery cache. You were given the correct co-ordinates but had to solve a riddle to get into the cache.'

I felt excitement rising in me, like when you're playing poker and the good cards keep coming. 'So, the riddle could get you into the casket?'

Jai folded his arms. 'Maybe. Guess where the co-ordinates led to.'

'The fallen tree where the metal casket was found?'

'Yep. And when do you think the cache was posted?'

'Jesus, Jai, am I suddenly on University Challenge? The day he died?'

'That's right, Meg-from-Cambridge. It was posted on the day Peter Hamilton was poisoned.'

'Oh my God. What was the riddle on the geocaching site?'

Jai shuffled his notes. '*In Piers's bane, the drops are steep, the pools are deep. Go there in vain, unless you know his middle name.*'

'P middle name,' I said quietly. 'He got the clue off the website, noted it down on that Post-it, and went to the location in the woods to find it. Steep drops and deep pools – that sounds very much like the old quarry. He could have just thought he was doing a normal geocache. And those lads in the woods must have seen it too.'

'Peter Hamilton must have known Piers's middle name,' Jai said.

'Do we know a Piers? With the middle name "Henry", presumably. Hang on, I think Piers is the answer to the riddle to get into the inner box,' I said. 'I've just worked it out.'

'Oh Christ, have you? Enlighten me.'

'Its "pi" – that's the bit about circles. Then "e", you know, Euler's number, pronounced like "oil". Then RS for Richter scale.'

Jai looked at his notes, then peered at me as if he was worried about me. 'Okay, not sure I'm familiar with Oiler's number but yes, one of our maths weirdos has written "PIERS" and a question mark.'

'Peter Hamilton must have put "HENRY" into the outer lock, opened the casket, seen the clue, put "PIERS" into the second lock, and that got him into the inner box.'

'So, it's like an extra layer of security just in case some random person found the casket and somehow got through the first lock.'

'I guess so. And the geocache thingy was definitely made public the day Hamilton died?'

'Yes, it was posted at 10am on October 12th. Then it was withdrawn later that same day.'

'Who posted it?'

'Thought you might ask that. According to the log-in information, Hamilton posted it himself.'

The door creaked open. Craig walked in, pulled out a chair and sat backwards on it in some kind of incomprehensible macho display. Those thighs were way too close for comfort. 'Heard your mother nearly blew herself up,' he said. 'You should look after her better.'

That was all I needed. My nasty internal voices manifesting as a fat copper.

I ignored him and spoke to Jai. 'And the cache was withdrawn from the website after Peter Hamilton died? From the same log-in?'

'Yes. So obviously, setting aside activities from beyond the grave, someone knew his log-in details.'

'Can they tell what computer this person logged in from?' I asked.

'They're looking into it. It's not necessarily easy.'

'So, this was definitely directed at Hamilton. It wasn't a random psycho who took a dislike to geocachers. And if they knew his log-in details, maybe they also got access to the Gmail account that sent the suicide note.'

'Maybe. And it turns out he logged on every Monday at around 12.30pm, so the killer probably knew that.'

I sighed and pushed my chair back, to put more space between me and Craig. 'It's very intricate,' I said. 'And whoever did this knew Hamilton quite well.'

'It's clever,' Jai said. 'I mean, if the dog hadn't found the body so quickly, the killer could have sneaked back and removed the casket and we'd have had no idea about any of this.'

'So, who knew him well enough to do it? I suppose his partners, his brother, and his wife would all know he'd be able to solve the second riddle, to get into the inner box, especially as he had Piers on his mind anyway. But it wasn't too unique to him. It was something quite a few geocachers would have been able to solve, but the chance of the wrong person happening on it and getting past the first riddle was incredibly slim, especially if the original GPS co-ordinates were only on the site for a few hours.'

Craig had been remarkably quiet listening to all this. He cleared this throat and said, 'Well, that's all very intelligent but you're wasting your time. We've arrested someone.'

I snapped my head round. 'What?'

'We've had a confession. Richard's delighted.'

'Who's confessed?'

'The homeless scrote who'd been supplying Hamilton with drugs.'

'Sebastian? Really? Why did he kill him?'

'Probably an argument over money. You know what dealers are like.'

'But Craig… Are you sure?' Nothing I'd heard about Sebastian made him seem right for this.

Craig curled his lip. 'Yes, he's confessed to doing it.'

'We have to catch the right person, Craig,' Jai said. 'It's not like in the good old days when you could beat a confession out of a random tramp.'

'Richard's not interested in your opinion.' Craig flounced away.

'I don't like the sound of this.' I stood up. 'I need another coffee. Have a word in my room, Jai?'

I leapt up and strode to our little kitchen area, banging the fire-door against its rubber stop. I rustled around to find mugs that were only lightly stained and moderately chipped, and made coffee for Jai and myself. Some bastard had been stealing my milk again. You would think in the police force you could leave a pint of milk in the fridge.

When I arrived at my room, the door was shut. I kicked it and it was opened by Fiona, looking furtive.

'Oh, it's you,' she said.

'Yep, my room.'

'It's okay, come in.'

'Oh, thanks.'

Fiona ignored my sarcasm and ushered me in, shutting the door behind me.

'Fiona was telling me about the so-called confession,' Jai said, taking his coffee and leaning against my desk.

I moved over and sat in my chair. 'Sorry, Fiona, I didn't make you a drink.'

'It's okay.' She glanced at Jai. 'I was just saying they taught us we should be extra careful with mentally ill people and I think that homeless man was mentally ill. Look I'd better go.'

'Thanks, Fiona,' I said. 'Jai can fill me in.'

She slipped out of the door, closing it softly behind her.

'She even wrote notes.' Jai lifted a sheet of paper from my over-flowing desk. 'In answer to the question, "What is your name?" he said, "I'm an oxymoron, an intelligent idiot, a confessing fugitive, impudently polite."'

'They kind of are oxymorons,' I said.

Jai gave me the kind of look a proud parent gives their newly toilet-trained kid. 'I knew I could rely on you to know what a sodding oxymoron is. So, in answer to questions about his whereabouts on Monday, he said…' Jai glanced down. '"I killed Peter. Poor Peter.

I killed Peter. He didn't fall. I'm a compassionate murderer. It was for the best. Am I going to prison? Can I have sausages?"'

'He's still after the sausages then. I'm surprised they've maintained the quality.'

'He's clearly a nut-job. And then they asked him how he killed Peter, and he said, "Killed Peter, yes, killed Peter." Apparently his competent adult woman intervened at that point but Craig carried on, and eventually he said something about poison. But I mean it's all over the internet about the poisoned cake. He didn't say anything else relevant. Nothing about the casket or anything.' Jai shook his head. 'It's so not him.'

'Yeah, unless he's capable of Oscar-winning performances, he doesn't sound like a calculating killer.'

'Agreed. And there's something else makes me think there's more to this than a drugs deal gone wrong. Look what's landed on your desk.'

I put my coffee down at speed. 'What?'

'Peter's will and life insurance details. In paper copy, like the olden days.'

'So, go on, what have we got?'

'Well, it's interesting.' Jai spread the papers on my desk. 'The life insurance only pays out for suicide if you've had the policy for at least five years. Which obviously they haven't. So, it is just about conceivable he killed himself and made it look like murder.'

'Okay...'

'And according to the will, the wife gets most of it, with some to the brother. There's also the big fat policy made out to his two partners. There was a critical illness policy and a permanent health policy too, paid for by the firm. Belt and braces. But, the really interesting bit.' Jai paused and looked at me.

'What, Jai, what? This isn't *The X-Factor* results.'

'There's a large bequest in trust for Rosie Carstairs.'

'Felix and Olivia's strange daughter?'

'That's the one.'

Chapter 25

I knocked on the rather fine, oak-panelled door of Felix and Olivia's barn conversion. It opened slowly and at first I didn't see anyone, but then the top of a head and some blue eyes edged out from behind it. Rosie.

'Oh, the detective,' she said, stepping sideways. 'Dad's at work and Mum's poo picking.'

'I'll just have a word with your mum then. She's what?'

'In the field. Picking up horse poo. I'd have helped her but I'm feeling a bit tired. I'm having a lie down.'

I imagined the thought of picking up horse poo would bring most teenagers over a bit tired. I scrutinised Rosie's pale face. Why would Peter leave a large bequest to his friend's daughter? Was that Felix's haughty nose? Or could it be Peter's? I'd only seen Peter dead, of course. Blue eyes were recessive so that didn't help us much.

I told her I'd go and find her Mum, and she pointed me in the direction of the furthest field (of course) situated up a steep hill (naturally). At least there were no precipices involved.

It was a bright, fresh day, the sun poking out intermittently from behind fast-moving clouds. Even while scooping up piles of horse manure, Olivia looked like something out of *Country Living* magazine, with her stylish Puffa jacket, topped off with an artfully arranged scarf and long, straight hair with just the right amount of dishevelment.

She looked up. A smudging around her eyes suggested she'd not slept. 'Oh. Hello. Is it true Peter's sister's dead?'

Curse Twitter. It was out already. 'I'm afraid so. We don't have any details yet.'

Olivia took a step towards me. 'But she was murdered?'

'There's no reason to treat it as suspicious at the moment.'

Olivia opened her mouth as if about to say something, then shut it again. She picked up her scraping equipment and took a step away from me. 'So, what was it you wanted to see me about? Do you mind talking to me while I finish this off? I need to get it done.'

I agreed, and offered to push the wheelbarrow, which was surprisingly heavy. 'Where was Felix on Sunday afternoon?'

'I've no idea. I was out all day with a friend. He didn't tell me what he'd been doing. Working probably. You don't think he...'

I looked at her retreating back. Felix's friends and loved ones weren't exactly leaping forward to vouch for his good character.

'I assume you know that in Peter Hamilton's will,' I said, 'there's a substantial bequest left in trust for your daughter.'

Olivia came to an abrupt halt. 'Oh. Yes, it's a bit awkward actually. You haven't told Felix, have you?' She hunched over and scraped at the ground with repeated strokes.

'No. Perhaps you could explain why Peter left money to Rosie.'

'Well, I'm sure you've guessed.' She straightened, and rubbed her lower back. 'Peter thought Rosie was his daughter.'

'And is she?'

'Well, possibly.'

Bingo. I knew it.

Olivia walked to a group of trees. I followed, struggling to push the wheelbarrow over the rutted ground.

'I don't know for sure.' She was talking at the ground. 'I know it sounds bad. I had a one-off liaison with Peter, and I started going out with Felix soon afterwards.'

I plonked the wheelbarrow down next to Olivia. 'And then you found you were pregnant?'

'Yes. And I mean, both Felix and I naturally assumed the baby was his. And if she is Peter's she must have been born late because it

173

was more than nine months since the thing with him.' She hesitated. 'Well, a little bit more.'

'Didn't you want to know for sure?'

'I never even doubted she was Felix's. She doesn't look any more like one or the other of them. I don't know why Peter suddenly started going on about her being his daughter.'

'When did he start going on about it?'

'Oh, about six months ago. Maybe a bit longer. He seemed to get it into his head she was his.'

'Is that why you were visiting him at his house, when he worked from home?'

Her head snapped up. 'God, you can't do anything secretly these days. Yes, it was. We weren't having an affair or anything. Just trying to decide what to do.'

'Does Felix know anything about this?'

'No. And I don't see why he has to find out.' She paused and shuffled loose hay on the ground into a pile.

A horse wandered over and nudged the wheelbarrow, threatening to tip it over. I felt slightly protective of the barrow, but there wasn't much I could do to influence the half-ton creature.

'Oh, bloody hell, Sam.' Olivia touched the horse on his chest and he tucked his nose in and backed up a couple of inches. 'Now he thinks I'm going to play with him.' The horse leant forward and grabbed Olivia's scarf with his teeth. She yelled and snatched it back, but not before I'd seen the purple bruising around her neck.

I caught her eye. She knew I'd seen. 'The sod bit me,' she said. 'He didn't mean it, just wanted attention.' She wrapped the scarf tight again. 'Like he did just now, but he misjudged it.'

I opened my mouth. An impenetrable force-field had shot up around Olivia. I let it go.

The horse gave us an *I'd-never-bite-my-mum* look and marched off.

'No, it's better Felix doesn't know,' Olivia said. 'I'd prefer to work on the assumption she's his. It makes life a lot easier for all of us, okay? He's her father, he brought her up. What good would it do now, raking up a lot of ancient history, when Peter's dead anyway?'

'Are you sure he didn't find out?'

She looked at me with those clear eyes that had gazed out of Peter's Cambridge photographs. 'You don't think…'

'Did his behaviour change before Peter's death? Or his attitude to Peter?'

'Look, he can be a bit… difficult. I think I'd have known if he'd found out.'

'Olivia, if he's aggressive—'

'It's fine,' she snapped. End of that subject.

I sighed. 'What about Rosie – does she know anything?'

'Of course not.'

'Olivia, we're going to have to talk to Felix about this,' I said gently. 'This is a murder investigation.'

She shot me a look that was hard to interpret but if I had to guess, I'd say she was scared.

★

I managed to parallel-park in a tiny space on the main road through Eldercliffe – reversed in and everything. I deserved a round of applause. The town was bustling with old and young, kids and dogs, prams and pushchairs. I crossed the marketplace and dragged myself up the hill and into the health centre.

Vivian was on reception, leafing through a magazine with a rainbow on its cover. I'd checked and we had received a complaint about Kate Webster helping a patient die, and police had indeed sniffed around, but it had come to nothing. I wondered if the complaint had come from Vivian. She shoved her magazine aside and confirmed that Dr Webster was back at work and had finished seeing patients for the day, so I could safely interrupt her without keeping the diseased of Eldercliffe waiting. She told me to go straight through to Consulting Room 4.

The room was small, with a desk pushed up against the wall, so Kate's view was of a chart about STDs and a poster exhorting her to give up smoking. She gestured to a seat next to the desk. She looked pale and thin, and her skin had lost its previous milk-and-honey look.

I felt vulnerable. Probably the smell. I reminded myself no one would be weighing me or asking me to lie on the bed and spread my legs.

'How are you?' I asked, sitting down with my knees clamped together.

'Not great. I thought it would be better to be at work but it isn't. They all seem like a bunch of malingering whiners today, with their non-existent illnesses and desperate need for attention.'

'Yes, maybe it's a bit early to be back.'

'Have you made any progress on Beth? Do you think it was an accident?'

'We've no reason to think it wasn't.'

She paused. 'I suppose you're here wondering if I knew about Rosie.'

'Partly, yes.'

'Well, I didn't.' She picked up a blood-pressure machine and repeatedly squeezed and released the bulb like a stress ball. 'Not until I saw his will. Then it was pretty damn obvious. I knew he had a soft spot for Olivia of course, but the father of her child? Jesus.'

'Peter never said anything to you about Rosie?'

'No. Nothing. I can't believe he was so damn secretive. I knew something was up. But this? It's been going round and round in my head, driving me nuts. He had a bloody child by another woman and he didn't think to tell me. I've realised he was actually a bit of a bastard, and now I can't even confront him because he's dead. Oh God, that sounds awful.' She fanned herself with her hand. 'Christ, is it hot in here?'

'Warmish.' It wasn't that hot.

'Sorry, excuse me!' She leapt up, kicking her chair backwards into a metal bin, and shot out of the room, dropping the blood-pressure monitor on my foot. I picked it up and squeezed it a few times. I turned to read about STDs.

A few minutes later, Kate appeared in the doorway. 'Sorry, just came over a bit queasy.'

'You are pregnant, aren't you?'

She froze by the door, then pushed it firmly shut behind her and sat back down. 'Oh, what the hell. Yes, it turns out I'm pregnant. Snooping old Vivian on Reception guessed too. Great timing, eh?'

'So, Peter's grandmother was right?'

'Yes, the mad old bat.' Kate's eyes watered. 'I'm pregnant and I've got no one to share it with. No husband, no family.'

'I'm sorry,' I said. 'Your parents died when you were young, didn't they?'

'Yes, there was a car accident.' She twisted her mouth as if trying not to cry. 'I haven't had much luck.'

I kept my voice low and soft. 'So, both you and Peter lost parents at a young age?'

'Yes, I suppose it was part of the reason we got on.'

I put the blood-pressure monitor on the table between us. Kate glanced at it, then picked it up and gave it a squeeze.

She continued, her voice harsh. 'Dad broke his neck. Survived three miserable, grotesque years, begging to die most days. And of course Peter's mum. It doesn't get much worse than that.' She folded her arms. It made sense that she was tolerant towards euthanasia. I wondered if my moon-faced religious visitors had ever spent three years nursing someone who was desperate to die.

'And I have to move house,' Kate said. 'Before the baby's born. I'm sure you think I'm being silly, but how could I let a baby be born into that?'

'What do you think's going on with the house? You don't really believe it's cursed?'

'No, of course not. But something's wrong there. I don't know what, but I'm not taking the risk with my baby.'

Chapter 26

I looked up from my computer to see Jai barrelling towards me. He threw himself into my visitor's chair and wheeled himself over. 'So… Beth Hamilton. PM says she died from the fall. Surprise surprise. There were no defence wounds and no suggestion anyone else was involved. But of course if someone just shoved her straight off the cliff, there wouldn't be any wounds. And she was only small.'

'Right.'

Jai tapped his fingers on the chair arm. 'Nothing at the top of the cliff either, but the scene was a mess, and you don't find much on rock anyway. As you pointed out, there are hardly any houses, and no one saw anyone. And there's nothing relevant on any CCTV, but again, there's not a lot round there.'

'We'll end up having to go for misadventure, unless any of the friends and relations come up with anything.'

'But she scrawled *GR* in the mud.'

'Maybe she fell,' I said. 'And she attributed it to the curse. How are we doing for alibis from the suspects in Peter's murder?'

'Working on it. Sebastian's been let out – obviously that one wasn't going to stick. Both Felix and Edward have alibis for when we think the casket was placed, albeit only from their wives.'

'I'm not convinced. Felix's wife is scared of him. And Edward's wife's a 1950s throwback who'd probably lie for him if he asked her to.'

'Well, we've found some interesting stuff on Peter. He seems to have been less of a dull dork that we thought.' Jai crossed his legs and bounced his upper foot. I could see why Craig got irritated if he had to put up with this all the time.

'Did we think he was a dull dork?'

Jai wrinkled his nose. 'Yeah, a patent attorney. I did, a bit. One of my dad's friends was one, and if he'd been killed, you'd have had to ask how they could tell. Seriously.'

'Okay, Dorothy Parker, what had Peter been up to?'

'He was accessing the Dark Web.'

'What? Why?'

'Well, these things aren't exactly transparent. He was going via TOR, you know, like Google but it keeps your identity anonymous. He seems to have been on the Silk Road 2 website, which is shut down now, and some other similar ones – Evolution and Agora.'

'Really? Can we see what he bought?'

'It's not that easy. You don't get a nice email confirmation, and you can't exactly use PayPal.'

'But what? Drugs?'

'Well, you can buy a Kalashnikov or arrange a hit man, but in view of what else we've discovered, yes, I suspect he'd been buying drugs.'

'Interesting.' I shuffled in my uncomfortable chair. I had a monstrous bruise on my hip which was bashing against the chair's plastic arm. 'He must have been technically savvy to use the secret search engines and everything, mustn't he?'

'Well, we already knew he was clever and technical, and it's not that hard. Craig even managed to get on it the other day. But there's more. Those drugs in his drawer – they can't identify one of them at all. They reckon it's new or experimental.'

'It could have been something from a client.' My mind flipped to pregnant Kate. How would she feel about Peter taking an unlicensed drug? If indeed he was taking it. Did she know?

'And the other one was called...' Jai looked at his notes.

'Aripiprazole. Sold under the Trade Mark ABILIFY. It's an anti-psychotic. Used for...' He held his notes closer to his face. 'The treatment of schizophrenia, bipolar disorder, major depressive disorder, tic disorders, and irritability associated with autism. I've asked the lab to have another look at his bloods.'

'But surely someone would have mentioned it, if he was psychotic?'

'His doctor knows nothing about it. Never saw him. But we've no suggestion he was dealing drugs, and the quantities in his drawer were small. Subject to confirmation from the lab, it does look like he was taking them himself.'

'Kate said he thought medication was for the feeble-minded.'

'Well, it looks like he changed his mind on that one, if he'd been taking both this ABILIFY thing and some dodgy, unknown drug as well. And look at this. I printed off an email exchange he had with someone who I think must be his client Lisa Bell.' Jai shoved a piece of paper over the desk at me. 'But note they're using their gmail accounts, not their work accounts.'

LisaB555@gmail.com: Peter, Just to let you know there are safety concerns with PK-634. Trials are on hold.

P.Hamilton@gmail.com: What safety concerns?

LisaB555@gmail.com: Can't say. But ALL those taking it must stop.

P.Hamilton@gmail.com: Assume patent application going ahead for now?

LisaB555@gmail.com: Yes.

P.Hamilton@gmail.com: Okay, so I still need more samples.

LisaB555@gmail.com: Like I said, ALL those taking it must stop.

P.Hamilton@gmail.com: And like I said, I NEED more samples.

'He wouldn't need samples for a patent application,' Jai said.

'So, he could have been taking this drug – getting it from Lisa Bell?' I'd known there was something dodgy about her, from the moment she'd elbowed me aside on that first morning. 'Maybe she wasn't having an affair with Peter, but she was supplying him illegally with untested drugs.'

'Maybe,' Jai said. 'I'd say that was the implication. And he didn't seem willing to stop.'

'Could he have threatened to expose her if she stopped supplying him? Could she have killed him to shut him up? It seems a bit extreme. I mean, I know drug companies have the morals of alley cats, but...' I put my coffee mug down with a bang. 'Unless this was part of a bigger cover-up. She'd been supplying other people illegally and maybe people got ill and it all started to get very serious and she wanted to keep it secret.'

'And Peter could have told Beth? To get a lawyer's view? Anyway, I've asked Lisa Bell to come in.' Jai looked at his watch. 'In half an hour. Shall we see her together?'

'Sounds good.' I looked again at Jai's print-out. 'Oh, and Kate's pregnant. Which suggests to me she didn't know he was taking the experimental drugs.'

'Yeah, and if she knew he was on them, why would he keep them in his desk at work?'

I started making handwritten notes. 'Okay, so we've got someone who, a year ago, was successful in a challenging job and who thought drugs were for sissies. And who, by the time he died, was taking experimental drugs, buying more drugs off the internet, smoking cannabis, drinking secretly, acting depressed, making cock-ups at work, not sleeping well...'

'What the hell happened to him?'

'Could he have developed bipolar or schizophrenia? You know the permanent health insurance policy he had through the company – that's for if you get ill and can't work, isn't it?'

'Yeah, I think so.'

'When did they take it out, and did it cover mental health issues?'

'Gimme that.' Jai twisted my screen around to face him and grabbed the keyboard. He tapped for a few moments, sucking on his lower lip.

'Well, it looks like they already had life insurance but they added permanent health earlier this year. I'd need to look into it some more. The small print on these things is a nightmare.'

'Yeah, would you check if it covers mental health?'

It occurred to me that there was someone I wanted to see after Lisa Bell. Someone I suspected might be an expert on illegal drugs and mental health problems, and who might even know what had happened on that roof in Cambridge all those years ago.

★

Lisa Bell tried to shift her chair forward, before realising it was attached to the floor. She huffed and stuck her elbows on the table. Obviously not used to chairs being regarded as potential weapons.

'Why have you brought me here?' she said. 'I'm just one of Peter's clients. I don't know anything about his death.'

'We're just making a few enquiries about his work,' I said in a friendly tone.

She gave me a wary look. 'Oh.'

Jai smiled at her – so much better than I could have done, so warm I could feel it even though I wasn't looking at him. 'Just to find out what was going on in his life,' he said.

She relaxed. 'Okay.'

I sent Jai a silent signal to keep going.

'We've been told his work quality went down in recent months,' he said. 'You'd found him slower with his work recently, hadn't you?'

'A bit, yes.'

'That must have been frustrating.'

'Well, maybe a little.'

'So, we heard you were working on a patent application for a drug PK-634.'

She stiffened slightly, her leg muscles shifting from the tone of raw meat to over-cooked. 'I think so, yes.'

'And Peter had samples of this drug?'

She raised her chin a little – almost a nod but not quite.

'But there were some safety concerns about the drug, weren't there?'

Jai's charm could only do so much. She was as still as a heron watching fish, and said nothing.

I smiled at her, and jumped in. 'So naturally you told him to stop taking the drug.'

She flicked her gaze to me and hesitated a moment too long. 'What? He wasn't taking it. He wanted samples of it for the patent application.'

'But he didn't have samples of the other drugs you were patenting.' This was a guess.

Again, a few too many milliseconds. 'No, but...'

Giving her no time to think, I said, 'You were giving him unlicensed drugs in return for free patent work, weren't you? Did he threaten to expose you when you asked him to stop taking the drugs?'

She shook her head. 'No! This is crazy.'

'Who else have you been supplying with unlicensed drugs?'

'No one. I just did what my patent attorney asked.' Her eyes flicked from side to side as if she was looking for a way out.

'We're struggling with your alibi for Sunday night,' I said. 'Watching TV alone.'

A flash of confusion on her face. She hadn't been expecting that.

'And the fact that you're lying about other things,' I said. 'Unfortunately it makes us suspicious. Whether you supplied him unlicensed drugs, that's not our area. But in our experience, people who lie about one thing... we have to wonder about them. Did Peter become inconvenient?'

Lisa blinked a few times, and shook her head. 'I didn't know he was going to take them...'

'You turned a blind eye?'

'Okay! I guessed he was taking the drugs. I let it go, and he reduced his charges. But I didn't kill him.'

'What was the drug for?'
'Movement disorders.'
'Was he ill?'
'I didn't ask.'
'But what did you suspect?'
'I wondered if he had the early signs of schizophrenia.'

Chapter 27

I drove to the less salubrious side of Eldercliffe. Brick terraces lined the narrow roads, and bin liners lay in piles in the doorways. Escaped drinks cans shone in the glow of the street lamps, and an occasional boarded-up house was decorated with graffiti of the non-Banksy variety. Despite the apparent poverty, the residents clearly all had cars – albeit some of them on bricks – because there was nowhere to park. I breathed in and drove through a tiny gap between rusting Ford Escorts, praying I wouldn't have to attempt to parallel park in front of a gang of feral youths. In the end, I turned round, drove back towards the leafier part of town, left the car and returned on foot.

A tiny sign identified the hostel. I pushed open a thick fire door and tripped up a step to stumble into a reception area which smelt of damp, just like home. A fluorescent light buzzed overhead and cast a clinical white light over a chipboard desk, behind which sat a young woman sporting pink hair and multiple piercings.

'Oh, mind the step.' Did she realise I'd already fallen over the step, or had it not yet happened in her brain?

'Thanks,' I said. 'I'm looking for Sebastian.'

She wore a badge saying *Shannon*. She looked at me through narrowed eyes. 'It's a bit late in the day. Are you his social worker?' Why was I always being mistaken for a social worker?

'Police, but don't worry, he's done nothing wrong. I just—'

She jumped up, with surprising sprightliness, popping out from behind the grey desk and standing as if to barricade the door leading into the rest of the hostel. 'Police. How can we help? They're a bit nervous of police here.'

'I just need to find Sebastian.'

'They frightened him the other day.'

I sighed. Bloody Craig. 'I'm sorry about that.' I said. 'I'll be nice to him. I only need a quick word.'

Her manner softened. 'He's really not here.' She moved towards me as if trying to edge me out of the building. 'He left. He never stays long.'

I stood my ground, passively, and she moved away and leant against the desk. Her T-shirt stretched tight over a waist which bulged over her jeans as if she'd been dropped into them from a great height.

'Does he often pop in and out then?' I asked.

'He's been coming here for years. But he doesn't usually sleep here. He'll be looking for somewhere to bed down now, I expect.'

'Why doesn't he sleep here?' It was a cold night.

'He likes to be in the open, away from other people.'

'What's he like?'

'He's a nice lad.'

I leant against the wall and looked at her with my softest and most un-threatening expression, the one I used with nervous cats, hoping she'd continue.

'He has problems,' she said. 'Gets paranoid. That's another reason he won't stay here. He thinks people are looking at him through the showers.'

'Is he schizophrenic?'

'I'm not sure if he's been diagnosed. We're always trying to get him to go to the doctor, get some medication, but he won't.'

'Does he take drugs?'

'Not the hard stuff, as far as I know. Cannabis, of course, if anyone's offering.' She seemed to remember who she was talking to. 'Not that we tolerate that here, of course.'

'It's okay,' I said. 'Do you know where he'll be staying tonight?'

She gave me a suspicious look. 'You want to find him tonight?'

I nodded.

'He's a good lad,' she said. 'Not a bad one.'

'I know,' I said. 'I promise I'll be nice to him. Buy him some sausages.'

She lifted her chin.

'It's not about him,' I said. 'He hasn't done anything wrong. I just think he may know something important.'

'To do with that dead man in the quarry? Or the woman?'

'Kind of indirectly. I know he wasn't involved.'

She looked at me as if weighing me up. 'Well, you could try the old railway bridge. And he does love his sausages. There's a café round the corner.'

She grabbed a dog-eared *A to Z* from a shelf by her head and pointed out a bridge only half a mile or so away. To my relief, she showed me on the map instead of giving me incomprehensible instructions involving pubs I'd never been to.

I thanked her and slipped out before she could ask any more questions, tripping down the step this time. Why couldn't I learn from my mistakes?

I decided to walk the half mile to the railway bridge, despite the foul weather and my aching bones. It felt right to walk when I knew Sebastian would be sleeping rough. Of course I should have phoned and asked someone to accompany me, but Sebastian would almost certainly be panicked into silence by two of us. Besides, I was wearing my Dr Martens boots – what harm could possibly come to me?

The pavement was narrow and the living rooms of the houses only arms-length away. I heard the muffled bass beat of music and saw the flickering of TV screens behind curtains as I walked past. I had a feeling of unease, like cold fingers on the back of my neck. I told myself it was just the blue glow from the TVs – horror movie lighting – but decided to avoid the maze of alleyways which was the quickest way to the railway bridge.

A flash of movement caught my eye, and I gasped. A tabby cat shot out from a passage between houses and I released my breath. I needed to calm the hell down. I contemplated turning back, giving up on the idea of talking to Sebastian. It's not as if information gleaned in an informal conversation with a mentally ill drug addict would be admissible in court. But I had a feeling Sebastian knew a piece of the puzzle. And if he told me the facts, I could find other ways to prove them.

I wrapped my coat tighter around me, wishing I'd brought a hat. A lone beer can skittered across the pavement, and the wind shook the trees above. It was a miserable night to sleep rough.

After about fifteen minutes, I reached the side road which led to the railway bridge. It was deserted apart from a few parked cars, and a shiver went through me. I steeled myself, walked to the top of a steep set of steps leading to the area under the bridge, and peered into the darkness. Something was scuffling down there. Either Sebastian or a family of rats.

My chest tightened at the sight of the steps plunging down away from me, only dimly visible in the orange light. I put my foot on the first step and eased myself down, then stopped to listen. There was definitely something under there. I carried on, step by step, looking at my feet and fighting my vertigo.

At the bottom, I gazed into the gloom. The ground underfoot was sandy, and a sharp urine smell hung in the air. A few old McDonald's bags wafted in the breeze, but there was none of the paraphernalia of homelessness I'd seen under the notorious Manchester bridges. A street lamp cast its sodium glow into the entrance, and my breath swirled yellow. I walked further into the dark under the bridge.

Something caught my eye. A man shifted from the inky black middle area towards the far side, which was lit by another street lamp. His ragged hair reflected the light. He turned to face me and I recognised him from the mug shots I'd seen.

'Sebastian!'

He walked away from me.

'Sebastian, it's about Peter Hamilton.'

He quickened his pace and broke into a jog.

I shouted at his retreating back. 'I need you to help me find who killed him. I'll buy you sausages!'

He slowed to a walk, but didn't turn around.

'There's a café up the road. It does all day breakfasts. I'll buy you one. I'll buy you two.' My shouts echoed from the curved roof.

Sebastian turned and stood while I walked very slowly and smoothly towards him.

'Poor Peter,' he said.

'Poor Peter,' I repeated.

He held a thin carrier bag and wore a huge coat. He looked tiny in the shadows, his body angled as if ready to dash away. I stood next to him in silence. Finally, he dropped his shoulders and lost the feel of a man on starting blocks.

'Shall we get sausages?'

He nodded and followed me as I re-traced my path, climbed the steps to the road, and walked the hundred yards or so to the main street.

Molly's Café was open for business, but quiet. I settled Sebastian at a plastic table by the door, where I hoped his aroma wouldn't come to the attention of Molly or her staff, and ordered two mugs of tea, two full English all-day breakfasts with extra sausages, and one veggie equivalent. Mine was just for the purpose of building rapport of course, and therefore calorie-free.

I brought the mugs of tea to our table. Sebastian sat on the chair nearest the door and fiddled with a ketchup container shaped like a mutant tomato. He looked like he was planning an escape, but I figured he'd stay until the sausages arrived.

'Loads of sausages on the way,' I said.

'Poor Peter.'

I didn't say anything, and focussed on him with my ears, not my eyes.

'Poor Peter, he wasn't feeling too good. Like me.'

I kept my voice quiet, and tried to sound like I didn't really care about the answer. 'What was up with Peter?'

'He wanted… No, no, he didn't.'

'Sebastian, you're not going to get into any trouble. And you can have sausages whenever you fancy.'

'He was a successful failure.'

Uh-oh, back to the oxymorons. I took a gulp of tea.

'He wasn't happy,' Sebastian said. 'Not happy.'

'No, he wasn't happy.'

'They're watching us, you know. I can't stay in that place. They watch us through the showers.'

The breakfasts arrived – piled high with extra sausages. Sebastian ate like he was on a paid mission. One plateful disappeared.

'Do they? And why wasn't Peter happy?'

'His head was full like mine. He needed some weed.'

'Is that what he wanted from you? Some weed?'

'Weed for Peter. Yes. It was the kindest thing. I saw him with the spikes in him. He didn't fall.'

'Who did you see? Who didn't fall?' That had been too direct, damn it.

Sebastian glanced up at me with nervous eyes, like a hunted animal. 'Are you one of them?'

'No,' I said, not looking directly at him.

'They all say that.'

He pushed aside the plate from the first breakfast and started on the second. Out of the corner of my eye, I saw the waitress staring. She brought over two more mugs of tea.

'On the house,' she said and shot off before I had a chance to thank her.

'So, he didn't fall,' I said.

No answer. His eyes were glassy. He ate the second breakfast and all the toast, including mine.

'Would you like another one?' I asked. 'Or a cake?'

He gave a quick shake of his head. I was relieved. It was like when you take in a stray dog. If you overdo the food, they puke on the carpet.

I paid quickly, with half an eye on Sebastian, and he was already standing when I returned to the table. I left a couple of pound coins by the tomato.

'Back to the bridge now,' Sebastian said.

I walked to the steps with him, trying and failing to extract more information. I waited at the top and watched him descend, hoping he had a sleeping bag. There was no point trying to persuade him to sleep at the hostel. It would just confirm I was one of them.

I waited while he found a spot, watched him walk around in circles like a cat preparing to nap, and turned to head back to my car. I tripped over my shoelace, swore, and squatted to re-tie it.

Was that the sound of voices? I froze. They were coming from under the bridge. The hairs on the back of my neck tingled. The voices were getting louder. Aggressive sounds, but I couldn't make out any words. Then a shout. Sounding scared. Sounding like Sebastian.

I crept towards the steps and peered down. Caught snippets of sentences.

'Tell the police and you're fucking dead... Fucking retard...'

I could make out three of them in the gloom, all distinctly Neanderthal. They were shoving Sebastian towards the tunnel wall. He was hunched over with his head down.

'. . . saying he didn't fall... he fucking fell.'

One of them pushed Sebastian harder and he dropped to the floor. Another one kicked him. I looked around. No one.

I ran down the steps.

'Police! Get off him.'

The men stepped away from Sebastian. One of them laughed. 'Oh look, it's the retard's girlfriend.'

It was so dark I could hardly see them. There was a shuffling of feet. Sebastian brushed past me and ran off through the tunnel towards the steps I'd come down.

I sensed a hesitation. Two of them looked at the third as if for guidance, then one of them lunged at me. I dodged and bolted after Sebastian. Charged through the sand of the tunnel and started climbing the steps. Made it to the top, my breath rasping in my throat. Feet pounded behind me.

A smack on the back of my head. Oh God, not again. I hit the ground. A sharp pain in my nose. I shielded my head. Someone kicked my stomach. I was lifted off the floor by the back of my coat. I snapped my arm around and made hard contact with something.

'Ow! Fucking bitch.'

He let go. I tried to drag myself away, but he caught hold of the back of my coat and slammed me against the stone wall that formed a boundary to the road. He lifted me by my coat, so my head was over the side of the railway bridge. I looked at the sickening drop. My breath came in hard bursts. My mind was full of the flashback again. Rope, ladders, dangling feet, panic, screaming. I was about to pass out. He lifted me higher.

Chapter 28

The tracks of the railway shimmered in the half-light far below. My terror turned to rage. I summoned all my strength, freed one of my arms and twisted round to face him. His breath smelt of hangovers and rancid meat. I stabbed hard at his eyes with my fingers. He yelped, let go of me and staggered back, clutching his head in his hands. I lunged at him and kicked his crotch with my big boots. He folded forwards and stumbled towards me.

'Leave her, you wanker!' One of the other men grabbed him and pulled him away. 'He said to rough-up the homeless twat, not attack some bloody copper.'

'She's no fucking copper.'

I was poised for him to run back at me, surprising myself with my fury-induced strength.

But they ran away into the night, their steps loud in the still air.

I collapsed onto the floor and lay by the roadside. The concrete beneath me was like ice. I prised myself into a sitting position and dabbed gently at my face. There was blood, but it was seeping, not gushing.

All the fight had gone from me. I leant against the stone wall and let the tears flow. As the adrenaline began to wear off, the pain kicked in. Every time I breathed, there was a jabbing in my stomach, and the bump on my head sent spikes into my brain. I must have scraped my hand on the wall – a layer of skin had come off and it felt as if it was on fire.

I couldn't face walking back to my car and driving with this hand. Mum's house was only about a mile away but that was quite a walk in this state, and she hated driving at night. I rummaged around in my pocket and fished out my phone. The screen was cracked but it still worked. My fingers struggled to find their way but I managed to stab 737 and his number.

'Meg? What's up?'

'I'm sorry. Are you busy?'

'Jesus, what's going on?'

I guess my voice sounded wrong. I explained the gist of the situation to him, and he told me to stay put. He was on his way.

I huddled into my coat and sat with my knees tucked to my chest, nursing my hand and trying to breathe shallowly.

After about fifteen minutes, I heard a car slowing and stopping. Surely it wasn't Jai already. I lifted my head. Wow, that made my brain throb. It was him.

He jumped out and ran to me.

'Holy crap, Meg.'

'I'm fine,' I said.

'You're bloody not. Who did this to you? Where are uniform?'

'I haven't called them.'

Jai's voice rose to an exasperated screech. 'Why not?'

'Please, Jai. Don't call them. I'm okay.'

He helped me up and into the passenger seat, pushed the door shut with a soft clunk, ran to the driver's side, and jumped in. 'We have to call. See if they can pick them up.'

'They're long gone. I can't even remember what they looked like. I was an idiot.' I gasped and clutched my stomach. 'Richard'll think I'm a liability. Craig'll think I'm a vulnerable little woman, and he'll be on me like a lion taking out the weakest buffalo.'

'But, Meg—'

'Seriously, they'll go mental over this. It's not worth it. Please.'

Jai huffed. 'I'll take you to the hospital.'

'No. Please. Just take me home. I'll be okay.'

'What if you've broken something? Or you're bleeding internally? Or you've made your head injury worse?'

'Honestly, take me home. I'll review things in the morning.'

'God, you're unbelievable.' But he set off towards Belper.

My head fell against the headrest and my mind went blank.

Jai used my keys to let us in and hurried to the kitchen to put the kettle on. I checked the living room, then trudged upstairs to check the bedrooms (stealthily so I didn't have to explain myself) and use the loo. In the bathroom, I peeled up my T-shirt and prodded my stomach. Nothing seemed dangerously wrong. And my face didn't look as bad as it felt. My hand was still burning but generally all the bits were in the right places. I swallowed two extra-strong painkillers and hobbled downstairs.

Jai was sitting on the chair in the living room, leaving the sofa for me. I lowered myself into it and he handed me a mug of tea.

'Meg, why's there a step ladder in the middle of your living room?'

'Oh.' I glanced at it. It squatted on the central rug where the coffee table should have been, dominating the room. A box of Quality Street balanced on the top platform. 'I've been meaning to start working on my thing with heights. Counter-conditioning.'

'In English?'

'I'm going to climb a few steps and then reward myself with chocolate. But I've been putting it off. Move it into the hall, can you? I can't face it right now.'

I looked up at the top of the ladder and noticed a cobweb the size of a dog trailing from the ceiling. Not a Chihuahua either – more of a spaniel. I didn't like to remove cobwebs when fresh – where else were the spiders supposed to live and hunt? But this one looked distinctly vintage and it occurred to me that the house might need a bit of a clean. I hoped Jai wouldn't be too horrified by me.

He stood and fiddled with the ladder. 'You're priceless.' He manhandled it into the narrow hallway.

'So…' he said, on his return.

'What?'

'You thought it was a great idea to meet a tramp under a dodgy railway bridge after dark, and ask him lots of difficult questions about a murder, even though you've already fallen on your head and nearly been blown up this week?'

'Come on Jai, I called you because I didn't want to go through this with my mum. Sebastian was fine. It was just bad timing. Can we discuss the case, not how much of an irresponsible idiot I am?' I held the mug with my good hand and took a sip of tea. He'd put sugar in it.

'Stop grimacing. The sugar's good for shock. Just drink it.' Jai took a gulp of his own tea and a bite of a biscuit from a packet he must have found in the cupboard. 'So, who did this to you?'

'I don't know. But I heard them threatening Sebastian. They didn't want him talking to the police.'

Jai let out a deliberate sigh. 'So, you heard them threatening Sebastian and you thought it was a good idea to pile in there, on your own. Two people are dead, Meg!'

'Seriously, Jai. Leave it. There was no time to get back-up. What if they'd killed him?'

'What if they'd killed you?' Jai put down his tea with a thud.

I collapsed back onto the sofa and let out a slightly hysterical laugh.

'What the hell are you on?'

'Must be the painkillers,' I said. 'No, I was thinking of that Robin Williams sketch where he takes the piss out of the British police. You know, *In England, if you commit a crime, the police don't have a gun and you don't have a gun. The police say, "Stop, or I'll say stop again."* So, anyway, it didn't work. I said, "Stop" and they hit me. And dangled me over the side of a railway bridge. Made me realise I really, really have a problem with heights.'

'Jesus Christ, Meg.'

'Anyway, I'm bored of my stupidity now. Sebastian's been saying something about someone who didn't fall. Did you notice in his interview? He said it again to me today. And the heavies were threatening him, trying to stop him saying that. And he said something about seeing him with spikes in him.'

Jai looked up from his tea. 'Spikes in him? Was he in Cambridge when the guy fell off the roof?'

'That's what I'm wondering.'

'Kate thinks Felix is dangerous. Could he have set the heavies on Sebastian?'

'Yes, I think he could.' I took a gulp of hot tea. Jai was right. The sugar was doing me good.

Jai sat up straighter in my slumpy chair. 'I wonder if Peter started threatening to come clean about whatever happened on the roof in Cambridge, and Felix killed him, then realised Sebastian knows too, so is now threatening him? He might even have persuaded Sebastian to confess to Peter's murder. For sausages.'

'We should definitely check it out. But I don't want us to zoom in too closely on Felix. You know about channelling, confirmation bias, inattention blindness, all that. We're not immune.'

'Don't let Craig hear you spouting all that graduate psychology stuff. He'll want to get Felix into the nick and bash him about until he confesses. Good old-fashioned policing.'

'Too accurate to be funny.' I forced down the last gulp of sweet tea and slapped the mug on the table. 'God, this hand hurts.'

'You're being very brave.'

I felt tears welling up. I cleared my throat. 'Did you check that permanent health insurance?'

'Yeah, it does cover mental health issues and it was taken out about six months ago by Peter Hamilton, whereas the life insurance has been in place for years.'

'That's interesting. So, about a year ago, say, Peter starts developing some mental health problem or other. Something you take ABILIFY for – maybe schizophrenia. He thinks mental health problems are for the feeble-minded so he doesn't tell anyone—'

'He gets ABILIFY and some dodgy experimental drug from Lisa Bell in return for free patent work. She said the drug was for movement disorders, didn't she?'

'Yes,' I said. 'Which can be an early sign of schizophrenia. Pass us one of those stale biscuits.'

'Yes, ma'am.'

'Sorry. I know you came here to rescue me, not to be given orders.'

'Don't worry, I know you can't help yourself.'

'No. Sorry. I'm a pain in the arse, I know.'

Jai smiled and shook his head slowly from side to side.

'Anyway,' I said. 'He was getting medication from Lisa Bell and keeping his illness secret.'

'Yeah. He probably also wanted to get the permanent health insurance in place, to give him a decent income if he was off work sick, but he needed to have had it in place a while before he told his doctor. Otherwise it wouldn't have covered what he had.' Jai took another biscuit. 'How old are these? They're rank.'

'They were in the cupboard when I moved in. Already open. One had a bite out of it.'

'Ugh, really?' Jai dropped his biscuit.

'No. They're not fresh though. So, anyway, he kept it quiet but self-medicated by drinking too much and smoking cannabis which he got from Sebastian. And he was acting different – his wife thought he was depressed, his colleagues noticed he was getting careless. And maybe the mental illness sort of changed his personality – he stopped being so cautious or something. Started talking about stuff that happened in Cambridge years ago.'

'Yes,' Jai said. 'And he started asking questions about Rosie.'

My thoughts strayed to Kate. Could she really not know if Peter had been developing a serious mental illness? 'His wife must know more than she's letting on. She's a doctor, for God's sake.'

'She could have killed him when she realised he was going off his rocker. Hoping to pocket the large insurance payment instead of getting lumbered with a mentally ill husband.'

'Oh, what a rosy view of marriage you have, Jai.'

'Based on experience, Meg. Based on bitter experience.'

★

Jai accepted my effusive gratitude and finally left around midnight, reassured that I wasn't oozing blood from any part of my body or suffering from a life-threatening brain haemorrhage. He urged me to get up late in the morning, and promised to come over and drive me to pick up my car when I was ready.

I was so exhausted I couldn't even face cleaning my teeth, but once in bed I couldn't sleep. When I closed my eyes, I saw the tracks of the railway below me, felt the man's hands on my neck, smelt his tobacco-breath.

I'd never in my life been scared of walking around at night on my own, and had always been irritated by the media making out women to be permanent victims, when most attacks were on young men. I'd certainly never worried about being in the house on my own. But this was different. If someone had put those heavies onto Sebastian to stop him talking, and now they knew I'd overheard, I was in danger. Beth could have been killed for knowing too much. I didn't want to be next.

I can look after myself, I'd said to Jai. How ridiculous.

My stomach and head were so sore they invaded my dreams, and I slept badly and woke early. When I tried to lift my face from the pillow, nothing happened. I tried harder – no movement, just a sharp, wrenching sensation in my neck. I shuffled onto my front, slowly and painfully, and levered myself up onto all fours and then into a sitting position. I lifted my nightshirt and inspected the mottled patterns of different shades of black on my torso.

I planted my feet carefully on the floor, heaved myself into a standing position, and hobbled to the bathroom for a facial inspection. Not as bad as it felt. A slight darkening under my left eye and swelling on my cheek, but not the stuff of horror movies.

After more industrial-strength painkillers, things started loosening up a bit. I fed myself a slow breakfast and felt much better with food inside me. I'd be in pain whether I sat at home or did something useful, so I decided I might as well carry on as best I could. I put on my normal, not-in-gut-wrenching-discomfort voice, and called Jai.

★

We arrived at my car, which had survived its night out better than I had. Jai turned to me. 'Are you going to be okay? You look like you're about to throw.'

'Oh. Thanks.'

Jai frowned. 'Look, I'm not sure you should be at work. You don't seem great.'

'Honestly, I'm better off doing something. I'll catch up with you later.'

I clambered out into the cold morning, and gave Jai a confident wave. He watched me fake a pain-free journey into my car, and then drove slowly away.

I called the Station and sat wondering if I was actually capable of driving. I'd been so adamant I was okay, I couldn't call Jai back. I took a deep and painful breath, wrapped my filthy windscreen rag around my bad hand, and stuck the car in gear. I drove (in meandering pensioner fashion) through the back streets to the centre of Eldercliffe, and parked on the pavement right outside Kate's surgery. I stumbled through the reception area and leant against the wall. There was no sign of Vivian today, and the receptionist gave me a startled look. 'Have you been hurt? Do you need a doctor?'

'I'm fine.' I flashed her my card. 'I just need a quick word with Dr Webster.'

Her expression changed to panic. 'She has patients.' Did she fear a patient revolt if I butted in?

'I'll be quick.'

She hesitated, and then picked up the phone. After a brief exchange, she raised her impeccably plucked eyebrows and turned to me. 'Okay, go through.'

I made my way to Consulting Room 4.

Kate looked up from her notes. 'Oh, hello.' Not unfriendly.

I sat in the patient chair, feeling less vulnerable this time, strangely since I was beaten and bruised.

Kate frowned. 'Have you been attacked?'

'Oh, it's nothing,' I said. 'Did you know your husband was taking ABILIFY?'

Her eyes widened. 'The anti-psychotic?'

'Yes.'

'No, I didn't.' She sat forward in her chair.

'He also seems to have been taking an experimental drug one of his clients gave him.'

She breathed in sharply. She hadn't known that.

'I think you know more than you've told me.'

She looked out of the window. The view took in the practice's tiny, steep, over-full car park (staff only) and behind that a rather fine Georgian pub. Her voice was soft. 'I suspected he might be developing schizophrenia.'

'Right. Why didn't you tell us this before?'

She turned back to look at me. 'He was such a proud man. He was ashamed. He would have *hated* everyone to know. I didn't see the relevance anyway. What does it matter now?'

'Why did you suspect schizophrenia? Doesn't it usually develop at a younger age?'

'Not always. He was irritable and depressed. Moody. Touchy. Obsessive. He became clumsy and his gait changed. He thought he was being watched. The list goes on. I tried to raise it with him but he wouldn't talk about it.'

'Is ABILIFY a schizophrenia drug?'

'Yes it is.' She stared out of the window again. 'Where did he get it from? And why is this relevant? Do you know who killed him?'

'We need all the facts. Is there anything else you haven't told us?'

'Are you thinking he committed suicide after all?'

'Well, the schizophrenia makes it more likely, don't you think? It would have been helpful to know about that.'

'I don't think he committed suicide. He wouldn't have done that to me. Or to his family.' She sighed. 'Maybe I'm kidding myself. People clearly *do* commit suicide and it's horrific for the relatives.'

'Yes, I'm afraid they do. And it is.'

But I didn't think he'd committed suicide either. Why bother with the permanent health insurance if he was going to kill himself?

'I think you know what happened on that roof in Cambridge,' I said.

The breath stopped in her throat, halfway to her lungs. 'I have patients waiting.'

'What happened? You need to tell me. You could be in danger.'

She gave me an appraising look and slumped back in her chair. 'I'll be done with these in an hour. Come back and I'll tell you.'

Chapter 29

An hour and two (non-skinny) lattes later, I sat again in the patient chair.

Kate picked up the blood-pressure stress reliever and squeezed it in and out while she talked.

'When I first met Peter, he told me about this friend who'd died falling off a roof in Cambridge. But he claimed he and Felix weren't there. He seemed pretty cut-up about it, but I thought that was just because he'd been good friends with the lad. But then about six months ago, he started talking about it again, saying he felt guilty and wanted to confess.'

'So, what really happened?'

'They were on the roof together, mucking about. Stoned. And the lad who died, George Matthews, made some comment about Olivia having slept with someone else. I'm thinking now it might have been Peter she'd slept with, but he didn't tell me that. Felix was always jealous about Olivia, and he shouted at George and shoved him. There was a scuffle and George fell. Since I found out about the situation with Rosie, I wonder if there was a bit more to it. But basically, Felix pushed the lad off the roof and he died.'

'My God. Didn't they call an ambulance?'

'He landed on spiked railings. Peter said they stood on the roof, obviously horrified, but it was clear there was no point calling an ambulance.'

I gave her a questioning look.

'I know. If he'd been on his own, Peter would have called for help. It's Felix. He's not normal.'

'So, Peter started going on about this recently?'

'Yes. And saying he wanted to confess.'

'Why didn't you tell us about this earlier? Don't you realise this could be a motive for murder?'

'I know, I know. I'm sorry. It was all so long ago. Peter made me swear on my parents' graves that I'd never say a word to anyone. I know it's bloody stupid – it's not like he cares now. But I made a promise… It felt important to keep my promise to him.'

I felt a stab of pity for this woman who'd lost so many people in her life. 'Don't worry. I understand.'

'I'm so sorry,' she said. 'I feel terrible. If this is relevant, I could be responsible for Beth being killed.'

★

My desire for Mum not to see my injuries battled with my anxiety about her and Gran. Anxiety won and I made my way over there after work.

I let myself into the house, which no longer felt safe and cosy, and hobbled down the hallway. I expected her to be in the kitchen, but as I walked past the little study on my left, I heard papers rustling and looked in to see her hunched over her desk.

'Hello!' I called, and she jumped so dramatically she nearly fell off her chair, arms and legs flying. She slammed her hands down on her papers.

'Bloody hell, Mum, what are you doing?'

'Goodness, Meg, what happened to you this time?'

'I'm fine, honestly. What are you up to?'

'You gave me a fright.' She looked at her hand, and tried to casually shift the papers away from me. I couldn't see what was on them.

'Sorry. I wanted to check you were okay.'

'What on earth happened to you?'

She didn't seem to realise there'd been another death. Thank goodness she was a techno-Luddite with no interest in social media or even the TV. I opened my mouth to reply, but was interrupted by a thud from upstairs. This time we both jumped, and looked wide-eyed at each other.

Mum leapt out of her chair and we sprinted up the stairs and into Gran's room.

I arrived first despite my injuries. Gran lay sprawled on the floor, tangled in her duvet. She looked tiny and broken. 'Oh Jesus, she's fallen out of bed,' I shouted.

I squatted on the floor. 'Gran, are you okay?'

Mum knelt next to me. 'I can't believe we're doing this again. Can we lift her back in?'

I prepared my shoulder for the onslaught. 'How is she so heavy? It's like she's made of uranium.'

We half dragged, half lifted her onto the bed, gasping with the effort.

Gran moaned gently as we shifted her pillows and tried to get her comfy. 'You're a good girl,' she muttered. 'I always said. Despite what they say. A good girl.'

It didn't seem the time to ask *Who said, and what did they say?* I let it go. She seemed unharmed but we agreed we'd ask the doctor to check her over again.

'Maybe the gas affected her more than they thought.' I pushed Mum onto the chair by the window. She was panting like a greyhound after a race. 'Sit down. I'll get us tea.' She complied for once, sinking onto the chair and putting her head in her hands.

I caught my breath and limped downstairs to the kitchen. The light switch sparked when I turned it on. I gave it a suspicious look. If it had done that when the gas was leaking…

I put the kettle on and indulged in some general fretting. I felt cold thinking about the light switch and the gas leak. The electrics in Mum's house were probably ancient. And how much longer was she going to be able to cope with Gran at home? I was helping as much as I could, but with work and everything… What if she'd had the gas leak or Gran had fallen when I hadn't been around? Guilt and helplessness gnawed at my insides. Gran had made it abundantly clear she'd rather die than go into a home, and we couldn't afford it anyway.

I forced my thoughts away from Gran, and they landed in another unsettling place – Mum's reaction when I'd arrived at the house. What had she been writing? There were no sounds from upstairs. I knew I shouldn't spy on her, but I was worried.

She always kept that room locked. When I'd jokingly challenged her about it, she said she'd picked up the habit from Dad, but she hadn't picked up his other OCD habits (apart from the occasional approved-method dishwasher stacking).

I crept through the hall towards the office, listening for movement upstairs. The door was closed – she must have pushed it shut behind us. The kettle was masking any noise I made, but it also made it hard to hear if Mum shifted. And if it boiled and flipped off, she'd hear me. I reached forward and turned the handle, pushed the door and stepped inside, leaving the door open behind me.

I saw the paper she'd been writing on – a few notes in her scrawly handwriting.

Nembutal/other barbs

Someone else take over Silk Road etc?

I stared at the scrap of paper, blinking repeatedly as if it would change the content. A floorboard creaked upstairs. I jumped towards the door. The kettle had boiled. I shot out of the office, pushing the door closed behind me, and slipped into the kitchen, just in time to avoid Mum. I made tea to the accompaniment of the click of her locking the office door, before ascending the stairs again.

My brain churned, trying to make sense of what I'd seen. The Silk Road was that Dark Web site, the one where you could buy drugs and arrange hit men. What in God's name was my mum doing writing notes about that?

I took the tea upstairs and we sat with Gran. She seemed fine – luckily she'd landed on her bundled-up duvet – but Mum and I discussed bed bars, and whether Mum needed more help coping.

'What were you doing in the office earlier?' I asked. 'You looked engrossed in something.'

'More to the point, what on earth happened to you?'

'Oh, nothing.'

'Meg, this is getting ridiculous. You're going to get yourself killed.'

'I'm okay. What were you doing in the office?'

'It was for our book group. I was making some notes on this week's book.'

I scrutinised her face. She looked completely calm except she kept blinking. The realisation that she was lying to me was like hot coals in my stomach. I kept my voice even. 'What was the book?'

She crossed her arms and said, 'Why don't you tell me what happened to you?'

'Honestly, it's not as bad as it looks.'

'Meg, please get yourself taken off that case. I'm worried about you.'

'What was the book, Mum?'

A swallow tracked down her throat. 'It was *Gone Girl*'.

A hollowness was opening up inside me, but I kept my tone casual as if making conversation. 'Did you like it? What did you think of the end?'

'I like it, but I haven't got to the end yet. It's for our book group on Sunday evening.'

I had actually read *Gone Girl* and there was nothing about Nembutal or the Silk Road in it. I had a stupid urge to cry. Mum was mixed up in something illegal, which meant she must be desperate. And she hadn't come to me for help.

I jumped up, scraping the chair back behind me. 'I'm going home.'

Mum looked up. 'Meg…'

'What?'

'Please look after yourself.'

I hesitated. 'Mum, if there's anything bothering you… anything you'd like to tell me… If you need money…'

'No,' she said. 'I just worry about you in that job.'

I walked down the hallway and paused halfway to the front door. 'Get that bloody light switch fixed in the kitchen. You'll end up killing us all.'

Chapter 30

Back home, I did my room checks, grabbed my laptop and sat at the kitchen table. I was really seizing up now, and felt shaky and panicky about Mum.

I confirmed that the Silk Road was now shut down but, as I'd thought, it was an online black market best known for selling illegal drugs. It was part of the Dark Web – the illegal part of the internet you couldn't find by normal searches – and you accessed it via TOR, a hidden service, so no one could trace you. What the hell? I raised my head and stared at my dated, orange-pine kitchen cupboards. Was my mother a drug dealer?

I stood, did a couple of agonising stretches, and put the kettle on, my mind spinning. Nembutal was a short-acting barbiturate, prescribed for insomnia. Mum had suffered from severe insomnia after Carrie died. And it was highly addictive. Could Mum be addicted to barbiturates? And be getting them illegally online? But she'd written, 'Someone else take over Silk Road etc'. Was she part of a drugs ring?

And what about her manic attendance of the book group over the years? She didn't read many books but she wouldn't miss her Sunday-night meeting. Could it be a cover for some sort of drugs operation? It couldn't be possible – not my Mum. I felt twitchy, like I wanted to pace up and down, but my body wasn't up to it.

I made tea, accidentally dropping the spent tea bag on the floor like some kind of halfwit, and then leaving it there because I couldn't face the journey to pick it up. I sniffed the milk.

Could any of this be relevant to Peter's Hamilton's death? In large doses, barbiturates could kill people, but they hadn't killed him. It was a strange coincidence that two apparently respectable citizens were talking about the Silk Road, and what about Mum's weird reaction to Kate Webster's name?

I lowered myself into one of the wooden kitchen chairs that I kept meaning to paint. This case was so complicated. And now it seemed that my own mum was somehow wrapped up in it. Words drifted across my vision – Tithonus, schizophrenia, Sebastian, Henry, Felix, cyanide, Piers's bane...

Hold on a minute. I pictured Kate Webster talking about Peter's ancestor, the Victorian who'd thrown himself into the quarry. Could he be Piers, the answer to the riddle in the casket? That would explain *Piers's bane*. *The drops are steep, the pools are deep.* The quarry would certainly be his bane if he'd thrown himself into it.

I tried googling *Piers, Victorian, mill owner, Eldercliffe,* and *quarry* but nothing came up. I tried combining these with *Henry* – the solution to the first riddle and possibly Piers's middle name – and *Hamilton*, in case he'd had the same name as Peter, but there was still nothing.

I texted Jai. *Did you speak to the man at the bookshop about Peter's ancestor?*

A reply came straight back. *There's a diary. He's bringing it in tomorrow morning.*

★

The next day, I plastered myself with all the foundation I owned and dragged myself in early to talk to the team, allocate actions, and avoid questions about my appearance.

Finally I was free to talk to Jai. 'Is Felix coming in? And have we got the diary from the dead Victorian?'

'Felix is coming in this afternoon,' he said. 'And as for the dead Victorian, as opposed to all the living ones, I'll go check if the diary's here yet.'

Jai wandered off at a frustrating pace and returned a few minutes later at high speed. 'Here it is. And what do you reckon his name was?'

'Piers.'

'It's only Piers Henry bloody Hamilton.'

A flush of adrenaline shot into my stomach, cold and sharp. It was him. He was the answer to the riddle.

'PHH,' I said quietly. 'So, who would know the story?' I said. 'I found nothing on the internet.'

'The diary's hand written, and the guy in the bookshop said it was never printed. Maybe it's not well known. He hadn't even shown it to Peter. He thought the content was too upsetting.'

'Can I see?'

Jai passed me a leather-bound book. The cover was worn but the gold lettering on the front was still readable – *Exclusive Diary*. 'It's okay,' he said. 'I don't mind if you read it first. I can see you're sweating with anticipation. You can tell me what it says.'

'I'm not sure that's any way to speak to your superiors.' But I took the book and started carefully flipping the pages.

★

Jai left me in peace and I read the last two entries of the diary in full.

Was there ever a man as wretched as I? My business is in ruins; my family has turned against me; my glorious rhododendron gardens are gone; and my house now teeters on the edge of the quarry like an unfortunate soul contemplating taking his own life.

I feel I am disintegrating before my own self. I know I am not long for this life, and today I have discovered the true cause. Our family is cursed, just as my grandmother told.

I have taken to visiting a healer who resides in a cave in the woods to the south of Eldercliffe. This kind soul does not shun me as my family does, and she has prescribed herbs for my sickness.

I have developed trust in this lady, and I believed she should possess all the facts. Therefore, I today mentioned the curse of which my grandmother spoke. Her face grew white, and she muttered under her breath and drew the sign of the cross.

'I have heard of such curse,' she said. 'It is spoken of among healers, because we seem powerless against it. I will tell you what I know.'

'Please continue,' I said, and settled back on my stone bench with a terrible heaviness inside me.

'Many generations ago,' she said, 'back in the times when there were witches in this land, a man accused his wife's sister of being such a thing. It was a very grave accusation, but it was made by a respectable man of the village, a married man with eight children. And the woman's own sister believed her husband, the accuser.

'This village was near to a place known as the Labyrinth; a terrible, dark, underground place of caves and tunnels, which had never been fully mapped. It was custom in the village to take suspected witches to the Labyrinth, and to find a noose which hung deep within. If the noose could be found, it was decreed that the woman was a witch, and her initials would be discovered hewn into the cave wall behind. In this case, the witch would hang. If the noose could not be found, the woman would be declared innocent and left to find her own way out, although sadly most women did not succeed. The villagers took this particular young woman into the Labyrinth. They found the noose and she was hanged to death.'

Not truly desiring to know the answer, I asked, 'And the curse?'

'The day after the woman was hanged, there was a strange occurrence. In this area, as you know, rocks jut from the ground in odd places, and one such rock the size of a small cart was situated outside the accuser's house. When he woke the day after the hanging, a carving had appeared on the rock. An image of the Grim Reaper, his scythe held aloft, and under it the man's wife and children.'

I shuddered as I envisaged the man waking to find such a thing. 'And that was the origin of the curse?'

The healer could not meet my eye. 'The man took a pick-axe and he hacked the stone to pieces, destroying the image and rendering the stone into a thousand fragments. But to no avail. His wife died young, as did many of his children. And his children's children.'

'That is my family?' I whispered. 'The family of the accuser?'

'So it is told.'

The next entry was a week later.

'After discovering the terrible news of our family curse, I raged against my fate. But now a certain calmness has come upon me. I have vowed to take my own life, although the healer begs me not to do so. She claims to have developed a fondness for me, and each day she makes a new potion to try to cure me. She has grown immensely thin, for which I feel deep regret. But I know what I must do. I will step from the cliff outside my own house.

First, however, there is something I am obliged to undertake. Although my children no longer speak to me, the thought that they may too be afflicted with this curse is troubling me greatly. The healer has spoken to her spirit guides and they have told her how I may remove the curse from my family.

I must carve a new image of the Grim Reaper. I must do it with care and diligence, no matter how long it shall take. I have decided I will practise in my own basement, and then I will carve it into the wall of the cave in order that I may spend my last times with the healer who has treated me with such kindness. When I am done, I shall be free to leave this world, and my children and their children's children will be spared. And that is what I will do.'

I closed my eyes and sank back in my chair. I pictured the healer growing thinner and thinner as she prepared potion after potion, trying to save her friend. Did her presence somehow remain in the cave? Maybe the emaciated ghost was more than a trick of light and shadows.

And I imagined poor Piers painting the awful image in his basement, and then hacking away at the cave wall, frantically trying to
remove the curse from his family. To no avail.

★

I called the health centre and asked for Kate Webster, my mind
full of the unsettling words from the diary. I wanted to know who
else they'd told about Piers. The murderer had known about the
tragedy or he wouldn't have written *In Piers's bane* on the mystery
geocache clue. Obviously Kate Webster knew, but I didn't think it
was her. There would be much easier ways to dispatch your own
husband, especially if you were a doctor. I wondered if Felix knew.

Kate sounded exhausted. 'Haven't you found who did it yet?'

'Who knew about the history of your house? About Piers
Hamilton falling to his death?'

'Oh, for goodness' sake, why?'

'Well, it appears the murderer knew. Obviously you knew.
According to the man in the bookshop, this was a pretty obscure
piece of knowledge.'

'Was it? I assumed lots of people knew it.'

'No. So, you can see from my perspective this isn't looking so
good.'

'What? You think I did it?'

I didn't think she'd done it. 'Who else did you tell about the
history of the house?'

'Oh God, I don't know. We mentioned it at our house-warming.
Close friends and family. I can't remember telling anyone else, but
I might have.'

'Who was at the house-warming?'

'Family-wise, there was Mark and Beth. And then work colleagues – Felix and Olivia, Edward and Grace. I think that was
about it. I don't know who else Peter told about the history, though.
His dad probably, if he didn't already know.'

'And what if the curse is on the family, not the house? It's just that the house stayed in the family. Can't genetic diseases be regarded as family curses?'

'There could be schizophrenia in Peter's family,' Kate said softly. 'All the suicides at the house. The paranoia about the Grim Reaper. Is that the curse? Schizophrenia?'

★

After I put the phone down, it immediately started ringing. A message from Olivia: 'I know I should have told you this before, but Felix lied about the Sunday night before Peter was killed. He went out about seven and got back about ten. And I don't know where he was on the afternoon Beth died. Please don't tell him I told you.'

Chapter 31

Felix leant back in the grey plastic chair and sighed, as if this was all far too tedious for him. 'Nice bruises. What happened to you?' His shiny-suited solicitor frowned at him.

I ignored the question. I was glad we'd ended up in our most uncomfortable interview room – the one that was always too hot, with the buzzy fluorescent light that gave you a migraine, and the smell of teenage car-thieves' old trainers and sex offenders' laptops.

Jai took Felix through the formal stuff, and sat back to let me conduct the interview.

'You should be more careful,' Felix said. 'And just to let you know, I'm not happy about being shipped in here and grilled like a common criminal. Put a foot wrong and I'll be down on you like a ton of bricks.' I had a mental image of him as a child at an expensive public school, twisting a smaller kid's arm behind his back.

'We'd like to know where you were the evening before Peter Hamilton died.'

'Oh, I don't know. Didn't I tell you before?'

'You lied to us before.'

Shiny-Suit said, 'If you don't have any evidence, I suggest you release my client.' Was that the best he could do for three hundred quid an hour?

'We know you went out,' I said. 'And we have an earlier witness statement from you saying you stayed in. You'd better explain.'

Felix was unnervingly still, like a cobra about to strike. 'Has that faithless wife of mine grassed me up? I'll have to deal with her.'

I pictured Olivia's bruised neck and felt a twinge of worry on her behalf. 'Where were you?'

He sighed. 'All right. I didn't tell you before because I thought you'd get all over-excited about it. Edward and I went in to the office to look through Peter's work. To find out if he'd made any more stupendous cock-ups.'

'Edward said he didn't go out that night.'

'Well, obviously, shock horror, he lied. We both agreed not to tell you. I'm sure if you confront him, he'll come clean. He crumples under pressure.'

'So Peter had been making mistakes which put you at serious financial risk?'

'Not necessarily.'

'And now he's out of the way and you have his life insurance money. How fortuitous.'

'I didn't kill him.'

'We know you pushed a young man off a roof to his death in Cambridge, didn't call for help, and then covered it up. Peter Hamilton was threatening to come clean.' We didn't know that for sure but it was worth a try. 'Yet another reason to want him out of the way. And what about Beth Hamilton? Where were you on Sunday afternoon?'

Felix shuffled in his seat, apparently losing his cool for a moment. 'I went out for a drive.'

'Where did you go?'

'Round and about the lanes. I can't remember exactly.' The screen came back over his face and his voice was as arrogant and confident as ever. 'You're on a fishing expedition. You've no evidence I had anything to do with Peter's death or that sister of his.'

'Ever heard of Piers? Remember his middle name?'

'I have no idea what you're talking about.'

'Really? Can anyone other than Edward verify where you were the night before Peter died, or on Sunday afternoon?'

'Well, I told that bi—' Shiny-Suit kicked Felix – actually booted him under the table, quite blatantly. Felix hesitated. 'I told my lovely wife exactly where I was going. Both times. I'm disappointed she didn't do me the favour of mentioning that.'

'Mr Carstairs,' I said. 'If you so much as lay an aggressive finger on your wife, we'll have you dragged in here in handcuffs faster than you can say *Get me my lawyer,* whether she wants to press charges or not.'

Shiny-Suit swallowed, with dramatic Adam's apple action. 'Can I have a moment with my client, please?'

★

The brightness of the morning had disappeared but the wind remained, dragging sluggish dark clouds across the sky as I headed south to Edward Swift's house. I noticed I was grinding my teeth. We needed more evidence.

Edward greeted me with no enthusiasm and led me through to the kitchen. He sat me at the table and placed himself carefully opposite. There were no offers of coffee and he didn't comment on my unorthodox, just-beaten-up look.

'We have reason to believe you lied about your whereabouts on the Sunday evening before Peter's death,' I said.

'Oh.'

'So, where were you?'

He tapped his fingernails against the table and spoke rapidly. 'I knew it was ridiculous to lie to you. It's Felix – he can be very persuasive. We went in to the office. We were discussing one of Peter's cases.'

'Why?'

'He'd messed something up. We were… We were trying to put it right.'

'Why all the secrecy then?'

Edward looked as if he was about to burst into tears. 'I knew we shouldn't do it. I told Felix.' He stood and walked to the patio door overlooking the fishpond.

'What did you do?'

Edward spun round and returned to the table. 'Oh, I can't lie any more. We were trying to cover up his mistake. Avoid the client realising. It happened during the period we had no insurance. It could have bankrupted us.'

'You'd better tell me exactly what happened.' I sat back in my chair as if I had all the time in the world.

Edward took a breath like he was preparing for a free dive. 'Peter missed the priority deadline for filing an international application. The client instructed him to do it by email and letter and Peter acknowledged and said it was all in hand, and then just didn't do it. It only came to light when the client asked for a status update. It was too late to do anything.'

I almost felt sorry for Edward. His face was damp with sweat.

'So, it was serious then? Peter had made a bad mistake? With big financial consequences?'

'Yes. And it got worse. Felix persuaded us not to tell the client. We filed an international application as soon as we found out. Tried to claim priority but we knew it would be rejected. We were too late. But they weren't the sort of clients who would check up on what we told them. They hadn't actually disclosed the invention, so the later date could still be okay, as long as no one else had filed a similar application in the meantime. So, we kept quiet and prayed.'

'But it turned out someone had filed a similar application?'

'It was awful. A direct competitor had filed something almost identical after our original priority date but before the filing date of our International. That evening, Felix and I were in the office arguing about what to do. Peter and I wanted to come clean but Felix wanted to fabricate some earlier prior art and persuade the client to withdraw the case based on that.'

'What effect would that have had?'

'It would have made it seem that the invention was unpatentable anyway, regardless of our mistake. Because someone else had already done it, even before the original priority date. They hadn't, of course. Felix was going to make something up.'

'So, he wanted to commit fraud?'

'Yes, I suppose so. It was a big-money case. Pharmaceuticals. And to make matters worse, early trials had been promising.' Edward put his head in his hands. 'It's such a mess. I've realised while we were all running around being busy, thinking everything was going well, Peter seems to have been going quietly mad. We trusted each other. It's only a small firm. We have systems but they only work if everyone behaves sensibly and uses them.'

'How long were you in the office that evening?'

'From about seven to about nine thirty.'

'So your wife lied when she said you were watching TV with her?'

'Yes. I'm sorry, it's not her fault. I asked her to.'

'And were you with Felix the whole time?'

'No, I was in Peter's room but Felix went to our Records department for about an hour. Working out what he could get away with.'

'So, he could have left the building?'

'I suppose so. I saw him at about seven thirty and then again at about eight thirty to nine.'

'Okay. Thank you. Do you know if Peter mentioned his mistake to anyone else? His sister was a lawyer. Would he have discussed it with her?'

'Probably. Are you going to report us?' He squeezed his eyebrows together and gave me a beseeching look.

'Look, it's not my main focus. But I strongly suggest you come clean to the client.'

Edward slumped in his chair and exhaled. 'Yes, we will. Of course. I knew we should.'

'Good. I just need to ask you a couple of other things. Do you remember Peter telling you the story about the Victorian who built their house, and committed suicide?'

'Yes, of course.'

'Did you mention it to anyone else?'

'No. Why?'

'Are you familiar with geocaching?'

'Yes. I used to do it with Peter and Felix sometimes.'

'Did you ever log into the geocaching website?'

'No. Peter always did that.'

'Did you know his password?'

'Of course not. What's this about?'

'Did you see Peter log in to the website?'

'Yes.'

'So, you or Felix could have seen his password?'

'Why would I care about his geocaching password? But yes, either of us could have seen it, I suppose, if we'd wanted to.' He froze and looked me in the eye, the first time he'd done that. 'Do you think Felix might have killed Peter?'

I didn't answer.

I stood and put my notes in my bag. I noticed a pile of books on the kitchen table. The top one was called *To Train Up a Child*. I felt a shiver of revulsion. I'd read about that book. It advocated 'training' children through a system of severe and escalating violence. I couldn't imagine for a moment they'd brought Alex up that way. 'Is that yours?' I asked.

Edward snatched the book and shoved it into a drawer in the kitchen table. 'Oh, good heavens, I told her to put it away. I don't want people thinking we believe in that nonsense.'

I gave him a questioning look.

'Oh, it's nothing,' he said. 'Grace had a few... issues. She's been seeing a therapist.'

'Oh?'

'Well, if you're interested, Grace's parents followed the teaching of a particular preacher when they brought her up.' Edward seemed relieved to be talking about something other than fraudulent patenting activities. 'It was before that book, but very similar. Her therapist asked to see the book, to understand more about the way her parents acted. You know what therapists are like. It's always about your childhood.'

Oh yes, I knew that for sure.

'How awful. I'm sorry. Are her parents still alive?'

'No, no, they're not. And she's fine, actually. Luckily she wasn't a rebellious child.'

I cringed at the sinister subtext about what happened to rebellious children.

Edward escorted me to the door. As I was leaving, Grace pulled up outside. She hopped out of her car and looked over at me. Her eyes widened and she hurried across the parking area, her feet scrunching in the gravel. She touched my arm and peered at my face. 'Inspector Dalton! Are you alright? Have you been hurt?'

I smiled at the contrast between her concern and Edward's failure even to notice my injuries. 'I'm fine,' I said. 'Thank you though.'

'Did Edward give you a drink? He can be so forgetful about—'

Edward shouted from the doorway. 'Come on, Grace.' His tone was harsh 'We need to talk. Felix has got us into an unholy mess.'

Grace set off towards the door. 'That man,' she muttered. 'He has demons inside him.'

★

The light was fading as I left Edward's house. The cloud sat so low it seemed like there was a block of concrete in the sky above the trees. The gloomy weather added to my exhaustion. I ached deep into my bones, and my head was spinning.

My mind wandered to the book on Edward's table. I'd read about it a few months ago. There had been at least three cases in America of parents following its teaching and beating children to death. Maybe that was what I'd sensed about Grace – why I'd thought she was a Stepford wife. She'd had all the rebellion beaten out of her as a child.

I arrived at Mum's, let myself in, and walked into the hall just as she emerged from her study. She gave me a warm smile, with a hint of furtiveness hiding underneath, and locked the study door.

She led me into the kitchen and gestured towards the table. I sat down, feeling prickly and hot like I was at a job interview. Mum walked to the sink and noisily filled the kettle. 'Do you want some supper, love?'

'No, I'll get some at home. Thanks.'

'You don't eat properly.' She stuck the kettle on and opened a cupboard above it, staring into it as if she'd forgotten what she was doing.

The words rose up in me and forced themselves from my mouth. 'Mum, I saw those notes you were writing yesterday. What was it about?'

She said nothing for so long I thought she was going to pretend she hadn't heard. She reached into the cupboard, rattled cups and fished out the best teapot, only to shove it back again. Finally she spoke with deliberate casualness, her back still to me. 'Sorry to disappoint you after your spying, but it was just for a short story I was writing for the book group.' She fumbled with tea bags and mugs.

'A short story?'

'Yes.'

'Really? What was the short story about? Someone who's addicted to barbiturates and joins a drug-trafficking group?'

She paused with a teaspoon in mid stir, and turned to me. 'Something like that, yes.'

I felt tearful, scared for her now and panicking that maybe there had been an intruder, maybe it was Mum they were after on those steps, maybe the boiler and the light switch had been tampered with, maybe I'd put her in danger when I was only trying to protect her. 'Mum, please tell me what's going on.'

'As I said, we decided to do a bit of creative writing in the group.

To make a change from reading books.' She stirred my tea, round and round, even though I didn't take sugar.

'I thought you said you were making notes on *Gone Girl*. Have you even read *Gone Girl*?'

'Yes, most of it.' She strode over and put two teas on the table. No table mats. That wasn't like her.

'Are you taking barbiturates, Mum? Did you start them after Carrie? How do you know about the Silk Road? What are you mixed up in?'

She scraped the chair viciously on the lino floor – she knew that drove me mad – and sat down opposite me. 'There's this thing called Google. You should check it out. It's great for researching stories.' Was this really Mum? She seemed like a stranger. 'You don't think I've actually gone on these websites, do you? How would I have any idea about that? I can barely even use a mobile phone, as you so often remind me.'

My belly churned like a concrete mixer filled with rocks. 'You would tell me, Mum, wouldn't you? If you were in trouble? After all we've been through.'

She reached across the table and put her hand on mine. 'It's just for a story, Meg. Don't worry about me, please. It doesn't affect you.' She gave me a bright smile full of fakery. 'Anyway, have you had any luck with that dating site?'

God, did I tell her about that? I didn't even remember. 'It's full of old, married men pretending to be single, lying about their age and looking for pubescent blondes.'

'You've not found anyone then?'

'You sound like Gran. Funnily enough, I don't actually need a man to complete my life.'

'You're not one of those lesbians, are you? I wouldn't mind if you were.'

I let out a sharp laugh. 'No. Sadly, my inclinations don't tend that way.'

'I often thought it would be much easier,' Mum said. 'You know, women are just… less bother to get along with.'

I smiled despite my frustration. 'I'm sure you're right, but don't think you can deflect me that easily with your surprisingly modern views. I still want to know why you were writing notes about barbiturates and the Silk Road.' I kept my tone light. 'And then lying to me about it.'

She looked into my eyes and I felt the world shifting. Mum had been the only solid, reliable thing in my life and I realised I didn't know her at all.

'Please believe me, Meg,' she said. 'I'm okay, and you don't need to worry.'

'But I do worry, Mum. What if that gas leak wasn't an accident? And the light switch. You need to tell me if you're in danger. I can do something about it.'

'Meg, don't be ridiculous. The gas man said it was wear and tear. It's my fault for not getting the thing serviced and checked. Same with the light switch. It was nothing to worry about. You've always had a tendency to over-dramatise things. You were always looking for mysteries and conspiracies even when you were a child.'

'Just because I'm paranoid doesn't mean they're not out to get you, Mum.'

'You have to accept I'm fine. Honestly, stop worrying.'

Chapter 32

The next day, I woke at five fretting about Mum. I crawled down-stairs, shoved the heating on, and set about making tea and toast for brain food. Hamlet bashed through his flap and yowled at me, pleased to see the staff up at a decent time for once. I opened *Organic chicken with rice and herbs* and left him dining while I carried my less exotic fare to the living room.

I slumped on the sofa, balancing my toast plate on its arm, and pulled the laptop off a pile of books on the coffee table. Of course I knew Mum had been lying, but short of hauling her in for question-ing, I couldn't see how to get the truth out of her. I just hoped I was wrong about the connection with Peter Hamilton.

The uncomfortable fact hovering at the edge of my consciousness was that Nembutal could be used to kill people. Mum couldn't have anything to do with killing people, but what about Kate Webster?

I stuck *Nembutal euthanasia* into Google. Yep, there it was – *the drug of choice for a quick and painless death*. Was Kate Webster getting hold of Nembutal to help people kill themselves?

Hamlet strolled in, licking organic chicken from his lips, and jumped onto the arm of my chair. With balletic grace, he walked over my toast plate, settled next to me, and purred obtrusively. I stroked him and clicked a link to an article about a recent right-to-die case. A video played and I sank back on the sofa and watched. An impeccably dressed young lawyer stood outside court, his pin-stripes gleaming in the sunshine. He spoke at the camera. 'It's wrong that this man should be forced to live a life of terrible pain, when all he wants is a dignified death. If he was able-bodied, he would be able to kill himself but the law denies him this right. It's horrifically cruel and we will fight on.'

The video flipped to the man who wanted to die. He slumped in a wheelchair, his head lolling to one side and his face slack. The man couldn't talk but his wife read a statement.

'Like Tithonus in the Greek myth, condemned to an eternal life of misery and torment, I am stuck inside my useless body, denied even the right to end my suffering.' A tear crawled down the man's face as his wife continued with a trembling voice. 'I wish those who deny me this right could spend just a day inside my body. I promise they would change their opinion.'

Tithonus. The note on the paper in Kate Webster's fire. The man who was given eternal life but not eternal youth, who was locked behind shining doors when loathsome old age pressed full upon him, who could neither move nor lift his limbs. The man who begged for death when death wouldn't come.

I grabbed a slip of paper and scribbled down the dying man's name. Could it be a coincidence that he was talking about Tithonus?

I hurriedly typed the man's name into Google. There he was. Motor neurone disease. Almost completely paralysed and getting worse by the day. A recent article reported he'd lost his case. The judges were sympathetic but were bound by the law. Any doctor who helped him die could risk fourteen years in prison.

'What's going on?' I whispered.

Hamlet stretched a paw in my direction and yawned.

I clicked a link to another article on the case. There was a quote from the man's lawyers, Templeton Law, a Nottingham firm. I peered at a tiny picture, hit 'control' and scrolled to zoom in. One of the lawyers was the pin-striped man I'd seen on the TV outside the courtroom. The other one was a woman.

I felt a chill like someone had chucked ice down the back of my neck.

It all crunched together in my mind. A group of people who helped patients die. Named after Tithonus, the wretched man cursed with eternal life. I'd finally worked out why Charity-shop-chic-girl had thought Kate was talking about typhus.

The lawyer was Beth Hamilton.

It felt like the substance of me had drained downwards, leaving my head empty. Mum was somehow involved in this. Of course I'd worked out she was up to something but it was still shocking to have it confirmed. Could this be the Sunday-night book group?

My mind shifted to accommodate this new information. It felt as if the room was spinning. I couldn't understand how Mum had got involved with this. How had she even met these people? I had to find out more.

It was still only seven o'clock, so I stuck some clothes on, jumped in the car, and set off for Mum's.

I headed out past East Mill. It was doing its full *dark satanic* number on me today, towering high above the road, its windows an ominous dark grey against the red brick. I normally found it beautiful but today it just brought to mind exploited workers and evil Victorian mill-owners. I took the road to Eldercliffe.

I pulled up outside Mum's house and opened the car door. I didn't want to get out. I sat with my eyes closed. There was a hint of smoke in the air, reminding me of those rare occasions in my childhood when Dad had decided it was a good day for a bonfire, and swept us all along with his manic enthusiasm. For a couple of hours, we'd stare into the flames and forget everything.

I found Mum in the back garden, weeding the patio, which seemed a strange thing to be doing when it was barely light. She didn't look up but I knew she'd heard me. I stood behind her, my hands scrunched into fists. 'Mum, you can stop lying to me. I've found out about *Tithonus*.' She rose slowly and turned, trowel in hand.

'Why didn't you tell me?' I said.

She clutched the trowel as if it was a weapon. 'Oh, for goodness' sake, Meg, why do you think? I was protecting my friends. A lot of people depend on us. And you're in the police.'

I wrapped my arms tightly around myself. 'Can we go inside? It's freezing out here?'

She hesitated as if wanting to make me suffer a bit longer, then wrenched open the tasteless plastic patio doors to let us into the kitchen. She strode around making tea, slamming mugs on counter-tops and bashing cupboard doors unnecessarily.

I sat at the table and crossed my arms and legs. 'You could have told me—'

She spun round. 'No, I couldn't. You'd have had to report it or risk your career. I could go to prison. What will happen to your gran if I can't look after her?'

'You could go to *prison*?'

'And the group will have to stop. And that will be a very bad thing.'

'I never knew you felt so strongly,' I said.

'I have my reasons.' She picked up the mugs and brought them to the table, sat down and looked straight at me. 'Honestly, Meg, I think if you give the matter some serious thought, you'll agree with me. People are being forced to stay alive, people who are begging to die. Have you ever seen a grown man crying because he's been suffering unbearably for twenty years and no one will allow him to end his suffering?'

I felt a chill as I remembered the man in the wheelchair outside the courtroom, tears seeping down his flaccid cheeks.

'If you did it to an animal, you'd be prosecuted for cruelty,' Mum said. 'Anyway, we decided we'd help these people. If the government won't change the law, we'll bend it a little.'

I warmed my hands on my mug. 'So, how exactly does the group work? You may as well tell me.'

Mum hesitated. 'Are you sure you want to know?'

'It's a bit late for that. Just tell me.'

She looked out of the window. 'Well, okay, you know the gist of it anyway. We have to be careful, obviously. We spread the word about ourselves very discreetly to doctors who share our views, and who have patients who want to die and aren't physically capable of committing suicide on their own. We have a website but you won't find it on Google. Peter did all that side of things.'

'Is that on the Dark Web?'

'Well, it's on a bit of the internet you can only get to if you know what you're doing. I don't really understand it.'

'And did Peter buy Nembutal from the Silk Road?'

'You've got it all worked out, haven't you? Yes, well, I think that one was shut down but others sprung up. Obviously Kate and Mark could get drugs through work but they had to be very careful. These things are monitored. So, we bought supplies online.'

So, Mark *was* involved. This explained the feeble alibis for Sunday night – they were all at the 'book group'.

I sat listening to my heart thumping, looking at this woman I hardly recognised.

I steeled myself. 'Is this something to do with Carrie?'

Neither Mum nor I had mentioned her until now, but she was there. Always there in the background, daring us to look at her. Thinking about her was like picking at a scab, except it was more like a stump where a whole limb had been severed. And I was loosening the tourniquet I'd had around it for the last twenty years.

Mum was stronger than me. She looked straight ahead. 'She asked us to help her die.' She took a breath, her face tight. 'We were selfish. We didn't want to lose her, we wanted every last second with her. Your father got angry. It was horrible. Anyway, you know what happened.'

'I didn't know she asked to die,' I whispered, wiping a tear from my face. So, maybe it wasn't my fault after all?

'She died too soon. If we'd have just said, *When you're ready, we'll help you go,* she'd probably have lived at least a few more months.

Lots of people never take the drugs we give them – they know the option's there. It allows them to carry on. If they ever can't bear it any more, it can be over.' Mum laced her fingers together and clenched her fists. 'People who don't get help, they go to Dignitas while they still can. They lose months or even years of life because they're scared to leave it too long.'

I pictured Carrie in those last few weeks. Emaciated and grey, her lovely hair all gone and her eyes huge and surrounded by shadows. 'I'm so sorry, Mum… for how it worked out.'

She sat up straight in her chair. 'Well, this is her legacy. *Tithonus*. No one who we help has to do what she did.'

'Kate, Beth, Peter and Mark all lost parents when they were young, didn't they?'

'Yes, and had to watch them suffer terribly. Mark remembers it clearly. He can't bear suffering. And Kate's father begged for death for years. He had a high neck fracture. Eventually died of pneumonia.'

'Beth was very young, wasn't she, when their mother died?'

'Yes, she doesn't really remember it well,' Mum said. 'Beth's very logical about it all. She can out-argue anyone. Most of the people against assisted dying are religious, even if the campaigning groups try to hide it. I just get impatient with them, but Beth focuses on logic.'

Mum didn't seem to know Beth was dead. I hadn't told her and it looked like neither Mark or Kate had. I hadn't the heart to break it to her now.

'I always thought you believed in God,' I said.

'I do believe in God. But he gave us free will and with that we invented medicines and so on, and we keep people alive way beyond when they would have died naturally. So, why wouldn't we use medicine to help them die when they want to? I don't see how a compassionate God could be against that. And, the thing is, if religious folk don't want to take advantage of euthanasia for themselves, that's fine – we're not trying to make them. But why should they stop others, based on their beliefs? They can believe what they like, they can believe in Santa Claus if they want, but don't use it as a reason to torture people.' She shook her head sharply. 'See, I'm getting annoyed again. I'm no good at talking to those people.'

I'd never really considered Mum's opinions about anything. Dad had opinions, I had opinions, but Mum was just Mum. She looked after everyone else. No one asked her what she thought. And all the time, she'd had these ideas – well thought-out and intelligent and brave. I felt a wave of sickness rising up in me. I'd never really *seen* her. I'd allowed her to be invisible, to fade into the background, to be defined in my mind only by her relationships with the rest of us, like so many women since the dawn of time. How could I have been so blind and self-centred?

'I've never seen this side of you.' I felt ready to cry. 'I always thought you stuck to the law.'

'You have to use your own judgement or you can end up like the Nazis.'

I swallowed and pictured Hannah sitting in her wheelchair, her lips tight as she told me people would think she wasn't worth the medical costs. 'But wouldn't old people or disabled people feel obliged to... you know... go. To save their relatives having to care for them?'

'We don't want to make it routine, love. We're happy that you'd have to apply for a court order. But at the moment, the judges' hands are tied by the law. And besides, now people feel obliged to stay alive, because they don't want their relatives to be prosecuted for murder if they help them die.'

My mouth was dry. 'Gran?'

Mum went totally still. 'If she asks.' It was so quiet I could hear her breathing. 'If she really wants it.'

I took a long, slow breath. 'So, what's your role?'

'I mainly talk to the applicants and their families. See if they meet our criteria and then if we agree to help them, I make sure they do it right. Get a video or something in writing making it crystal clear how ill they are and that they really, really want to be dead. We give it a while, check they don't change their mind. Videos are good. We keep copies of them all as evidence.'

I stood and walked to the window. 'I can't believe you've been doing all this. Secretly, without telling me.'

'I might have told you if you hadn't been in the police.'

I stared at the autumn leaves swirling above the lawn, defying gravity. I thought about the times I'd felt the darkness come over me. The desperation to be done with it all, to choose oblivion over pain. 'What about mentally ill people? Do you help them?'

'No, we refer them on to people who can help them get better. Besides, we don't help people who can easily get themselves to Beachy Head and jump off. We're just giving people who can't physically do it the same rights you or I have. If you want to commit suicide, you can do it.' I turned and looked at her, feeling myself blush. Her eyes flicked to mine and I looked away again. 'It's not illegal. Why deny that right to someone who's paralysed?'

I opened my mouth, but realised I had nothing to say.

'Would you watch some videos?' Mum said.

'That fence panel's come off again. Remind me to sort it at the weekend.'

'Come on, love. I'll make some coffee.'

I moved away from the window and trailed after Mum. She unlocked the office, ferried me in and sat me in front of her monitor. She unlocked a sturdy metal cabinet and fished out a DVD, which she stuck into the computer.

'Watch that. I'll be back in a minute.'

A video played. A man lay in a single bed in a small, white-painted room. His head was propped on pillows and a computer screen perched on a cantilever a couple of feet in front of his face. He was so still he looked like a photograph.

A woman sat on a small chair by the bed. Lank hair tangled

around sharp cheeks and hollow eyes. She spoke softly. 'He's only forty-six. He had a stroke three years ago. He's completely paralysed.'

I couldn't see Mum but heard her voice. 'And your husband wants to die?'

'Yes.' The woman's voice rasped as if she'd been shouting. 'He wants it to be legal but we can't afford to go to court. Besides, we've seen the other cases. We wouldn't win. I just want a doctor to help us – you know – do it the best way so he doesn't suffer.' She wiped her face. 'He can't even talk. Only move his eyes.'

'So, Steven, can I ask you, are you absolutely sure you want to die?' Mum's voice had exactly the right mix of compassion and practicality.

The man's eyes flicked to the screen. The camera followed them. A cursor moved between groups of letters, directed by the man's gaze. It was slow.

A robotic voice spoke. 'Y... E... Yes'. The tone of the voice was smug and inappropriate, as if it was pleased with itself for getting it right. The man's words appeared on the screen. I could see *yes*, plus words he must have said previously. *Cant go on shit life they should try it not worth living no pressure my decision had enough.*

The camera scanned back to the man's face. I could hardly imagine his frustration but of course there was little expression on his face – he couldn't move his muscles. Only his eyes flicked to and fro. The shot zoomed in to his right eye. I looked deep into it and felt a terrible heaviness in my centre. I blinked back tears.

The camera scanned around the room, to the piles of painkillers, the rubber gloves, the drip, the label on the *Nimbus advanced dynamic flotation system*, and back to the woman, who was openly crying now.

'I want to keep him alive,' she said. 'But it's for my own sake, not his. How can I know what he's going through every day? I have to respect his decision.'

The robotic voice spoke again. 'Please ... Let ... Me ... Die.'

'He wants me to take his tube out.' The camera focussed on the woman's face, her rough skin, her expression of despair. 'But

I don't want him to die like that. I want his last thoughts, his last dreams, to be of good times he had, of loved ones, not of thirst and desperation and fear.'

I jumped. Mum pushed the office door open, two cups in her hands. She placed them on the desk and stopped the video.

I picked up a coffee mug and swirled the hot drink around pointlessly. 'Did you help him die?'

Chapter 33

We moved to the kitchen and sat nursing our coffees.

I sent Jai a text to say I had a family crisis and would be late. He replied immediately.

No prob. We've got Felix. Search team found his glove near where Beth died. Will keep you posted.

'Well, it's good news on that,' I said to Mum. 'I think we've got the bugger.'

'You should go in to work.'

Part of me desperately wanted to go in; this was the good bit. We'd finally got Felix.

'They can handle it without me,' I said. 'You need to tell me what's been going on with Tithonus. Did you help that poor man die?'

'No. He's still alive.'

'Oh, God.' He was still there, now, in that bed, unable to talk, unable to move, desperate to die. He couldn't even shout or scream.

'We always wait at least a month and go back to make sure they feel the same way. He was why I went to Chester. You realised Sheila next door didn't really borrow the sat nav. I'll have to visit him again before we give the go-ahead.'

'Mum…' I wiped my eyes aggressively. 'I'm not sure I can think about him still there like that. It's too much.'

I couldn't explain. It was like when people shared pictures on

Facebook of dogs in a lorry in Korea, all rammed together, all innocent and terrified, waiting to be tortured and killed. Or a pig in a crate so small it couldn't turn round for its whole life, just so people could eat cheap bacon. Or little girls in countries where they were mutilated by their own mothers and grandmothers, and married at age twelve. And it was too much, and I'd get this feeling that I couldn't bear it, the weight of all that suffering pressing down on me, and that's when things would start spiralling into a vortex, and I had to catch myself, or I didn't know how far I'd go. I wanted to tell Mum all this but the words wouldn't come. So I just said, 'What will happen if the group gets closed down?'

'I don't know.'

'But it's illegal?'

'Yes, nobody can legally help him kill himself.'

I took a sip of burning coffee. 'Are all the videos that bad?'

Mum looked into my eyes. 'They're pretty awful. Do you want to see more?'

'Not right now.' I hugged my warm mug between my hands. 'I know it's a weird time for one, but could I have a bath?'

★

I lay in the comforting water. Steam sat heavily in the warm air, fragranced with Mum's eucalyptus bath oil. I reached forward to turn the hot tap, then flopped back, remembering something from the book *The Diving Bell and the Butterfly*, dictated (astonishingly) by a man who could only blink one eyelid. He'd talked about his nostalgia for the baths of his former life, when he'd soaked for hours, manoeuvring the taps with his toes. I imagined the horror of being bathed by a nurse, unable to move or talk, recalling a previous life taken completely for granted. How did a person cope with that? The answer was they had no choice. They were imprisoned, without even the ultimate option of choosing to die. I couldn't face watching the videos. Lucky me. I could walk away.

And then there was Carrie. Deep down, I'd still been blaming myself – that was clear. But if she'd been asking to die, maybe it wasn't my fault after all?

Memories flicked in front of my eyes like photographs in an album. The early years were in colour – the BC (before cancer) years. Images of Carrie and me, Mum and Dad, happy and normal. Dad swinging me around, me laughing like a maniac, with no idea how precious it was. Then the cancer years, in sepia tones. Hospital corridors, drips, sick buckets, doctors with their sad, sympathetic faces. Mum crying, Dad withdrawn, me in the background, being quiet for Carrie. Finally, the AD years. Black and white.

As I watched the memory images, I gently experimented with the possibility that it wasn't my fault. Tried lifting the guilt, to see what life would be like. For a few seconds, I was infused with a strange lightness, but then the guilt came flooding back over me. I didn't even know who I was without it. I sank into the hot water and closed my eyes.

★

I padded downstairs, warm from my bath, and found Mum in the living room. She'd taken one of the chairs and moved it so she could stare at the off-white wall as if it was a cinema screen.

I sat on the sofa – the same one we'd had when I was a child, with worn arms and a musty smell that reminded me of evenings in front of the TV.

'What are you doing?' I said.

'I find it calms my mind.' She swallowed. 'The nothingness of the wall.'

'Right.'

'But then you notice it's not really nothingness at all. You think it's just white but there's colours and contours in it if you look deeply enough.'

The soft light passed through the bay window from the garden and shimmered on Mum's wall, giving it a pink glow.

'Are you alright, Mum?'

'White's a funny colour. All colours and none.'

'How did it all start? You getting involved with this Tithonus group?'

She took a breath that went right into her stomach. 'After your sister died, you know, I kept blaming myself. If we'd only listened to her, she—'

'But you weren't to know, Mum. I blamed myself too. I never told you.'

She snapped her head round. 'Why on earth should you blame yourself?'

I stared down at my fingers. Long, piano player's fingers, but I'd never learnt to play the piano. 'I said something terrible.'

Mum rose from her wall-viewing chair and sat next to me on the sofa. She tucked her feet under her so she was facing half towards me. 'Come on, Meg, nothing you said would have made any difference. You were only ten.'

'I know.' The dull thunk of the dishwasher churned away in the kitchen. 'It doesn't matter, Mum. Tell me about Tithonus.'

'What were you going to say? Why did you feel guilty?'

Oh lord, why had I said that? A prickly sickness came over me. Could I really tell her? I rubbed my fingers on the worn cloth of the sofa, back and forward, forward and back.

'Go on, Meg. Tell me. And I'll tell you all about Tithonus.'

I felt a weird exhilaration. The sickness subsided. I spoke quickly before the feeling deserted me, looking at the wall again. 'Sometimes I hated her.' My voice sounded calm and unnatural, as if it was coming from somewhere far away. 'I was so jealous. I wished I was ill instead of her.'

Mum clutched the sofa as if afraid she'd blow away. She reached forward and touched my arm with her fingertips. 'Oh, Meg, I'm sorry.'

239

'She got all the attention. I had to be quiet, be good, I was invisible after she got ill.'

'It was impossible for us to get it right,' Mum whispered.

'I know. I know. I told her…'

'Go on, Meg, it doesn't matter. It won't have made any difference.'

'I told her…'

It was like standing on the edge of a cliff, watching the waves crashing on the rocks below. I was ready to jump. I took a deep, gasping breath. 'I said I wished she'd just hurry up and die.'

Mum moved up the sofa and gently touched my arm. She pulled me to her and held me tight.

'I couldn't stop thinking about it all day at school.' I spoke into Mum's shoulder. 'I rushed home to tell her I didn't mean it. And that was the day…'

'Oh no.' Mum moved away slightly and held me at arm's length. The air between us felt brittle, like it could smash. 'Oh, no, Meg, no.'

'That was the day.' I pressed my hands to my face. 'She did it because of me.'

Mum held me again, briefly, then sat back and looked at me. She took a tissue from her pocket and blew her nose loudly. 'No, she didn't. It wasn't because of you. She'd been talking about it for a while. We should have taken her seriously. She was sick of being ill, it was only getting worse. There was nothing more the doctors could do. She'd had enough, Meg.'

'Have you got another tissue?'

She foraged in her pocket and passed me a scrap of toilet paper. I took a deep breath and blew my nose.

'We should have listened to her,' Mum said. 'If she'd known we'd help her… when she was ready. She wouldn't have had to do it herself.'

'Could you really… you know, have done that?'

'Maybe not. But we should have at least considered it.'

'She didn't say goodbye.'

'I know.'

'I've always hated goodbyes. I prefer to just sneak away.'

'Well, that's what she did I suppose. She sneaked away.'

I rose and walked to the bay window. Stared at the velvet autumn lawn. I felt that peculiar lightness again.

'Can we get a coffee, Mum?'

'Yes of course.' She jumped up and we moved to the kitchen.

I sat at the table. 'You'd better tell me how you got involved with Tithonus.' It was easier to talk in here with the noise of the dishwasher dulling our words.

Mum made instant coffees and placed them gently on the table. No mats again. 'Please don't blame yourself, Meg. Is this what it's been about? Why you've been so... down?'

I sighed. The weight inside me had already lightened. 'I think so.'

'She was dying anyway, Meg. I know that sounds brutal, but it's the truth. You're alive, and I love you, and I don't want you to feel bad.'

'But Mum...'

'What she did – it was horrific. But think about the alternative. For her. And then decide if it was such a terrible thing. Or if maybe it was a blessing.'

My mind swirled and churned, trying to make sense of every-thing. Could it be a blessing to die? 'Tell me about Tithonus. Please?'

'Afterwards,' she said, 'I needed something to focus on. I started thinking about it and looking into it. Whether it's right to help someone die. If that's what they really want. I wrote an article for a magazine, about our experiences with Carrie.'

'Really? And you never told me or Dad?'

'No. And then I suppose I just forgot about it and got on with life. Then when I moved here, I heard rumours that the doctors at that surgery had a reputation for, you know, helping people, when they were ready.'

'Go on.'

'Anyway, I mentioned it to Kate Webster but of course she wouldn't tell me anything. Pretended she didn't know what I was talking about. So I told her about Carrie and showed her the article I'd written years earlier. Said I supported her. Said if there was anything I could do to help, to let me know. I wasn't expecting it to come to anything, I just wanted her to know she had... Oh I don't know, that I was behind what she was doing.'

'And, what, she asked you to be part of her group?'

'No. Not at first. We kept in touch. The group sort of evolved. We all have to be very careful.'

'How many people have you helped to die?'

Mum tapped her fingers on the pine table. 'Not that many. Quite a few have the drugs but haven't taken them.'

'But what'll happen to you if you get found out?'

'It's okay, Meg. I know you have to report this.'

'You won't go to prison, will you? You've only helped people who were dying anyway. I know it's illegal but judges are lenient, aren't they?'

'It doesn't matter. You can't risk your career. You have to tell your boss about this.'

'Just tell me what you think will happen.'

'Well, I don't know for sure.' She looked at the table. 'It's not... It's not that clear cut. We've helped some people who weren't terminally ill. A young man paralysed in a rugby game, a deaf man who was going blind.'

'But how did you know they wouldn't change their minds in the future?'

'We didn't. Not with absolute certainty. Mark's vet says to pet owners, *Better a month too early than a day too late.* It's better to prevent suffering than to prolong life for the sake of it. And I agree.'

'With animals, yes. But, for people... Oh, I don't know, Mum. Not everyone's going to agree with you there.'

'I know. And, well, there's another thing that complicates it.'

'What, Mum, tell me?'

A red flush crept up her neck to her face. 'A few people have left money in their wills. To Kate.'

'Money? Why just Kate? Why not all of you?'

'I don't really know. I guess she befriended them more. She says she's going to give it away. But it looks bad. It looks bad for the whole group. If you did this for personal gain, a judge would take a dim view, obviously. Not that Kate did. It's just how it looks.'

'Jesus, Mum, what have you got into? Are you saying you could go to prison?'

She didn't reply.

'If you go to prison… oh my God. And what about Gran?'

'I've always done what I thought was right.'

'But what if the rest of the group aren't so scrupulous? What if they *have* been doing it for personal gain? You don't know for sure.'

'Well, we're all in it together.'

'You're right,' I said. 'I do have to report it.'

I jumped up, strode into the hallway and grabbed my phone from my coat pocket. My finger hovered over the keypad. I felt a knot of anger in my chest. How could she have done this? If Mum went to prison… I couldn't bear to think about it. And what about Gran? Who would look after her? I couldn't possibly care for her and work. I remembered when she'd first been diagnosed with stomach cancer. I'd spent an almost unbearable few hours on the internet researching what would happen. I'd read a horrific story by a man whose wife had suffered in agony at the end, the man tormented that he'd prioritised their wedding over the trip to Dignitas she'd requested. What if Gran ended up like that? Dying in agony because I'd turned in the only people with the courage to help her.

I walked back to the kitchen and dropped my phone on the table. 'I can't do it. You haven't the first idea what prison would be like. And what about Gran? I can't do it.'

The phone rang. Jai. I picked up instinctively.

'We've got some question marks over it being Felix. There should be CCTV if he left his office on that Sunday night, and there isn't.

243

And we've got some concerns about Kate. They found searches on her computer. She's been googling about drugs that can be used to kill people.'

'Oh. Jai, that might not be...'

'What?'

Now was the time to tell him. I had to tell him. I could be holding back the investigation. Why wasn't I telling him? It was as if, having made the decision two minutes ago, my commitment to it was now solid. I knew the psychology, knew what my brain was doing to me. But it didn't change anything. I thought of Gran. 'Nothing, Jai. Sorry. I'll catch up with it all tomorrow. I'll be in early.'

'It's fine. I'll fill you in then.'

I placed the phone gently on the table and sunk into my chair, stunned at the enormity of what I'd done. I'd compromised a murder investigation. My insides were twitching like a dying fish.

'You should have told him,' Mum said.

'I know.' I pictured Gran's tiny body; Steven's eyes flicking to and fro in his little white room. 'I couldn't do it.'

I spent the rest of the day with Mum, watching more videos and talking about Tithonus, and a little about Carrie and Dad.

I eventually bedded down in the spare room, wearing one of Mum's T-shirts, at 2am.

I woke to the sound of the phone early the next morning. I broke free from the tangled sheets and pressed the handset to my ear. Jai's voice came through the speakers so loud I had to hold the phone away from my head.

'Meg. Rosie's gone missing!'

Chapter 34

I slammed the phone back to my ear. 'What? What do you mean she's missing?'

Jai's words tumbled out on top of one another. 'She didn't come home last night. And we can't locate Kate Webster either. I think Kate might have killed Peter and Beth, and now she's taken Rosie too.'

I felt a jolt of adrenaline like an electric shock. 'Kate?'

'She left work on Sunday earlier than she said. She could have pushed Beth off that cliff. And the stuff the geeks found on her laptop. She'd searched how to get hold of cyanide.'

I threw the sheets off and stood, my mind whirring and swirling with all yesterday's revelations. 'Hang on a minute, Jai. That might not be...' My brain was fogged up. I gave my head a shake and winced at the pain.

'She'd deleted her search history but they found it eventually. She was looking at how painful it is to die of potassium cyanide poisoning.'

I felt a rising panic that I hadn't told anyone about the group yesterday. 'Jai, that might not be about killing Peter.'

'What do you mean? He died of bloody cyanide poisoning, and she's googling it. It's nearly always the spouse. Why didn't we see it?'

I started pulling on underwear with one hand. I was going to have to tell him. I hesitated, picturing Steven's hollow eyes, his wife's desperation. But no, it had gone too far now. 'I've found out Kate's part of a group.' I stood on one foot, dragging on one of yesterday's socks. 'A group with doctors and a lawyer.' I lost my balance and fell onto the bed. 'They seem to have been getting hold of illegal drugs to help people die.'

'Oh God, that doesn't sound good.'

'People who are really ill, though. It doesn't mean she killed her husband.'

'Sounds pretty bad to me, Meg.'

'I know. Yes, it does now. God.'

'When did you find this out? Why didn't you tell anyone?'

'I know, I know.' I could hear blood rushing in my ears. 'I'm coming in. I need to see Richard.'

I ended the call and collapsed backwards onto Mum's super-soft guest bed. A wave of sickness washed over me. I'd been so focussed on Felix, I'd allowed myself to overlook Kate. Maybe she was the killer. And now she could have Rosie. If I'd reported her murder-group yesterday when I first discovered it… I rose and stumbled around the bedroom in the grey dawn light, putting on the rest of last night's clothes. I'd always known I was going to be found out eventually and now it had happened. It wasn't Imposter Syndrome after all. I really was incompetent. My judgement was off. I'd protected my mum, who I realised I barely knew, and now a girl could be dead because of it.

I smeared toothpaste around my mouth and splashed water on my face, which was tinged with yellow and green bruises. My head was throbbing and I was on the edge of tears. I shouted a goodbye to my confused mother and left the house.

I sat for a minute in the car, hands on the wheel, eyes staring, then took a breath and set off. I headed straight for work, knowing if I went home I wouldn't get myself out of the house again. I had to come clean before I thought any more about the consequences for Mum and Gran.

The hills were particularly beautiful that morning. The sun

shone on the peaks, but mist had settled in the valleys and draped itself over the lower hills like a white tablecloth. In contrast, the Station had never looked more dreary. I parked and limped into the building and straight to Richard's office before I could change my mind.

I pushed the door closed behind me, and it shut with a dull thud. I knew I was defeated when I sat voluntarily in the chair. It smelt of stale sweat – or maybe that was me.

Richard looked surprised. I wasn't sure if it was at my presence, my appearance, or my choice of seating. Jai clearly hadn't told him about the group.

I explained about Tithonus. Richard's face became redder and damper as my tale progressed. I finished with a little shrug.

Richard wheeled himself forward on his fancy chair and tweaked one of his piles into perfect alignment. 'So, our prime suspect has been obtaining lethal drugs illegally?' He fixed me with a stare that could have drilled concrete.

I cleared my throat. 'Well, I wouldn't say she was the prime suspect. I'd say Felix was the prime suspect. But the victim's wife, yes.'

'And you found out about this when?'

I was sinking into the chair. 'Yesterday morning. But she wasn't buying cyanide.'

'Bloody hell, Meg, you can't know that.' He picked up a cactus and hurled it onto the floor. It splatted onto its side, spewing tiny lumps of soil. It was strangely sad. 'You know she's gone missing, as has the first victim's illegitimate child?'

I nodded. 'So I understand.'

So I understand, for God's sake. Did I think I was going to get out of this by talking like a lawyer?

'And you put the information on HOLMES? About this killing group?'

'Not yet.'

The tendons in Richard's arms stretched like metal wires under

247

his skin. 'And you say your mother's a member of this group? So you were protecting her.'

'I suppose so.'

'You know I'm going to have to suspend you, don't you?'

I thought about all the lectures we'd been given. *Honesty and integrity is key. It's okay to make mistakes if you admit to them.* I could have argued my case, but I didn't have the energy or conviction. Besides, he was right – I should have said something yesterday. I'd prioritised my own family over the investigation. I nodded, feeling like I'd been kicked in the stomach.

I hauled myself out of the chair, left Richard's office, and shuffled into the toilets. Every bit of me hurt, from my brain to my toes.

I let myself into a cubicle, locked the door behind me, flipped down the lid of the toilet, and sank onto it. I folded my upper body forward onto my thighs and sat staring at the floor, a huge emptiness opening up inside me. Suspended. Dad would be so ashamed if he found out. I could never tell him. Tears clogged my eyes.

I knew if I cowered much longer in the cubicle, I'd hear someone talking about me, so I let myself out and hurried down the corridor towards the exit.

My vision smeared with tears, I thudded into a body.

'Whoa, Meg!'

It was Jai. I tried not to look at him. I couldn't handle sympathy.

'I can't believe you didn't report that group immediately,' he said.

I looked up. 'What did you say?' I tried to shuffle towards the door but he blocked me.

'They were *killing* people, Meg.'

It was like another kick in the stomach. I leant against the wall of the corridor. 'People who were begging to die.'

'But it's wrong.'

This wasn't Jai. It was like he'd been taken over by an alien. I straightened and looked him in the eye, anger bubbling inside me. 'Why's it wrong, Jai? Come on, tell me.'

He hesitated. 'Well, it's illegal for a start. And it's wrong to play God.'

I shoved past him, then turned to look at his unreadable face. 'I'll tell you what's wrong. You telling me you've let go of all that religious crap when you clearly haven't. Some poor bastard who can't even move, who can only blink one fucking eyelid, and you want to keep him alive, to torture him. Where was God when he had his stroke aged forty-three? Tell me that. Actually, don't. Just fuck off.'

I ran to my car, choking back a sob.

I fumbled for my keys and threw myself into the driver's seat, desperate to get away from anyone who might see me. I turned the key and the car stuttered and then died. I swore and smacked the steering wheel, tears misting my vision. I shouted a few threats and tried the ignition again, and the car started. I shoved it into gear and accelerated away.

The day was the opposite of my mood – rich with autumn colours, the leaves red and gold and the sun glistening on the damp road. I drove slowly, eyes fixed straight ahead, hands clamped on the steering wheel. I couldn't believe Jai had turned on me. I couldn't rely on anyone. First my mum, now Jai. What was the point of it all?

Back home, I did my room checks and crawled into bed fully clothed. There was a part of me that always screwed up my life – that didn't even want a life – and she'd taken charge. I'd not seen her for a while. The other part – Sane-and-Functional-Meg – was watching with a kind of dispassionate interest. She knew a whole armoury of psychological tricks and techniques to feel better, but they weren't coming out today. Fuck-Up-Meg was in control again. I fished my sleeping pills out of the bedside drawer. Five left. I took them all.

Chapter 35

Something was ringing in my dream. And Hannah was there. I was gazing up at her as if from under water. She was drifting further away. The ringing was coming closer. I tried to focus. Hannah was talking about her friend – the one who could no longer move. This mattered somehow. But the ringing was too loud. Hannah's lips were moving but I couldn't hear any more. She faded away. I forced my eyes open. The light was painfully bright. I closed them again. The ringing battered my ears. I pulled the duvet over my head.

It was inconceivable that I could answer the phone. It was as if I was hearing it through layers of glass and there was simply no possibility of getting myself to the receiver, never mind speaking. My answer-phone message came on, sounding like somebody else completely. How had I managed that? Then Jai's voice. 'Meg, pick up. I'm worried about you. Please. Pick up.'

I didn't pick up. But when he hung up, I crawled up onto my knees and squinted at the phone. I'd slept through eight calls and five answer-phone messages.

I collapsed back into bed and shut my eyes. The full horror of the situation swam into my consciousness. Rosie was missing. Kate could be a murderer. If she killed Rosie after I'd found out about the death group, it was my fault. I rolled into a foetal position and put my head under the pillow.

The phone rang. I pressed the pillow to my ear.

A muffled voice left an answer-phone message. 'I'm coming round.' I felt a wave of sickness. It was Jai. 'And I know the safe code for your spare key.'

Shit, shit. I shoved the pillow aside, hauled myself into a sitting position and looked into the mirror beside my bed. I winced at my swollen eyes and green-tinged skin. Maybe he was bluffing, trying to get me to pick up the phone. But he didn't ring again.

I lowered my feet experimentally to the floor. A wave of nausea came over me. I ran to the bathroom and retched into the toilet, bashing my forehead on the toilet seat. I clawed my way up to the basin, swilled and brushed my teeth, then found myself retching again. What the hell did they put in those sleeping pills?

Jai couldn't see me like this. I brushed my teeth again, staggered back into the bedroom and pulled on clean knickers and jeans, a stretchy bra and a white T-shirt, trying to make myself feel clean. Then collapsed panting onto the bed again. I didn't have time for a shower and didn't think I could stand for that long without vomiting. Shame, because I must have smelled shocking.

I lowered myself downstairs, clutching the banister. Why were my knees now hurting as well as my face, head and hand? It was cold downstairs. I twiddled the thermostat in the hall, more in hope than expectation, and made my way to the kitchen to put the kettle on.

The door-bell rang. I tucked my hair behind my ears, smoothed down my T-shirt, walked purposefully down the hallway, and pulled open the door.

Jai pushed into the house. 'Fucking hell, Meg, why didn't you answer the phone?'

'You'd better come in,' I said, even though he already had.

What to say, what to say. Whilst it genuinely didn't matter to me at that moment whether I lived or died, it did matter that Jai didn't see how screwed up I was. Why hadn't I rehearsed a convincing lie?

I walked towards the kitchen. 'I think my phone must have gone wrong. The first call I heard was this morning. Sorry.'

'Why didn't you bloody answer it then?'

'Oh, er, I was in the bathroom and by the time I saw the message I figured you'd be nearly here.'

'Right.'

'Sit down,' I said, waving vaguely at the kitchen table and chairs. 'I'll make tea. Have they found Rosie?' I put tea bags in cups and peered at him sideways from the corner of one eye, as if this would help if it was bad news.

'They're still looking. You don't look well.'

'Yeah, you know… bruises. They go all yellow and green before they get better. I'm okay.'

'I'm sorry about what I said.'

'It doesn't matter.'

'No, it does. You were only protecting your family.'

A wave of self-loathing came over me. 'Yeah. Cos that's what people do, isn't it? Fuck everyone else.'

'Don't beat yourself up, Meg.'

I let out a slightly crazy laugh. 'Why not? I was selfish and dishonest, and now a girl could be in danger. Why shouldn't I beat myself up? I put my own family first. All my supposed morals and values – it was all for nothing when it really came to it.'

'It's only natural to look after your mum and your gran, Meg.'

A huge anger welled up inside me, not just at myself but at humans in general, evolved beyond our level of competence, full of lofty ideals we couldn't stick to. 'Yeah. We look after our own.' I didn't know why I was banging on at poor Jai. I realised I was standing over him and waving my arms around. But I couldn't seem to stop. 'It's like when you read arguments in favour of vivisection. It's always, *So, you crazy anti-vivisectionist, would you sacrifice your granny for a rat?* Well, no. But what about *a* granny for *your* rat? Someone else's granny or your dog? It's not about *a* granny versus *a* rat. It's about *yours* versus *someone else's*. We're all selfish shits when it comes to it. Would I sacrifice my cat for a random granny? No, I fucking wouldn't.'

Jai frowned. 'Are you okay? I should have supported you. Anyway, I—'

252

'You know I'm suspended.'

Jai looked at his feet and nodded almost imperceptibly. I planted the mugs on the table and sat opposite him, hoping he couldn't smell me. I felt calmer after my ridiculous rant.

The wisteria smacked against the kitchen window like someone trying to get in. It was raining again, in horizontal sheets. A trickle ran down the inside of the window from a leaky frame or dodgy lintel or something.

'They've predicted a storm,' Jai said. 'The edge of Hurricane something or other.'

'Great. That's more tiles off the roof and rain in the attic. They always give them such innocuous-sounding names, don't they? Apparently more people get killed when they call them girly names. They don't take them seriously. How fucking retarded are people?'

Jai smiled uncertainly, as if he was dealing with a dangerous lunatic. 'They should call them all Hurricane Adolf,' he said. 'Or Hurricane Osama.' He must have decided to humour me.

'Or call them all Hurricane Daisy and let the sexist morons die. Natural selection.'

'Are you sure you're alright?'

'I don't blame Richard,' I said. 'He couldn't do anything else. Have they found Kate?'

'Not yet.'

'Are there any clues where she's gone?'

Jai bashed his heel repeatedly against the wooden chair leg. 'I'm not supposed to be talking to you about it, Meg. Richard says you need a rest. Get away from it all.'

'I don't need a rest,' I said. 'It doesn't help being stuck here feeling useless. Did Rosie leave any clues on social media? When did she disappear? Has she got a boyfriend? Do you really think Kate's got her?'

'I really don't know. They're doing all the usual stuff, combing the area, they've put out an appeal. She's been gone a while now. Since Thursday evening.'

I slumped in my chair. 'Do you think she found out Peter was her father?'

Jai shrugged. 'I should go...'

'Jai...'

He looked at me, all wide-eyed concern.

'Oh, nothing.'

'Meg, are you all right? Why don't you go over to your...' He broke off and rubbed his nose.

'You've remembered my mum's conspiring with the prime suspect?'

'Yeah, okay.'

The dream from this morning slipped into my brain. Hannah's friend. Something about genetic diseases. Something important. 'Did you find out any more about Lisa Bell's company? I'm not convinced Hamilton had schizophrenia. There's more to this—'

'Meg, you're supposed to be having a rest. And you're suspended.'

Resting was the worst thing for me now. Resting could kill me.

'Go on. I'm fine. Really.'

He hadn't even taken his coat off. I was shivering in my white T-shirt. I saw him to the door and closed it behind him with a click, before heading back upstairs. I'd thought he was a friend, but he was just a colleague. I shuffled under the covers, closed my eyes, grabbed a pillow and wished I had more sleeping pills.

I was slipping down. I recognised this state. I had to catch myself before I sank too low. I had to save Rosie.

Sometimes I had lucid nightmares – realised I was dreaming and needed to wake up to escape the nightmare, but waking was like clawing myself from a vat of tar. This was the same. It took hard, physical force to make my eyes open. The lids seemed to have weights attached. I did it though. Raised my leaden body and propped myself on pillows. My laptop was by the bedside. I reached for it and pulled it slowly onto my chest. It felt twice its usual weight.

I had to stop the bad thoughts. The best thing for me now was to concentrate on the case, if only I could make my brain work. I had to save Rosie. Kate hadn't taken her – why had I allowed myself to believe that? Something else was going on. Peter Hamilton hadn't been suffering from schizophrenia.

Lisa Bell's company was called Pharma-Kinetica. I clumsily typed the name into Google. An expensive-looking website popped up. I blinked and tried to get my exhausted eyes to focus. The website discussed the development of treatments for *orphan diseases*. These were rare conditions. I felt a tingling in my fingers.

Deep in the website I found reference to drugs for *hyperkinetic movement disorders*. The experimental drug Peter had taken was for a movement disorder. We'd been assuming it was the beginnings of schizophrenia. But the curse was something else – something genetic that had blighted Peter's family for generation after generation, something even worse than schizophrenia, something neither an ancient healer nor the best of modern medicine could help. And finally there it was.

Chapter 36

I popped into a sitting position, my lethargy evaporating, and stared at the laptop, my heart beating fast.

Huntington's Disease. A genetic disorder that affected muscle coordination, getting worse and worse over time and eventually leading to death. The early symptoms included personality changes, mood swings, fidgety movements, irritability and altered behaviour.

I wiped the laptop's screen, which was reflecting the morning light back at me, and clicked to another web page. Could Huntington's explain Peter's behaviour? It typically came on in mid-adult life and seemed to fit his symptoms.

I searched my sluggish memory for the name of the other drug Peter had been taking. ABILIFY. I googled *ABILIFY Huntington's* and held my breath while I read that ABILIFY was used for the chorea (abnormal movements) associated with Huntington's, and was often used in the early stages of the disease.

I threw off the covers. Sweat prickled my back. These symptoms sounded just like the ones Peter had exhibited – and that Kate had interpreted as schizophrenia. I remembered her saying in our first meeting that Peter had been drinking but denying it. Staggering when he stood up. The staggering could have been caused by Huntington's and he could have been telling the truth about not drinking. Felix might not have pushed him in the StairGate incident. And the experimental drug could have been for Huntington's

– someone with that disease would have been desperate to try anything.

So, where did that leave Rosie? If she was Peter's daughter… Even though I'd only met her a few times, I couldn't bear the thought of her having this disease. I clicked page after page, frantically reading the horrifying words. The gene was dominant, so any child of an affected person had a fifty percent chance of inheriting the disease. About six percent of cases started before age twenty-one. What had Rosie said on the stairs? *There's something wrong with me but nobody knows what it is.*

I lay back on my pillows, feeling sick and panicky. The prognosis for Juvenile Huntington's was appalling. If she had it, she'd go into a slow decline, gradually losing movement until she could no longer walk or move her arms, and eventually couldn't talk or swallow. Finally, she'd be unable even to breathe and would die, probably in her twenties or thirties.

I pictured Rosie in Grace's kitchen, rolling her eyes at Alex. I couldn't accept this as her fate. Although I knew it was ridiculous, I wished again that I'd lied about the probabilities in the card game, and made her think she was right. I could at least have given her that.

I shoved the laptop aside and stood, feeling the room spin as if I was drunk. I needed to go and talk to Olivia. If Peter had been showing early signs of Huntington's and Rosie had found out, who knows how she might have reacted. Maybe it could help us find her.

The task of dragging myself to Olivia's felt impossible, but I decided to take it one step at a time. I could abort at any point. I stood and tried not to think about the fit Richard would have when he found out.

My mobile rang. Fiona. I hesitated, then pulled it to my ear.

'Meg, it's Craig. Don't hang up.'

My knees softened and I sank back down on the bed. 'Craig. Hello.'

'I borrowed Fiona's phone. I didn't think you'd take my call.'

'Could be right there, Craig.'

'Well. I wanted to say… I'm sorry you were suspended.'

'What?'

'I thought it was unfair. Anyway, I'll see you when you get back. Bye.'

'Hang on, Craig...' But the phone had already gone dead.

What was that all about? Was it a figment of my imagination? He could have been playing evil games with me but he'd sounded genuine. I realised I was feeling a little more positive. The task of getting out of the house and over to Olivia's felt slightly less monstrous.

★

I pulled up at the end of Olivia and Felix's lane, feeling like I'd run a marathon. I put on my most waterproof raincoat, hauled myself from the car, and crept on a puddled footpath which led to the back of the house, to avoid being seen by any other detectives. I paused to quell a wave of sickness, then walked past a window towards the kitchen door. Olivia must have seen me through the rain-smeared glass and she flung the door open.

Her voice was high and desperate. 'Have you found her?'

I shook my head quickly. 'I'm sorry.'

Her shoulders sank and she backed into the kitchen, waving me in after her.

I walked in and saw Grace Swift, Edward's wife, sitting in one of the chairs. She smiled and jumped up.

'Inspector Dalton. Is there news?'

I gave another shake of my head.

Grace wilted. 'Oh. I'm so sorry.' She glanced at Olivia. 'I'm sure they'll find her soon. If there's anything I can do—'

Olivia's voice was flat. 'It's fine. Thank you, Grace. It was good of you to come over.'

Olivia's hair was tangled, and make-up was smeared around her eyes. She gestured towards the chunky wooden seats at her farmhouse table. I sat down and dripped rainwater onto the kitchen floor.

'Well, I'd better go.' Grace gave Olivia a rather awkward hug. She turned to me. 'You don't need to ask me anything, I assume?' Worry lines creased the skin around her eyes. 'I haven't seen Rosie since last week.'

'Have you seen Kate Webster at all? Peter's wife?'

'No, not for weeks. Why?'

'Don't worry,' I said. 'We'll be in touch if we need to talk to you.'

The door from the hallway crashed open, banging against my chair, and Felix took a step into the kitchen. He obviously didn't notice me; I was sitting behind him, partially shielded by the door. He shot a look at Grace. 'I suppose you knew.'

Olivia's voice was contemptuous. 'Of course she didn't know.'

Grace shuffled closer to the external door. 'Know what?'

'What my bitch of a wife hadn't bothered to tell me. That my daughter isn't actually my daughter.'

Grace stuttered. 'No... I didn't have any idea...'

'Well, she knows now,' Olivia said. 'You stupid bastard.'

Felix spun round and lunged with his hand outstretched towards Olivia's neck. She jumped up and backed away.

I leapt from my chair. 'That's enough, Felix.'

He froze and then pivoted to me. 'What the fuck are you doing here?' He turned to Olivia and spat the words at her. 'This bitch tried to frame me. Put one of my gloves in the woods near where Peter's idiot sister fell off the cliff.'

I ignored Felix and walked to Olivia. I touched her arm. 'You don't have to tolerate this, Olivia. He has no right to do this.' Her scarf had fallen to the floor and I saw the bruise on her neck, yellow and green.

Felix stood rigid, his breathing fast and audible. He fixed me with his reptilian eyes, and spoke with slow, measured menace. 'Why don't you get out of our business, or I'll call your boss.'

A brief panic – did he know I was suspended? I guessed not. It was just bravado from a habitual bully. 'Be my guest. He'll want to talk to you about assaulting your wife anyway. You'll save me a call.'

Felix advanced towards me. 'You fucking interfering—'

I stood my ground, trying to keep my voice firm. 'I can have uniformed police here in thirty seconds. With handcuffs. They're right outside your house. Would you like me to call them?' I sincerely hoped he wasn't going to say *Yes*.

Felix hesitated, glanced at Grace standing open-mouthed by the door, and shot me a look of the purest loathing. He stormed from the kitchen.

Olivia collapsed onto her chair. Grace rushed to her. 'Are you okay?'

Olivia nodded. 'I'm fine, Grace, honestly, I'm used to him. His bark's worse than his bite. You should go.'

'Don't worry, Grace,' I said. 'I'll make sure she's alright.'

'Well, if you're sure...' Grace smiled nervously and disappeared through the back door.

'She brought me one of her stupid bloody magazines,' Olivia said. 'As if that's going to help.' She picked up a magazine and flung it across the table. 'Look at the lead article.'

I reached for the magazine. Bright red letters stood out over a picture of a man and a woman standing hand in hand and gazing wistfully at the camera. 'When God Challenges Us.' It was another *Life Line* magazine, an older edition than the one featuring the godly business woman.

'For Christ's sake.' Olivia snatched the magazine from me and hurled it over her shoulder. She was acting as if the incident with Felix had never happened.

'Olivia, you can get help,' I said gently. 'You don't have to put up with it.'

'I know. I know. I will. I've seriously had enough. All this... It's put everything in perspective. But right now, I need to find Rosie.'

'I understand. Just be aware it's abuse and it's a crime.' Our eyes met and a flash of understanding passed between us. I remembered her shining out of Peter's Cambridge photographs, and wondered how it had all gone so wrong.

'Anyway,' I said. 'As you say, we need to find Rosie. I came round because we're trying to work out more about what was going on in her life.'

'I've already told your people everything I know. They've searched our whole house. What do they think? That we're hiding her in the attic?' Olivia tapped her fingers fast against the table and leant forward. 'And wanting to know if she's *vulnerable*. Of course she's bloody vulnerable. She's fifteen. She's not the sort of girl to run off. She must have been taken. Or had a terrible accident.'

'Rosie was having some health problems, wasn't she? Did you find out what was wrong with her?'

The tapping stopped. 'The doctor didn't know.'

'Did he mention genetic diseases at all?'

She spoke slowly. 'He asked us if there was anything in the family but there wasn't.'

'I know this is hard,' I said. 'But did Peter ever talk to you about Huntington's Disease?'

Olivia froze. 'No! Rosie does not have Huntington's.'

'Olivia, please. It might be relevant.'

She put her head in her arms and her shoulders shook. I sat pathetically across the table, not sure how to react. Should I put my arm round her?

'I'm so sorry.' I stayed put.

She looked up. Mascara trailed down both cheeks. 'Peter was talking about it.' She spoke so quietly I could hardly hear. 'A few times, Rosie's legs went rigid and then collapsed from under her. And once she had a kind of fit.'

'Oh my God.'

I looked down and noticed the magazine sprawled on the floor. I read the other headline articles. It certainly didn't look like a comforting read. 'Bringing up Godly children in modern times', 'Balancing work, family and God', 'Care, not killing,', 'How to be a good Christian wife'. Something about the phrase 'good Christian wife' made me shudder. What would a good Christian wife do when her husband tried to strangle her?

Olivia gulped. 'And she's been feeling so down about everything. . .'

'Does she know about Peter's suspicions?'

'No, of course not.'

'What if she found out? Could it have anything to do with her disappearing?'

'Oh God,' Olivia said. 'Do you think she overheard me talking to Mark?'

'Peter's brother?'

'Yes, I asked him about it.' She clawed at her knotted hair. 'It was just before she disappeared. But I was sure she was in the shower. Do you think she heard? If she googled it. Oh Jesus...'

'Have you heard from Kate Webster?'

'No. Why?'

'We're having trouble locating her too.'

Olivia brightened a little. 'She's a doctor, isn't she? Do you think Rosie contacted her to ask about the Huntington's and then they've gone off somewhere together?'

I decided not to share Kate's new status as Prime Suspect.

Chapter 37

I sat in the car at the end of Olivia's lane and called Jai. 'Any sign of Rosie?'

'No, we're combing the area.' I could hardly hear him above the noise of the rain smacking on the roof of the car. 'But Meg, I'm not supposed to be talking to you. Have a rest.'

'I don't want a rest, Jai. Listen, I think Peter might have had Huntington's Disease. And that means Rosie could have it too, if she is his daughter. Just get them to look at her laptop – was she googling Huntington's? What if she guessed that she has it?'

'You think it's relevant?'

'If she found out she had a terminal disease? Of course it's relevant. She's had no help or counselling or anything. She'll be feeling utterly desperate. And, Jai, Felix is abusive. Olivia could be in danger from him.'

I hung up, unsure whether Jai had listened to any of that, or had dismissed it as the deranged ramblings of a madwoman. For once, I wasn't feeling sorry for myself or my family. This was so much worse. If Peter had developed the early stages of Huntington's, his behaviour started to make sense – taking the experimental drugs, setting up the permanent health insurance, losing his judgement at work, even reading Stoic philosophy. If he knew he was dying, could it have also made him want to come clean about the boy on the roof in Cambridge? And what about the Rosie situation?

He must have seen her having problems. I could only imagine the horrific realisation that she might be his child and could have the condition. But it still didn't explain why he was found dead in a cave, or where Rosie was.

I wiped my face with the back of my hand and stuck the car in gear. I knew who I needed to talk to.

It looked like Jai had been right about the storm. As I headed north, the wind buffeted the tiny car and rain came down in sheets, obscuring the hills. The effort of staying on the road filled my brain.

Twenty minutes later, I parked outside Peter's father's house and ran to the door, hair flying.

Mrs Brown let me in and muttered about the shocking weather while she led me through to the gloomy living room.

Laurence didn't even look up. His head was slumped forward onto his chest. The rats were in the cage this time, digging holes in their sawdust.

Whilst I was full of pity for this poor man who'd lost two children, I had to get the information from him as quickly as possible. 'Is there Huntington's in your family?' I said.

He raised his head slowly and frowned at me, the folds in his face deepening. 'What makes you say that?'

'Did you know Peter had a daughter?'

'What?' He took a cotton handkerchief from his pocket and wiped his face. 'Has she... ?'

'Has she got Huntington's? I don't know. She's only fifteen, and she's gone missing.'

'Oh no, no. My mother's right. This is a curse.'

'Did Peter know? What about Mark? And Beth?'

'What do you mean she's gone missing?'

'We're looking for her. Did Peter know about the Huntington's?'

He spoke quietly into his chin. 'He realised about a year ago. I thought it kindest not to tell them when they were young. You don't understand unless you've lived with it.'

'You kept it from them?'

'You think I don't feel terrible?' Laurence grasped a chunk of his fleshy stomach. 'Why do you think I'm like this? It's a punishment. My guilt embodied.'

'So, your sons and daughter didn't know until recently?' I tried to imagine what it must have been like for Laurence. Keeping a secret that big. It was as if his body had expanded to cope with the magnitude of the deception.

'I thought they could have at least half a normal life, without this horrific sword of Damocles hanging over them. How do you tell your children they have a fifty percent chance of a ghastly premature death, just like their mother?'

'But didn't aunts and uncles die too? They must have noticed lots of illness in the family?'

'Lily was an only child. They knew her father had died young but it wasn't unusual in that generation. It was a small family. Luckily, they never asked to do a family tree.'

'But what if they'd had children? Without knowing?'

'I kept meaning to tell them… It was never the right time. They all seemed happy. I was going to tell them if ever they talked about having children. But none of them did. Who's this girl? I can't bear it.'

'She's Felix's daughter. Only it seems she may actually be Peter's daughter.'

He let out a tiny puff of breath that seemed to contain a lifetime of sadness. 'My God. Is she showing signs?'

'Maybe.'

He put his head in his hands and let out a low groan, like an animal in pain.

'Did you know Kate's pregnant?' I said gently.

'Oh, it's too much. My mother… she was rambling. I thought she was confused. Does Kate know?'

'She's disappeared.'

Laurence sank deeper in his seat, his folds of fat spreading as if they were melting. 'I've messed up everything,' he said, his voice rough. 'I thought it was for the best. I just wanted them to have normal lives for a while, after losing their mother. And it was different a few years ago. People were ashamed, discriminated against. You know it used to be called the Witchcraft disease, and even when I was a child, they were talking about compulsory sterilisation.'

Witchcraft. The young woman in Piers's diary who was accused of being a witch. The sister who turned against her was married to the accuser. The supposed witch must have had the disease, and her sister must have had it too, but showed signs later. She'd passed it on to some of her eight children, who'd passed it on to the subsequent sufferers under the 'curse'. Poor Piers Hamilton must have had it too. No wonder his carving didn't work. And the man who'd sketched the images of the Grim Reaper. He'd probably had it too, and committed suicide.

'The Grim Reaper... and the curse... it was all about this.'

'Look, if I'd told them, they might not have been able to get life insurance, mortgages – even getting a job can be hard. And most people who know they're at risk don't want to find out if they'll get it. So, I figured people prefer not to know.'

I had read this. Most people who knew they had a fifty percent chance of having the disease chose not to take the test. Laurence had a point. But he should have told us last week.

'So, you knew exactly what your mother was talking about with the curse,' I said. 'That's why you didn't want me to talk to her.'

'Mark asked me not to say anything. It would give the life insurance company an excuse not to pay out. Mark said he and Kate have started a charity to help sick people. He said she was going to put the insurance money towards it. It was a huge amount of money – I wanted it to go to them.'

'This could be relevant to Peter's death. And possibly Beth's too. We've been conducting this whole investigation in the dark.'

'I just did as Mark asked. What does it matter anyway? They're both dead now.'

★

The gravel outside Mark Hamilton's house had turned to a river bed. A wide ribbon of water flowed past his house and towards his barn. I parked in the shallowest spot and battled my way against the wind to the door.

'Mark!' I hammered on the rain-soaked wood. The dogs were throwing themselves against the living room window on my left, but I couldn't hear any in the hall behind the front door. There was no sign of Mark. I hammered again. The dogs' barks reached frenzied levels. Where the hell was he?

I tried the door handle and it turned. I gave the door a shove and pushed my way into the hallway, which was dusty and smelt of damp. I peered through the glass living room door. It was being battered by a wall of dogs. No sign of Mark. Christ, was he dead too? I smacked the glass with the palm of my hand.

A door at the far end of the living room swung open and Mark appeared, wearing leggings and a jumper that looked like it belonged to a tramp. He shuffled over and opened the door. The dogs charged through and a Saint Bernard knocked me to the floor. Mark stood silently and watched while I scrabbled up.

'Are you all right?' I said, although he probably should have been saying that to me.

'Why are you in my house?'

I brushed dust and hair from my trousers. 'Did you know Rosie Carstairs has gone missing?'

He froze, his face blank. Then he spoke in a coarse voice, like something heavy being dragged over gravel. 'Yes. You'd better come into the kitchen.'

We trailed through to the slightly warmer kitchen, and Mark pulled the solid, Georgian door closed behind us. I found myself a chair with just a few magazines and no cats on it. I shoved the magazines on the table and sat down. In a corner of the room sat a tin bucket, into which drips fell noisily from the ceiling.

'Sorry about the attire.' He plonked himself on a chair, on top of a small stack of *British Medical Journals*. A tortoiseshell cat crawled onto his knee. 'I'm not having a great day. Losing all your siblings can do that to you.'

'I know,' I said. 'I'm so sorry. And sorry to disturb you.'

He stroked the cat meditatively, as if he'd forgotten I was there.

'You need to help us find Rosie,' I said. 'I know about the Huntington's. Does she have the juvenile form? Did she find out?'

'I barely even know Rosie.'

'But you know she might be Peter's daughter.'

'Yes. I do know she might be Peter's daughter. In fact, judging by the symptoms she's been having, I'd say she's almost certainly Peter's daughter. And what an almighty fuck-up that is.'

'Do you know where she is?'

'Why are you so desperate to find her? What's the point? All these police swarming all over the countryside, and appeals to the cretinous public. Rosie's doomed anyway. There are no happy endings for her.'

'What do you mean?'

'Rosie's fucked.' I winced as if he'd slapped me. 'The only blessing is she won't reproduce, and this torment will die out, at least in our family.'

I instinctively shuffled back in my chair, putting an extra inch between us. What had happened to him? Where was the kind man I'd met before? 'Do you know where she is? Do you think she's in trouble?'

'She's in trouble all right.'

'Do you know where she might be?'

He sighed. 'Of course not.'

'Mark, did you know Kate's pregnant?'

He looked at me, his eyes black and a muscle twitching in his cheek. 'No. She can't be.'

'It's probably very early days.'

Mark carefully lifted the cat from his knee and placed her on the table. He stood, walked to the far side of the room, and bashed his head against the exposed stone wall. Hard. And then again. I jumped from my chair and rushed over to him.

'Mark! Stop, please.'

He turned to me, clutching his stomach. 'When will this end? I thought she'd been spared.'

'Do you know where Kate is?'

'What do you mean?'

'She's gone missing too.'

All the life went out of him. He returned to the chair and the cat jumped back on his knee. A red dribble oozed down his face.

I sat back down, wishing I had a cat to stroke too. 'Kate didn't know about the Huntington's?'

'No. I told her on Thursday, because of Rosie. I didn't know she was… Oh God. Peter swore they weren't trying for kids. I mean, he was taking those bloody drugs from his client. He thought they were helping. Jesus, why wasn't he more careful? For fuck's sake. Poor Kate. She'll be devastated. She'll have to take the test. She'll have gone on a walk in the Peaks to think, and then she'll go to the mill.'

One of Mark's dogs, a Jack Russell, tried to crawl onto his knee, obviously not noticing the cat. Mark sat oblivious while the cat hissed and smacked the dog hard across its nose. The dog whined and skulked away. The cat gave it a smug look and cleaned her face with a front paw.

'You mean she'll have gone to her holiday home?'

'I don't get it,' Mark said. 'People think life's so fucking sacred. What's sacred about turning into a demented, angry monster, who can't move or talk or even swallow, who eventually dies of suffocation?' A vein pulsed in his neck. 'Life's not sacred. Life's an evolutionary bloody accident.'

I stared at him, not even sure what point he was making now.

'God,' he spat. 'They think there's a *benevolent* God. More like a sick fuck. Let's do it on the throw of a dice. You? Oh, we'll give you a normal life. You? Let's go for horrific illness in middle age, and premature death after excruciating suffering. You? Oh, let's add a bit of spice and kick it off at age fourteen, just when you should be brimming with health and have your whole life ahead of you.'

I looked into the black centres of his eyes. What could I say? Nothing could make this any better. 'I'm really sorry about your family.'

'Yeah. Thanks. It's life. You're not religious are you?' He gave a humourless laugh.

'No.' I remembered Carrie in the weeks before she died – her body so thin it could snap, her wispy hair just beginning to grow back because there wasn't any point in chemo any more. 'No,' I repeated. 'If I thought someone had created this world deliberately, I don't think I could live with my fury. So, no. No benevolent gods in my little construction of reality.'

Mark looked at me as if inspecting an exhibit in a museum. 'Good. We have to find Kate.' He wiped a smear of blood from his forehead. 'She can't take the pregnancy to term if it's got Huntington's. This suffering's gone on for enough generations. It has to end.'

'The police think she killed Peter and now she's possibly taken Rosie.'

'I thought you were the police?'

I didn't answer and he just gave a slight nod. 'Kate didn't kill him. She loved him, and she didn't know he had HD. I kept telling him to say something to her. He promised over and over, but he could never make himself do it. That's what we argued about before he died.'

'Do you think he killed himself?' I asked.

One of the magazines I'd moved from my chair was familiar. The Godly business woman again. She was everywhere.

'Isn't that religious?' I nodded towards the magazine.

'Oh. Yes. One of the receptionists at work gave it to me. How hilarious is that? She thinks she's going to save me. I told her it was too damn late for that. Anyway, thought I'd have a look. Know thine enemy and all that, but it's incoherent.'

'Which receptionist gave it to you?'

'Oh, the main one, Vivian. Chuck it on the floor.' He leant over, picked up the magazine and dropped it onto a clump of dog hair on the terracotta floor tiles. 'No, he didn't kill himself. He wouldn't have done it at this stage. He was still deluding himself he could find a magic cure. There was plenty of torment for both him and Kate to go through before he got to that point. People always think they'll just have a few more days or a few more weeks. Unless they have to go to Dignitas, of course, because no one's got the guts to help them in this country. Then they're forced to go too early.'

'He was reading Stoic philosophy though?'

'I took that as a positive sign. I gather he was spending time sitting in that cave smoking weed and reading Epictetus. *I must die, but must I die groaning?* He could have done worse.'

'Did he have the test for HD?' I asked. 'Without it getting onto his medical records?'

'We all did. Privately and secretly. It's the best way.'

I looked straight into Mark's eyes. He didn't tell me his result.

'Beth had the gene too,' he said. 'She'll have killed herself. She was brave like that, different from Peter. Why do you think so many of our family end up going over that cliff? It's not about the house. It's just that the house stayed in our family.'

No, the curse wasn't about the house. Beth had known that. No wonder she'd been so keen to shut Kate up. She hadn't wanted anyone to realise what the curse was really about, for fear of losing Peter's life insurance.

'I know about Tithonus,' I said.

'I know. Your mum told me. They suspended you.'

I glanced up. 'You knew I was suspended? Why are you even talking to me?'

'Thought I owed you that much in the circumstances. I know

271

you tried not to get us into trouble.' Mark smiled, his earlier venom gone. 'Sorry I ranted on at you.'

'It's okay,' I said. 'There's some terrible things going on. Mark, if the test shows the baby has HD...'

'The foetus. The rule is that Kate would be required to terminate.'

Chapter 38

My mobile rang as I drove away from Mark's house. I snatched it illegally to my ear. Olivia's voice, fast-paced and panicky. 'I was looking again at her Twitter feed and she tweeted this weird thing, just before she disappeared. I think it might mean something.'

'What did it say?'

'I am both Theseus and the Minotaur.'

'Theseus and the Minotaur? As in the Greek myth?'

'Yes.'

'I am both?'

Her voice was high pitched. 'Yes, yes, what does it mean?'

'Do you have any idea? Didn't you say she was into Greek myths?'

'Yes, she is. But I don't know what it means.'

'Okay. Let me look into it. Speak soon.'

I ended the call before she could ask me anything awkward, and called Jai.

'For God's sake, Meg, what are you doing?'

'Have you found her?'

A momentary pause. 'No.'

I told him about my conversation with Olivia.

'Why did she call you?'

'Her choice.'

'Do you know what it means?' Jai said. 'Why all the Greeks? We've had Tithonus, Epictetus, now Theseus.'

'I'm just thinking…'

'You're not on this case, remember.'

I winced. 'Yeah, well, have the rest of you even *heard* of Theseus?'

'Yes, actually. The Minotaur in the Labyrinth.'

I swerved to avoid a vast puddle that had appeared in the road. 'Jai. I think I know where she is.'

★

Jai reluctantly agreed to pass my suggestion on to Richard. They would have looked at her Twitter feed anyway, but it might not have meant anything to them. I also suggested they look for Kate in her holiday home. I didn't know the address, but there couldn't be many converted windmills near Bakewell. I was desperate to get started, but didn't know exactly where the start was, and of course I couldn't go in to the Station. I drove home with my fingers clenched and my breath coming in short bursts.

I let myself in and hobbled through to the kitchen, slipping on the dusty hall floor. My laptop sat on the kitchen table. I wrenched the lid open and started searching. Surely there'd be a caving site with details. But there was nothing. Increasingly frantic, I sifted through pages and pages of results, my clammy fingers slipping on the keyboard.

The reactive sergeant would know. The tattooed one. Ben Pearson. I pictured him telling me about it in the quarry, and then the next day, telling me about the girl who'd hanged herself. It seemed like years ago, when I'd first heard about the noose in the Labyrinth.

Where teenagers go to commit suicide. Deep inside the Labyrinth. But where was it?

I grabbed the phone. Of course I didn't have his number, and had to go via numerous layers of mouth-breathers to get through to him, but eventually there was his voice.

'Pearson.'

'Oh, thank God.'

I explained, without burdening him with the suspension thing, and asked him where the Labyrinth was.

I could sense a trace of anxiety thrumming down the phone line. 'Why?'

'We think a girl's gone in there. It's urgent. Please.'

'Are you sure? It'll be terrifying in there at this time of year. And it'll flood if these rains continue.'

'Yes, we want to get her out. Where is it?' If he'd been in front of me, I would have shaken him.

'The landmark that people know is above it,' he said. 'It's called The Devil's Dice – a load of square-shaped rocks that look like they've been chucked out of a spaceship. You'll find reference to that if you google.'

'Oh, I was stupid. I remember now.'

'But I'll give you a map reference too,' he said. 'It's the most accurate way. The exact location's hard to find if you don't know where you're looking. And the main entrance is sealed up, you know, after that poor girl. But there's a way in through the top. The cavers still know the way in. And no doubt so do the local teenagers.'

'Thanks so much. That's brilliant.'

I took the details and put them into an OS map. The Labyrinth was only half a mile from Mark's house, along a footpath.

I phoned Jai with the details. 'You've got to get them to look in there.'

'Richard didn't seem very interested, Meg. I'll do my best. But we've had a more promising lead.'

'What?'

'Rosie was seen by a postman at Mark Hamilton's house this morning.'

'At Mark's?' I sank down on one of the kitchen chairs. Pictured the darkness of his eyes. He'd been lying to me the whole time. 'Jai, the Labyrinth is right by his house.'

'Neither of them are there now. They think he might have taken her.'

'Seriously, Jai, I think Rosie's going to the Labyrinth.' Why was I doing this, sticking my neck out? I couldn't afford another screw-up.

Jai sighed at unnecessary volume.

I carried on. 'She said, *I am both Theseus and the Minotaur.* She feels like she's a monster – like the Minotaur. But she's also Theseus. So she's going to kill herself. In the Labyrinth.'

A pause. 'If you say so, Meg.'

Jai told me police were crawling all over Mark's house. There was no sign of Rosie or Mark. This lead had taken priority – they weren't going to look in the Labyrinth. Past caring about my career or future, I told Jai about my visit to Mark's house.

'Sounds like he's gone a bit mental,' Jai said. 'Rosie must have been at his house when you were there. That's creepy. You shouldn't have been there on your own with him.'

'Blah, blah. The thing is, Jai, I really don't care. I just want to find her.'

I ended the call, and opened and shut the fridge door a few times. When had I last eaten? It must have been days earlier. I grabbed a piece of moderately mouldy cheese and was about to cut off the best bit when the phone rang. Jai. I snatched it with my non-cheesy hand.

'They say they're already searching that general area, but there's no way into the caves. It's all blocked off.'

'Oh for God's sake.' I hurled the cheese at the kitchen wall. 'You told them about the way in over the top. She tweets about the bloody Minotaur and they won't check the Labyrinth? Christ almighty, Jai.'

I slammed the phone on to the table. I'd go there on my own and find her.

I folded my arms and paced up and down the kitchen. It was really too small for proper pacing, and I bashed my thigh on the table. The dusky light had dulled the edges of things.

Right. What did I need to do? Find the Labyrinth, go in there, find the noose…

How big was the Labyrinth?

This was ridiculous. How would I find her? Labyrinths weren't known for their ease of navigation.

I sat down and put my head in my hands. Maybe she wasn't even there. Maybe Mark had her. Or Kate had her. Or both of them.

I called Ben Pearson back. 'Look, I know this is a weird request, but is there any chance you could help me find the entrance to the Labyrinth? I need to look in there.'

'What? Aren't Section doing it?'

'They can't find it.'

'But it's getting dark and this weather's terrible. If it keeps on like this, it'll flood.'

'There's a young girl in there. I think she's going to kill herself.'

Three beats of silence, then, 'Oh God.'

'I'm really sorry, I don't know who else to ask. Please can you help? Just to find the entrance, not to go in there or anything.'

'I really think you should get Section to—'

'They won't!' I could hear myself getting overwrought. 'They say they can't find it. They're following another lead. Please.'

'It's a bad place,' he said softly. 'I swore I'd never go in there again.'

'I'm sorry. You don't have to go in. Just show me the entrance. I'm so worried about this girl.'

The line went silent for so long I thought we'd been cut off. Then, 'I'll meet you at the lower car park in twenty minutes. Bring every torch and every coat you own. And waterproofs and walking boots. And a couple of spare jumpers. And bear in mind, this is one of the most dangerous cave systems in England, and that's when it's not raining.'

Chapter 39

Jai called back while I was limping around the house, gathering clothes and torches.

'What are you plotting, Meg?'

'I'm going to search the Labyrinth myself.'

'What? You can't go in there on your own.'

'I think there's a vulnerable girl in there. Besides, I'm suspended. If I want to go caving in my own time, I can.'

Silence for a couple of seconds. 'I'm coming with you.'

'No, Jai. There's no need.' I scuttled towards the door and beeped the car open.

'Well, I am. Please don't argue with me.'

'Okay, if you insist. I'll see you at that car park I mentioned, soon as you can. Bring torches and waterproofs and boots. And spare jumpers. Ben Pearson's going to show me where to go.'

Dusk was falling as I drove, and the rain came down in sheets, steaming up the car and overwhelming the aged wipers. I remembered Ben's comment about the tunnels flooding.

There was one other vehicle in the car park – a Land Rover. The rain bounced off its roof as Ben emerged wearing professional-style waterproofs and a head torch.

'I really appreciate this,' I said, but my words were whipped away and scattered by a gust of wind sweeping across the car park. 'Here's Jai.'

Jai pulled up and pushed his car door open against the buffeting wind. He stamped through the puddles and exchanged a look with Ben.

'Are those the Devil's Dice?' I asked. High on a hillside above us, silhouetted against the setting sun, were chunks of rock that did indeed look like huge dice.

'That's them. And the entrance to the Labyrinth is underneath.'

Ben led us up a footpath, and across a tussocky field to a rocky outcrop at the base of the dice. An obvious cave entrance huddled in the hillside, but it was barricaded with robust bars. I shone my torch in. The cave went further back than I could see, the dark effortlessly swallowing the light beam.

'Up here,' Ben shouted, scrambling on his hands and knees up the rocks at the side of the cave entrance. 'Watch out, it's steep.'

Jai and I followed, crawling up the slippery rocks. I blinked rain from my eyes. Was that thunder in the distance?

'I don't like this weather,' Ben said. 'There are parts of the Labyrinth that you can't get to when it's wet, not without diving.'

'Diving?' Jai's voice was almost inaudible against the rain and wind. A streak of brightness lit his face, highlighting every line of worry. The thunderclap came soon after.

'Uh oh,' I said. 'The storm's not far away.'

Ben stood on the rocks, looking into the night. He muttered something under his breath, and did something with his arm. Was he *crossing* himself? I felt a shiver go through me.

'I'm just going to put this out there,' Ben said. 'I absolutely do not recommend going into this cave system. It's huge, virtually impossible to navigate, and it floods when it rains. It's extremely dangerous.'

'I'm going in,' I said. 'But please don't feel you have to come with me. You've shown me the entrance. I know you said you'd never go back inside.' I glanced at Jai. 'And you, Jai. Don't risk it. Please. I'm kind of semi-suicidal – it's different for me.'

I heard the shake in Ben's voice. 'You'll kill yourself if you go in alone. Follow me.' His face was unreadable in the gloomy light.

'No,' I said. 'You can't—'

He gave a quick shake of his head, and disappeared. I realised he'd lowered himself into a gap in the rock. It was only just wide enough for a person, and was invisible unless you knew exactly where you were looking. I wasn't surprised Section had missed it.

A crack of thunder shook the rocks under us.

Jai's head torch dazzled me. 'I'm coming too,' he said.

'No, Jai, really. You don't—'

'Shut up and get in that hole.'

I smiled and shook my head. Looked at him again. He meant it. I shrugged and slithered into the gap.

Jai plopped down beside me. 'Jesus Christ. I'm not even getting overtime for this.'

We stood in a gloomy cavern the size of a small room. Water dripped from the roof onto the slimy floor and our bodies cast uneven shadows on the walls. A bat whisked past my face.

'This is a very nasty cave system,' Ben said. 'Even experienced cavers get lost.' He took a chunky coil of rope from his backpack and tied one end of it to a metal ring attached to the cave wall. 'And drowned.' He looped the rope through a tree root that twisted down from the roof of the cave. He checked it several times for solidity. It was a very long rope, thin but strong, like something you'd tow cars with. The length chilled me – just how far in were we going?

'Like Theseus,' I said.

'Not worth taking any chances down here. Come on.'

Ben led us towards the back of the cavern. A passageway about four feet high sloped down into the blackness. We ducked and shuffled through, the light of our torches flickering against the cave walls, which sparkled in the half-light. I thought of the women forced in here, accused of witchcraft. Imagined their terror as they were led deep into the rock, towards the noose.

'Rosie! Rosie!' Our voices bounced back to us, 'Rosie, Rosie,' as if they were ridiculing us.

The cold was shocking. It passed straight through my clothing to my bones.

'Do you really think she's in here?' Ben said. 'It seems unlikely.'

'I just think—'

There was a scuffling noise. Like the sound of footsteps, but in the distance as if it was coming from a place deep within the ground. Jai jumped and hit his head on the roof of the tunnel. 'Oh my God, is that her?'

'Rosie!' I shouted. I heard only the echo of my own voice in return, and a dim rumble of thunder that seemed to shake the whole hillside.

We carried on shuffling down the narrow corridor, hunched over, and came to a T-junction. Guessing as to where the noise had come from, we took the left fork. A whimper echoed through the passageway but I couldn't tell if it was near or far. I already felt confused and disorientated, and was glad of Ben's rope. I turned to him. 'Where's the noose you told me about?'

'It's a long way in. You don't think—'

'Can you take us to it?'

Ben turned towards me, the beam of his torch swooping along the damp wall. I was glad I couldn't see his face. 'It can be hard to find.' His voice had a harsh edge to it and he spoke quickly. 'And the tunnels flood. With all this rain—'

'Look. If you want to go back…'

'Come on.' Ben's voice was firm. 'We've got this far.'

We kept inching down, though tunnel after tunnel, twisting and turning deeper into the rock. I had no idea how Ben had remembered it all.

Eventually, the path branched in two, but Ben indicated a gap in the rock straight ahead of us. The opening was only about two feet high. 'Short cut. This should avoid the underground river.'

'Underground river?' Jai said, in the voice of a condemned man.

'We need to get a bloody move on.'

I crouched down and crawled on my belly into the gap. It led into a tunnel about three feet in diameter, extending down into the rock. It reminded me of a nightmare I used to have where I was stuck in a world where all the ceilings were waist height. This was far worse. I shuffled down, trying not to think about all the rock above me and the water flowing into the cave system. Brutally cold water seeped down the tunnel floor below me, and as we crept lower, the bottom of the tunnel started filling. I knew cavers died in flooded tunnels.

The tunnel floor now sloped upwards and it became even harder to drag myself along. I wedged my arms against the walls and clawed myself up the slope, gasping for breath, suddenly sweaty despite the freezing conditions.

Finally I emerged into a cavern.

There she was.

A chain-link noose was looped around her neck. She'd already done it. I couldn't go through this again. A scream started forming in my throat. Then I realised her hands were gripping the noose. She stood on a square piece of rock, rather like one of the Devil's Dice, and held one foot out over the edge of the rock as if about to step off it. A torch was propped on the rock beside her, directed up towards the cave roof. Rosie looked tiny and frail, skinny jeans and loose-laced trainers emphasising her stick-thin legs; huge eyes staring.

'No! Rosie, please. Wait a minute.'

She removed her hands from the noose, leaving it around her neck, and looked straight at me, her foot hovering over the edge. I remembered her tripping down the stairs, and Olivia saying her legs had collapsed under her in the past. The noose was attached high above her to a ring that looked like an ancient version of the kind of thing you'd attach a horse to. The chain was long, giving the noose a good drop for an instant kill. I knew my suicide methods. If I tried to make a grab for her, she could step off and her neck would be broken instantly.

'Rosie, please wait.'

'What are you doing here?' Her voice was surprisingly loud.

Jai shuffled through the opening and gasped when he saw Rosie. Ben followed. Our torches shone in her face, and on the cave wall behind. It was uneven, marked with something. Initials. Cut into the rock.

'Why have you come?' Rosie said. 'I want to die. I'm dying anyway. Why shouldn't I choose my own death?'

I spoke quickly to Jai and Ben. 'Switch the torches off for now.' I didn't want them shining in Rosie's face, and the thought that the batteries could run out was twitching at the edge of my brain. I turned mine off and popped it into my pocket.

I looked back at Rosie's face, made sinister by the upward light of her torch. 'You don't know you're dying,' I said. 'Please, Rosie, come out with us.'

'I *am* dying. I heard Mum talking, I've got Huntington's. I'm not stupid.'

'You might not—'

'I said I'm not stupid. I googled it.' She let out a little gasping sob. 'I should be able to choose when I die. I'll end up paralysed and then I'll be totally helpless and dependent, and they'll be able to keep me alive, even if I really, really don't want...' She tailed off, and leant over the edge, her neck still in the noose.

My heart pounded in my ears.

'I'm just going to do it,' Rosie said.

Jai lunged forwards. I grabbed his arm.

'No,' I hissed. 'It won't work.'

Jai stopped. He didn't carry on towards Rosie but neither did he move back.

'You haven't even had the test,' I said. 'It might be something else. Please. Just have the test and give your parents a chance to talk to you.'

'I'm not coming down,' she said. 'I hate them.' I couldn't see her expression in the peculiar up-light. Only her eyes were clearly visible. 'Mum didn't even tell me what was wrong with me, and

Dad doesn't want me because I'm not his proper daughter. I'm Peter's, and he's dead.'

'Rosie, please…'

I could hear water flowing somewhere behind us. I pictured the tunnels filling.

I took a deep breath of the tomb-like air. 'My sister hanged herself.'

Rosie's gaze darted to me, and she placed her hands back on the noose. 'I just wanted my death to be under my own control,' she said, her thin voice echoing off the cave walls. 'The Devil's Dice. How perfect is that for me? The throw of a dice. And I lost.' She clutched the noose tightly in her small hands. 'Why did your sister kill herself?'

'She was dying of cancer. She didn't want to go through the last few months.' The dark helped me say it. 'And I said a terrible thing to her, Rosie, and she never gave me the chance to take it back.'

Rosie shuffled her weight from one foot to the other, keeping the noose around her neck.

'I found her,' I said. Jai took a sharp breath next to me. 'I found her in her bedroom, hanging from a beam. She'd climbed a ladder. I tried to get her down but I couldn't.'

'Sorry,' Rosie said.

I wasn't sure if the rushing in my ears was my own blood, or water gushing into the cave system. But I had Rosie's attention.

'I still blame myself,' I said. 'It was horrific for our family. It's really screwed me up.'

'Yeah, she's damn screwed up,' Jai said, and I thought Rosie actually smiled.

'If you come back with us now and talk to your family, I promise you…' I took a moment to wonder what the hell I was doing, and then carried on anyway. 'I promise you on my sister's grave – you won't be forced to live a moment longer than you choose to. And we're the police.'

'What if Mum doesn't agree?'

I hesitated, watching my career saunter away. 'I'll talk to her and persuade her. But even if your mum doesn't agree, we'll help you anyway.' If I wasn't sacked for what I'd done so far, I would be now.

'I don't want to end up in a wheelchair,' she said. 'Do you promise, promise?' She suddenly sounded much younger. I was overcome with a wave of despair at her situation – that the best she was hoping for was a dignified death. I prayed to a God I didn't believe in – *Please don't let her have Huntington's.*

'Promise, promise,' I said.

She reached to un-loop the noose from her neck. I released my breath.

She slipped. Her feet dropped from the edge of the rock and she slammed downwards. She was caught, her neck still in the noose, hands clutching at it. She was making a terrible wheezing noise.

I screamed and lunged towards the dangling legs, my head full of that other time. I snatched at Rosie's calves, trying to push her up to release the pressure on her neck.

A crash and it was dark. Completely dark, like I'd been blinded. Rosie's torch was gone. My heart battered my ribs like a wild animal trapped in a cage. My eyes stretched wide in their desperation to detect any hint of light. I couldn't find my torch in my pocket without releasing Rosie's weight.

Something grabbed me from behind. I yelled and flung my head around but could see nothing. My breath came in desperate gasps.

It was Ben, and he was helping me support Rosie.

A torch clicked on. Jai was beside us. He scrambled past.

Rosie gasped and choked. I tried to lift her higher, but she collapsed at the waist, so the weight of her upper body was suspended by the noose. I saw Jai behind, scrabbling to climb onto the rock Rosie had fallen from.

I shouted into Ben's ear. 'Can you hold her any higher?'

Jai yelled and crashed to the floor. 'Shit, it's slippery!' I was dimly aware of him at the edge of my vision, hauling himself to his feet, and up onto the rock, standing, pulling at the noose with frantic hands.

'Rosie, help him,' I shouted. She tensed and got heavier.

We crashed to the floor, Rosie's weight forcing the air from my lungs.

Jai jumped from the rock, panting heavily. 'Jesus Christ.'

Ben extracted himself from the pile of us and leapt to his feet. 'Right. Quick. Follow me! We could be in the shit here.'

I stood and grabbed Rosie's hand. 'Come on.' She staggered to her feet, gasping and clutching her neck.

Ben moved towards the tunnel.

'I can't go in there,' Rosie's voice was panicky. 'It's this way out.' She pointed to a roomier pathway to the left.

Ben reached for Rosie's arm and tried to pull her. 'That other way's longer and it might be flooded.'

Rosie resisted and started crying. 'I can't go in there.' She was going to get us all killed.

'Wait there.' Ben dashed off to the left. The three of us stood in the gloom, shivering.

A couple of minutes later, he reappeared. 'Totally flooded. No chance.'

Rosie's sobs grew louder. You could want to die but still be scared. I knew that.

'Come on,' Ben grabbed Rosie. 'Go behind me. Hang onto my legs. We're going.'

Rosie cried gently but did as she was told. Ben turned to us. 'Hold the rope,' he said. 'Pull yourself through with the rope. The lowest section might be flooded.'

Jai's voice was quiet. 'What do you mean, flooded?'

'I mean, to get through, you may have to hold your breath whilst dragging yourself through the lowest part of the tunnel underwater.'

Rosie started to whimper. I wasn't far off whimpering myself. 'Can't we sit it out?' I said. 'Wait for the water to go down?'

'Aside from possible hypothermia,' Ben said. 'This whole cave floods. Right to the roof.'

I said nothing, but pictured us freezing and frantic, the water rising.

Ben shuffled into the tunnel, pulling Rosie behind him. Jai hung back and let me burrow in after Rosie's skinny legs. His panicked breathing was loud as he crawled in behind.

The air inside the tunnel felt thick. The walls were slimy against my fingers and the roof sat low over my head. I shuffled through, gasping with fear, trying to keep up with Ben. Then he stopped.

'Okay,' he shouted. 'A ten-foot section's flooded. It'll be rising all the time. We need to go. Follow me. Take the deepest breath you can, and pull yourself through on the rope. It'll be easier than crawling. Just do it. I've got a diving torch so stay as close as you can if you want to see anything.'

And he disappeared with a soft gurgle.

My breathing came faster and faster. I couldn't do this. But Jai was behind me. I couldn't let Jai die. He actually valued his life. He should have gone first. I took a huge breath and pulled on the rope. Entered the water. The cold was a physical shock, like being punched. I wanted to gasp. It was almost impossible not to gasp.

I pulled myself forward through the freezing water, my eyes shut and panic rising in my chest. I crashed into something. Rosie's leg. She was blocking my way through. What the hell was she doing? I flailed around, trying to feel what was going on. I opened my eyes in the murky water. A faint, diffuse light was coming from ahead but nothing was clear. Rosie's legs thrashed against the sides of the tunnel. My need to take a breath was almost overwhelming. I tried to push myself backwards and crashed into Jai behind me.

I felt something pulling at my ankles, but I couldn't seem to let go of the rope. The harder my ankles were pulled, the harder I hung on. A part of my brain knew this was wrong. But I couldn't let go. Darkness was closing in from all sides. I was beginning not to care, to feel remote from it all. I felt an odd incredulity and slight embarrassment that this would be how it ended. Stupid people dead in a cave. All the suicidal thoughts I'd had over the years and now I was going to die accidentally. And I realised I wanted to live.

Chapter 40

In my moment of extreme calm, I saw Rosie's shoelace caught on a protruding nose of rock. I tugged it towards me and it popped free. Rosie's legs thrashed around my face and then disappeared into the darkness.

I gripped the rope with both hands again and knew I had to take a breath. I opened my mouth and gasped. Water flooded my throat. I coughed and more water gushed into my nostrils. I felt pure, white terror.

The rope jerked in my hands. I didn't let go. It moved, pulling me through the water. Something grabbed me. My face scraped on rock. I was out of the water, lying on the cave floor, coughing, panting, gasping. Tears streamed from my eyes. My stomach constricted and I vomited a violent stream of water.

Rosie was hunched beside me, her body bent forward with huge wracking coughs.

Then Jai was crouching down, saying something I couldn't understand. Grabbing me and trying to get me to my feet.

Ben's voice sounded far away. 'Come on!'

I forced myself up and teetered on jelly legs. I was dimly aware of Ben lifting Rosie to her feet and dragging her forward. My brain felt black; nothing made sense except coughing and coughing and getting this water out of me. But with Jai clutching my arm, I stumbled after Ben's retreating body.

I passed into a kind of auto-pilot, staring at Rosie's legs and putting one foot in front of the other, hunching over to avoid the cave roof, still spluttering but feeling the blackness gradually lift as we stumbled through the dreadful passages of the Labyrinth.

Eventually, we reached the final cavern, and Ben helped us drag ourselves out. We staggered across the car park and piled into Ben's Land Rover, Jai in the front, Rosie and me in the back. The car was filled with towels, blankets, spare jumpers, and even those foil wrap things they give marathon runners. I muttered incoherent thanks and admiration.

Ben ignored me. 'Get out of your clothes. All of them. Quick.'

We did as we were told, with freezing, swollen fingers and in silence, bashing each other with awkward elbows and knees. We stripped off our wet clothes, the extreme situation making us unselfconscious.

Ben twisted in his seat to reach for a T-shirt. And there was his tattoo. I hadn't meant to look, but then I couldn't look away. I sat open-mouthed. It covered his whole chest and stomach.

He paused with the shirt ready to pull on. 'Do you know what it is?'

It was drawn in blacks and greys. It evoked the forbidding feel of the place, but also showed the route through. All the twists and turns. 'It's the Labyrinth,' I whispered.

Rosie didn't look, and Jai flicked his head round briefly, then reverted to staring forwards in the manner of men forced to get naked near each other.

Ben pulled on his T-shirt. 'I couldn't seem to let it go. After… that girl.'

'That's why you remembered the route through.'

He gave a quick nod. 'Get yourselves wrapped up.'

We sat with the engine running and the heating on full, shivering like spinning washing machines. Our teeth actually chattered.

Jai turned in his seat. 'What the hell happened in there when you got stuck?'

My voice shook with cold. 'Rosie's shoelace caught on a bit of rock.'

'Christ almighty,' Jai said. 'Why won't teenagers tie their bloody laces properly?'

The question hung in the air unanswered. I gave Rosie's leg a reassuring rub.

'I tried to pull you out backwards,' Jai added. 'But I couldn't shift you.'

'Sorry. I think I was hanging onto the rope in a sort of deranged panic.'

'Trainers aren't your serious caver's footwear of choice,' Ben said.

Jai laughed. 'Oh my God,' he said. 'I'll be having nightmares about that till the end of my days.'

I laughed too. Then we were all laughing, shakily, even the recently suicidal amongst us.

'Yeah, thanks for that,' Ben said, 'Next time you fancy a bit of caving, count me out.'

★

Half an hour later, we were warmed up, dried off and clothed in towels and our spare jumpers. After thanking Ben so many times he started to get irritated, Jai and I walked across the freezing car park to our respective cars. Rosie came with me and I gave Jai my house keys so he could let himself in and put the kettle on.

I phoned the Station and arranged for a sympathetic uniform to meet us outside Rosie's house. Before I could be asked any awkward questions, I invoked the *Peak-District-mobile-signal-effect,* and ended the call.

'Sorry about my trainers,' Rosie said as we pulled out of the car park.

I turned to look at her, huddled in the passenger seat in the oversized jumpers. 'Don't worry. You didn't ask us to come and rescue you.'

The roads had turned to rivers and the rain was still lashing down. Twigs and small branches drifted down with us like flotsam and jetsam as we drove along in our little bubble of light.

'My initials weren't on the cave wall,' Rosie said quietly. I glanced at her and she gave me a quick smile. 'I didn't mean for anyone to understand that tweet. I don't know why I did it.'

'What did it mean?'

'I'm going to turn into a monster, aren't I? A useless drooling monster who can't walk or talk or—'

'No, you won't.'

'But I was going to be Theseus too. I was going to kill the monster.'

'Rosie, you might be unwell, but you'll never be a monster.'

'Well, maybe the Minotaur wasn't either. Maybe he just needed to eat. Anyway, Mark helped me. Talking things through.'

'You stayed there Thursday and Friday nights?'

She gave a little nod. 'I like the dogs and cats. And Mark. He's not all hysterical like my mum can be.'

'He encouraged you to kill yourself?'

'No. He didn't try to make me do anything. But he was angry with that other lady. He spoke to her on the phone after you came, and he kept saying, 'You've got to have the test, you can't go through with it.' I got a bit scared and sneaked out.'

'You knew I was there?'

She nodded. I felt sick. She'd been so close and I'd missed her. Trusted Mark Hamilton.

★

I left Rosie in capable hands but didn't go inside with her, since I was clothed only in a towel, four jumpers, and a piece of tin-foil. I told her I'd be back the next day to talk, and set off for home. Jai had thoughtfully left the parking space right outside for me, so there was no need for a half-naked dash.

Once inside, I banged the thermostat up to twenty-eight degrees even though I knew it never made it over nineteen, and found Jai in the kitchen making tea. I was still shivering.

I dug out a sartorially uninspiring collection of clothes for Jai, including a pair of comically short jogging pants and a fleece Gran had bought me one Christmas, bafflingly and insultingly in women's XXL. We withdrew into the kitchen, closed the door and stuck the fan heater on.

Hamlet marched up and down, shouting as if I'd been missing for days. In fact, it had only been a couple of hours, but I couldn't believe how much more positive I felt.

I rooted around in the cupboard to find oats, while Jai sat at the kitchen table with a stunned look on his face. Hamlet crawled onto his knee and gave him one of his slightly spiky massages.

I grabbed the bag of oats and squinted at the sell-by date. Only a year over. Oats couldn't really go off, could they?

'So, you discovered your sister?' Jai said hesitantly.

I turned to him, oats in hand. Looked down at the packet. 'Yes. I was ten.'

'Oh my God, that's terrible. I mean, I knew there'd been a suicide in your family, but that's just—'

'I got home from school, went up to her room to see her...'

'You don't have to tell me.'

'No. I want to. Bottling it all up hasn't worked so well for me.' I shuffled oats and milk into a pan in random quantities and stuck the mix on a hob. 'I'll probably cock the porridge up, you know.'

'It will be fine. As long as it's hot and vaguely edible.'

'That's top level in this kitchen. But I'll stick cream in it, that'll help.' There were few dishes that weren't helped by cream. 'Anyway, so, I wanted to apologise. I'd said something terrible to her. It seems ridiculous now but I was actually jealous of her. She got all the attention and I thought my parents preferred her. I thought they wished it had been me who'd got ill, not her.'

293

'Oh, Meg. You didn't want Peter Hamilton's brother to think he committed suicide. You knew how that felt.'

'They'd had an argument too. He'd have blamed himself just like I do.'

'It was kind of mean of your sister to do it that day. Before you'd had a chance to make things right.'

I'd never thought of it like that. Never thought about Carrie's responsibility in all this. But it was true. I'd only been ten. She was fifteen. Hadn't she thought about the effect it would have on me?

I gave the porridge a final stir, dished it out into bowls and poured double cream on the top. I even found some Demerara sugar. I sat down and skidded a bowl across the table to Jai.

'A culinary triumph,' he said.

'It is for me.' I added copious amounts of sugar and stirred my porridge round and round but didn't start on it yet. 'I don't know why I'm telling you all this. I suppose my career's in ruins, so what the hell. I think deep down I've always felt like I basically murdered my sister. Except the rational part of me knows I didn't. She wanted to kill herself, and it was nothing to do with me. She'd spoken to Mum and Dad about it.'

Jai stopped chewing. 'They knew she wanted to die?'

I nodded. 'I only just found out.' I lifted a spoonful of porridge, then put it down again. 'Anyway, on that day, well, I walked into her room and… we had this big A-frame ladder that lived in the spare room, for when you had to change light bulbs. The ceilings were those high ones you get in barn conversions. The ladder was in the middle of her bedroom. She had the best room, with the vaulted ceiling. To make up for all the other stuff she didn't have.' I stirred my porridge. Could I do this? I took a gulping breath. 'So, she'd rigged up a noose from the highest beam and she was hanging from it.'

'Oh my God,' Jai whispered.

'So, I ran and climbed up the ladder. I don't know why really, maybe I thought I could save her or it was just an instinct. I grabbed hold of her but she was dead. I started screaming and fell off the ladder. Broke my ankle and it got overlooked, with… you know, with everything else going on. So it set wrong.'

'Your limp.'

'Yes, my limp.'

'I always wanted a limp when I was a kid. Or maybe a withered hand.'

'You *what*?'

'There were so many of us children, I wanted to be different.'

'My God. That's a new perspective.'

'I know. I'm weird.'

'It's not that great actually.' I lifted my ankle and placed it on my knee. 'See how it grew this big chunk of callous where it didn't heal right. It means the joint won't move properly and I'll never have a slim, ladylike ankle.'

'It makes you unique.' Jai was unusually still. 'It must have been really hard though. With your sister.'

'It was.' I swallowed. 'You've heard I had time off with stress a couple of years ago?'

Jai paused mid-chew.

'It's okay, Jai. Everyone seems to know. I had a sort of break down after I was called to a suicide. A young girl who'd hanged herself. It triggered all sorts of memories. I had counselling and apparently I need to let go of my guilt over my sister. But how am I supposed to do that?'

'Was that why you left the Manchester force?'

'Partly. Everyone knew about it. They were fine but I felt like they were treating me differently. But then everyone seems to know about it here too.'

'Craig has a friend…'

'Yeah. Good old Craig. Did you know he phoned me earlier? Anyway, it was partly to be near Mum too. My dad left shortly after I started uni and she's been on her own since then. Which is fine.

But now she's having to look after Gran. When the chance came up to move back here, it seemed to make sense.'

'And the scenery's better here.'

'It is. Although there are too many heights for my liking, and I've kind of gone off the caves.' It was such a relief to talk, as if I'd been carrying a bag of bricks around with me, and now I was unloading it, brick by brick. 'And this recent fear of heights, I think it's all about my sister too. I've had some flashbacks.'

'Jesus Christ. And this is why you have to check every room when you get home.'

'Oh, you noticed that. I thought I was being subtle. I know it's ridiculous and not rational, but I have this urge to check them. The ceilings.'

'It's okay. I understand. Well, kind of.'

'So, when I saw Rosie—'

'My God, you handled it so well.'

'I think it did me good. I had to focus on her, and it forced me to just get on with it. But I'm thinking now, why were we so desperate to save her? She'd chosen to kill herself.'

'It's natural I suppose,' Jai said. 'To want to rescue people.'

'I'm not sure Mark sees it like that. He doesn't seem to think life as such has any value. Avoiding suffering is his thing. But, I mean, everyone suffers, maybe we'd all be better off dead.'

Jai shifted Hamlet higher up his knee. 'I suppose most of us end up slightly on the positive side, on balance.'

'Probably not when you look at the whole world, and the whole animal kingdom.' Hamlet purred like a power tool. 'Although cats must push up the average contentment levels.'

'But think of the mice they torture.' Jai looked down at Hamlet and touched one of his neat, white front paws. 'You were right, you know. When I said it was wrong to kill people, it was a knee-jerk thing from my upbringing. I'm sorry.'

'It's okay. I'm sorry I told you to fuck off.'

'The whole religious objection doesn't stack up anyway, does it?

It should be about avoiding pain, not prolonging it to make some stupid point.'

'That's what Mum says. She still believes in God. I don't get it though. If there was a god and he was a nice guy, why would he have arranged the whole deal like this? I mean, like the set-up with prey animals and predators. You'd make everyone a herbivore, wouldn't you? Unless you were a sick bastard.' I smiled. 'But now I'm sounding like Mark.'

'Well, maybe he has a point.'

A wave of affection swept over me as Jai sat there in my terrible clothes with the cat drooling on him and kneading his legs. He was tactfully trying to rearrange Hamlet to minimise the effect of the needle-sharp claws.

Suddenly ravenous, I stuffed porridge into myself. 'Kate's not the killer,' I said. 'Should we be worried about Mark? Where is he? I remembered he had cut-up wellies in his pantry.'

'You think it could be him?'

'Could he have attached smaller soles to bigger boots like the Unabomber, so he left medium sized footwear marks, even though he had size twelve feet? And he had a machine for sealing plastic food bags. He uses it to make dog food.'

Jai spoke quickly. 'After what happened to his mum, he was desperate for his family not to suffer, and also Kate.'

'If he doesn't think death's a bad thing, only suffering, then killing him would have done Peter a huge favour, saving him and Kate from the next few years, which were going to be horrific. Beth had the gene too. Could he have killed her as well, to save her from suffering? He was very quick to say she'd committed suicide. And look at how he behaved with Rosie. Do you think he let her walk off into the night to kill herself?'

'The set-up would make sense – he wouldn't want Peter's death to look like suicide because he wants Kate to get the life insurance. So, he'd try to make it sufficiently unclear that there'd be an open verdict.'

'He goes geocaching,' I said. 'And he could easily have known Peter's password. And he knew about the history of the house.'

'Oh my God, it really could be him.' Jai stroked Hamlet faster.

I paused with my spoon halfway to my mouth. 'I think Kate's in danger.'

Chapter 41

Jai clearly wanted to leap up, but Hamlet had him pinned. He stayed perched on the chair. 'Would Mark harm Kate?'

'Only to protect her, and future generations, from suffering,' I said. 'I think something's going on at her holiday cottage in Bakewell.'

I rushed to the living room and grabbed the laptop, prising it open as I dashed back into the kitchen. A converted windmill near Bakewell had been for sale two years ago. I scrawled the address on a scrap of paper.

I was still officially suspended, pending being sacked when they found out what else I'd been up to. I shouldn't have been rushing around trying to rescue people. But I had to do something. I called and asked Richard if they'd been up to the mill to see if Kate was there.

'We're checking it out, Meg. Calm down, you're supposed to be having a break.'

I'd thought I was calm. So much for that performance.

I smacked the phone down and turned to Jai. 'They're not taking it seriously.'

'Come on then.' Jai looked like a special kind of superhero in my appalling clothes. 'Let's go. Bring your crazy scarf, we're going to be cold. Have you got the address? Where's your radio? Mine's in that bloody cave, somewhere.'

I grabbed my scrap of paper. 'It's at the Station, charging. I wasn't thinking straight when I left…'

'Oh.'

We paused and stared at each other. 'We'll have to rely on the mobiles.' I tried not to think about the state of the signal in the wilds of the Peak District.

'We'll phone in and tell them where we're going,' Jai said. 'Just in case.'

'Let's take your car,' I said. 'My hand's all torn up.'

We bustled out of the house and ran to Jai's car. I shot round to the passenger side and Jai threw himself into the driver's seat and eased us out of the tiny parking space and off down the cobbled street.

Unlike a traditional hero racing to save the damsel, I put the address into the sat nav. 'Jai, I'm going to be sick. You can slow down a little bit.'

Jai pulled out onto the A6, way too close to the front of a quarry lorry. 'Just how desperate is Mark that Kate doesn't have a baby with Huntington's?' he said.

I pictured Mark's black eyes. 'He can't cope with more suffering. He doesn't value life for its own sake. And Rosie heard him arguing with Kate on the phone. He was angry. It sounded like Kate was refusing to test the baby.'

Jai glanced round at me. 'Why wouldn't she want the test?'

'You have to agree to an abortion if it turns out positive.'

'Oh God. And Mark's determined to wipe Huntington's out of his family.'

'Okay, you can speed up a bit.'

The rain turned to sleet and the roads were slick with water. We'd lost five degrees since we left Belper. I wrapped Carrie's scarf around my neck and sat quietly as we drove through the night. My brain whirred. Snippets of conversation and disjointed images flashed through my mind, as if I was in a cinema watching a film made by a madman. I shut my eyes and let everything shift and juggle in front of me. The cave house in the woods, Olivia's face in Peter's photographs, Sebastian under the railway bridge, the godly business woman everywhere, Hannah saying it got nasty at the religious group, Felix pushing a man off a roof onto spiked railings, Edward being arrested at an anti-abortion march, GR scratched into the dirt...

'Oh God,' I whispered. 'Maybe it's not Mark after all. Maybe—'

'There,' Jai yelled.

A rutted lane led off to the right over the moor, and in the distance a windmill stood out against the night sky. Jai swung the car onto the lane and accelerated.

Lights were on in the top of the old mill tower. They cast a glow through the wet air onto the surrounding hillside, through huge windows.

A shape came into view in the pool of light around the base of the tower.

'Mark's car's there,' I said. 'And I think that's Kate's behind it. And is that another car?'

Jai looked ahead at the mill, and sped up abruptly.

A flash from the headlights shone onto stone. Right in front of us. I gasped. The dry-stone wall ahead had collapsed onto the lane. 'Watch out!' I shouted.

Jai swerved. The car slewed sideways, tyres screeching. I slammed my right foot to the floor in an imaginary braking action. The car bounced and jolted under me with shocking force, throwing me up so my head smacked onto the roof. Finally we pitched down and smashed to a halt, the noise of metal on stone filling my ears. Something smacked me in the face – hard, like I'd been punched – and then everything went quiet except for an ominous hissing.

I groaned and clawed the spent air-bag away from my face. An acrid smell filled the car and a thin powder lay on me like fine snow. The car was making a strange clanking noise like expanding metal.

I rubbed my head. 'Jai, are you okay?'

'Get out of the car.' His voice was muffled and I could barely see him through the dust.

I unclipped my seat belt and levered myself sideways. My head was spinning as if I'd had too much to drink. I staggered forward and clutched onto a collapsed part of the dry stone wall we'd ploughed into. The front of the car was strewn with rocks and concertinaed into half its previous length. And it was still producing that unnerving hissing and clanking.

I looked up and saw Jai's head emerge from the far side of the car, but then it dropped out of sight. I stumbled over to him, and found him slumped on the ground.

'I think I might have broken some ribs,' he said.

'Oh crap. Can you stand up?'

Jai levered himself up, with much wincing and shallow breathing. He wasn't normally a wimp, so it must have been bad. I helped him hobble away from the car and we sank onto the wet grass. The cold ground bit into me, and I realised I was shivering. I wrapped my coat and scarf tight, and pulled my phone out of my pocket. Not even the sniff of a signal. Just the no-entry sign that indicates you've got no chance.

I tried 999 in case I could get through on another network, but there was nothing.

I pictured my radio sitting charging. It had an orange button on it. If I'd pressed that button, it would have used its GPS to radio my precise location to our colleagues, who would have absolutely floored it to come and save us. I cursed myself.

'I think we're on our own,' I said. I typed a text anyway, in case a temporary signal appeared.

Jai sat clutching his chest. 'Jesus, we'll have to wait for backup. You can't go in.'

'But—'

'Seriously, Meg. How many times have you screamed at the TV when Morse goes in alone?'

He had a point.

I rubbed my head and inspected my hand. 'I think I'm okay. I'll just go and take a look. We need to get help for your ribs anyway. If they're badly broken, you could puncture a lung. There'll be a landline in there. And we're probably over-reacting – Mark and Kate could be settling down for a nice cup of tea.'

'I don't like it.' Jai prodded his ribs. He let out a tiny gasp.

'Don't try to move, Jai.'

He groaned. 'Be bloody careful. You don't have to be a hero. You've got nothing to prove.'

Jai was so wrong. I had everything to prove.

I made sure my phone was on silent, and limped towards the base of the tower. A raw wind sucked the warmth from me. I leant and picked up a fist-sized rock, which I gripped with my good hand.

The tower was cylindrical and an oak panelled door faced me as I approached. I reached out and pushed it. It resisted, but I gave it a harder shove and it opened, tipping me into the room. I caught my balance and edged forward one tiny step. Inside was a gloomy, cavernous space, about thirty feet across. I crept in, the door thudding shut behind me. I shivered and tried to keep my breathing steady.

The floor was laid with old flagstones, so cold I could feel them through my boots. I took a step forward. Something lay in the centre of the room, hard to make out in the dark. As my eyes adjusted, I could see it was a wooden board about three feet square – like a trapdoor up to an attic. It sprawled on the floor, its edge shattered as if it had crashed down from above.

My gaze was drawn upwards. There seemed to be only two rooms in the tower – the one I was in, which was at least forty feet high, and another room at the top, above this one. The light we'd seen flooding over the moors must have been coming from the room at the top, which was reached by stairs which spiralled around the cylindrical inner wall of this room.

Was that the sound of someone above me? I peered up into the darkness.

Hairs prickled on my neck and arms, and I could hear my own breathing, ragged and fast. I couldn't make sense of what I was seeing.

The ceiling of this room must have been the underside of the floor of the upper room, but something seemed to be hanging from it. As far as I could make out, there was a hole in the middle of the ceiling and a bundle draped down through it.

I saw feet. Something hanging and feet. I took a step back, ready to scream, not daring to look up in case I saw Carrie's face. My heel caught on the edge of a flagstone. I fell back and crashed to the ground. My brain resisted what my eyes were telling it. There was a person hanging from the ceiling.

Chapter 42

I stood again, legs wide apart, taking deep breaths. It wasn't Carrie. I inched towards the centre of the round room, craning my head upwards. It slowly came into focus – a bundle hanging from the ceiling. A person in it, encased in netting. Not Carrie. It was Kate Webster.

There was no way I could access the bundle from this room. It was far above me. The only way to it was through the hole in the floor of the room above.

I had to go up. I knew I was being reckless and stupid and I should wait for back-up, but I couldn't just leave Kate hanging in the net.

The stairs wound their way up the inside of the tower. They were stone, built into its structure, cantilevered out over the drop and only about two feet wide. My left ear was buzzing. I wasn't scared of what was up there – only at the thought of going high.

I pushed my shoulders back and clutched my rock tightly. I wouldn't be controlled by this fear. I started to tip-toe up, trying to keep my breathing quiet. Only a flimsy wooden banister separated me from the ever more dramatic drop to the right. Something seemed to be congealing in my throat. I gulped it away. Didn't look down. I pictured the steps in my living room and the tin of chocolates. Just some steps, one at a time.

A soft moaning came from the bundle. Kate was trapped in the net and dangling from the ceiling like a fly in a spider's web. There was something else in there with her. It looked like a rug, crumpled underneath her.

The net hung about six feet down from the ceiling. It was too low for Kate to reach the rim of the hatch in the floor above her, and the net was too fine to provide any purchase to climb up it. Kate seemed to be frozen, terrified to move in case the whole net ripped apart.

I inched higher and made the mistake of glancing down. The flagstone floor was far below me now, glistening like ice. My vision went fuzzy and I cringed away from the edge and pressed myself against the outer wall. I closed my eyes and sank down into a sitting position, my face on my knees. My head was full of the sight of my dead sister, myself falling from the ladder, screaming, knowing it was my fault. I ground my knuckles into my temples.

I opened my eyes and saw Kate staring at me, her pupils vast in the darkness. I took a huge breath, right down into my stomach, stood up and put my foot on the next step up. And the next.

I was okay. I was doing this. I crept up the steps, higher and higher, not looking down, concentrating on the feel of the stone under my feet, staying right there in the moment, not picturing the depth below me. I heard muffled voices from the room above – a man and a woman.

The stairs led to the circular room at the top of the mill, the one with the huge windows from which light had been flooding out over the moor. I crept up the final few steps, trying to see whoever was in the room before they saw me.

I gulped. Mark stood with his back to one of the vast, curved windows. His face was distorted and his expression wild. I froze. He turned towards me and looked straight into my eyes. Sweat trickled down my back.

I tried to read Mark's expression. He flicked his gaze towards the centre of the room. I looked where he'd gestured with his eyes. A waxed wooden floor, a couple of leather sofas. A person.

I felt a glimmer of relief at the familiar clothing. My first instinct was that this was a friend. Someone wearing the protective suit of a crime scene investigator, kneeling by the hatch in the middle of the floor, looking down into the dangling net in which Kate was trapped.

She raised her head to look at me. The relief flooded away like water through a broken dam.

'Grace,' I said. 'What are you...'

She held a ten-inch hunting knife, its silver blade sparkling in the light. It was next to the top of the net. By her side were three small wooden trunks, each about the size of a hand-luggage-approved case. On top of one of the trunks were a couple of dice, also wooden. I blinked, trying to work out what she was doing. My heart thudded to a fast rhythm.

'Please, Grace.' I inched closer to her. 'Put the knife down, and help us get Kate out.'

'No!' She shifted the blade down slightly. It was millimetres away from the netting. 'I'm doing God's work. These people have been committing murder.'

Mark's gaze was fixed on the knife. 'We were helping people,' he said. 'Stopping them suffering.'

My eyes flitted side to side, looking for options. I placed my rock on the floor. It wasn't going to help.

Mark turned to look at me. 'She's playing some weird game with the dice,' he said quickly. 'If I try to move closer, she threatens to cut the net.'

Grace kept the knife by the net, but with her other hand, she gently stroked the top of one of the trunks. I could see numbers cut into its lid: '1, 2'. The second trunk had the numbers '3, 4' on its lid, and the third the numbers '5, 6'. What the hell was she doing?

I tried to keep the panic out of my voice. 'Grace, we've got to get Kate out of the net.'

She gave me a furious look. 'No! They've been playing God. By killing them, I'm saving others.' Her arm was rigid, the knife hovering by the top of the net. One flick of the wrist and Kate would fall and be smashed apart on the slabs beneath us.

Kate's voice shot through my thoughts. It was shaking with fear, coming from the net hanging below us. 'Please, Grace. Please help me. We won't do it any more. I promise. We'll let God decide when people die. Please...'

Grace leant forward over the hatch. 'You're right!' Her voice echoed from the high roof. 'That's what I'm doing – letting God decide. I couldn't make my mind up whether you should live. You're evil but you have an innocent soul inside you. That's why I need the dice. God will decide through them.'

I took a sharp breath. She knew Kate was pregnant. That was the reason she hadn't just killed her. Vivian from the health centre must have told her – they were in the Life Line group together.

'Please, Grace,' I said. 'Think of the innocent baby. Give me the knife.'

She looked straight at me. 'Don't come any closer! Any of you, or I swear, I'll slash right through this net.'

I stopped. The air seemed to crackle with Grace's energy. I looked around the room again. Both Mark and I were about six feet away from Grace, and her knife was millimetres from the net. Any move towards her and she could slice through the net before we could get anywhere near her.

I noticed a twenty-pound note on the oak floor behind Grace. She must have planted it so Kate would see it when she arrived at the windmill, and walk to pick it up – straight across the trap door, which must have been sabotaged and covered with the rug that was now in the net with Kate. And I remembered Olivia saying Grace was a whizz with burglar alarms. Had she set this one to send her a message over the internet when Kate arrived, so she could come up here and play her lethal games?

I spoke quietly. 'What are the trunks and the dice for, Grace?'

She looked at me and smiled, reminding me of the woman I'd thought she was. 'One of these three trunks has a picture of Our Lord Jesus inside it, to represent mercy and forgiveness,' she said. 'If God chooses that trunk, he wants this woman to live because she has an innocent soul inside her. In the other trunks... well, I think you'll recognise the pictures in those.' She smiled again, and this time there was just a hint of her madness in it. 'Oh yes, you'll definitely recognise those. If God chooses one of those trunks, then we'll know he wants this woman to die for all the evil things she's done. A one-in-three chance of living. I think that's fair.'

'Please,' I said. 'You can't do that. Just help us get—'

'I know which trunk contains the Lord Jesus, you see, so we'll have to throw the dice to let God decide.' Grace picked up one of the dice and examined it. 'God does play dice – we know that now. Einstein was wrong.'

'No!' I couldn't believe she was actually doing this. 'Just help us get Kate out of the net. God wouldn't want this, Grace.'

She didn't seem to hear me. 'But once the die has chosen, I'll give you the chance to change its choice. God can work through you.' She pointed at me, and our eyes locked for a moment. 'Yes, you can make the choice. It's a little game. I like that idea.'

'No. Grace. There's no time for games. Please...'

Grace tossed the die onto the floor by her knee. 'It's a five,' she said. 'God has spoken. Trunk number three. I wonder if the Lord Jesus is in trunk number three. On the other hand, maybe there's something else in there. Something bad...'

She moved her knife closer to the net. It looked sharp enough to cut throats, never mind netting. 'You have to decide whether to stay with trunk number three or change.'

I glanced at Mark. My heart was pounding. We didn't have time for this craziness.

'I'll make it easier for you to decide,' Grace said. 'I'll make it a choice of just two trunks. She flung open the lid of the second trunk and whipped out a piece of paper. She laughed. 'Jesus isn't in this one, see?'

I glanced at the paper as she tossed it away. My stomach froze at the sight of the familiar image.

'Now do you want to change trunks?' Grace said. 'Or stick with the choice of the die? If you don't choose the trunk with the Lord Jesus inside, we'll have to let Kate fall, I'm afraid. That would be God's will.'

Mark inched closer to Grace. She was so distracted by her insane games, she didn't seem to notice him.

Her eyes were fixed on me. 'Choose now or I cut.'

I realised with a sick jolt that this was the same game Alex had played with me in Grace's kitchen, what seemed like years ago, when I'd thought she was the too-perfect wife and mother. The probabilities were the same. The roll of the die had only had a one in three chance of selecting the trunk with Jesus in it, so I should change its choice. All this darted through my mind in a microsecond.

I was hot and cold and sick and panicky. Even if I changed my choice, there'd still be a one-in-three chance that Kate would die.

'Choose now!' Grace flicked her knife towards the net.

The words stuck in my dry mouth 'Yes! Change the choice. Go for the first trunk. And please hurry.'

Grace laughed again. 'Clever! Yes, you should always change your original choice.' She whipped open the lid of the first trunk and grabbed a piece of paper from it. She held it up to me and smiled.

It was the same as the picture in the second trunk. The image so horribly familiar. Sketched in pencil but almost identical to the one on the cave wall and in the basement of Kate's house.

'I thought you'd like it. I think I got the expression right. I've been following the case – of course I have.' Grace glanced down at the image. 'It's a shame for you, because you did the logical thing, but the die chose Our Lord Jesus the first time. And you changed its choice to this. But I'm glad you got to see my drawing.' She flipped the paper away and leant over the hatch in the floor. 'Bye bye, Katie.'

Something dashed across my peripheral vision. Grace plunged the knife down. Mark crashed into her and shoved her away from the hatch. He grabbed her arm and tried to wrestle the knife from her. I jumped to help him.

A ripping noise. Kate screamed. Grace must have cut enough of the net for it to start tearing.

I flung myself onto my hands and knees and leant into the hatch, trying to reach for Kate's hand. The net was still mostly intact, and Kate was supported by it, clawing desperately upwards. I stretched down as far as I could reach, but could only touch her outstretched finger-tips.

I glanced behind me. I couldn't see Mark or Grace. I felt sick. I couldn't reach Kate. She was going to fall. That image of Carrie flashed again into my mind.

Carrie. Carrie's scarf.

I wrenched if from my neck, folded it over so it was double thickness, and fumbled a knot into it. My fingers were thick with cold and panic, but I managed to tie a second knot. I pulled at it to check it would hold. It was my only chance to reach Kate, but I didn't know if it would be strong enough.

'Kate, grab this!' I leaned into the hatch and dangled the scarf down. 'It's knotted. Wrap it around your wrist.'

Kate reached up with one hand, hanging onto the net with the other. She put her hand through the loop and twisted her arm to wrap the scarf tightly around her wrist.

With all my strength I hauled on my end of the scarf, but I couldn't get any purchase. The oak boards were too slippery. There was nothing to grab hold of and pull against. I could see Kate's terrified face. She was hanging onto the scarf but the net was tearing.

The net ripped and Kate's weight slammed onto the scarf. I felt a sickening jolt in my shoulder and crashed onto my stomach.

I was being pulled slowly forwards by Kate's weight. I tried to cling onto the floorboards with my other hand but they were polished smooth and there was nothing to grip. I clawed my toes down but there was no purchase. I was inching closer to the hatch.

My head was at the edge of the opening. I looked down and saw Kate hanging from the scarf below me.

If I held on to her, I'd be dragged through the hatch and we'd both fall onto the icy slabs below.

I caught Kate's eye. She knew I was going to have to let her go. I'd be responsible. Again.

Something thumped onto my legs. A moment of panic, then I realised that whatever it was, it was holding me firm and stopping me being dragged any further into the hatch.

'Hold on, Meg, I've got you.' Jai had never sounded so much like an angel. He must have hauled himself up the tower with his broken ribs.

Jai's weight pinned me. I was held with my arm dangling into the hole, Kate's weight dragging on my hand, my shoulder screaming at me to let her go.

I wouldn't let her go.

But I couldn't lift her to safety alone – Jai would have to help me pull her up. And to do that, he'd be forced to take his weight off me, and I'd start slipping again. In his few seconds of hesitation, I realised he wasn't going to do it. He was going to let Kate fall.

Kate's terrified voice cut through my swirling thoughts. 'I can't hold on to the scarf much longer!'

'Jai,' I gasped. 'You can get off me for a moment. Reach into the hatch, grab the scarf, and help me pull Kate up.'

I felt him hesitating. Cops didn't risk each other's lives. I couldn't breathe properly with his weight on me. I thought of his poor ribs. My voice rasped. 'Go on! Quick.'

Jai hesitated a moment more, then I felt his weight lift off me. I started slipping forwards. Jai leaned into the hatch and I finally felt a lightening of the pull on my shoulder. I took a huge breath, lifted myself onto my hands and knees, and reached for the scarf with my good arm. Together, Jai and I scrabbled and yanked and dragged Kate up to safety.

I lay on my side, panting. My ears were full of Kate's rasping breath next to me. The sweat was cold on my face, and I realised an icy draught was wicking it away. I looked to the far side of the room and saw a gaping hole shattered out of one of the windows. Mark and Grace were gone.

Chapter 43

I wrenched myself into a sitting position. Jai was next to me, crumpled over and clutching his chest. His face was a peculiar shade of green.

'Jai… oh my God.' My breath was coming in desperate gasps. 'Your ribs… all that way…' The words stuttered out incoherently. 'You okay?'

Jai clenched his teeth and nodded. 'Hmm. Kind of. How about you?'

I glanced at my shoulder and a wave of sickness almost overwhelmed me. I nodded.

I turned to Kate. She was still panting, and was sitting way too close to the hatch in the floor. Her gaze flitted around the room. 'Mark,' she whispered. 'Where's Mark?'

I looked at the shattered window. 'He was trying to get the knife from Grace…'

'He's fallen? Oh God. Oh no…' Kate stood and swayed backwards towards the hatch. I didn't even have the energy to warn her. That would be true irony, if she fell through it now, although maybe not suitable for Alanis's song. What was my mind rambling on about? I needed to think sensible, detective thoughts.

Kate hobbled towards the steps at the edge of the room. She looked back at Jai and me. 'Are you alright?'

I nodded and forced myself onto my feet to follow her. 'You stay there,' I said to Jai, with no confidence that he would.

He nodded and reached stiffly to get his phone from his pocket. 'I've got one bar up here. I'll call for help.'

I limped down the steps as fast as I could, round and round, such a long way. I pushed through the huge oak door, which Kate had left swinging open, and stepped outside onto the freezing gravel. It had stopped raining and the air smelt of wet trees. The sky had cleared, and stars pin-pricked the deep blackness above.

I saw Mark first, lying still on the ground. Kate was hunched over him.

Grace was behind. She looked wrong. Was I seeing her body or Mark's body in front? My brain wouldn't accept the angle of her head in relation to her torso.

The soft noise of a distant siren pierced the night air.

★

The hospital smell propelled me back in time with such nauseating force it made my head spin. I shut my eyes and indulged in a moment of regret for my lost years, my non-childhood. But for once, I didn't feel guilty that Carrie had lost so much more.

'Well, she was a bloody lunatic.' Jai leant forward, cradling his ribs.

We had a small waiting area to ourselves, and there were no doctors in evidence. 'Do we need to make a fuss?' I said. 'Get you seen more urgently?'

'No, I'll live. But I need to take my mind off it, so you can tell me what the hell Grace was doing with those boxes.'

'It's a probability thing called *the Monty Hall problem*,' I said. 'Maths professors fall out over it, and write stern letters to *The Times*.'

'Jesus, Meg. Craig's right – you are an ubergeek. You were

working out probabilities whilst dealing with a raging psycho. I was surprised how strong you were though. For a geek.'

'I'm not feeling so strong now.' I looked down at my arm, lying like a dead animal in my lap. As well as the shoulder being dislocated, the elbow was battered and bruised. 'But I do upper-body exercises with Hannah.'

'Of course you do. And thank God for your sister's scarf.'

'I know. If only she could realise. I never thought she was great at knitting, but it was pretty strong.'

Jai shifted in his seat.

I smiled. 'This is killing you, isn't it? Not being able to fidget properly? Anyway, do you think between us we could manage to obtain some of the toxic coffee from that machine in the corridor? And chocolate?' Surely tackling a homicidal maniac whilst simultaneously solving probability questions must have used some calories.

We rose, wrestled coffees and chocolate from the machines and returned to our brutal chairs.

'So,' Jai said. 'Grace was targeting members of the assisted dying group?'

'Looks like it.' I took a bite of my Yorkie bar. Annoyingly advertised junk had never tasted so good. 'She must have pushed Beth off the cliff. And I didn't tell you, but when I fell down those steps, someone had run up behind me. I was wearing Mum's coat. I'm pretty sure now that Grace was after Mum.'

Jai sighed. 'Nothing surprises me any more. I won't ask why you didn't tell me this at the time.'

'Thanks. Appreciate that.' I decided not to mention the rest of it. But I suspected Grace had been in Mum's house and had tampered with the gas and the light switch. 'I knew Mum was anxious about something, but she wouldn't tell me what. I should have made her tell me.'

'Well, you thought she was a normal mum. You didn't know she was mixed up with a criminal gang. But the time you got beaten up? When you were with the sausage-eating tramp.'

'I don't think that was anything to do with Grace. Just Felix's heavies going above and beyond.'

'Strong work ethics,' Jai said. 'Do we know for sure Felix sent them?'

'Not a hundred percent. I'm pretty sure though. Kate even said he keeps in touch with dubious characters so he can get occasional recreational drugs. They'll blab if we can find them.'

'We'll find them.' Jai scrunched his chocolate wrapper and hurled it inaccurately at a bin. 'But Grace planted the geocache and wrote the suicide email?'

'She must have done. She could have seen Peter put his password in when they all went geocaching, and he had the same one for that Gmail account. She knew he couldn't resist cake. But she probably didn't expect his body to be found so quickly. Didn't count on a greedy Labrador snuffling around the woods. She'd have thought she could get rid of the casket before anyone saw it.'

'And she was wearing Felix's boots?

'Looks like it. She must have stolen them from the shed. And she took his gardening gloves at the same time, and planted one in the woods near where Beth was found.' I took a swig of the truly awful coffee.

'GR,' Jai said.

I nodded. 'She started writing Grace's name. It wasn't the Grim Reaper at all.'

Chapter 44

A week later, I sat opposite Edward Swift in one of our bleak interview rooms. He was slumped forward on his blue chair, arms resting on the bolted-down table, chin in hand. The place smelt of cherry disinfectant, as if someone had puked on the indestructible grey carpet.

Richard had been obliged to un-suspend me when I'd become a minor public hero. News of my exploits had spread, alongside pictures of the mill, and trunks and dice people had set up to illustrate my dilemma. Online debates and a few pub fights had taken place over *the Monty Hall problem*.

I wasn't enjoying being *Mighty Meg* – it was too much like a nickname I'd had when I went through a chubby phase as a child. And Craig had already come up with some unflattering variations. But I was glad to be back at work.

Edward seemed to have aged several years since I'd last seen him in his sparkly kitchen. 'I just need to ask you a couple of questions,' I said.

He sat up and folded his arms. 'Go ahead.'

'Did you know about Peter's assisted dying group?'

'No, I didn't.'

'No idea at all?'

'I knew he was in favour of it, but no more than that.'

'But Grace obviously knew?'

Edward pursed his lips. 'Obviously.'

I folded my arms too, and waited.

Edward shifted back an inch, and something seemed to flip inside him. Like someone had turned on his Bluetooth to allow communication. 'I think Grace must have got the information from the receptionist at the health centre,' he said. 'They were in some religious thing together. And from following your poor mother about the place, of course.'

'Did you realise she felt strongly about assisted dying?'

'Not really, no. She got a little excitable about abortion a few years ago, got me going on demos outside clinics. But I thought she'd calmed down.' Edward examined his neat nails, and then ran his fingers over a scratch in the cheap beech veneer of the table. 'I'm trying to make sense of how she could have done those things. It must be her upbringing. She had a terrible time.'

'Yes. *To Train Up a Child.*'

'It's not surprising she was damaged, but honestly, I had no idea...'

An image popped into my mind. Grace as a little girl, cowering in the corner of a room, her father looming over her.

Edward glanced up quickly, then looked back down at his hand, drawing imaginary shapes on the table. 'She wasn't a bad person, not really.' He knotted his eyebrows together as if working on mental arithmetic. 'I've been researching it. We tend to think it's the primitive side of the brain taking over, but it's not. When someone kills like this, it's the executive function over-ruling the emotional brain. It's based on group identity, and obedience to an authority.'

Poor Edward. He was coping by taking an analytical approach. I sympathised. 'Yes, I've been reading some recent research. In relation to terrorists.'

His expression brightened, and he actually looked me in the eye. 'Me too!'

If I started losing him again, I knew to get more technical. I could quote scientific papers with the best of them.

I shifted back a little in my chair. 'Were you aware she had access to potassium cyanide?'

'For the jewellery business? No. But I've looked into it, and it seems normal. In fact, if you want to murder someone, being a jeweller gives you quite an advantage. But, she was so intelligent, she'd have found a way, no matter what. All that business with the casket and the mystery geocache. It was clever. Peter used to type his password right in front of us. And we often used to go to a café after we'd been out. Peter always had something to eat – chocolate cake or Bakewell pudding.'

'So Grace knew he liked chocolate and almond.'

'Yes. And she had a wonderful memory. And the net trap. If Mark hadn't turned up…'

'She'd seen the set-up with the floor when you borrowed the holiday cottage?'

'I suppose so. They mentioned the trap door – something about reinstating the mechanism in the future. I never saw it though. I gather it was secured with some very big bolts.'

'Yes. It was perfectly safe. Well, it would have been if the bolts hadn't been undone.'

'It was very ingenious, what Grace did.'

How charming when a husband's admiration for his wife could survive the discovery that she was homicidal. Although he did have a point about her brains. I'd been right about the burglar alarm – she'd set it to send her a message via the internet when anyone entered the house, so she'd known when Kate arrived.

'She could have cleared it all up afterwards,' Edward said. 'And it would have looked like a terrible accident. But I gather she had a bit of fun with *the Monty Hall problem*?'

Fun? What a strange man he was. 'It wasn't a lot of fun for me.' I placed my splinted arm on the interview table. It turned out I'd dislocated my shoulder and sprained my wrist but hadn't broken any bones. *Did you keep the shoulder-joint immobilised after the injury?* the doctor had asked. *Not exactly*, I'd said. It felt much better now it was back in its proper place, but I wouldn't be doing any arm exercises with Hannah for a while.

'Will you be able to keep the patent attorney business going?' I asked.

'With Peter dead, Felix possibly going to jail, and a major professional negligence claim?' Edward sucked a breath deep into his lungs. 'I don't know. I really don't know.'

'And what about Alex? How's he coping?'

He let out the air. 'Poor Alex. It's been terrible for him. Grace's Life Line group offered to help, but I think I'll be giving that a miss.'

★

Mark Hamilton was propped on hospital pillows, his legs surrounded by a framework which wouldn't have looked out of place in a steel works or a modern art installation. I breathed the tangy, disinfected air and felt almost no guilt. My head spun with the unfamiliarity of it.

'Both femurs,' he said. 'I've got pins in my legs and everything.'

'Sounds nasty.' I shuffled my chair forward so I could see him clearly. He had stitches in his lip, just below his nose, and two black eyes. 'Is it very painful?'

'My face is actually more painful than my legs, and I've got stitches inside my mouth so it's hard to eat. The food keeps getting stuck in the stitches.'

I grimaced.

Mark lifted his hands and waved them around. 'But amazingly, my arms are fine. I count myself lucky. I seem to have landed on my legs and then bounced onto my face. It's common to break your spine in falls like that.'

'Yes. Grace… I'm not sure if you've been told, but she didn't make it.'

'I heard. But it was a C2 fracture. Horrific. She'd have been completely paralysed. So it's probably for the best… Even after everything, I'd have hated her to go through that.'

I pictured Grace lying battered and broken, her head forced back at a sickening angle. I focussed on the flowers and grapes beside Mark's bed. 'Even though she killed your brother and sister?'

'In a way, she did them both a favour. Ironic, really, in the circumstances.'

I couldn't reconcile this person with the man who'd hidden Rosie in his house while half of Derbyshire was searching for her; who'd let her walk off into the night to commit suicide.

It was as if he'd read my mind. 'Rosie made me promise,' he said. 'On Peter's grave. She appeared at my door and said if I didn't promise not to tell a soul where she was, she'd be gone and no one would see her again. Ever.' He touched the stitches in his lip. 'I couldn't break that promise, even when you appeared. She hid upstairs.'

I thought of myself in the Labyrinth, making all kinds of promises just to get that damn noose off Rosie's neck. 'I understand,' I said.

Mark shifted higher on his pillows. 'I didn't encourage her to commit suicide. She sneaked out while I was on the phone. I had no idea, honestly…'

The heavy hospital door swung open and Kate Webster walked in. She gave Mark an uncertain smile, and her eyes flicked to me.

'Meg!' She hurried to my side. 'Can I call you that? I don't know what to say. How do you thank someone who saved your life? I'd hug you if you didn't look so bruised.'

I waved my good arm dismissively. 'Oh, all part of the service. UK police – best in the world.'

'Seriously. Thank you. And I'm so sorry about your shoulder. I seem to be the only one who came out relatively unscathed.'

'I'm just sorry I chose the wrong trunk.'

Kate laughed. 'That'll teach you to be good at probability. Anyway, I owe you my life. She wouldn't have let me go even if you'd chosen the right trunk. I think we all knew that. So thank you.' She touched my good shoulder, walked around Mark's bed and sat in the chair on the opposite side.

'Mark and Jai played a fairly major part too,' I said.

'I can't believe it,' Kate said. 'Grace trying to kill us. I thought she was kind of... inoffensive.'

'She was a nutcase,' Mark said.

Kate gestured towards Mark with a neat thumb. 'Did you know he was in the clear with HD?'

'Oh.' I turned to Mark. 'I assumed when you grabbed a homicidal lunatic and hurled yourself out of a forty-foot window that you must have had the gene?'

'No, I was just being reckless.' Mark gave me a stitch-stretching smile. 'I had the test at the same time as Peter and Beth, and it came back clear, but I didn't feel like celebrating in view of their results.'

'It's so awful losing Peter, and then Beth too, so soon after,' Kate said. 'And I'm angry I never got the chance to say goodbye to my husband. I know he'd made some bad decisions but he was a good man really. And he never got to make a Bucket List and swim with dolphins or whatever people do.'

Mark shifted on his pillows. 'I know what you mean. I knew I was going to lose my brother and my sister, but not so quickly, and with no time to say goodbye. There's lots of things I wish I'd said to both of them.'

'It's just...' Kate brushed her cheek with the back of her hand. 'Oh, I don't know. It's been a lot to take in.' I thought about everything Kate had to cope with – not only Peter's death but his disease, his possible daughter, and a pregnancy too.

'It must be really tough,' I said.

I allowed myself a brief thought about Carrie. The usual hole inside me seemed to be missing.

'I've decided to have the pre-natal test as soon as I can,' Kate said. 'When I thought about the poor child growing up with a fifty percent chance of HD, I changed my mind. And at least if the baby's in the clear, it will have an uncle.'

'That sounds like a good decision,' I said.

Kate crossed her arms. 'I feel terrible for Rosie though. I'm praying she doesn't have it.'

'Me too,' I said. 'Do you know how she's doing?'

'A bit better. Olivia asked me to have a chat with her. I told her some other things that should be tested for. But she's thinking about whether she wants the HD test.'

'So, she's not talking about... you know, wanting to die?'

'No, not at the moment. If it does turn out she has it... who knows.'

'I kind of promised her, in that cave, that if she did want to die...'

'We'll worry about that if it comes to it. She may change her mind. They've made some progress with epigenetics and gene therapy recently. Someday, there'll be a cure. And people often say they couldn't live if they were paralysed or whatever but then they find they do still value life.' She glanced at Mark. 'We'll support both Rosie and Olivia any way we can.'

'You do know the police have to carry out an investigation into Tithonus?' I said. 'But I'm not involved.'

'I know. I understand. And I'm not taking those bequests, just so you know. Are you back at work?'

'Yes. I've had enough written warnings to last a whole career. But yes. I'm back.'

★

Jai pulled up outside the hospital doors. I slid into the passenger seat. The radio blared out something poppy and cheerful, and the car smelt of its mirror-dangling air-freshener.

I told Jai about Mark's test result.

'I do like a nice, happy ending in a murder enquiry.' He smiled, but I could tell from his rigid posture that his ribs were hurting.

We drove out of the car park and set off for Belper. The centre of Derby was very grey compared to the glistening, green hills I'd become used to.

'Is your mum being okay with you? You know, for grassing up her group, as it were?'

I sighed. 'Yeah, not too bad. She's coming over to mine actually.' I looked at my watch. 'Pretty much now.'

'She must know you couldn't have done anything else when Rosie disappeared. And when we suspected Kate.'

'I suppose so. But I keep thinking about if she goes to prison. She'd never cope. And what would happen to Gran? And there's this man she showed me a video of. Trapped in a horrible white room in a body that won't work, with no one to help him. Sometimes I wish I wasn't a cop.'

'Well, you nearly weren't, what with your vigilante performances and everything.'

I shuffled around to get comfortable. 'How are the ribs?'

'Should be fine. Breathing's a bit of an issue but otherwise I can do most things.'

'Great. What a team. People will think we've had a fight.'

We drove past the rows of mill-workers' cottages which towered above us in Milford. I let my eyes go soft and gazed at the pattern of light and shade on the velvet hillside behind.

Jai turned the radio down. His voice eased its way into my head. 'Grace didn't make it then.'

'No.' I shifted to give my bad arm more support. 'I know it sounds ridiculous but… I feel a bit sorry for her. Even though she tried to kill my Mum. Did you hear about her childhood?'

'Yeah, grim. I had a look at the reviews of that "child train-ing" book on Amazon.' Jai turned and gave me a horrified look. 'Unbelievable. Telling you to hit *babies*.'

'Look at the road, Jai. You nearly crashed into a taxi.'

Jai laughed. 'Oops. Yeah, I hate it when they do that in films. Give each other long, meaningful looks when they're supposed to be driving. How are viewers supposed to concentrate on the simmering passion when they're waiting for the horrific, head-on collision?'

I laughed. Then we both fell silent.

'Anyway,' I said. 'Did you know Olivia left Felix? Turned out he'd been abusing her for years, quietly behind closed doors. She only stayed because of Rosie and having no money of her own.'

'What a bastard.'

I relaxed back in the car seat, letting the warmth from the heater seep into me. 'Would you come in for a coffee? Help me cope with Mum?'

'Are you sure?'

'Yeah, it'll make it less tense. She'll have to be relatively nice to me if you're there.'

'Okay. Let's see if we can get you to the top of that ladder before she turns up, then we can have chocolates too.'

★

Mum was pulling up as we arrived at my house. I watched her leave the car and walk over the cobbled road. I'd been expecting her to be angry, but she just looked old and fragile.

I looked round at Jai. 'Actually, do you mind? I think it might be better if I tackle her on my own.'

Relief darted across his face. 'Of course. I'll drop you off.' He double-parked next to Mum. 'Save me some chocolates.'

I hesitated. Should I give Jai the 'friend kiss'? I decided not, patted him briefly on the arm, and levered myself out.

I let us in, ushered Mum through to the kitchen, and shoved a cushion onto one of the wooden chairs. 'Sit down. I'll do tea.'

'Can you manage? How's your shoulder? You shouldn't overdo it.' She clenched her hands together and rested them on the table, interlocking the fingers.

'If I can't manage to make a brew, I'm in serious trouble. Without a regular input of tea, my body completely shuts down.'

She smiled, but there was an invisible screen between us, like we were talking through glass. I stepped to the sink, filled the kettle, and stuck it on. I stared out at my windswept garden. The storm had ripped the wisteria off the side of the house and it lay forlornly in a puddle, but the un-killable shrubs were thriving. 'I am sorry, Mum,' I said. 'You know... about Tithonus. Are you angry with me?'

Mum let out a sharp laugh. '*Angry* with you? You are a strange girl. Two people were dead. You saved Kate's life. You're a public hero. And besides, if you hadn't stopped Grace, I could have been next.'

'But I'm sorry about the way it worked out. You know. That I told everyone about the group.'

She said nothing. All I could hear was the boiler doing its extravagant burning routine and the rain tapping against the window. Finally she took a deep breath and said, 'You thought Kate had that girl. You did the right thing.'

The kettle pinged. I dropped tea bags in mugs and poured water over, still not looking at Mum. 'I'm having nothing to do with the investigation into the assisted deaths, obviously.'

'It's okay, Meg. Losing two friends is the terrible thing, not the fact that you reported the group. I only wish I'd realised earlier someone was targeting us. I thought I'd seen someone following me but assumed I was imagining it. If I hadn't been so quick to dismiss my fears, maybe I could have saved Beth.' Mum picked up a mug and swirled the tea round. 'No, I'm not angry with you. I'm just worried about the people we can't help any more.'

A flash of memory. The camera panning deep into Steven's eye. 'That video you showed me – the man who wanted to die?'

Mum's tone was brisk and practical. 'His wife removed his feeding tubes.'

I sat down with a thud. 'What about Gran? If she wants to...'

'I'll find a way. She won't be forced to stay alive.'

There was a crash followed by a yowl louder than anything

327

heard outside of teen horror. Mum jumped and slammed her mug on the table, spilling tea. 'Oh, good lord…'

'Jesus, Hamlet,' I said. 'You'll break the cat flap again.' He charged to the middle of the room, stopped and stared at me with a crazed expression. I patted my knee. 'Come on, do your cat job. Sit here.'

Not usually one to follow suggestions, Hamlet jumped up and settled himself on me, his purr so loud it drowned out the boiler. I rubbed under his chin, and felt a flush of satisfaction when I realised I hadn't checked the rooms.

Mum reached to stroke Hamlet, and the tension dropped out of her shoulders.

'Is the milk fresh?' she asked. 'I know what you're like.'

'Ha. Yes, I went shopping. There's even some vegetables in the fridge that don't have bizarre foreign bodies sprouting from them. In fact…' I reached behind me, careful not to dislodge Hamlet, and took a pack of chocolate digestives from the shelf. 'Brand new, unopened, not-even-slightly-stale biscuits.' I stuck them on the table in front of Mum.

'So, all in all, you're enjoying being back in Derbyshire?'

I glanced at my splinted arm. 'Yeah. I mean, it's obviously a bit dull, but I think I'll cope.'

ACKNOWLEDGEMENTS

Thank you to my incredible agent, Diana Beaumont, for being brilliant, and for making it fun too.

I'm hugely fortunate to have HQ as my publisher. Thank you to my fantastic editor Sally Williamson, and to the whole HQ team for being so professional and enthusiastic, as well as lovely to spend time with.

Thank you to Jo and Ducky Mallard, who know more about crime scenes and maggots than seems quite healthy, but who were okay with me being inaccurate when the story needed it. I'm not sure there would have been a book without my amazing early critiquers. Big thanks to Alex Davis, Beccy Bagnall, Sophie Snell, Gemma Allen, Fay Gordon, Katherine Armstrong, Alice Hill, Robyn Arend, and Hjordis Fischer. Also to Scribophile, and to Writing Magazine for choosing me to win a critique from James McCreet.

Thank you to The Festival of Writing, Joanna Cannon, and Claire McGowan for liking my first chapter and contributing to one of the most astonishing weekends of my life.

My fabulous friends have been endlessly supportive throughout. Thank you Louise Trevatt, Corrine Baker, Fran Dorricott, Jo Jakeman, Glenda Gee, Ali Clarke, Lucy Padfield, the members of White Peak Writers, and the Narmies. In contrast, my animals have been an endless pain-in-the-neck throughout, but have prevented me from becoming welded to my chair. Apart from Minnie-Minx (RIP) who co-wrote the book.

Thank you to my mum and dad, and Julian and Marina, for ongoing encouragement, and occasional urgent editing and proof-reading services.

And finally to my wonderful partner Rob for listening to me banging on about my book for more hours than any man should have to endure, and for staying supportive throughout.

Printed by RR Donnelley at Glasgow, UK